W9-AXM-917

Hallmark PUBLISHING

A WATERFRONT Wedding

A HEART'S LANDING NOVEL
FROM HALLMARK PUBLISHING

LEIGH DUNCAN

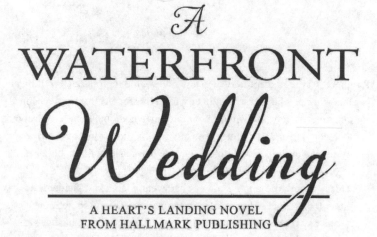

A Waterfront Wedding

Copyright © 2021 Leigh Duncan

All rights reserved. Except for use in any review, the reproduction or utilization of this work in whole or in part in any form by any electronic, mechanical or other means, now known or hereinafter invented, including xerography, photocopying and recording, or in any information storage or retrieval system, is forbidden without the written permission of the publisher.

This is a work of fiction. Names, characters, places and incidents are either the product of the author's imagination or are used fictitiously, and any resemblance to actual persons, living or dead, business establishments, events or locales is entirely coincidental.

Print ISBN: 978-1-952210-14-3
eBook ISBN: 978-1-952210-15-0

www.hallmarkpublishing.com

Chapter One

THE HEEL OF EVELYN HEART'S shoe snagged the carpet runner the moment she crossed the Library's threshold. She teetered precariously for a moment before regaining her balance.

Regrets played tag in her head. Why in the world had she agreed to manage the Captain's Cottage while Jason and Tara were on their honeymoon? She'd never worked one-on-one with the brides who had their hearts set on getting married in her family's ancestral home. She could have, *should* have, stayed right where she belonged—tucked away out of sight in her own office in jeans, a T-shirt, and a comfy pair of flats. If she had, her toes would be thanking her right about now.

Kind of forgetting something, wasn't she? Like, it had been her idea to take over in her cousin's absence?

Lately, working behind the scenes at the most popular wedding venue in Heart's Landing, the town known far and wide as "America's Top Wedding Destination," had grown too confining. Evelyn sensed a change in the wind. Stepping into Jason's shoes while he and Tara were away for a month offered the chance to unfurl her wings a bit, to prove she was capable of more than just keeping track of the books and inventory. So, yeah, she'd stepped up.

Too bad she'd nearly fallen on her face in the process.

She glanced at the couple who'd remained so entranced by the ornate carving on the mantelpiece they hadn't noticed her near pratfall. *Thank goodness.* As she'd done a hundred times in preparation for their meeting, she reviewed the pertinent facts. Devon Stanley the Third, partner in a New York law firm. Sherry Banter, his fiancée, the head of a charitable foundation. The two planned to exchange vows in an elaborate winter ceremony in a little over eighteen months. Their guest list topped 250, making it one of the larger events of the season.

Evelyn closed her eyes and took a second to envision the perfect wedding for the duo. Her heart warmed. She cleared her throat and stepped forward.

"The Library will be at your disposal during the reception. Many of our couples opt to duck in here to enjoy a private moment or two before they're introduced as Mr. and Mrs. for the first time." She didn't bother to mention how romantic the intimate space would look with candles flickering and champagne chilling by the fireplace. From the dreamy expression Sherry wore, the bride-to-be already had the picture firmly planted in her mind.

Sherry pressed a fluttering hand to her heart. "It's perfect. Absolutely perfect." Her fiancé beamed down at her.

"The Captain's Cottage *is* the premier wedding

venue in Heart's Landing," Evelyn pointed out. It had been for more than fifty years—ever since her great-grandfather Heart had moved the family quarters to the third floor. Not long after, he'd begun hosting weddings for nearby Newport's rich and famous in the two spacious ballrooms downstairs.

Evelyn's heart rate settled into a steady rhythm as the image of Devon and Sherry's picture-perfect wedding firmed. "Let's go to the office and get the paperwork out of the way."

"But darling." Devon leaned down to his bride-to-be, whispering so softly Evelyn strained to hear his words. "We agreed we wouldn't make a final decision today."

Sherry's expression dimmed. "You're right." She turned to Evelyn. "Dev and I feel we owe it to ourselves to consider all our options."

Evelyn blinked. That wasn't the way the conversation had played out in her mind. Devon and Sherry should've jumped at the chance to hold their wedding in the 125-year-old mansion overlooking the rest of Heart's Landing. "I can't hold the date for you," she said. "Not without a deposit. I'd hate for you to be disappointed if some other couple reserves the space before you do."

Which was a real possibility. From movie stars to secretaries, women across the country dreamed of saying their "I do's" at the Captain's Cottage. She'd checked the schedule this very morning. Turner and Stewart. Williams and Ortega. Suzuki and O'Hanrahan. Paired names filled the calendar for the foreseeable future. Others, who hadn't acted fast enough and had missed their chance, crowded a long waiting list. She didn't want to write Dev and Sherry's names at the bottom.

Across from her, Sherry worried one perfectly manicured nail. She gazed up at her intended, tears pooling in her blue eyes. "Honey, I know we were going to wait, but I've dreamed of having my wedding here since I was a little girl."

"Hmm." The tall attorney scanned the room, no doubt weighing his choices. His gaze dropped to his fiancée. "Everything about this place meets all our criteria. Let's do it!"

Sherry's tears evaporated. She threw her arms around Dev's shoulders. "Oh, honey! You're the best. We'll have such a beautiful wedding!"

Evelyn bowed her head. *The perfect wedding for every bride.* It was more than just a saying in Heart's Landing. It was the rule everyone in town lived by. By choosing the Captain's Cottage as their venue, Dev and Sherry had made the best possible choice.

"Alicia Thorn coordinates all our events. She'll be in touch with you next week," Evelyn said as she bid the young couple goodbye an hour later. Watching them go, she hid a niggle of concern behind a warm smile. People rarely made the four-hour drive from New York, spent hours touring the grounds, measured the ballrooms, and oohed and aahed over the Cottage's luxurious honeymoon suites, without locking in their date. Yet Devon and Sherry had nearly done exactly that. They weren't alone, either. Just last week, a different couple had driven off without making a decision.

Was it something she'd said? Some change she'd made?

She fought an urge to run her fingers through her hair. Not that she could. As she had every morning for the past two weeks, she'd wrestled her unruly curls into a sleek chignon. She'd pulled the requisite slim-fitting business suit from her closet, slipped her feet into the toe-pinching high heels. She shook her head. No. She'd dressed the part, stuck to the script, listened attentively, and assured every couple they'd have the wedding of their dreams at the Captain's Cottage. So why the hesitation?

Still pondering the question, she headed to the dining room for a pick-me-up. Coffee, for sure. Lunch would be nice, too. But peering into the cheery room, where tiny flowers adorned the wallpaper above dark wainscoting, she paused. At a table in the far corner, six young women sported sleek updos and fresh manicures as they chirped and cooed around a beaming bride-to-be. The Martin party. Tonight, they'd dance the night away in the Green Room. Across from them sat the parents of a couple who'd sashayed down the aisle last night to the tunes of a country-western singer.

"Duty calls," she murmured. As hostess of the Captain's Cottage, she'd stop by both tables and say hello. She breathed in the tantalizing scent of the stuffed rolls prepared by the kitchen staff every Saturday. Ignoring an empty gurgle from her stomach, she slowly started making the rounds.

She complimented the group who'd wiled away the morning at Perfectly Flawless Day Spa and cheerfully jotted down the bride's request for a last-minute seating change. At the parents' table, she accepted several compliments for how smoothly things had gone the night before and promised to pass the praise along to the staff at their weekly meeting. As she moved away, the foursome resumed their conversation. Evelyn smiled. The two couples came from opposite ends of the country and moved in different social strata, yet they were already strengthening the bonds they'd share throughout the lives of their children and, if they were blessed, their grandchildren.

Jenny Bell, Alicia Thorn's new assistant, sat alone at another table, her attention ping-ponging between the screen of her laptop and a check-off list. Not wishing to interrupt the petite brunette, Evelyn stepped toward the plates stacked at one end of the sideboard. Instead of fixing herself a snack, though, she stepped aside when new arrivals wandered into the room. Gmal Kahn and Josie Blackwater had driven up from Charleston to finalize plans for a ceremony that combined his Egyptian roots with her Native American heritage. After greeting the pair, Evelyn chose to forgo lunch and settle for coffee, leaving Josie to study the lobster rolls while Gmal eyed oven-roasted turkey on buttery croissants, platters of cookies, and stacks of brownies. She was doctoring a cup with cream and sugar when Jenny joined her.

"Hey," the young woman whispered.

"Hey, yourself. You looked busy. I didn't want to bother you."

"You wouldn't have. I was going over the list for the Johnson wedding."

"Everything under control?" She knew it would be. Jenny's stint as the personal assistant to one of Hollywood's top actresses had taught her how to get things done. Already, staff bustled about setting up tables and chairs beneath a white tent on the back lawn. Sarah Allgood and Sam Johnson would exchange their vows on the veranda at noon tomorrow, then head for a scenic spot high over the Atlantic Ocean for their garden-themed reception.

"We're all set. And you? How'd things go with Devon and Sherry? Did they have any special requests?" Throughout Heart's Landing, people went out of their way to fulfill the wishes of every bride. Jenny had only been at the Cottage a few months, but she knew what was expected.

"Not them, but the Martin bride wants Aunt Clara to sit at her parents' table." Evelyn relayed the change to the seating arrangements, then frowned. "Sherry and Devon put down a deposit, but I don't know... something seemed a little off. Like they weren't sure." She stirred her coffee. "I don't get it. That's the second time I've gotten an odd vibe from a couple since I started filling in for Jason. It makes me think I'm doing something wrong."

"Maybe they couldn't make up their minds. The occasional bride has that problem, you know." Jenny gave an innocent shrug.

"You have some experience along those lines, do you?" She grinned. As far as wishy-washy brides went, Jenny had taken the cake *and* the icing. Her wedding to Nick Bell had been far different from the one she'd come to Heart's Landing to plan.

"I might." Admiring the diamond-and-gold bands on the third finger of her left hand, Jenny giggled. "Hey, Sherry and Dev signed on the bottom line. That's what counts. When she walks down the aisle in the Green Room in front of all their family and friends, they'll know they made the right choice."

"Maybe." She shook her head. "But I had the feeling they were checking out other venues. That can't be right, though. Not if they want to get married in Heart's Landing, and Sherry insisted on it. Rustic Weddings off Boston Neck Road is big enough, but I can't imagine holding such a posh reception in a barn. They don't seem like the type to risk an outdoor wedding in the winter, either. Where else is there?"

"Well..." Jenny hesitated.

She stared into the other woman's wide brown eyes. Jenny knew more than she was saying. "What?"

"It's Ryan Court," she said softly. "You know him, don't you?"

"Jason's friend?" Evelyn stirred her spoon with a little more force than necessary. Coffee sloshed over the side of the cup. "Oh, shoot!" She grabbed napkins and mopped.

Growing up, she'd spent countless hours with Jason and Ryan—sliding down the sturdy banisters of the Captain's Cottage, skating on the pond out back in the winter, collecting shells along the beach on hot summer days. They'd been best buds all through grade school, but when the boys had moved on to middle school and had left her behind, her friendship with Ryan had dissolved. Two years younger, she hadn't moved in his social circles once they'd hit high school.

She still didn't. She'd seen him around, of course. In a town the size of Heart's Landing, it'd be hard not to run into each other. The last time had been at her cousin's wedding.

“He bought the Boat Works,” Jenny said. “He, um, plans to open it as a wedding venue.”

“You’re joking, right?” Once home to a thriving business, the building had sat vacant for more than three decades, ever since Mr. Farley, God rest his soul, had retired and padlocked the doors. She’d been inside on a dare about fifteen years ago. Once had been enough. The place had been full of rotted floorboards and mildew. She shivered. “I’d never want to get married there.”

When Jenny nodded agreeably, she stopped to reconsider. Even if Ryan had bought the property, it’d take years to repair the damage done by the wind and weather. Unless... Her stomach sank a notch as she recalled the Court family business. She closed her eyes, imagining crews of construction workers demolishing the old timbers, hammering new drywall in place, painting and spackling. With all that help, Ryan could probably turn the project around in no time. “Huh. I wonder why Jason didn’t mention it.”

“Maybe he didn’t know. He was a little distracted by Tara.”

Despite her concerns, Evelyn smiled. Tara was the best thing that had ever happened to her cousin. The woman had come to Heart’s Landing on a secret assignment to expose the supposed lies surrounding Captain Thaddeus Heart. But the journalist’s insistence on finding the truth had forever dispelled any doubts about the legendary seafarer.

“Oh, before I forget, Alicia asked if you could stop by her office around one-thirty.” Jenny poured hot water into a cup and added a tea bag.

Evelyn glanced at her watch, then gazed wistfully

at the couple who still lingered at the sandwich trays. Lunch would definitely have to wait.

As for Ryan Court, he wasn't going to be a problem. No matter what he'd done to the dilapidated building at the marina, it would never rival her family home. The Cottage's reputation as the best wedding venue in Heart's Landing was secure.

"It's a beautiful location. I love the water, the view. I can practically see the lights from the marina twinkling in the background when I walk down the aisle." Catherine straightened the engagement ring on the third finger of her left hand. "But..."

Ryan Court winced. *But.* There was that word again. So far, it had tumbled from the lips of every bride-to-be who'd toured the restored Boat Works. Whenever it did, his hopes of landing his first booking for the newest wedding venue in Heart's Landing had dimmed a bit more.

"But...I'm not sure you'll finish construction in time for my wedding." Ryan had grown up with a hammer in one hand, a sheet of sandpaper in the other. Like any good carpenter, he knew the importance of meeting a deadline, and he'd meet this one. Of that, there was no question. He hadn't sunk every dime he owned into the waterfront property or spent more than a year restoring the once-dilapidated building only to fall short this close to the finish line. He hadn't hammered blood, sweat, and—yeah, he'd admit it—a tear or two into new shingles, siding, or drywall to give up

now. By week's end, he'd tick off every item on a very short punch list. The Boat Works would be in tiptop shape long before this bride's big day.

"But...I can't imagine what it'll look like. I need pictures!" He stroked the neatly trimmed scruff along his jaw. Maybe he should scatter linen-draped tables and chairs throughout the reception area. Bring in floral arrangements and floor runners. Hire a photographer.

He gave his head a barely perceptible shake. All of that took money. Too much money for a guy whose savings account stood as empty as a midwinter swimming pool. No. Staging the Boat Works would have to wait until he landed a booking or two. Trouble was, it sounded more and more like he'd need those photographs to attract customers. He resisted an urge to rub his aching temples.

"But...I had my heart set on getting married in the Captain's Cottage." He suppressed a groan. Didn't everyone? Once Captain Thaddeus Heart's granddaughter had glided down the staircase of the so-called Cottage to marry into the Rockefeller clan, the mansion-size home at the end of Procession Drive had become the most well-known wedding venue in Heart's Landing. Each year, hundreds of brides and grooms said their "I do's" beneath white tents erected on the acres of manicured lawns. Hundreds more exchanged vows in the library or on the veranda before dancing their special night away in one of two massive ballrooms. How had he expected to compete with that?

He glanced over Catherine's shoulder to the docks and the water beyond. He stilled. The Boat Works had something no other wedding venue in Heart's Landing could offer—a scenic waterfront view. Enormous plate glass windows looked out over the bay, where birds turned and wheeled against the blue sky. At night, those same windows took full advantage of the lights that sparkled like diamonds along the piers and the boats that bobbed at anchor in the quiet harbor. The lapping of gentle waves provided a backdrop soothing enough to calm a jittery groom's nerves. Polished cedar walls would cast the bride and her wedding party in a rosy glow.

"But..." This particular bride cleared her throat. "How many weddings have you held here?" Tiny lines creased her brow.

His focus sharpened. "As you can see, we're still finishing up a few minor details." He gestured to a pair of doors propped against a nearby workbench. By close of business, they'd swing between the main room and a kitchen that would make professional chefs drool with envy. "We'll hold our official grand opening at the end of the month."

"In other words, mine would be your first booking?" The faint lines on Catherine's face deepened.

"Yes." No sense denying the obvious. "But don't worry. If there's one thing Heart's Landing does well, it's weddings." From Forget Me Knot Florist on the corner of Procession and Bridal Carriage Way to The Glass Slipper on Union Street, shop owners throughout the area prided themselves on providing the perfect wedding for every bride. They delivered on that promise so often that the small town, a stone's throw from Newport, had been hailed as America's Top Wedding Destination by none other than *Weddings Today* magazine. "If you choose the Boat Works, you'll be glad you did. On that, you have my word." He held his breath.

Catherine thought a moment longer before, with a breathy sigh, she extended her hand. "Thank you for spending your time with me this morning. I really do love this venue." She cast a wistful glance toward a sixteen-foot Farley tied up at the dock next door. With cream-colored decking above a brilliant blue hull, the sailboat was a thing of rare beauty. "I have a few other places to see before I make a decision. I'll get back to you."

Suspecting it was a fruitless effort, Ryan nonetheless doled out business cards and contact information. As he escorted Catherine to the door, he added, "Wherever you decide to hold your ceremony and reception, you can't go wrong in Heart's Landing."

He lingered in the doorway while Catherine's heels sounded a speedy retreat on the freshly painted deck that stretched to the parking area. Behind him, a door opened. He turned in time to see a familiar dark-haired figure emerge from a back room. The electrician slipped a pair of wire cutters into the tool belt he'd hitched over a belly that wasn't quite as flat as it'd been when they'd both played baseball for Heart's Landing High.

"How'd it go?" The rubber soles of Norman Hawk's work boots squeaked against the glossy wood flooring.

"If I were a betting man, I'd wager she won't be back." Ryan rolled his shoulders, a move that did little to ease a mounting tension. The June wedding season had kicked off two weeks earlier. But the calendar he'd hung in the back office was still as blank as fresh drywall.

Norman's heavy eyebrows lifted. "Really? This place is awesome. I'd get married here in a heartbeat."

"Oh? Can I pencil you in?"

Norman snorted. "I'm not even in the market." His dark oval eyes pinned Ryan with a look that meant business. "Us single guys gotta stick together. There aren't many of us left."

"Truth." He grinned. One by one, the rest of his high school teammates had traded in their baseball gloves and cleats for shiny gold bands until only he and Norman remained unattached. Now that they'd reached their thirties, he guessed that made them both confirmed bachelors.

Not that he'd object if the right woman did come along. A woman who'd love him for himself. Someone who'd laugh at his jokes and share his secrets, his dreams. Same as he'd share hers. A real Heart's Landing love for the ages...that was what he wanted. He wouldn't settle for anything less. But all that meant his mystery woman would have to be truly special.

So far, he hadn't met anyone who even came close.

Okay, there might have been a girl. Ages ago. Back then, timing and circumstance had worked against him. For now, he had more important things to do than fret about women. When he'd announced his plan to resurrect Heart's Landing's abandoned boat factory as a wedding venue, his brothers had looked at him like he'd lost his marbles. His dad had merely folded beefy arms across a broad chest and exhaled a long, slow breath that only confirmed what he already knew—he'd let his father down. And not for the first time. Since that day, his family had watched and waited for him to fail. There'd been times over the past year when he'd feared he might. Stripping the building down to its bare studs and transforming it into someplace a bride and groom would be proud to hold their wedding, yeah, that had required far more effort than he'd anticipated.

His gaze drifted across the hardwood floor he'd spent three months restoring. He'd scoured lumber yards from here to Maine searching for the perfect hardwoods to fill in the gaps where the original slats had rotted through. He'd spent weeks bent over an orbital sander, stripping the old flooring down to bare wood. It had taken another week to apply the stain and longer still to finish it with multiple coats of polyurethane. Those were just a few of the thousands of jobs he'd tackled, mostly on his own, over the past year. But now, with wide wooden beams soaring across the ceiling and light glinting from chandeliers, the Boat Works was the perfect place to hold a wedding or a reception…or both.

All of which didn't amount to a hill of beans if no one ever got married here.

"I just wish one of these brides-to-be would take a chance on it." He pushed hair overdue for a trim off his forehead. "So far, they've all wanted something with a proven track record."

"You can't blame them, can you?" Norman nodded toward the workbench Ryan had erected at the back of the room.

"Nah." He shook his head. The average couple spent a fortune on their wedding. With that much money in play, he'd be just as leery as the next guy when it came to taking a risk on an unknown.

"Hang in there. The right bride will come along. Someone who sees all the potential and none of the risk."

"I hope it happens sooner rather than later." He crossed his fingers. He'd exhausted his savings in getting this far. If he didn't line up a few weddings soon, he'd be hard-pressed to make the mortgage payments. But that was more than his friend, more than anybody, needed to know. He straightened. "You finished up in there?"

"Yep. I ripped out the old wiring and ran a new line to handle the extra load for the double ovens. You're all set." Norman brushed his hands together. "I'll personally vouch for the electrical wiring in this place."

"You better." He grinned. Following in his father's footsteps, Norman had become a first-rate electrician. His services were in high demand throughout Heart's Landing.

"There's just one thing."

There usually was. "What is it this time?"

"You sure I can't interest you in a backup generator? Now's the time to put one in if you're going to do it."

"I'd love to, man. But the price tag on one of those babies is a bit steep." And here he was with little more than two extra nickels to rub together. "Maybe later, once I have a few weddings under my belt."

"Give me a holler if you change your mind." Norman hefted his toolbox and headed for the door.

"Will do." He flipped off the lights. "I'll walk you

out. Alicia Thorn called. She asked me to come see her at the Captain's Cottage."

"Oh?" His expression curious, Norman rubbed his chin. "What's up with that?"

"No idea."

"Maybe she double-booked a wedding and wants to send a bride your way."

It was far more likely she'd discovered damage in one of the Cottage's rooms and needed him to make the repairs. He was, after all, a carpenter at heart. Despite that, he mentally crossed his fingers.

"One can only hope." He kept his voice light and teasing, all the while acknowledging that the odds of the best event coordinator in Heart's Landing making that sort of mistake were practically nonexistent.

Chapter Two

FEELING A LITTLE BIT LIKE she'd been told to report to the principal, Evelyn made a beeline for Alicia's office. Her heels tapped across the century-old wood floors. She trailed her fingers along the top of dark wainscoting that lined the wide corridor. On either side, doors opened into offices at regular intervals. The sameness of the rambling mansion that never changed despite a daily influx of brides and their wedding parties normally settled her. Today, it stirred an achy reminder of how monotonous her days had become. By taking on more responsibility while Jason was on his honeymoon, she'd hoped to change that, but taking prospective clients on tours of the grounds didn't thrill her any more than adding columns of numbers or keeping track of the Cottage's inventory. She was ready for a new purpose, a new direction. But what?

Reaching the first office on the left, she flung the door wide without bothering to knock. "You wanted to see me?"

She saw the back of Alicia's head, with tight gray

curls that held more salt than pepper, and then realized the wedding planner was on the phone.

Phooey. Evelyn beat a hasty retreat. She'd spent the entire morning projecting cool, calm professionalism, and here she'd gone and interrupted Alicia in the middle of a call. Would she never tame her impulsive side? She slumped against the wall, prepared to wait, but not more than thirty seconds passed before Alicia's voice rang warmly through the hall.

"Evelyn?"

"Yes?" She straightened.

"Come on in and have a seat. I'll be right with you."

Aware of the woman's busy schedule, Evelyn moved quickly.

"Let me get this down before I forget it." Alicia pushed a pair of wire-rimmed glasses higher on her nose, squinting at the monitor while the pink tips of her fingernails flew over the keyboard.

"Take your time." Evelyn settled onto one of the three guest chairs arranged in a semicircle before a sleek, modern desk. She marveled that even during the hectic bridal season, when the Captain's Cottage hosted more than a dozen weddings each week, Alicia's workspace remained as pin-neat as the woman herself...unlike her own office, which even on a good day, looked messy and disorganized. Self-conscious, she opened a notebook crammed full of Post-It notes and reminders. A slip of paper made a mad dash for freedom when the air conditioner kicked on. She lunged for it and barely caught it in her fingertips.

"There." Alicia turned away from the computer. "That was the Sutter bride. She wants to have a photo session under the willow tree between the ceremony and the reception. We'll need to make sure the area is freshly raked and trimmed. Can't have our bride snag her veil on a low branch now, can we?" Behind her glasses, a mix of humor and concern swirled in dark eyes.

The Sutter/Fox wedding. Six bridesmaids, an equal number of groomsmen. Plus, the flower girl and ring bearer. The parents, possibly the grandparents, would all be in the photos. Add in a couple of close friends, and suddenly things were getting very crowded on the west lawn. Evelyn thumbed through her day planner, searching for her notes on a wedding three weeks in the future. By some miracle she found them and rummaged for something to write with.

"Don't bother." Alicia offered a pen from a nearby caddy. "I made a note for the gardeners and sent you a confirmation email."

"Thanks." She sighed. Alicia was the absolute best. "What would we ever do without you?"

"You'll find out one of these days. As soon as Jenny's ready to take over, I'm going to retire."

"You're leaving us?" Evelyn squeaked. Alice had planned events at the Captain's Cottage for as far back as she could remember. With an unflappable calm, she'd risen to meet every challenge, from wishy-washy brides to grooms who suddenly developed cold feet. She was the reason they'd never had a wedding fiasco. "Does Jason know?"

At Alicia's nod, Evelyn fought down questions that rushed through her head like an incoming tide in Heart's Cove. She shoved all but the most important concern aside. "You're sure Jenny's up to the challenge?"

"She's doing great." The laugh lines etched into Alicia's cheeks deepened as their eyes met. "Remember the Smith wedding?"

"How could I forget?" Three hundred guests had filled the Green Room that night. Ships' flags had hung from the rafters, blue-striped life preservers had adorned white chairs, and tiny sailboats had served as place cards for the nautical-themed wedding. The evening had led to Jason and Tara admitting their true feelings for each other.

Now, sitting in Alicia's office, Evelyn sighed at the romantic notion of it all. One day, she'd like to discover her own true love. One day. But not now. Not when Jason was away on his honeymoon. And not when she was too busy to eat, shc mentally added when her tummy growled.

"Jenny handled that wedding all by herself. She's been taking on more and more responsibility ever since. You'll see—by this time next year, you won't even miss me."

"I doubt that!" The protest slipped out of her mouth before she could stop it. Planning the hundreds of weddings and events held at the Cottage each year required mad skills. "What if something goes wrong? What'll we do without your expertise? What if—" The thought of disappointing even one bride brought her to the brink of tears. She sucked in a steadying breath.

"Hush," Alicia soothed. "I'm not moving across the country. I'll be close if you need me."

The planner's reassurance calmed the butterflies

that had taken flight in her stomach. She sank into her chair and tried to come to grips with the idea that Alicia was moving on to the next stage in her life while she was... What was she doing, exactly? Once Jason and Tara returned from their honeymoon, everyone would expect her to quietly return to her role behind the scenes. But what if that wasn't what she wanted?

Unable to put her finger on what came next in her own life, she noted the two empty seats. "Who else are you expecting? What's this meeting all about, anyway? Jenny didn't say."

"You'll see." Alicia's smile was full of mystery. "If I'm not mistaken, here comes one of our other guests now." The event planner propped her elbows on her desk and stared expectantly at the door.

Ryan mounted the wide steps. At the top, an impressive set of double doors opened into the three-story mansion known as the Captain's Cottage. He suppressed a whistle. Restoring the Boat Works had given him a fresh appreciation for the effort required to maintain a place this size. At the turn of the century, the rich and famous had established a number of similar estates in nearby Newport. More often than not, those summer homes had been converted into apartments or razed to the ground when family fortunes had changed. But not this one.

In the foyer, he nodded to a life-size portrait of a swashbuckling seafarer, Captain Thaddeus Heart, merchant sailor and founder of the town that bore his name. The captain had plied the seas between London and New York for more than a dozen years, and by selling his cargo on both ends of the trip, he'd amassed a sizable fortune—enough to buy land and build a suitable home for his wife and thirteen children. Through careful husbandry, the Hearts had maintained the cottage and the land surrounding it for more than a hundred years.

Nearly as familiar with the rambling estate as he was with his parents' more modern home, Ryan headed deeper into the building. A smile tugged at his lips when he passed the spiral staircase that led to the family's living quarters. He and Jason had raced down those stairs as kids, each trying to outdo the other. Passing the dining room, he chuckled softly. How many times had he snuck cookies from one of the trays meant for guests while his pal had stood guard? They'd been in their teens before they'd realized Jason's dad had known all along what they'd been up to and had instructed the staff to let them be.

At the entrance to the Blue Room, he checked the soundness of the wood out of habit, but he needn't have bothered. He might not be able to build a house from scratch like his father or his brothers, but he could take something broken and make it good as new. Once, a pipe had burst and flooded the ballroom, and he'd repaired the damage to such a degree that not even the most discerning eye would ever see the difference.

Staff in black pants and white shirts bustled about the Green Room, straightening gold bows on the backs of the chairs and arranging centerpieces on the tables. Two women consulted seating charts and worked their careful way through the tables, leaving place cards at each setting. A soft clink drew his attention to Ashley and Alexis, the owners of Favors Galore. In the back of the room, they arranged a tantalizing array of sweets on pink-and-gold platters. One of the dark-haired twins—he'd never been able to tell them apart—caught sight of him and waved him over. He mouthed an apology while pointing to his watch.

Turning away from the preparations, he made his way down a long hall to the office of Alicia Thorn, Event Planner. The door stood ajar, and he recognized one of the voices coming from the inside. He gulped.

Evelyn Heart. The one who'd gotten away.

Not really, he told himself, though his feet sank into the floorboards, refusing to move. Evelyn and Jason—Ryan's best friend—were more like brother and sister than cousins. That made Jason's younger cousin off-limits. Sure, back when he'd been a foolish teen, he'd asked her out on a date. Once. He'd been half relieved when she'd turned him down. Although, even after all these years, he had to admit her abrupt dismissal had stung a bit.

Not that he'd spent the intervening years pining after her. He'd been popular enough in high school. Captain of the baseball team. Vice President of the student council. He didn't like to brag, but he'd known some of the girls thought he was good-looking.

But not Evelyn.

He'd often wondered if she considered herself above him. He was, after all, destined to make his living with his hands. But if that wasn't good enough for her—if *he* wasn't good enough for her—it was her loss, wasn't it? Regardless, he'd taken the hint and kept his distance.

Even now, he avoided her company as much as possible. Considering the size of Heart's Landing, that wasn't always easy...like now, when it looked like they'd be in a meeting together. He risked a quick study while the conversation continued. Evelyn had always worn her hair long and still did. Today, she'd slicked the thick masses into a knot that highlighted her slim neck and fine features. As he watched, she leaned forward, one hand moving animatedly. He was too far away to hear her words, but from the way a bright intelligence gleamed in her green eyes, she was passionate about the topic. He grinned as, with the other hand, she gave an unconscious tug on the hem of her skirt.

As often as not, Evelyn had tagged along while he and Jason had battled imaginary pirates on the Cottage's third-floor balcony or dug for mussels along the shore. She'd been more tomboy than girly-girl in those days. Now, though, there was no denying her softer, feminine side.

At that thought, he swallowed hard. The woman moved in an entirely different sphere from his own. He didn't even approach her level—a fact he needed to keep in mind.

But while he was lost in thought, the conversation in the office must've drifted to another topic. Alicia's gaze lifted. Evelyn's head swiveled. Ryan started, barely managing to get his feet in motion before the two of them caught him gawking.

"Alicia. Evelyn." Wondering what job they had in store for him, he nodded to both women.

Alicia's office chair spun in his direction. "Good. You're here. JeanMarie texted. She'll join us in a minute. Can I get either of you anything?"

"I'm fine," Evelyn murmured. She straightened, slipping her foot into the high heel that had dangled from her toes.

"Yeah. Me, too," he said, though he wished he'd grabbed a bottle of water from the dining area. He swallowed dryly as he glanced around. Why was he here? For the life of him, he couldn't think of any repairs at the Captain's Cottage that'd require Evelyn's input. He chose the chair farthest from her and lowered himself onto it.

Seconds later, muted footsteps sounded in the hall. They grew closer. Within seconds, a petite woman wearing a helmet of brown hair and a pair of well-broken-in work boots burst into the room. The tail of her khaki blouse hung loose over dark green slacks, giving her a slightly disheveled look. "Sorry I'm late." Breathless, she smoothed her wrinkled shirt, straightening the Parks and Recreation logo over her pocket. "It's been a crazy morning."

"No problem." Alicia pointed to her watch, reminding everyone she ran a tight ship. "We were just getting started." Once JeanMarie had taken the vacant seat, the woman in charge cleared her throat. "I'm glad you all could make it. You're probably wondering why I've asked you here. I'll get right to it. We need to discuss the Wedding-in-a-Week event."

Huh? Ryan crossed and re-crossed his legs. If it'd been anyone else sitting behind the desk, he'd assume he'd been summoned by mistake. Alicia Thorn did *not* make mistakes. He fought an uncommon urge to squirm beneath her penetrating gaze.

Heart's Landing played host to a number of events throughout the year. He'd participated in most. Once he'd won an Honorable Mention during the spring chili cook-off. Each fall, he helped build the set and cheered from the wings during the annual reenactment of Captain Thaddeus's famous battle with a hurricane. He shopped for Christmas presents among the booths at the winter craft fest. But the Wedding-in-a-Week festivities? He'd never had anything to do with that. And he didn't plan to—not until he had the Boat Works solidly in the black. His curiosity rising, he folded his arms and sat back in his chair to listen.

"As you might remember, *Weddings Today* runs a Wedding-in-a-Week contest every year. Thousands of engaged couples from all over the world enter. Every one of them hopes to win an all-expense-paid wedding. The magazine chooses the couple they deem most deserving from the applicants. Because we've been named America's Top Wedding Destination again this year"—she paused to let the significance of the honor sink in—"we host the event. Business owners throughout Heart's Landing participate by donating their goods and services. I'm sure you remember filling out your forms last fall."

On his right, JeanMarie and Evelyn nodded, while Ryan tried hard not to scratch his head. He knew good and well he hadn't dropped his name in the box. He'd considered it. In fact, he'd spent hours weighing the benefits of throwing his hat in the ring versus the risk of failure. But he'd barely finished demolition on the Boat Works by the deadline at the end of September. That had given him another ten months to transform the building into a wedding venue. A lot of people would consider that an adequate time frame. He hadn't. Like death and taxes, construction delays were inevitable. In the end, he'd decided the odds were too great that he'd hit a snag and let the town—and the bride and groom—down.

So, if he hadn't entered, why was he here? He stirred, prepared to ask, but Alicia barely paused for a breath, much less for questions.

"This year's lucky couple will arrive tomorrow. Over the course of the next week, the participating Heart's Landing business owners will present our bride and groom with three options for their wedding—three menus for their reception, three music choices, three floral motifs, three gowns and tuxes. Everything they could possibly need or want in order to have the wedding of their dreams. A photographer from *Weddings Today* will be on hand to document the entire process for a special late-summer edition, which will showcase the businesses that contributed to this year's special wedding."

Ryan drank in a deep breath of air and slowly exhaled. This situation grew stranger by the minute. He certainly didn't have three choices to provide the bride and groom. The best he could offer was one not-quite-finished Boat Works.

"That's where you come in," Alicia said. "Each of you is in charge of one of three venues. The Captain's Cottage," she said with a nod to Evelyn. "Statue Park." She offered a smile to JeanMarie. "And the Boat Works," she said, finally looking straight at him.

Ryan gave the faces of the other two women a quick scan. Evelyn leaned forward, her eyes bright, her lips pursed in a small, round O. JeanMarie's face had tensed into a not-so-pleasant shape. His eyes narrowed.

"When did you say this was happening?" asked the woman in charge of the parks scattered throughout Heart's Landing.

"The lucky couple and a photographer from *Weddings Today* are scheduled to arrive"—Alicia referred to her computer screen—"on the 4:30 train tomorrow afternoon. JeanMarie and Ryan, since this is your first experience with Wedding-In-A-Week, I'll go over the schedule. And Evelyn, I know you've helped Jason with the contest before, but as the Cottage's sole representative this year, this is all good information for you, too."

The wedding planner plunged ahead. "Each of you and other business leaders from Heart's Landing will be on hand to greet this year's couple at the train station. Jenny and I will escort them to the Union Street Bed and Breakfast, their home for the week. Starting bright and early on Monday, we'll tour the three venues. Tuesday through Friday, they'll visit some of the best shops in town, starting with Eat, Drink and Be Married. Saturday, the bride and groom will tell us which of the options they've chosen, which will give us exactly twenty-four hours before the wedding Sunday afternoon."

"Next Sunday?" JeanMarie straightened, her expression glum. "A week from tomorrow?"

"Yes." Alicia tilted her head. Concern knitted her eyebrows. "Is that a problem?"

"Actually, it is." When JeanMarie's words faltered, Ryan braced for bad news. Her voice barely a whisper, she said, "Lightning struck The Ash last night."

The room took a collective breath. One of the oldest trees in Rhode Island, The Ash had already weathered many winters by the time Captain Thaddeus had first made landfall in nearby Heart's Cove. He and his wife, Mary, had carved their initials into its thick trunk. Families had picnicked in its shade for more than two hundred years. Visitors to Heart's Landing gawked at the tree that towered over the town.

"That's why I was late. I spent the morning assessing the damage. I've consulted with several specialists. There's nothing to be done. No hope at all. It can't be saved."

Ryan's jaw clenched. JeanMarie, her shoulders slumping, stared at her lap.

"That's not the worst part," she murmured.

He shifted. How much worse could it get? He was pretty sure he wasn't the only one in Heart's Landing who'd shared a first kiss in the shade of that old tree. Or had rested his head in his arms against its rough bark, his eyes closed, while he'd played hide and seek with friends. Every spring, the youngest and oldest students at Heart's Landing Elementary made a special field trip to Statue Park. After the docents regaled them with stories of Captain Thaddeus's exploits, the kindergartners would join hands, while the fifth graders marveled at how many of them it took to circle the massive base. Its loss was a crushing blow.

"The Ash is so big we've had to call in experts from Providence to remove it. They won't get here for at least ten days, possibly longer. Until then, we've blocked off the area with cones and barricades, but it's quite a mess. Limbs and debris everywhere. We couldn't possibly hold a wedding there next weekend."

For a long moment, all four of them sat quietly, each absorbing the news in their own way.

Evelyn was the first to break the silence. "I'd like a cutting to plant on the grounds here."

"We're one step ahead of you." The tiniest flicker of light shone in JeanMarie's dark eyes. "We've been harvesting and planting seeds for more than a decade. We have quite a few saplings available."

"I'll take one." Ryan smiled. He had just the spot for it near the Boat Works. The idea of baby Ashes taking root throughout Heart's Landing stirred a warm feeling in his chest.

"Me, too."

They all swung toward Alicia, whose expression had grown pensive.

"I hate hearing about The Ash," she said, her voice heavy. "But I'm also concerned about how this will affect our Wedding-in-a-Week plans. I'll notify all the sponsors, though I'm sure word has already spread through town." She grabbed a blue binder from a stack on her desk and paged through it. After a minute, her shoulders lifted and dropped in an acquiescent shrug. She closed the notebook. "According to the rules, we can move forward with two venue choices. I don't like that, but we're at the start of the wedding season. At this late date, every other venue in Heart's Landing is booked solid."

"You're right about that," JeanMarie confirmed. "We had two weddings scheduled in the park this week. My secretary's been on the phone, trying to find somewhere else to hold them. There wasn't a single opening anywhere in town."

Alicia's dark eyes widened. Stiffening, she clamped a hand over her mouth. "What are you going to do?"

Ryan shifted on the chair that had suddenly grown uncomfortable. The thought of disappointing two brides in one week actually made his chest ache.

"It's all right," JeanMarie soothed. "I've spoken to both of our couples. They've agreed to hold their ceremonies in the green space across the street. They actually prefer it."

He could see why. Red maples ringed the open grassy area that was normally reserved for picnics and family outings. If anything, the location was even prettier.

At JeanMarie's soothing reassurance that the brides in question would still get their perfect weddings, Alicia's horrified expression cleared. She tapped her fingers on her desk. "Well, since we know for sure there aren't any other venues available, that leaves the Captain's Cottage and the Boat Works. It's all up to you, Evelyn and Ryan. Can Heart's Landing count on you?"

"Absolutely." Evelyn's voice firmed. "The Captain's Cottage would be honored to participate."

Ryan pressed his shoulders into his chair. The question of how he'd landed a spot in the prestigious contest remained. Another guy might keep his mouth shut, sit back, and thank his lucky stars, but his mom hadn't raised him to take unfair advantage of a situation. He leaned forward. "Alicia?" When he had her attention, he pointed out the problem. "Don't get me wrong—I'd love for the Boat Works to be involved. But I never signed up for this." He shrugged. "I thought you should know."

On the other side of her desk, the older woman peered at her computer screen. "Everything was in order with your application." She adjusted her glasses on the bridge of her nose. Behind the lenses, brown eyes focused sharply on him. "You'd be leaving me—leaving Heart's Landing—in the lurch if you withdrew. Is that what you want to do?"

"Never," he blurted. He swallowed. A bit slower, he added, "Not at all." He still had no idea who'd submitted his name, but he could figure that out another day, another time. For now, he'd been given an opportunity. He wasn't fool enough to turn it down.

Alicia's gaze swung between his and Evelyn's. "Then I can count on both of you?"

For a chance to have the Boat Works featured in a national magazine? Was she kidding? He'd cleared his schedule in order to knock out the punch list this week, but he'd take care of every single item before the sun came up Monday if he had to pull back-to-back all-nighters to make it happen. He grinned and shot Evelyn a challenging look. "Unless you'd like to make things simple and back out now," he teased, knowing full well she wouldn't even think of such a thing.

"Not on your life." She paired her answer with a cocky thrust of her chin, accepting the dare with a sparkle in her green eyes.

He grinned. *Game on!*

Chapter Three

STILL SEATED ACROSS FROM ALICIA'S desk ten minutes later, Evelyn thumbed through a blue binder brimming with information about the Wedding-in-a-Week contest. A cursory glance told her the rules hadn't changed from last year, when she'd served as Jason's assistant. Satisfied, she pulled the Participation Agreement from the back, signed it, and slid it across the wide desk to the Event Planner. "This looks great. I'll go over it in greater detail this evening, but the directions seem pretty clear." No surprise there. Alicia had coordinated the town's efforts for the very first Wedding-in-a-Week and had overseen the festivities for the past ten years. "I guess I'll see you tomorrow at the train station." She gathered her belongings.

"Jenny and I will both be there." In answer to Evelyn's raised eyebrow, the coordinator offered a reminder. "She'll shadow me this year. By this time next year, she'll be in charge."

Another change. Lately, everyone around her was moving on to the next thing in their lives. First, Jason and Tara had found true love and gotten married.

Next, Alicia planned to retire. The woman they all depended on wasn't just thinking about it, either. She was actually putting plans in motion.

Evelyn inhaled. When she'd left New York, she'd known exactly what she was supposed to do next. Now, restlessness plagued her, but she didn't know which direction to head. For a while, she'd satisfied her creative bent when she'd dressed as Mary Heart and performed with Jason, aka Captain Thaddeus, at weddings and receptions. But when her cousin and his new wife returned from their honeymoon, Tara would take over that role. She'd become the Cottage's official hostess, as well.

Where did that leave her? She didn't know. But handling the books and inventory for the Cottage wasn't enough. Not for forever, anyway.

"You and Jenny then," she echoed. "See you tomorrow."

She eyed the tall man who blocked her exit. Ryan's broad shoulders rounded as he bent over his own blue binder, his intense concentration showing in the way his lips parted, the barest bit of his tongue caught between even, white teeth. She couldn't help but smile. There was a time when she'd thought he might be the one. When the sound of his voice or a single glimpse of his blond hair had set her heart racing. But nothing had ever come of it, and like most schoolgirl crushes, she'd outgrown hers. "Ahem."

"You need to get by?" Ryan glanced up from the manual.

She stared into a pair of piercing blue eyes. Her heart shifted into overdrive. *Oh, man.* He still had it. She'd never been able to define that elusive factor, but once it had made all the girls at Heart's Landing High sigh whenever Ryan had walked past. Not that she'd been one of them. Simpering wasn't exactly her style. Instead, she'd feigned indifference to his charms. A ploy that had worked so well, Ryan had never even looked twice in her direction.

His attention dropped to the blue binder. He turned another page. "How are we supposed to memorize all this stuff *and* get everything ready by Monday morning?" He wiped his brow.

She smothered a smile. She'd asked Jason the same question last year. Her cousin had warned that committing the information in the binder to memory was a colossal waste of time. The book covered every contingency, from what to do if a bride got food poisoning to how to handle a bad case of cold feet. Most of it would never happen. If something did go wrong, they could always refer to the manual.

Still, if anyone else had asked the same question, she probably would've left them to their studies. But this was Ryan. Her cousin's best friend. She hadn't talked to him much in recent years, but she'd known him forever. It wouldn't be right to let him sit there, paging through the thick booklet as if he needed to memorize every line.

She moved forward, gently taking Ryan's copy of the book and closing it. "Sure, there are a lot of rules. Pages of them. But they all boil down to a handful of guidelines. Let me treat you to a cup of coffee." Her smile shifted into a grin. They both knew coffee flowed freely in the dining room. "I'll go over what you really need to know." Not that it'd matter. His Boat Works didn't stand a chance. The bride and groom always chose the Captain's Cottage. Always.

Interest flickered in Ryan's blue eyes. "Throw in a couple of cookies, and you've got yourself a deal."

She laughed. He wore his sandy blond hair longer than he had in high school. The lean form he'd sported then had grown more muscular. Crow's feet now tugged at the corners of the blue eyes that once gave her heart palpitations. But some things hadn't changed. Ryan had had a fondness for the cook's macadamia fudge bars ever since he and Jason had their first play date in grade school. Today, he was in luck. She'd caught a whiff of chocolaty goodness coming from the kitchen on her way downstairs this morning. "There'll be plenty of your favorites," she said. "C'mon, then."

"I don't get it," Ryan said once they'd filled coffee cups and plates at the sideboard in the dining room. "Why the secrecy? Why not tell us at least a little bit about the couple before they get here?" Alicia had refused to divulge even the simplest bit of information about the pair.

Evelyn raised one finger while she swallowed a bite of chocolate-and-rosemary scone that melted in her mouth. "Mmm." She licked her lips. "Delicious." She gave the rest of her dessert-slash-lunch a longing glance but settled her fork on her plate. The scone could wait. She'd promised to answer Ryan's questions, and that was what she'd do. "I've only helped with the festivities once before, but Jason said someone once got hold of the couple's names and leaked the information on social media. It ruined the magazine's big reveal. From then on, information was provided on an as-needed basis."

"They're afraid someone in Heart's Landing would spill the beans? Don't they know us at all?"

Ryan's guileless expression brought a smile to her lips. The man had a point. The town frequently hosted the weddings of the rich and famous without anyone being the wiser. Once they met the lucky couple at the train station tomorrow, no one in Heart's Landing would even consider revealing their identities. She forked up another bite of scone.

Across from her, Ryan chewed a bite of brownie and swallowed. "We don't know *anything* about them?"

"Just that they deserve the very best we can provide." She couldn't fault him for his curiosity. She'd like to know more, too. She dabbed at her lips with a napkin and told him what she could. "Every couple has their own special story. Maybe the bride has recovered from a major illness and can't afford the wedding of her dreams. Or the groom was in an accident. One year, the couple came from an area that'd been devastated by a hurricane. The church where they'd planned to get married had been destroyed."

"Man, that's rough." Sympathy swam in Ryan's eyes. He clucked his tongue.

"It's not always a hardship, though," she hurried. "No matter what the circumstances, weddings are happy occasions. They deserve celebrating."

For the Wedding-in-a-Week couples, the town pulled out all the stops. Only a true Heart's Landing bride received more attention. Those were so rare, she'd only met one in all the time she'd worked at the

Captain's Cottage. At that, her chest tightened the tiniest bit. She'd love to identify a true Heart's Landing bride one day, the way Denise had discovered Jenny at I Do Cakes. She sighed dreamily.

"Um, you were saying?"

"Hmm? Oh, sorry. I was thinking about something else there for a minute." Shaking herself, Evelyn hauled her thoughts back to the present. "Now, where was I?"

"Other winners of the Wedding-In-A-Week contest?" Ryan prompted.

"Right!" She'd give him one thing: Ryan had always been able to keep his wits about him. She shook aside the thought and focused on the contest. "Our lovebirds last year were childhood sweethearts who'd drifted apart after high school. He went off to college. She took a gap year to travel. They fell in love with other people, got married, and raised families. Thirty years later and on their own again, they both showed up at their high school reunion. They reconnected and discovered they'd been given a second chance at love." She swiped a sudden dampness from her cheek. Love, that was what Heart's Landing was all about. Her voice hoarse, she added, "There wasn't a dry eye in the house when they walked down the aisle."

"I hated to miss their wedding. I was on a buying trip, trying to find replacement lumber for the Boat Works. When I got back, it was the talk of Heart's Landing for weeks."

"About that." She pushed her scone from one edge of the plate to the other. Now that Ryan had opened the door, it was time for a little information-gathering of her own. "What on earth made you buy a derelict place like the Boat Works?"

"Do I sense a bit of skepticism in your tone?"

He tilted his head, and she felt a sudden urge to brush away the few strands of blond hair that spilled onto his forehead. Which was ridiculous. They'd drifted so far apart over the years, she barely knew the man. She busied herself with her fork. "It's a surprise, that's all."

"The building had good bones, a ton of natural light, great potential. Besides, Heart's Landing needed a waterfront venue."

"To compete with the Captain's Cottage." She tsked. "Are you trying to put us out of business?"

"What?" A shadow fell over Ryan's face. His eyes darkened. "You know me better than that."

"Do I?" she challenged. She used to think she did, but years had passed since she and Ryan had done more than exchange casual greetings.

"Of course you do." He nudged her elbow with his own. "The Cottage is steeped in history. It has elegant surroundings. It's the premier place to get married in Heart's Landing. It always will be. The Boat Works doesn't offer the same experience at all. But..." He hesitated.

"But?" It was her turn to prompt.

"But some brides want something a little more down-to-earth. They can have that with the Boat Works. Being on the water is another huge plus."

"Hmph." She softened, wanting to believe him. But that still didn't explain how he'd carried off all the repairs without anyone being the wiser. "I couldn't figure out why the town wasn't buzzing with news about your plans. But I guess, what with your dad and your brothers pitching in, word just hasn't gotten around yet. You must've remodeled the whole thing in record time."

"No." Ryan's forehead wrinkled. His lips turned down at the corners. "I'm on my own with this one." He wolfed down another bite of brownie.

Evelyn took a beat to study him while he ate. There was more to that story, she was sure of it. But whatever it was, he wasn't in the mood to share. She toyed with her biscuit. "Well, you always did have a thing for old buildings." Letting him off the hook for now, she reached for memories of long-ago summers, when they'd spent days on end together. "You practically rebuilt the old tree house you and Jason discovered in the woods out back." Her cousin had been all for tearing it down, but Ryan had insisted on patching the holes in the floor and replacing the broken rungs in the ladder.

"I'm surprised you remembered," he said, his voice low.

"It'd be hard to forget. You turned it into a great fort. I was so jealous whenever you and Jason spent the night out there. But Mama said I was too young." She laughed.

"You *were* two years younger," he chided.

"And yet I won every race."

"That's not the way I remember it," Ryan sputtered.

"I guess we'll have to agree to disagree on that one," she conceded. "But you were always repairing something. Remember that red wagon you and Jason used to haul your gear around? The slats kept coming off, and all our stuff would tumble out. You fixed it more than once. Then you and Jason would load it up and take off again."

"Seems to me you rode in it a time or two."

"Yes, well." She cleared her throat, determined not to let the conversation veer too far off track. "So you rebuilt the Boat Works on your own? I've only been inside the place once. When we were in middle school, Chuck Middleton bet me a dollar I'd be too chicken to crawl in through that broken window in the back."

"He should've known better than to dare you."

Her tummy shimmied when a throaty chuckle emerged from somewhere deep in Ryan's chest. She'd always enjoyed his sense of humor. "That was ages ago," she agreed. "But you're right, I never was one to turn down a challenge. I like to think I'm a little bit smarter now. Anyway, my point was, the place was a disaster. Part of the roof had collapsed. I stepped in a hole in the floor and almost fell through it. What have you done to it?"

Ryan pulled a slim phone from his back pocket. "See for yourself." He pressed a button, and the screen lit up.

She stared down at a picture. Even though the image was slightly out of focus, the shingles on the Boat Works glistened in the morning sun. She thumbed to the next shot. Soaring ceilings above glossy wood floors stole her breath. "This is beautiful," she whispered. "You did it all yourself?"

"As much as I could." The tiniest hint of pride edged the corners of Ryan's voice. "I brought in a crew to tear out the old timbers and the wood rot. A company that specializes in marine work checked the foundations and laid the new deck. But the rest, that's all me."

"It must've taken forever."

"A year." Ryan shrugged. "The better part of one, anyway."

"From the looks of these, you could hold a wedding there tomorrow."

"Almost. I have a few small projects to finish—a door to hang between the main hall and the kitchen, some touch-up jobs to do." His eyes filled with an earnest promise. "I'll knock those out before anyone steps foot in the building on Monday."

She eyed him carefully. For the first time since she'd walked into Alicia's office, a shiver of doubt passed through her. Was this the year the Captain's Cottage lost out to another competitor? *Impossible.* She shook off the thought and squared her shoulders. She'd promised to fill Ryan in on the important aspects of the contest. It was time to get down to business and do just that. "About Wedding-In-A-Week. The blue binder covers every possible contingency, but there are only three things you really need to remember."

Ryan blinked as if reeling his thoughts back in from a place he hadn't intended them to go. Patting his shirt pocket, he located a pen.

"No badmouthing the competition." She ticked the first item off on one finger. "The whole reason the vendors in town participate is to showcase their products and services. If one of us makes a negative comment that finds its way into the *Weddings Today* article"—she shook her head—"people won't sign up next year." She waited until he nodded before she held up the next finger. "No bribery or other undue influence. It's okay if Mildred Morrey provides a light snack when the couple visits Forget Me Knot, but if she treated them to dinner at a steakhouse, that'd be a problem."

Ryan's blue eyes twinkled. He snapped his fingers. "Guess I'd better cancel those season tickets at Fenway. And here I thought I'd found the perfect bribe."

"Exactly. Something like that would get you thrown out of the contest."

"Well, we can't have that!"

They both shared a laugh. She'd hadn't realized how much she'd missed being around Ryan. It felt good to laugh with him again. She shook her head. "Last and most important, live up to the Heart's Landing promise and deliver a perfect wedding. No matter what happens along the way."

"Got it." Ryan clicked the end of his ballpoint pen. "So how much of this is our responsibility? Are we expected to accompany them throughout the week?"

"Not usually." Evelyn started to run her fingers through her hair, thought better of it, and tugged on an earring instead. In years past, Jason had shown up at the train station to greet the arriving guests, given the lucky couple an in-depth tour of the wedding venue in Heart's Landing, and had known his work was done when he'd seen a sparkle in the bride's eyes or heard the groom ask for a tape measure. He'd left instructions for her to do the same. But after seeing Ryan's photographs, she wasn't sure the usual routine would do the trick. This year might call for all hands on deck in order to save the day for the Captain's Cottage.

Ryan peered into the depths of Evelyn's green eyes and faltered. He'd forgotten the smattering of freckles across the bridge of her nose. Or how a single glance from her could tie his tongue in knots. She'd given a breathy little sigh a moment ago. Why was that? He straightened. It didn't matter. They might've fallen out of touch, but he still knew her well enough to be certain of one thing—she hadn't been sighing over him.

He snatched what was left of the nearly forgotten brownie from the tiny dessert plate. Cramming the tasty tidbit into his mouth, he chewed furiously. It made a good enough excuse for not speaking, and it certainly kept him from blurting out something incredibly dumb. Like telling Evelyn how pretty she was. That would only lump him in with other guys who'd lost their heads over her. The ones who'd complimented her iridescent green eyes, or commented on the thick red curls that even now threatened to escape the knot she'd trapped them in. He wouldn't be one of those.

He wouldn't ask if there was someone special in her life, either. Women like Evelyn weren't alone and unattached. Not in this day and age, when social dating apps guaranteed even the shyest wallflower a perfect match.

Not that anyone had ever accused Evelyn of being shy. She said what she meant, meant what she said, and let the chips fall where they may. He liked that she didn't keep the people around her guessing. They always knew exactly where they stood with her.

He always knew exactly where he stood with her.

Which was how he knew he had as much chance with her as a builder had of constructing a new house without a hammer. Yeah, neither was ever going to happen. Friendship, though, that was an entirely different matter. The three of them—Evelyn, Jason, and him—had been thick as thieves once upon a time. He and Jason were still best buds.

But him and Evelyn? Nah.

The two of them had drifted apart after… Well, after he'd foolishly asked her to the homecoming dance within earshot of her posse. The girls had found something uproariously funny in the idea of a baseball player dating the queen of the drama club. They'd laughed out loud while Evelyn had coolly turned on one heel and walked away. He supposed that part had hurt the most, although there hadn't been anything pleasant about the entire experience. But a dozen years had passed since then. Now, the faded memory served as nothing more than a faint reminder that he and Evelyn would never be more than friends.

He supposed she was offering that—friendship. Why else would she be sitting there, sharing the ins and outs of the Wedding-in-a-Week contest like they were pals again? He was good with that, wasn't he? He'd missed having her in his life. Missed being able to turn to someone he trusted to give her honest opinion. Missed her sassy wit. Missed how she was always ready for the next adventure. He scooped a few stray crumbs into his hand and brushed them onto his plate. He supposed, if they were going to do this, it was time to start getting to know one another again.

His appraising glance swept over the guests who wandered in and out of the dining room. "So you're in charge while Jason's away?"

Evelyn nibbled on her scone. "I'm filling in till he

and Tara get back at the end of the month. Then, things will go back to normal."

"And what's normal for you? What do you usually do here?"

"You don't know?"

At her confused glance, he shrugged. "Humor me. It's been a while. Jason and I stayed in touch while he was in college. We'd catch a hockey game together or grab a pizza when he came home for a weekend. But after he moved to New York and I headed for Maine, we almost never made it back to Heart's Landing at the same time. So, fill me in. What's been happening with you?"

Across from him, Evelyn's forehead crinkled. "Okay. But tell me this first—why Maine?"

He smiled. Playing catch-up had been the right move. She hadn't kept tabs on him any more than he'd kept up with her comings and goings. "I went to work for my dad straight out of high school. Stayed on until I got accepted into an apprentice program with Josh Morgan, the top restoration specialist in the country. Lives,"—he paused to correct himself—"lived in Maine. I spent a dozen years working with him. I'd still be there if he hadn't retired. He moved to Florida. He has family down south."

"So you came back here? Didn't want to stay in Maine?"

"I missed seeing all the brides." He grinned as if he was just joking around, but the truth was, there was no place quite like Heart's Landing. He liked watching couples meander up and down the tree-lined streets, ducking in and out of shops with names like I Do Cakes, The Glass Slipper, or Favors Galore. He enjoyed the laughter and good wishes that spilled out of Bow Tie Pasta whenever a wedding party arrived for a rehearsal dinner. And the church bells—they rang out day and night in celebration of couples who'd just exchanged their "I do's." He'd missed the lighthearted air of a town that put its best foot forward twenty-four seven. He'd wanted to be a part of it all. Turning the Boat Works into a wedding venue let him do that.

"The brides, huh?" Laughter danced in Evelyn's eyes.

"That, and winters up north are brutal." Another truth.

"You've been here how long?"

"Two—no, three years. Dad thought I'd come back to join Court Builders. I suppose that was only natural." With his entire family in the construction industry, he'd learned to calculate board feet over dinner the way other kids recited their multiplication tables. "I worked for Dad through high school and summers, then full time for a while. My brothers wouldn't think of working anywhere else."

"But you had other plans?" Evelyn prompted. She toyed with the remains of her dessert.

"I never saw the point of building something new. So many houses could be perfect with some TLC. Dad and I didn't quite see eye to eye on the subject." Ryan exhaled. When he'd announced his intention to branch out on his own, start his own restoration business, his old man had acted like he'd had the rug pulled out from under him. "I guess buying the Boat Works was the last straw. Proof I was never going to be what he wanted me to be. Things have been strained between us ever since."

Evelyn put down her fork. "They should be proud of you. I've seen some of the work you've done here at the Captain's Cottage. If those pictures you showed me are any indication"—she pointed to his cell phone—"you've done an outstanding job with the Boat Works."

"Thank you. That means a lot." But he'd monopolized the conversation when he really wanted to know more about her. "How about you?" he asked, turning the tables as deftly as he could. "Last I heard, you were headed for Julliard. From there, the sky was the limit. We all expected to see your name on the marquee of some big show on Broadway."

"Well." Across the table, the redhead expelled a long, slow breath. "Julliard's one of those places where you learn if you've got the 'it factor' or not." With slender fingers, she framed the phrase. "Some of the other students in my class had more talent in a single strand of hair than I had in my entire body. Being around them, I had to lower my expectations. I'm local-theater good. Not big-stage good."

He opened his mouth to protest. She'd always been a star. While he and Jason had taken turns as the swashbuckling heroes of countless backyard plays, she'd stolen show after show with her feisty heroines and swooning damsels in distress. Later, she'd captivated audiences in school plays and pageants. At sixteen, she'd landed her first lead role as the youngest actress ever cast as Laurie Williams in the Heart's Landing Little Theater presentation of *Oklahoma*. She had talent and plenty of it. But a dismissive wave of her hand silenced his protest.

"I didn't give up right away." Evelyn fussed with

her napkin. "I figured I owed it to myself to try, so I headed to New York. I gave myself two years to make it." Her lips turned down. "I answered every casting call, went to at least fifty auditions that first year. Every once in a while, I'd land a bit part. But I had to work temp jobs and short-term assignments to pay the rent."

"That must've been rough." Ryan shook his head as he pictured her rushing from job to job, from tryout to tryout.

"Yeah. At first it was. There's not much call for untrained office staff, even in New York, so I enrolled in a few night classes." Evelyn grinned. "I discovered all those hours in Mrs. Cunningham's math class weren't wasted after all. I was pretty good at bookkeeping. That led to better paying jobs, ones that—surprise, surprise—paid the rent *and* the grocery bill. I started answering fewer casting calls and taking more temp work. Soon, I got to the point where I was ready to chuck the whole acting gig." She steadied herself with a breath. "That's when Uncle Dave got sick."

"And you moved home." Ryan nodded. As the eldest in his generation, Jason's dad, David Thaddeus Heart, had inherited the Captain's Cottage from his father.

"My family needed me." Evelyn straightened her napkin. "I quit my job, gave my roommate two months' rent, and was home by the end of the week. Thanks to my newfound skills, I was able to take over the books here. Which let Jason concentrate on spending whatever time was left with his dad."

Ryan grimaced. David Heart's loss had shaken Heart's Landing. "He was a good man, your uncle. He passed too soon." He set his own crumpled napkin on the table beside his plate. "He was the one who got me interested in restoration."

Evelyn raised an eyebrow. "I did not know that."

Ryan tipped back in his chair while he gestured to the hallway and beyond. "There's always something to fix in a place like this. The finish on a banister wears thin. Someone drops a plate and nicks a floorboard. A piece of wallpaper lifts. Somewhere else, the owners might see that as an excuse for replacing the banister, laying down new flooring, ripping out the paper and painting."

Evelyn's forehead wrinkled. "Not here."

"Right." Preservation was the name of the game at the home that had housed generations of Hearts. "Your uncle liked that sort of work and did a lot of the repairs himself. Sometimes, he'd commandeer Jason and me as his helpers. Uncle Dave noticed I shared his interest and encouraged me to pursue it."

Curiosity flickered in Evelyn's gaze. "I always wondered why you hung around, even when Jason wasn't here."

Ryan nodded. There'd been other reasons. She'd been one of them—not that he'd ever tell her that. "Your uncle was the first to show me I could have a future doing what I love." Unhappy with the way the conversation had once more focused on him, he swallowed. "And now you."

"I handle the payroll and accounting for the Cottage and make sure we have everything on hand to keep this place running."

"You don't miss it—the stage? The limelight?" As a kid, she must have known she was talented. But it hadn't gone to her head until high school, when she'd started running with the drama crowd. Their main purpose, as far as he could tell, was stroking one another's egos. He'd steered clear of her after that. Now, he was having trouble reconciling the diva he hadn't liked very much with the woman who'd swapped an acting career for one in a back office.

"Not so much," she answered, her tone matter-of-fact. "Four years at Julliard and two more as a broke, struggling, would-be actress—it kind of drove the point home, you know? Besides, Jason and I, we've put together a little act portraying Captain Thaddeus and Mary. We perform it for weddings and receptions. We sing, we dance. It's a ton of fun, and it means so much to the bride and groom and their families. That's been enough to satisfy my creative side."

He brought the front legs of his chair down, his thoughts racing. With an elfin face surrounded by rich, red curls, Evelyn possessed a rare beauty. As for talent, he had no doubt hers would take her as far as she wanted to go. But if entertaining wedding guests made her happy, he certainly wasn't going to argue. As her friend—or someone who wanted to be—he'd support whatever decisions she made.

Right now, though, they needed to focus on the matter at hand. He leaned forward. "I have quite a bit of work ahead of me if I'm going to make the Boat Works look its best by Monday. Can we talk about Wedding-in-a-Week for a little bit?"

Across the table, Evelyn's lips thinned.

"What is it?" He'd seen that expression before. It usually meant trouble.

"Well, it's that name. 'The Boat Works,'" she said,

surrounding the words in air quotes. "Are you married to it?"

"You don't like it?" The building at the marina had always been known as Farley's Boat Works. He hadn't seen any need to change it.

"I'd think something with a little more pizzazz would be nice. Maybe Harbor Weddings. Or Sea View Ceremonies. Or, oh, I know, what about Waterfront Weddings?"

"But what if people want to hold other events there? Retirement or birthday parties. Town meetings." Ryan scratched his head. The handcrafted sign proclaiming to one and all that the Boat Works was open for business lay on sawhorses in his work room. He'd planned to hang it this evening.

"You think no one orders birthday bouquets from Forget Me Knot Florist? Or Favors Galore never provides gift bags for retirement parties? Every business in town advertises their connection to weddings. It's what we do. Why mess with a good thing?" Evelyn sipped the last of her tea.

He'd wanted her opinion, hadn't he? Now that he had it, he should probably trust her intuition. "Waterfront Weddings has a nice ring to it," he conceded. Daring to let her see how much he wanted to win, he let hope fill his eyes. "It'd look nice splashed across an article in *Weddings Today.*"

"It's a nice name." But even as she said the words, Evelyn's eyebrows drew together. She spoke through lips that had firmed. "I wouldn't get my hopes up about any Wedding-in-a-Week article, if I were you."

"I wouldn't count it out," he shot back. The Boat Works, or whatever he ended up calling it, might not have all the charm of a centuries-old home, but the building was part of the history of Heart's Landing. It was also a beautiful place to get married, even if he did say so himself.

"Look." Evelyn straightened. "Heart's Landing has played host to the Wedding-in-a-Week contest for the last ten years. Ever since we were named America's Top Wedding Destination. The winning couples have run the gamut. Their weddings have, too. Some brides have walked down the aisle on their own. Others had six attendants. We've thrown receptions for anywhere from ten to two hundred guests. There've been stately affairs. One was a circus—I kid you not, trapeze artists and everything. But no matter what kind of wedding they wanted, every one of those couples had one thing in common. They all chose to get married at the Captain's Cottage. Every. Single. Time."

Ryan stiffened. His entire future might rest on the publicity that came from having the couple pick his venue. "There's always a first time."

"I wouldn't bet on it," Evelyn said lightly. Pushing away from the table, she rose. "I'm just saying."

He'd almost forgotten how competitive she could be. When they were kids, she'd insisted on doing whatever he and Jason did, going wherever they'd gone. Despite the difference in their ages, she'd matched them step for step as they'd raced through the halls of the Captain's Cottage. Stacking his coffee cup and saucer atop his dessert plate, he challenged, "Why don't we do exactly that?"

Evelyn's head tilted. "Do what, exactly?"

"How about a friendly little wager?"

"Depends." She rocked on her heels. "What did you have in mind?"

"Oh, I don't know." Mimicking her tone, he cupped his chin. "Dinner at Bow Tie Pasta, and the loser picks up the tab?" Sooner or later, everyone in Heart's Landing dined at the Italian restaurant on Bridal Carriage Way. As wagers went, it made the perfect bet. But the slight cooling of Evelyn's demeanor told him he'd said something wrong. Pretty sure he knew what it was, he corrected, "For the winner...and the date of their choice."

Immediately, her face softened. "Now you're talking." She grinned. "You'd better save your pennies. You know I'll order the lamb."

Some things never changed. Not at all surprising that she'd pick the slow-braised lamb...the most expensive item on the menu, Ryan licked his lips. "Yum. My favorite. I might need a double order."

"You'd have to win first. And you won't."

"I guess we'll see about that." He flashed her enough of a smile to confirm their friendly rivalry before he sobered. "All kidding aside, this stays between us, right?"

"Afraid your reputation will suffer when you lose?"

"I'm serious." He pulled himself erect and peered down at her. "Because it's Heart's Landing."

Evelyn shook her head even as her lips quirked into a smile. She gave a stage-worthy flick of her wrist. "Just as long as you know I'm looking forward to lamb for dinner." With a saucy swing in her step, she headed for the door.

Watching her go, Ryan allowed himself a wistful smile. He'd been right after all—she had someone special in her life and he, not Ryan, was the one she intended to take to dinner at Bow Tie Pasta. Which was okay, because he didn't want anything more from her than friendship. That and making sure she didn't win their little wager. His smile shifted into a genuine grin.

Going toe-to-toe with her in the competition was going to be fun.

Chapter Four

EVELYN SETTLED THE STUDS ONTO their velvet cushion and stirred one finger through the remaining choices in her jewelry box. She pressed her lips together, dissatisfied. Nothing seemed right. A pair of plain pearls had gone quite well with the teal shirtwaist she'd worn to church this morning. But for the afternoon, she'd changed into a floral print that made her feel feminine and pretty. She wanted the right accessories to go with it. Something that would impress Ryan when he saw her at the train station.

Wait. No. She wanted to impress the Wedding-in-a-Week couple. Ryan had nothing to do it with it. He was a childhood friend, her cousin's pal, an acquaintance. Nothing more.

Her hand hovered over the earrings. Okay, maybe there was a little bit more, but it was all in good fun. They were both eager to have the winners of the Wedding-in-a-Week choose their venue for their ceremony and reception. And the stakes were high, weren't they? Dinner for two at one of the swankiest places in all of Heart's Landing. She inhaled deeply. She could practically smell those lamb chops now. Not that she intended to eat them herself. Or that it mattered one iota what Ryan had done to the old Boat Works. He didn't stand a chance of winning.

But the celebration dinner was a week away. In the meantime, it couldn't hurt to give him a few friendly pointers. She owed him that much, didn't she?

Watching him sweat over the rule book yesterday had stirred a memory straight out of her childhood. She must've been five or six at the time. She remembered, because she'd been in Mrs. Collins's kindergarten class, where every student had long since learned to tie their shoes. Every student but her. After nap time each day, the other kids had put their sneakers on and run out to the playground. Not her. She'd stood there, her cheeks burning with shame, while she'd waited for the teacher to tie the two neat bows. She'd tried to teach herself, but she'd needed help. Only the more people she'd asked, the worse things had gotten. Her dad had said, "Loop, swoop, and pull," but her laces had gotten tangled. Her mom had told her a story about a squirrel and a tree while putting the strings through an intricate dance that had made no sense at all. Resigned to learning on her own, she'd practiced for hours with no success. Every time she'd thought she'd mastered the task, her bow had fallen apart in her fingers.

Until Ryan had taken pity on her. She remembered that day like it was yesterday. She'd been sitting on the bottom step, tears streaming down her cheeks, when he raced down the stairs. His feet had skidded to a stop on the hardwood floors. Instead of teasing her or calling her a baby, he'd walked right over, sat down beside her, and patiently taught her to make bunny ears with each lace and tie them together. She'd never admit it to a soul, but to this day she couldn't tie her shoes any other way.

She'd been indebted to him ever since. By helping him now, she could finally even the score. Not that it'd change the outcome. She hadn't been trying to trick him into backing out when she'd told him the couple always chose the Captain's Cottage. No matter how much time and effort Ryan had poured into the Boat Works, he didn't have a chance of winning their bet. But as long as they were in the competition together, she'd lend him a hand. Because she owed him. Because it was the best thing to do for Heart's Landing.

That her childhood friend had grown into the most attractive man she'd seen in quite a while? Yeah, that had absolutely nothing to do with it.

Her phone chimed a reminder that she had places to go and people to see.

Returning to her jewelry box, she held up delicate dragonflies on fine gold chains that nearly reached her shoulders. The gossamer wings caught the light streaming through her bedroom's third-story window. As much as she knew the pair would go perfectly with her dress, she frowned. She'd promised Jason she'd at least try to maintain a proper, businesslike air in his absence. Dragonflies didn't exactly fit that image. Reluctantly, she traded the dangly pair for some that would earn a business school's seal of approval.

Slipping them on, she glanced at the itinerary wedged into the corner between her dresser mirror and the frame. According to the schedule, Jason and Tara were supposed to check in later. Which was a good thing. She had lots of news to share with them, as well as a few questions to ask. Like why Jason hadn't mentioned Ryan's plans to turn the old Boat Works into a wedding venue. She jotted that down at the top of her mental list and hustled out the door.

Poking her head into the kitchen five minutes later, she immediately spotted the bustling figure who'd been a fixture in her life as far back as she could remember. As kids, she and Jason had used every excuse in the book to pass through the kitchen, where as likely as not they'd snagged a cookie on their way.

"Hey, Connie," she called. Even as an adult, she didn't dare step foot into the head chef's domain without an invitation.

"How was church? Did you and your friends enjoy lunch?" Connie's round face beamed a friendly greeting.

"Excellent, and yes." When Connie gave a brisk nod, Evelyn smiled to herself. Most people thought that, tucked away in the kitchen, the chef stayed too busy to keep track of the comings and goings in the Captain's Cottage. In truth, not much in the house escaped her notice. Evelyn's weekly brunch with friends following the morning service was only one of many examples.

"Good. You deserved a bit of a break. Seems like you've done nothing but work while Mr. Jason's been gone." The cook swirled a tiny spoon through a pot of soup, tasted, and nodded her approval. Dusting her hands on her apron, she asked, "Now, what can I do for you?"

Evelyn smiled. As usual, Connie knew she hadn't simply stopped by to shoot the breeze. "I'm on my way out again. Jenny's going to meet me in the foyer. We're headed to the train station to meet the folks from *Weddings Today.*" She waited a beat. "They'll be here before lunch tomorrow."

"Oh, yes." Connie grabbed a pair of potholders from a stack beside the oven. "I have it on my calendar. Essie and Fiona will bake extra when they do up the cookies." Connie's two helpers put out trays of baked goods for guests of the Captain's Cottage to enjoy each afternoon. "Any special requests for our special guests?"

"Nope." She thought better of her answer. "On second thought, the heart-shaped ones would be nice. With red sprinkles."

"As if you didn't know we make those every Sunday." Grinning, Connie aimed a potholder at her and gave it a good shake. Most guests spent only a night or two in the Cottage's bridal suites, not long enough to grow aware of the menu's weekly rotation. "I'll tell the girls to add some of those mini-éclairs everyone likes. They'll probably put out a few other tidbits, as well."

"Thanks, Connie. You're a treasure." Like Alicia, Connie was another of the reasons the Cottage continued to maintain a stellar reputation. Evelyn had no doubt that when the lucky couple stopped in at the dining room tomorrow, they'd swoon in delight.

"Aw, get on with you now."

Evelyn replied with good-natured grin. She wouldn't take up any more of the cook's valuable time. The Cottage seldom had overnight guests on Sundays, but that didn't mean the staff took the day off. Connie and her crew would spend most of the afternoon prepping meals for the busy week ahead.

"I'll probably be at the train station for a couple of hours." She patted her dress, reassured when she felt the outline of her phone in the pocket. "If anything comes up, call me on my cell," she finished.

"You just go on, Miss Evelyn. We'll hold down the fort."

After saying goodbye, she continued her trek toward the front of the house. Her footsteps slowed as she drank in the quiet. It was rare to schedule a wedding on a Sunday afternoon, and today was no exception. Her footsteps echoed in the empty corridor. The distant sound of a vacuum hummed, confirmation that the housekeeping staff was busy cleaning the bridal suites in preparation for Monday's new arrivals. A low buzz of conversation came from the few guests who lingered over final cups of coffee in the dining room. Knowing she'd spoken to everyone there earlier, she didn't bother to stop.

In the foyer, a portrait of her great-great-grandfather greeted every visitor to the Cottage. From thick brows to high cheekbones and on down to a chiseled jaw, Thaddeus Heart's face reflected determination and success. The man had been every inch the captain of his own ship. Though he'd spent a dozen years at sea, his love for his wife and family were legendary. He'd sworn an oath to celebrate Mary's birthday at home each year, and he'd kept that promise. His love for her was so great that one year, he'd even braved a hurricane in order to drop anchor in Heart's Cove on time.

"You have his lips. You're tall like him, too."

Evelyn jumped. “Oh my goodness, Jenny!” She’d been so lost in thought, she hadn’t noticed her friend approach.

She looked nothing like her successful ancestor. Was that why, at thirty, she was still adrift and unsettled? Peering up at the picture again, she shook her head. “People have always said I favor Mary a bit more. Jason’s the one who inherited his looks from the Captain.”

Jenny, who held an armload of bulky packages, canted her head. “Hmm. I still say there’s a strong family resemblance.”

The idea that she shared something in common with her ancestor was oddly comforting, even if Evelyn couldn’t see it. She turned toward Jenny. “Let me help you with some of that.” Taking half the boxes from the petite brunette, she peered into one that stood open. “What is all this stuff?”

“Name tags so our guests don’t have so much to remember. Brochures for the new arrivals. Extra copies of the weeks’ schedule so everyone knows what’s happening and when. A few odds and ends.”

“You’re prepared for just about anything, aren’t you?” They stepped out beneath the porte cochere.

“When I was working with Kay, I had to be,” said the woman who’d spent several years as the personal assistant to a Hollywood megastar. “But Alicia’s showed me a few new tricks. She’s a great teacher.” Jenny shifted her lightened load to one hand. “It’s such a pretty afternoon. I thought it’d be nice to walk. That’s okay, isn’t it?”

“Sure.” The sun rode lower in the sky than it had when she’d come back from lunch. The air remained pleasantly warm. She started down the long, curving driveway that led to Procession Drive, while a gentle ocean breeze chased wisps of white clouds across the blue sky.

They hadn't gone far before Jenny said, "You look extra nice today. Is that a new dress?"

"You like it? It has pockets!" The moment she'd tried the dress on and discovered the slits, she'd known she had to have it.

"Every outfit ought to come with pockets," Jenny declared, hooking a thumb over one at her side.

"I'm glad we didn't have to dress up too much today." She ran her free hand over the skirt that brushed the tops of her knees. For the past two weeks, she'd stuck to business attire, her curls pinned and slicked into a bun. The summery dress and sandals made a pleasant change. "I'll probably regret leaving my hair loose. Between the wind and the humidity, it tends to get a bit wild."

"Isn't that the way? If we have curly hair, we wish it were straight. If it's straight like mine, we wish for curls." Jenny laughed as she shaded her eyes with one hand. "Oh, look! Mildred Morey is changing out her window display."

She followed Jenny's gaze to the window of Forget Me Knot Florist. Sure enough, curtains had been drawn across the plate glass to hide the work from passersby. "Mildred always comes up with the dreamiest arrangements. I absolutely adored the one she created last month."

"The man down on one knee?" Jenny gushed. "I loved how she had him holding out the ring, the bouquet hidden behind his back. Like the flowers were the most important thing. Brilliant!"

"It's no wonder she's the most popular florist in Heart's Landing. What do you think she'll do this time? Maybe something for Wedding-In-A-Week?" Hoping for a peek, she stopped beneath the awning of the floral shop, but it was no use. No matter how hard she squinted, she could only make out vague shadows behind the curtain. She'd barely taken a step farther down the sidewalk when she felt a sharp poke in her ribs. "Hey!" She shot an accusing glance at Jenny, who answered with a sly grin.

"So you and Ryan sure looked cozy in the dining room yesterday. Anything going on there?" Jenny wiggled her eyebrows.

"With Ryan?" She snorted. "Hardly. We've known each other practically all our lives. He's Jason's best friend."

"And why is that a problem?"

She shrugged, ignoring the question as she got her feet moving again. She made it as far as the entrance to I Do Cakes before she realized Jenny was still waiting for an answer. "We never saw each other that way," she explained. "Or at least, he never did. I might've had a tiny crush on him when I was younger, but he was two years older, so nothing came of it." She didn't have to close her eyes to imagine her parents' reaction if, as a sophomore, she'd told them a senior had asked her out on a date. She could hear her dad's bluster, the concern in her mother's voice. Not that it mattered. "Ryan barely knew I was alive back then."

"Well, he was sure giving you a second look yesterday." Jenny tossed her head. Her dark hair shifted on her shoulders. "I think he threw in a third for good measure."

She nudged Jenny's elbow. "Quit teasing. There's nothing going on between me and Ryan." Although the idea was worth considering. The way his hair had fallen onto his broad forehead while he'd spoken had stirred a desire to push the strands out of his clear, blue eyes. The urge to trace the angle of his jawline or cup his square chin in her hand had been more than a passing fancy. She might even have suppressed an urge to brush her fingers down the length of his muscular arm and see if his muscles tensed beneath her touch. But she hadn't done any of those things. Chances were, she never would. Not now. Not ever.

"He's a friend. That's all," she insisted. Despite her efforts, a tiny bit of doubt crept into her voice. "At least, I hope we'll be friends again."

"Sounds like there's more to that story."

"Not really." What more was there to tell? She and Ryan had been close once. Then they weren't. Now it sounded like they might renew their friendship, at least for the time being. There wasn't much more to say about it, and as they passed Bow Tie Pasta, she attempted to change the subject by pausing to inhale the heavenly scent of tomato and garlic that permeated the air under the covered walkway. But Jenny only tapped her foot, obviously wanting more details.

"There's Helen!" Hoping to distract Jenny, Evelyn waved furiously at a slight figure in the window of The Memory Box. "Do you think she entered the Wedding-in-a-Week competition?" she wondered aloud.

"She always does. Remember the gorgeous boxes

her brother made last year?" Handcrafted from the finest materials, they were perfect for storing wedding memorabilia.

While they waited for the opening bars of "The Wedding March," the signal that it was safe to cross Honeymoon Avenue, Evelyn crooked a tiny smile, satisfied her ruse had worked and Jenny had forgotten all about Ryan. However, once they reached the sidewalk again, the other girl cleared her throat.

"I believe you were going to tell me more about a certain relationship?"

"I was?"

"You know you were. Stop procrastinating, and out with it. Otherwise, we'll be at the train station and I still won't know what's going on."

She sighed heavily. The girl was as stubborn as a dog with a bone. "Okay, but there's really not much to tell. We palled around when we were kids—Ryan, me, Jason. In the winter, we'd build snow forts and have massive snowball fights that went on for days. Or, once the pond froze over, we'd race around the ice pretending we were Bruins in the playoffs for the Stanley Cup. Summers, we'd pretend an old tree house was the *S.S. Mary Shelby* and we had to fend off pirates. We put on talent shows and plays. My uncle Dave let us rummage through the wardrobes in the attic for costumes to wear. When we could convince Connie to pack us a picnic lunch, we'd pick wild blueberries and eat them until our lips turned blue. We had so much fun." Thinking of those days, she sniffed.

"What changed?"

"I've asked myself that question a time or two."

She studied the clouds that looked like streaks of paint against the clear blue sky. "We drifted apart, I guess. We got older, got interested in different things. Jason and Ryan started playing sports—hockey in the winter, baseball in the summer. I joined the drama club and chorus. The guys used to hang out at the Cottage some, but after they graduated and Jason left for Cornell, Ryan went to work for his dad full-time."

In her teens and early twenties, it had seemed critically important for her friends to share the same interests, the same likes and dislikes. Life had taken her and Ryan in very different directions, so it was only natural her friendship with him had faded. But wait. There had to be more to it than that. Ryan and Jason had very little in common, yet they'd remained fast friends. So why hadn't her friendship with Ryan survived? She couldn't put her finger on a specific reason, but she suspected there was one. What it was, she had no clue.

Just beyond the candy-apple-red awnings of Perfectly Flawless Day Spa, someone had blocked off the sidewalk with yellow tape. "The Ash," Jenny whispered, her voice turning funereal. "We have to go around."

Evelyn craned her neck, but a row of buildings blocked her view of the downed tree. Silently, she turned. In minutes, they'd backtracked to Honeymoon Avenue and headed west toward Union Street.

They were halfway down the block when Jenny said, "You two are going to be able to get along, aren't you? I mean, you'd make a cute couple, but as long as you're not interested in each other, it's important that everything goes smoothly this week."

She chortled. "Ryan and I grew up in Heart's Landing. We both know better than to let anything interfere with delivering a perfect wedding for every bride." The town's motto was so deeply ingrained in every citizen, she wouldn't be at all surprised to learn that mothers sang it as a lullaby when rocking their babies to sleep. "Don't worry. We'll behave. Ryan's a good man, a good worker. Remember when we had that leak in the Blue Room?"

Jenny shook her head. "Before my time, I'm afraid."

"That's right." She shot her friend a wry glance. Jenny had slipped so seamlessly into the fabric of Heart's Landing, she sometimes forgot Nick's new bride hadn't even lived here two years yet. The woman still had a way to go with learning thc town's history. She scanned the block ahead. A banner welcoming the Wedding-in-a-Week couple stretched across the street. Farther down, bunting lined the railings of the Union Street Train Station, and hundreds of helium-filled balloons tethered by long strings bobbed in the light breeze. "Okay, I'll give you the short version, seeing as we're nearly there.

"Less than two weeks before one of the most important weddings of the season, the Blue Room flooded during a storm. Jason was out of town, so Alicia offered to move the festivities to the Green Room free of charge. It's larger and I think it's prettier, so it was a really good deal. But the bride got so upset at the change in plans, she had a complete meltdown. She and her fiancé got into a huge fight, and he called off the wedding. That left us with an opening in the Cottage's calendar. I don't have to tell you how rare those are." She waited until Jenny nodded before she proceeded. "As it so happened, this one got snapped up by a certain Hollywood celebrity who sent you"—she pointed to Jenny—"here to Heart's Landing to plan a simple, quiet ceremony."

"Which didn't turn out simple or quiet." Jenny snapped her fingers as an important piece of her history slid into place. "But what does that have to do with Ryan?" she asked a moment later.

"Jason hired him to make the repairs."

Jenny gave a low whistle. "I've been in that room a million times. I never even knew there'd been a problem."

"I hear he's the best restoration specialist in the state. Maybe even in New England."

"And now he's restored the Boat Works."

"Yeah, that." She heaved a breathy sigh. "If the Boat Works is half as good as it looked in the pictures he showed me, the Captain's Cottage could lose quite a few bookings to him." Which would probably put a damper on any hope for renewing their friendship, since she and Ryan would both be competing for the same clients.

"You know..." Jenny said slowly. She stopped and gave her head a shake. "Never mind. It's probably not my place to say anything."

Less than a block remained before they reached their destination. She shot Jenny a sidelong look. "Go on. Say whatever's on your mind."

"It's just that I haven't been here all that long, but I've dealt with a couple of brides who were hoping for a waterfront wedding. The Cottage is great, and we definitely have the best location. With an ocean view, though?" She shrugged. "Not so much."

Evelyn nibbled on her lower lip. Much as she might want to, she couldn't deny that Jenny made a valid point. Up until now, whenever a couple wanted to say their vows within sight of the ocean, the staff had erected tents overlooking the sea. Trouble was, that high up, things tended to get a bit breezy. She knew Alicia and Jenny cautioned brides to avoid long veils and billowing dresses when planning an outdoor ceremony, but she'd seen more than one bride fight to hang on to gauzy fabric when the wind blew.

Enter the Boat Works, and problem solved. With enormous plate glass windows offering both protection from the elements and a beautiful view, brides wouldn't have to give a second thought to the wind or the rain ruining their wedding day.

"So you're saying the Boat Works fills a need."

"Don't you think so?"

She supposed she did. It fit in with Heart's Landing's promise to provide a perfect wedding for every bride and groom. She felt small when she realized she'd been selfishly thinking about the Cottage so much that she'd lost sight of the town's number-one goal.

She shifted Jenny's packages from one arm to another. Opening the Boat Works marked a change. But this was one change she could accept...as long as the Captain's Cottage retained its status as *the* spot to get married in Heart's Landing.

Chapter Five

RYAN LIGHTLY TAPPED THE CASING with a closed fist. The wood frame popped into place over the swinging door he'd spent the afternoon hanging between the kitchen and the main hall. He stepped back, brushing a few flecks of sawdust from his shirt while he admired his handiwork. Not bad, if he did say so himself.

The stain he'd used matched the floors perfectly. The polished brass push plate gleamed against the darker wood. He gave the handle a slight tug. The door swung inward, then rocked back into place exactly as it should. Warmth spread through his chest. He might not be able to build a house from the foundation up, but he could install a door with the best of them.

He turned, casting a critical eye over the interior of the Boat Works. When he didn't spot so much as an inch that required a repair or touch-up, he tugged a wrinkled paper from his back pocket. Running a finger over each item on the punch list, he counted off the completed tasks. Twenty-seven switch plate covers installed. Check. Comfy chairs, makeup tables, mirrors—all assembled and arranged in the bride's dressing lounge. Check. Every squeaky hinge on the kitchen cabinets oiled. Check and check.

Tonight, while the rest of Heart's Landing slumbered, the cleaning crew would scour the building—mopping floors, cleaning sinks, and polishing tall glass windows—until the Boat Works shone like a brand-new copper penny from stem to stern. And he hadn't stopped there. After the meeting in Alicia's office yesterday, he'd stopped by Forget Me Knot, where Mildred had kindly agreed to lend him a few floral arrangements for the showing. He'd bartered future repairs at Favors Galore to have Ashley and Alexis work their magic in the reception area, too. By the time the Wedding-in-a-Week contingent walked through the doors bright and early tomorrow morning, boxes of handmade chocolates would dot long tables adorned with what the girls had assured him was the trendiest in wedding decor.

He splayed his fingers along his lower spine, massaging an uncommon stiffness. He shook his head. His back could complain all it wanted about the effort he'd expended over the last twenty-four hours, but if the Wedding-in-a-Week couple chose the Boat Works as their venue, it'd be worth every twinge.

As important as that was, he hadn't pulled an all-nighter to impress a couple of strangers. No. Unable to sleep, he'd worked through the night to keep his mind from dwelling on a certain redhead with an elfin face and a wide slash of a smile. He'd been in a state of shock from the moment he'd walked into Alicia Thorn's office and seen Evelyn seated in the guest chair. He'd been too focused on her long legs, the spiky heels that cupped her feet like gloves, and the expressions that flitted across her face like lightning to pay attention to a word the event planner had said. Thank goodness JeanMarie had taken the middle chair when she had. Otherwise, he might've done something incredibly stupid, like reaching out to wrap Evelyn's fingers in his or tuck that one loose strand of hair behind her ear.

He hadn't been able to believe his luck when she'd offered to fill him in on the details of the contest. But sitting in the dining room with her afterward, he'd felt as tongue-tied as a thirteen-year-old boy coming face-to-face with his favorite movie star. Which had led to him stumbling around, groping for words until he'd made that foolish bet. Why, why had he done that?

He groaned. He knew the answer to the question as well as he knew every callous and scar on his hands. He'd been hoping she'd have dinner with him. In one of the most romantic settings in all of Heart's Landing, he and Evelyn would laugh and talk and share a great meal. By the time they finished their second glasses of wine, she'd realize they were made for one another. And that, as they said, would be that.

Yeah, right. Not. Gonna. Happen.

He should have his head examined. Evelyn hadn't been waiting around for him any more than he'd been pining after her. Hadn't he convinced himself that she meant nothing more to him than any of the dozens of other friends he had in Heart's Landing? While he lived in Maine, she so rarely crossed his mind, he felt certain he'd have no problem returning to the town he'd grown up in and going about his life without her in it. Why not? He and Evelyn moved in different social circles. They had different interests. The odds that he'd even cross paths with her more than once or twice a year were so slim, he hadn't even given the matter much thought.

He should have. Because now that he was here, now that he'd spent his life savings restoring the Boat Works, he was a goner. Just being in the same town together had stirred nearly forgotten feelings for the impish redhead. He'd been as surprised as anyone when they'd sprung to life again. Yet he'd kept them at bay by avoiding Evelyn whenever possible and, when it wasn't, he'd kept his focus tightly on the job at hand.

But now...

Now, the Wedding-in-a-Week competition had thrown them together. Worse, he had a sneaking suspicion Evelyn wanted to renew their long-dormant friendship. While that might seem like a good idea, he was pretty sure just being friends with her would be the death of him. He hadn't been able to think of anything but her all night.

He shook his head. He'd been right to keep his distance the past couple of years. He needed to stick to that plan. At the same time, he'd have to do everything in his power to have his venue chosen for Wedding-In-A-Week. If he failed at either task, he'd soon find himself standing in the unemployment line nursing a broken heart. Something he simply could not allow to happen.

He dusted his hands and bent to gather up the last of his tools, satisfied that both he and the Boat Works were as ready as they'd ever be for the competition. The clock had been ticking while he'd stood here woolgathering. If he didn't hurry, he wouldn't make it to the train station on time to greet the Wedding-in-a-Week couple. The last thing in the world he wanted right now was to lose out on the contest—or his bet with Evelyn—before things even got started.

Striding up to the train station a scant hour later, Ryan did a double take at the sea of white balloons bobbing in the breeze like foam dancing atop ocean waves. Streamers and bunting decorated the railing that led from the sidewalk to the tidy brick building just off Union Street. To say nothing of the crowd. He'd expected a good turnout. Heart's Landing was nothing if not eager to give a hearty welcome to every guest. But this...he hadn't expected this. So many people crowded the platform there wasn't room for them all. He peered through the windows of the tidy train station and spotted even more figures milling about inside.

A mild relief washed through him. It should be easy enough to avoid Evelyn in this crowd. Loosening the sleeve of the polo that had bunched slightly at his biceps, he scanned the area. He was supposed to meet the mayor under the *Welcome to Heart's Landing* banner but didn't see him. However, Walter Headly stood on the outskirts of the crowd. The former owner of the Honeymoon Hotel looked rather out of place with his shirttail flapping over baggy beach shorts. Ryan cut across the grass toward one of Heart's Landing's most-loved citizens.

"How you doing, Walter?" The older gentleman had propped his arms on the business end of a metal detector. "Find anything interesting lately?"

"Aye-yup. The storm night afore last stirred up a bit of sand. Found a chain with the prettiest locket." Walter dug in his pocket and drew out a thin necklace. "Pure gold, I'm thinkin'. Hurts my heart that someone let it get away from 'um. You'd think folks would take better care of the things they value."

Despite having been born and raised in Heart's Landing, Ryan needed a second to sift through the muted *r's* of the old-timer's thick accent. "Maybe you'll get lucky and Georgia will know who lost it." The clerk at the train station ran the town's Lost and Found department.

"Aye-yup. That's what brought me he-ah. Didn't expect all this, though." Walter swept one age-spotted hand at the crowd that had spilled out onto the lawn. "Quite the pah-ty."

"Important guests and reporters from *Weddings Today*." He checked the double-sided clock that hung from a cast-iron mount decorated with the town's standard hearts-and-flowers motif. "They're on the 4:30 train. It's due in any minute. I have to get on up there." Ryan gestured toward the far end of the platform. "You should stay. It'll be fun."

"Don't have much time." Walter stepped back, sand sifting down from the metal detector he'd hefted over one shoulder. "Walter Junior's bringing the grands over for dinner. I'd best be getting home. I'll come back when things are quiet-ah."

Watching the portly widower shamble off at a surprisingly quick pace, he couldn't help but wonder if he was catching a glimpse of his own future. Forty years from now, would he spend his days scouring the beach for things people had lost and dispensing advice about holding on to what was precious? He gave his head a slow shake. Walter was one of a kind, a Heart's Landing institution.

An overhead speaker broke into his reverie with a burst of loud static. His attention shifted as, in her most official voice, Georgia addressed the crowd.

"Attention. Attention. Amtrak Train 165 is due to arrive in ten minutes. All passengers planning to board the train, report to the platform." After a slight pause, she continued in a far less formal tone. "Here she comes, folks. Let's give our Wedding-in-a-Week couple a hearty Heart's Landing welcome."

Time to get moving.

Exchanging greetings with friends and acquaintances, he made his slow way toward the mayor, who faced the opposite direction while he spoke with someone Ryan couldn't see. As he moved closer and the group milled and shifted around the man, he caught flashes of a bright spring dress, but it wasn't until he was nearly upon the couple that he spotted cinnamon-colored hair and knew he was about to come face-to-face with the one person he'd sworn to avoid.

He had to say hello. It'd be rude to do any less.

"Mr. Mayor. Evelyn," he said, extending his hand as he cut through the last of the crowd.

"Ryan Court. Always a pleasure." Greg Thomas ignored Ryan's outstretched hand. Instead, the man who divided his time between running the town and the largest tux shop for miles around administered a hearty backslap. "I was happy to hear your Boat Works had been chosen for this year's Wedding-in-a-Week competition. Always good to have new businesses in Heart's Landing." The mayor leaned close enough to whisper in Ryan's ear. "You have your permits, don't you?"

"Yes, sir." He grinned. "Passed all the final inspections. I'm good to go."

"Well, now. That's great. I have a couple of people I need to speak with, but I'll look forward to seeing what you've done with the place. Rumor has it, it's a beauty."

"Come by anytime," he started, but he was speaking to thin air. The mayor had already moved on. Which left him standing alone with the one woman in Heart's Landing he wanted to spend less, not more, time with.

"Cutting it a little close on that Occupancy Permit, weren't you?"

The observation caught him off guard, but then, Evelyn had a knack for saying the unexpected. "I was sweating bullets," he joked, pretending to mop his forehead. The move must've been the right one, because she aimed that wide smile at him, the one that kicked his heart into overdrive. "To be honest, I hadn't planned on getting it for another couple of weeks. In time for the Grand Opening at the first of the month. But I called the Building Inspector's office after our meeting with Alicia, and I got lucky. He swung by late yesterday and signed off."

"I guess that gave you a little time to relax before all this." She tilted her head to the crowd.

"I wish." If she had any idea how much he'd accomplished since they'd last seen each other, she'd be amazed. "There were still a million and one things left to do."

Not one to be outdone, Evelyn piped, "Meanwhile, I was working my fingers to the bone at the Cottage."

He coughed to cover a hoarse laugh. With thick curls cascading around her shoulders and all dolled up in a sundress that barely skimmed the tops of her knees, Evelyn hardly looked worse for wear. But then, she could probably make a ratty pair of jeans and a stained T-shirt look like couture. A sudden tension ran across his shoulders. He straightened. "I was working like a fiend to finish up before our guests arrived."

As if he'd shared a secret, she leaned a little closer. "That explains why you're late. For a minute there, I thought you weren't going to make it."

So she'd noticed his absence, had she? Stifling a smile he had no business wearing, he scanned the area. "And miss all this? Not a chance. Not when there's so much at stake."

"For Heart's Landing. For the Wedding-in-a-Week couple." She nodded as if she understood what he'd meant.

He lifted an eyebrow when Evelyn's deadpan delivery trailed off. "Have you forgotten our bet already? Or were you just hoping I had?"

"You wish." Challenge glittered in the green eyes she lifted to meet his. Her usual teasing grin deepened. "I'm planning to enjoy every bite of my *free* dinner."

"We'll see about that." He couldn't help ragging on her in return. He enjoyed her company more than he should. Deliberately, he tore his gaze from hers while he gave himself a stern reminder that he'd sworn to keep his distance from Evelyn. Hoping to do just that, he stared over her head. At the edge of the platform, Greg Thomas spoke quietly with an Amtrak representative. "With everything that was going on, I haven't had time to study the program. What happens next?"

Evelyn sobered. "You haven't been to one of these in a while, have you?"

"Not in the last..." He studied the bunting, the stringed quartet warming up on one end of the platform, the crowd of well-wishers. The truth was, this was his first. Although brides had vied to get married in Heart's Landing for decades, he'd moved to Maine two years before *Weddings Today* had hosted its first Wedding-in-a-Week celebration. "Actually, no," he corrected. "And this turnout"—the hand he swept through the air took in everything from JoJo Moss aiming her camera down the tracks to the masses of balloons that bobbed in the breeze—"is a bit more impressive than the last time someone met me at the train station."

"Huh. So all this really is new to you." Evelyn scanned the crowded platform. "There's not much to tell. Mayor Thomas will kick things off with the usual speeches and introductions." Cupping one hand over her mouth, she leaned closer. "He likes to keep things short and sweet, so that part won't last too long. Thank goodness." Her hand fell away, and she straightened. "After that, Alicia and Jenny will organize a reception line inside for our special guests."

Her movement filled the air with the sweetness of fresh flowers combined with a tangier smell of grapefruit that went straight to his gut. He swallowed. Casting about for a safe topic, he peered through the station windows. Beyond the glass, servers in white shirts and black pants moved between tables. “Any chance for a bite to eat?” In his rush to get the Boat Works in tip-top shape, he’d skipped lunch. Come to think of it, he might’ve skipped breakfast, too.

“Get serious.” Evelyn’s lips curved. “You forget you’re in Heart’s Landing or something? Food Fit For A Queen is catering today’s event.”

He all but smacked his lips. He’d be hard pressed to choose between the offerings at the Captain’s Cottage and those of Chef Hubbard’s. Rubbing his hands together, he asked, “What are we waiting for?”

“Um, the train?” Evelyn’s eyes sparkled with humor. She plucked at his shirt sleeve. “Hold on. What’s that you have all over yourself? Run a hand through your hair.”

He did as he was told and gave a sheepish grin when white flecks rained down. “Sawdust. I told you I was working right up to the last minute. Now do you believe me?”

Smiling up at him, she reached forward just as he dusted a few bits from the front of his shirt. The brush of her fingers against the back of his hand sent a heart-stopping charge of electricity straight through him. He couldn’t help but tense. The instant he did, her hand dropped so fast, he’d have sworn she’d burned herself on a hot stove.

“You’ll do,” she announced tightly. Her smile evaporated. Confusion sifted onto her face as she widened the gap between them.

“Thanks. Uh, for the help,” he said, doing his best

to ignore the fact that he'd never felt so uncomfortable in his life. An urge to reach out, to explain, surged through him. But standing in the midst of half of Heart's Landing while they waited for the arrival of two people who could change his entire future was neither the time nor the place. To cope, he mustered his best, most good-natured smile while he searched for some quip or comment that would wipe the storm clouds from her eyes. His mind drew a blank, but he refused to give up. He was still trying to come up with a solution when a distant train whistle blew.

"Oh!" Evelyn breathed. Her focus shifted away from him. "They're here."

Anticipation rippled through the crowd. From one end of the platform to the other, people straightened. Smiles grew brighter. Those holding "Welcome!" signs lifted them higher.

He followed Evelyn's lead when she, along with everyone else, leaned toward the wide turn. A clump of trees blocked his view of the tracks. For several long seconds, nothing happened. Then, he heard it. The clackety-clack of metal in motion. A bell rang out. The engine nosed around the curve into sight.

As the heavy diesel roared loud enough to make the gravel dance in the flower beds, more than one person put their fingers in their ears. At last the engine whooshed past and, with a final squeal of its brakes, slowed to a stop. The passenger cars slid to a halt, their doors aligned perfectly beneath overhead signs. The noisy engine, which had moved well beyond the station, throttled down.

"Make way. Make way!" Emerging from the station, Georgia cleared a path through the crowd. Conductors stepped from between the cars to assist departing passengers. Ryan caught movement out of the corner of one eye and turned just in time to see the mayor mount the first set of steps behind the engine. An excited hush fell over the group. Evelyn leaned forward, her brow furrowed with anticipation.

A spattering of applause broke out the moment a man wearing a brown fedora appeared in the doorway of a passenger car. "Sorry to disappoint, folks, but I'm not the groom," he called. The collective groan that greeted his announcement didn't seem to faze him. He hustled past to the baggage claim area.

For several long minutes, nothing else happened. Ryan shifted his weight from one foot to another as time dragged on with no sign of the Wedding-in-a-Week entourage. Around him, people murmured questions. "What if they missed the train?" "Where are they?" "What's taking so long?"

Five minutes passed. Then ten. Beside him, Evelyn danced on the balls of her feet. Finally, the door of one of the passenger cars opened with a noisy creak. A familiar figure stepped into the vestibule area. Smiling broadly, Greg Thomas lifted a microphone.

"Welcome, welcome. Thank you all for being here today. I've just met with our Wedding-in-a-Week couple, and I don't mind saying you're in for a treat! You're going to fall in love with Brianna and Daniel, just like the judges at *Weddings Today* did. You'll get to meet them in a minute, but first—before I introduce them—let's find out a little bit more about the winners of Heart's Landing's Wedding-In-A-Week!"

Greg tugged an envelope from the pocket of his suit. Hampered by the mic, he slid one finger under the flap and ripped it open. Inside was a single sheet of paper, which he held up to the crowd. "Um, bear with me," he said. "This is the first time I'm seeing this, so don't expect a perfect delivery."

"Like all your other speeches, Greg!" someone shouted.

The comment earned scattered chuckles before, with a throat-clearing harrumph, the mayor began, "This year's winners of a Heart's Landing Wedding-In-A-Week, courtesy of *Weddings Today*, have traveled all the way from Geneva, Florida. They've been best friends ever since their teacher, Mrs. English, assigned Daniel the seat next to Brianna's in first grade."

His voice as clear as a radio announcer's, Greg continued, "Daniel and Brianna spent an idyllic childhood growing up in Central Florida. Along with a close-knit group of friends, Daniel and Brianna enjoyed the best the area had to offer—fishing in nearby lakes, kayaking and swimming in the crystal-clear water of artesian springs, picking oranges in the citrus grove owned by Daniel's family, and drinking root beer floats at the local diner run by Brianna's parents.

"Once they entered high school, both Brianna and Daniel began to think about the future. Brianna planned to help run her family's business while she pursued a culinary degree. Meanwhile, Daniel had set his sights on a career in the military. But their plans changed when... Oh, my." Greg's voice halted abruptly. Clearly struggling to maintain his composure, he gazed toward the station, his eyes damp. After a long pause, he shook the paper and cleared his throat. His voice dropped an octave. “When Brianna’s parents were tragically killed in a car crash the summer before her junior year of high school.”

Sympathy rippled from one end of the gathering to the other. Ryan studied his feet. His heart went out to the bride-to-be.

Eyes lowered, the mayor resumed speaking. “More than anyone else, Daniel was there for Brianna. He stood beside her at the funeral and stuck by her side during the days and months that followed. It took time, but with Daniel’s help, Brianna eventually settled into her new life with her aunt and cousins. While the two remained good friends, they headed in different directions after graduation.

“Brianna got her degree from the local college. There, to honor her parents, she studied emergency medicine. After graduating, she went to work as an EMT at the hospital where her folks received treatment the night they were killed. Daniel attended college on the other side of the state. He earned his degree in Criminal Justice. This helped him fulfill a lifelong dream when he enlisted in the Marines.”

Applause erupted for the young man who’d chosen to serve his country. When it died down, the mayor waited a beat before he continued, “Remembering how supportive he’d been when she’d needed someone to rely on, Brianna sent letters to her friend while he was at boot camp. Daniel claims her letters gave him the strength he needed to make it through one of the most rigorous training programs in the military. Once he’d completed basic training, he headed home on leave with one thing on his mind—to ask Brianna out on their first real date. That night, an enduring friendship blossomed into love. Daniel and Brianna have known they were meant for one another ever since."

Several women sighed audibly into the pause when Greg stopped to take a breath. Ryan rocked on his heels. Brianna and Daniel's story had all the hallmarks of a true Heart's Landing love for the ages.

"The couple will soon report to Camp Geiger, where Daniel will undergo further training." The mayor lowered the paper. His eyes crinkled, and he practically beamed at the crowd. "But not before Heart's Landing—and *Weddings Today*—gives this very deserving couple a perfect wedding!"

A round of thunderous applause echoed from one end of the platform to the other.

When it died down, Greg said, "And now, without further ado, I give you Private First Class Daniel Johnston and his lovely fiancée, Brianna Smith." The mayor hustled down the steps. A photographer followed and stood at the foot of the stairs.

Ryan joined the others in raising a heartfelt cheer for their guests while, beside him, Evelyn did the same. He craned forward, eager to learn more about the bride and groom, as a young couple stepped from the train car into view.

According to the introduction, Brianna worked as an EMT, but the woman at the top of the stairs looked as though she couldn't possibly be old enough for such a big responsibility. Blond hair framed her face and fell in soft curls around her shoulders. A long, lean frame only added to her youthful appearance. Her mouth gaped slightly, and she viewed the crowd through eyes so wide, Ryan wondered if this was her first trip north of her home state.

An equally young Adonis stood beside the bride-to-be. Tall, with shoulders broad enough to carry a heavy load, he wore his brown hair buzzed so short, it was barely fuzz. While Ryan watched, Daniel straightened the collar of his uniform and bent to whisper something in Brianna's ear. Whatever he said must've steadied her, because she tipped her head to his and pressed a kiss to his cheek. Like the homecoming queen in a parade, she waved and blew kisses to the crowd while Daniel descended the steps. Then, rather than offer her his hand, the young Marine lifted Brianna as if she weighed no more than a feather and tenderly lowered her feet to the ground beside his own. Their arms wrapped around each other's waists, they followed Mayor Thomas into the station.

Ryan tracked Brianna and Daniel until they disappeared. Around him, people shifted. The crowd broke up, half skirting around the building to the sidewalk and beyond, the rest flowing toward the doors. A reception line formed inside.

Beside him, Evelyn grabbed his arm. "Hey! Are you going to stand there all afternoon? Let's go inside."

He shook himself. "What?" He eyed the redhead standing next to him. "Sorry. I was kind of caught up by their story."

Evelyn pressed a hand over her heart. "True love. Isn't it wonderful?"

"When it's right, it's right," he agreed.

"Come on." She headed for the entrance. "We need to get in line to say hello."

Minutes later, the mayor introduced him as the

owner of the Boat Works and excused himself. Ryan and the groom-to-be exchanged firm handshakes. His plan to move on stalled, along with the people in line behind him, when Evelyn and Brianna stopped to chat like two long-lost friends.

"What do you think they're talking about?" Daniel asked when the women shared a laugh.

Ryan smiled. The young man's Southern drawl was thicker than maple syrup on a cold winter's morning. "I'm pretty sure Evelyn's telling your fiancée all about the Captain's Cottage."

Understanding dawned in Daniel's dark eyes. "Ever since we found out we were coming here, Brianna's been studying brochures, trying to imagine where we'd get married." His forehead creased. "I don't remember seeing any pictures of the Boat Works."

"We don't officially open until the first of the month. That's when the website is set to go live." In his haste to get everything else ready on time, he'd forgotten to have his web designer bring the site online earlier. He'd correct that oversight before he turned in for the night. "It was originally the home of Farley Boat Works. That business died out long ago. I've spent the past year turning the building into the perfect wedding venue. The views are spectacular."

"Waterfront, then?" When Ryan nodded, Daniel rubbed his chin. "Sounds like something I'd like."

"Can't wait to show it to you." Ryan grinned. Beyond the reception line, Mildred Morrey shook her head in response to some question Greg had asked her. His jaw set, the mayor locked arms with Nick Bell next. Despite an uneasy feeling that shifted in Ryan's stomach while the two engaged in a whispered sation, he focused on Daniel. "I hear you did fishing back home. If you get a chance this week, come on down to the marina. I keep a couple of rods in my office. We can try for some stripers." The fish was a local delicacy.

Daniel's grin widened. "Now you're talking."

They talked about fishing for a few more minutes before Ryan stepped aside to let the next person in line take his place. On the other side of the room, the mayor was still making the rounds. Whatever the man wanted, he didn't seem to be having much luck. Glad to stay out of it, Ryan headed in the opposite direction. At the buffet table, his stomach rumbled when he added Chef Hubbard's famed sausage balls to a heaping plate.

"Hold it! Don't move." At his elbow, a photographer snapped a picture. "Thanks," he said, lowering the camera. "You don't mind if your picture appears in *Weddings Today*, do you?"

"Not at all." The more publicity, the better. He balanced his plate in one hand and stuck out the other one. "Ryan Court. Owner of the Boat Works."

"Curtis Webster." The photographer squinted, then whipped a small notebook out of a back pocket and scribbled in it. "Sorry. It helps me later if I jot things down as I go." He swung, searching. "Oops. Gotta get a picture of that. I'll see you around, Ryan." Curtis headed toward whatever had caught his attention on the other side of the room.

Ryan's stomach sent up another reminder to feed it. He was just about to take his first bite when the mayor, along with Evelyn, Alicia, and Jenny, appeared at his elbow.

"A word, please," Greg Thomas said. He marched to a corner without checking to see whether he'd been followed.

With a last, wishful glance at his food, Ryan joined the others.

"I had a quick minute to speak with our winning couple, and I must say Daniel and Brianna are absolutely adorable," Greg said once he made certain no one else lingered close by. "But they're so young and so inexperienced, I'm concerned they might not have what it takes to make it through the week."

Ryan eyed their guests of honor. Surrounded by well-intentioned townsfolk, they were so ill at ease he was surprised they hadn't already bolted for the door. "They do seem a little lost. Makes you wonder why *Weddings Today* chose them."

"Everything's done online," Alicia offered. "Couples submit a video along with their application. Junior staff weeds the entries down to ten. Senior editors conduct online interviews with them, but no one actually meets the winning couple until they arrive in New York for a photo shoot."

Greg Thomas ran a hand over his balding head. "Brianna and Daniel come from a small, rural town where everyone knows everyone. She barely stepped foot outside of Geneva before this trip. Nothing in Daniel's background has prepared him for all the hoopla, either. It's a lot to handle."

"Planning a wedding can overwhelm any bride and groom. Having to do it all in a week, well, we all saw how that worked out when I did it." Jenny grinned. Her not-so-simple wedding had thrown the entire town into an uproar.

"I suppose you have a solution." He waited for the mayor's response. The man rarely pointed out a problem without having a plan to deal with it. Whatever it was, Ryan didn't think he was going to like it.

"I want you to take them under your wings, guide them through the whole process."

"Me?" He stepped back. Ask him to repair a busted window or change a flat tire, and he was your man. But he couldn't do what the mayor was asking. There were rules against it. "Aren't you worried I might try and sway Brianna and Daniel to choose the Boat Works?"

"That's why we're asking you and Evelyn to work together. So neither of you has the upper hand," Greg soothed.

"I can't afford to be away from the Cottage for an entire week," Evelyn objected. "I'm already filling in for Jason. Plus, I have my own work to do."

He wasn't at all surprised to hear her protest, but he couldn't help but wonder if it was the assignment or working with him she disliked the most. He quashed the question. She wasn't any happier with Greg's idea than he was—that was the important thing.

The mayor frowned. "I know it's a lot to ask. I'd get someone else to do it if I could, but there isn't anyone. I've asked practically everyone here. With the wedding season in full swing, Nick and his staff are working around the clock to make sure every cake gets delivered on time. Mildred Morrey's so busy, her niece took a leave from her job in New York to help out at Forget Me Knot. Ashley and Alexis have hired two new people to help out at Favors Galore, and they're still concerned about filling all their orders."

So that was what all those whispered conversations had been about. That still didn't mean he was the right choice. He scanned the rapidly emptying room. There had to be someone better qualified to take his place. "This seems like the kind of job a wedding planner would do, doesn't it?" He eyed the two women who flanked the mayor.

"I have my hands full with other aspects of the contest. Coordinating visits at the participants' shops, communicating with the editorial staff at *Weddings Today*. There are a million details that'll require my personal attention." Alicia passed the baton to her assistant.

Jenny stepped forward. "While Alicia devotes her time to handling the behind-the-scenes efforts, I'll be in charge of all the other weddings we have scheduled for the Cottage this week. And I'll take as much of your load off your shoulders as I can," she said, directing the comment to Evelyn. "I'll show prospective clients the grounds, answer phone calls, oversee the staff."

"And don't forget, the photographer from *Weddings Today* will be right there with you, too," the mayor added.

"Sounds like you've thought of everything," Evelyn mumbled.

Ryan wasn't convinced. "I don't have any experience planning a wedding. What makes you think I can do this?" He fought an urge to sidestep when Greg pinned him with a steely gaze.

"Daniel already likes you, Ryan." Greg turned the

same unflinching gaze on Evelyn. "And you seemed to hit it off with Brianna." Raising his hands, the mayor aimed a finger at each of them. "I saw the way they opened up to you in the reception line. Believe me, they hardly said more than two words to anyone else."

He shook his head. Working with Evelyn was a bad idea on so many fronts, he couldn't even count them. And then there was the not-so-little matter of the couple who stood like two abandoned puppies in the middle of the room. How was he supposed to help them? "This is beyond my comfort zone, Mr. Mayor."

"Even with Jenny's help, I have my hands full," Evelyn objected.

Greg said, "I wouldn't ask, but Heart's Landing needs you. The Marines have given Daniel extra time off because of all the good publicity he'll generate for the Corps. That only adds to the pressure this couple will be under this week. Can you imagine what would happen if they cracked? Maybe *Weddings Today* would take their contest somewhere else next year." His firm features said he wasn't taking no for an answer. "You both grew up here. Weddings are ingrained in your blood. You're young enough that Brianna and Daniel can relate to you. And there's one more thing you have in common with them that no one else does—you've been friends since grade school. Just like Brianna and Daniel. In my book, that makes you not just a good choice, but our only choice."

He scuffed his foot against the floor. He'd been right—he didn't like the mayor's solution. But if it meant that much to Heart's Landing, he supposed he didn't have a choice. He'd have to help out. "Okay, I'll do my part, as long as…" He let the rest hang. Before he committed, he had to make sure of one thing.

"Yes?" Equal amounts of relief and doubt swirled in the mayor's eyes.

"As long as the Boat Works stays in the running for the wedding venue."

"The Captain's Cottage does, too," Evelyn insisted.

"Absolutely." Greg Thomas gave his head a firm nod. "Now, don't advise them on their choices—that's up to them. Just be there if Daniel needs someone to talk to, Ryan. If Brianna needs a shoulder to lean on, make sure it's yours, Evelyn." The man rubbed his hands together. "I want one of you with them when they visit every shop. "You can take turns if you must—"

"We will," Evelyn blurted before Ryan had a chance to say the same thing. He agreed with an emphatic nod of his head.

"Good. I knew you were the right people for the job. Now, don't let me down. We're all counting on you to get this couple through all the Wedding-in-a-Week festivities and give them the wedding of their dreams."

Ryan eyed Evelyn. His fingers clenched. He deliberately relaxed them. "I guess we'd better meet. We need a plan on how we're going to handle all of this."

"Sure. Jenny wants to go over a few things right now, and I need to be at the Cottage for Jason's phone call in a bit." She slipped her phone from her pocket and held it up. "I'll call you as soon as I'm free."

"Tell Jason I said hi." He nodded. He still had some things to take care of at the Boat Works and could use the time between meetings to knock a couple of them off his list. His stomach muscles tightened as the group broke up, and Jenny and Evelyn headed for a corner, their heads together.

Heaven help him, what on earth had he been thinking? He'd just agreed to spend an entire week shepherding a couple he'd barely met through their very own Wedding-in-a-Week. Worse, he'd promised to work closely with the one woman he'd sworn to avoid.

He squared his shoulders. For the good of Heart's Landing, he'd do his best to make sure Brianna and Daniel got the wedding they deserved. He had no doubt he could help them survive this week. But would *he*?

He glanced down at the plate still balanced in one hand. His appetite for cheesy sausage balls or fried wontons had dulled. Not even the macadamia nuts sprinkled atop a fudge bar tempted him. After making sure no one was looking, he dumped the food in a nearby trash can, wiped his fingers on a napkin, and ducked out the closest exit.

Chapter Six

EVELYN PROPPED HER PHONE AGAINST a stack of fabric samples on her desk so she could multitask during her video call with her cousin Jason. In the darkness beyond his and Tara's hotel room, she spied the lights of a soaring church tower. "So how was Cambridgeshire?" she asked.

As she listened to his answer, she went through the stacks of paper on her desk. Thanks to the hundreds of suppliers who had business dealings with the Captain's Cottage, her office floated on a sea of samples. Despite that, she could usually put her finger on exactly what she wanted. Ever since Jason and Tara had embarked on their monthlong honeymoon, though, she'd lost more than one battle against the clutter.

If that were all, she wouldn't worry about it. She could deal with messy. But she'd fallen behind on some of her own responsibilities, and Jason had only been gone two weeks. She flipped through the reminders that had appeared on her desk while she was at the train station. The kitchen had run out of crème fraiche. Housekeeping wanted more buffing cloths.

The landscapers needed more mulch. Each item was critical to the smooth operation of the Captain's Cottage, and it was her job to supply it. Now that Mayor Thomas had added to her workload by practically shaming her into working with Brianna and Daniel, she didn't see herself getting caught up anytime soon.

The full weight of running the busiest wedding venue in Heart's Landing pressed down on her shoulders. Maybe, if she asked Ryan nicely, he'd take over the whole job of showing Brianna and Daniel around Heart's Landing. She shook her head. Not if she wanted the couple to choose the Captain's Cottage, she wouldn't.

"Everything all right?" Jason stared out from the screen, his gaze slightly off-center.

She straightened. "Sure. You're in Eli, right? At the Poet's House?" Jason and Tara had chosen the snug hotel because of its fabled views.

"Eee-lee," Jason corrected. "Yes. We're in the north of England. We have to be up bright and early tomorrow. Our tour of the Ely Cathedral starts at nine." He turned to his wife.

"I can't wait to see it," Tara gushed. "The octagon is considered one of the marvels of medieval architecture."

"After that, we'll ferry across the Channel to France," Jason continued. "Then, it's on to Florence and our final destination, the Duomo."

"Jason arranged a private tour of the Dome and Terraces. It's supposed to be breathtaking," Tara chimed in.

"That sounds positively..." *Boring.* Evelyn bit her tongue. Traipsing through dimly lit churches had never been her cup of tea, but Jason and Tara shared a passion for flying buttresses and majestic naves. She supposed that was part of what made them perfect for one another. As for herself, she could think of a dozen better ways to spend her first month of married life.

Not that she had time for a relationship, what with the busy bridal season heating up. Plus, the added responsibilities of looking after Brianna and Daniel. Her pulse thudded. Two more weeks. She only had to get through the next two weeks before Jason and Tara returned from their honeymoon. She could do it. *Piece of cake.*

She sniffed the air. The smell of Connie's freshly baked cookies wafted into her office. Her stomach growled insistently. She hushed it and peered at the screen. On the other side of the Atlantic, Jason and Tara shared a loving glance.

"You're having a good time?" she asked them.

"Oh yes!" Tara's sweet smile filled the screen. "It's been wonderful!"

Warmth blossomed in her chest. Tara and Jason deserved all the best.

Her cousin brushed a kiss onto Tara's forehead before his expression turned serious. "How are things going there? Any problems?"

She toyed with an earring. "Nothing I haven't been able to handle. The Hoovers asked if we could sing at their reception. They were disappointed to learn you were out of town, but they perked right up when I told them 'Mary'"—she enclosed the original Mrs. Heart's name in air quotes—"would make a special appearance at no charge. We had a great time at the reception on Friday."

"I'm sorry we left you with so much to handle." Regret played across Jason's face.

"I'll fill in for you when we get back," Tara offered. "I already know the songs for the performances. Now that I'll be living at the Cottage, I probably ought to learn everything else, too. From the financial end on down."

Jason's expression brightened. "You can finally take that nice, long vacation you've been putting off."

"Maybe," she hedged. Jason and Tara meant well, but their suggestions only highlighted a growing concern. Now that her cousin had found his true love, his wife would rightly assume the role of hostess of the Captain's Cottage. As for the skits and pageants, it was only fitting for Tara to play Mary opposite Jason's impression of the swashbuckling captain. But where exactly did that leave her? Without a firm goal in mind, looking at the future made her feel uneasy and unsettled. In a move that normally calmed her thoughts, she stroked her ponytail while she filled Jason in on the Wedding-in-a-Week festivities.

On screen, he grinned. "That's great news, Evelyn. Can't you just picture it? Daniel in his uniform. Brianna all decked out. They'll look wonderful on the cover of *Weddings Today* with the Captain's Cottage in the background. The publicity will generate a ton of new business. Maybe enough to pay for that new roof."

"You think so?" Replacing the slate on a one-hundred-year-old home was no easy feat. Artisans skilled enough to hand-shape the tiles were hard to come by.

The few they'd located were horribly expensive. She'd nearly fainted dead away when Jason had shown her the first cost estimate. But her cousin was right, she decided, running the numbers in her head. With the added business a big, splashy article in *Weddings Today* would generate, they might even have the work completed before the June bride season started next year.

She sat for a long moment after she and Jason said their goodbyes. Despite her efforts to forget about it, the question she'd asked herself during the call wouldn't go away.

What came next for her?

She'd never become the kindly maiden aunt tucked away in the family wing, living off her cousin's charity. For one thing, she spoke her mind too often for anyone to mistake her as kindly. Then, there was the not-so-little matter of earning her keep, something she insisted on doing. She squared her shoulders. In order to prove she was still a vital member of the team, she needed to drum up new business for the busiest wedding venue in town. Which meant making sure Brianna and Daniel chose the Captain's Cottage for their wedding venue. No matter the cost.

She tugged on her lower lip. Short of breaking the rules, that was. She'd never do that. But she couldn't afford to let her friendship with Ryan get in the way of what was best for the Captain's Cottage. Or winning that dinner at Bow Tie Pasta. She grinned.

The time had come to find out more about her competition. And, thanks to the mayor's little plan, she had just the excuse she needed. If that meant she had to spend a little bit more time around a certain hunky carpenter who made her heart race, all the better. Right?

She reached for her cell phone and punched Ryan's number.

The sun rode low in the western sky by the time Ryan climbed the ladder into the old tree house. In the small copse of woods near the Captain's Cottage, cool air and shade provided a welcome relief from the summer heat. He stood at the railing and scanned the path that led from the trunk of the sturdy red oak to the mansion's manicured lawns. A figure rounded the corner of the house. *Evelyn.* He didn't need to see the red hair she'd twisted into thick braids to know it was her. He'd recognize her long, lean silhouette anywhere.

He checked his watch. She was running a few minutes late. But then, punctuality had never been her forte. Still, there she was, striding toward him. How had he let himself get trapped into working with her? Especially just after he'd sworn to keep his distance? Maybe he should have his head—and his heart—examined.

But no. He was doing this for the sake of Heart's Landing. For Brianna and Daniel, a couple who deserved their very own perfect wedding. For the Boat Works. The Wedding-in-a-Week competition was a once-in-a-lifetime opportunity. He'd be a fool not to put his all into it. Even if it did mean working with Evelyn. Besides, it was only for a week. He'd do his part and she'd do hers, and when the seven days were up, he'd walk away with his heart intact.

"Knock, knock." Evelyn's voice floated up through the hole in the floor of the tree house. A light tapping sounded as she rapped on the ladder.

"You need a hand up?" He peered down at her. When they were kids, climbing up the ladder had felt like climbing Mount Everest.

"I've got it," she grumbled.

Same old Evelyn. Competition was part of her nature. He stepped back as her head popped through the square hole. With an effortless grace, she hoisted herself up the rest of the way.

"You sure picked the strangest place to meet. Frankly, I wasn't sure you knew our old fort still existed."

"Oh, I knew, all right." They'd spent a lot of time in the tree house when they were younger. He had a thousand good memories of the place. "I checked it out soon after I came back to Heart's Landing. A couple of the steps on the ladder had come loose. So had one of the railings. I replaced those. Otherwise, it was in decent shape considering how long it's been here."

"Hmmm." She folded her arms across her chest. "You don't have to do that. I can have the gardening crew give it a thorough look every so often and make whatever repairs are necessary."

"I don't mind." He paused, uncertain whether or not he was saying too much. "I stop by from time to time. It's a good place to think and clear my head."

"Really?" She peered up at him, surprise flickering in her green eyes. "I've been too busy lately, but last summer, I'd fill a thermos and come out here first thing in the morning at least once a week. I like listening to the birds, watching the Cottage come to life."

Memories from their childhood came back in a rush. "We had some good times here when we were kids, didn't we?"

A wide grin broke across Evelyn's face. "We'd pretend the tree house was a pirate ship and sail the seven seas."

He glanced toward a wooden lean-to in one corner. "Jason was always trying to get you to stay in the cabin so we could rescue you." He laughed. "But you rarely went along with his plans."

"I wanted to be captain of my own ship." She flicked a thick braid over one shoulder.

He shook his head. He and Jason had had a lot to learn about girls back then. Fortunately, Evelyn had been more than willing to teach them. As a matter of fact, she'd actually insisted on it. When they'd tried to tell her girls couldn't captain a ship, much less be a pirate, she'd grudgingly abided by the rules. But not for long. One rainy afternoon when they couldn't go outside to play, she'd dragged them both into the Library. There, she'd hauled down a book that was nearly as big as she was. She hadn't even been able to read yet, but she hadn't let that stop her. She'd pointed to pictures of Anne Bonny, an infamous *lady* pirate of the 1700s. After that, Evelyn had demanded they all take turns playing the role of captain. He chuckled. He'd always admired her spunk.

Standing, she wandered over to the railing. "I

wonder what happened to our flag. You remember it? Your mom made it for us."

"I have it." His heart expanded at the thought of their initials stitched into the corners, and he smiled. Once, long after they'd outgrown their pirate days, he'd taken a shortcut through the woods on his way to visit Jason and had spied the tattered piece of cloth hanging from an old fishing rod they'd used as a flagpole. He'd retrieved it and, later that night, he'd tucked it among the mementos he kept in a footlocker by his bed.

"You do?"

"I thought my children might like it for their own tree house someday." He cleared his throat. "If and when that day comes, that is." He shuffled his feet. Why on earth had he mentioned children? Any discussion along those lines was bound to lead to talk of hopes and dreams for the future. That was not the kind of conversation he wanted to have with a woman who'd long since made it perfectly clear she wasn't interested in him.

Hoping to change the subject, he grabbed the bags he'd brought with him. "I guess we ought to talk about this Wedding-in-a-Week thing. Have a seat?" He gestured to the bare planks where, as kids, they'd spent long hours shooting marbles and playing card games.

"Well, I'm glad someone ended up with the flag." Evelyn settled on the edge of the rough flooring, her feet dangling in the air above the ground.

"I brought sandwiches." Paper rustled as he plopped one bag between them on the boards. "I hope you don't mind, but I'm starving." He'd gotten so lost in putting the finishing touches on the Boat Works this afternoon, he hadn't eaten.

Evelyn stared at the brown paper bag. "Is that what I think it is?"

He grinned. "If you're hoping for grinders from The Aisle, this is your lucky day." A sign over the tiny storefront read Down The Aisle of Sandwiches, but everyone simply referred to the sub shop as The Aisle. From the time they were old enough to pedal their bikes along Procession Avenue, he and his friends had ridden as often as they could.

"Oh, man. I'm dying for one of those." Grabbing the bag, Evelyn stuck her nose inside and breathed in. "The best smell ever," she declared, handing it back.

She was right, and he didn't bother to deny it. He pulled out two subs wrapped in thick white paper. "You want chips?"

"And ruin a perfectly good sandwich? No thanks. You asked for extra hots, didn't you?"

"Of course." The pickled red peppers added an extra kick that set the subs apart from all others. Eagerly, they peeled back the layers of paper to reveal classic Italian grinders stuffed full of salami, ham and provolone atop a bed of shaved lettuce. The air filled with the aroma of The Aisle's secret dressing. The smell made his mouth water almost painfully.

"Dig in," he suggested, barely able to wait for her to go first.

She did, and they ate in silence for a few minutes. After they'd devoured the first salty, tangy bites, he pulled out two bottles bearing the familiar anchor of a popular Rhode Island brand.

Eyeing the drinks, Evelyn squealed, "Oh, my goodness. You remembered."

"How could I forget? It's still my favorite." His mom made sure the old-fashioned metal cooler on their back porch held an assortment of Yacht Club sodas whenever Jason and Evelyn came over to his house. The three of them had made a game of sifting through the melting ice until each of them found their favorite flavor. He and Evelyn had always been partial to cream soda, while Jason preferred root beer. He pried the top off his and drank deeply. Evelyn did the same. The cool, refreshing taste made the perfect accompaniment to the spicy sandwiches.

At last, he sat back, his arms angled behind him to support his weight. "The Aisle and cream soda. I think I missed those the most when I lived in Maine."

"That, and the brides," Evelyn teased lightly.

"And the brides." He laughed, feeling more at ease than he'd expected after confessing that his love for Heart's Landing had drawn him home.

She handed him a napkin. "Thanks," he said, and mopped his face. When they'd gathered the trash into bags, he returned to the subject they'd met to discuss. "They really stuck it to us with this one, didn't they?"

Beside him, long shadows played across Evelyn's face. "Yeah, but what choice do we have? We have to help. The whole town's depending on us."

"True. But I meant it when I said I had no clue how to handle this. How about you? You have any ideas?"

She shrugged. "Most of the meals are covered. The mayor's taking Brianna and Daniel to the White

Dove tomorrow. They have a lunch meeting with Alicia on Tuesday. And so on and so forth. Nights, we're off duty. Alicia or Jenny will go with them to check out their choices for the rehearsal dinner early in the week. The other evenings are set aside for date nights—we don't have to worry about any of those."

"That's good to know." With the others pitching in, he and Evelyn wouldn't have quite as much to do.

"That leaves the vendors for us. Tomorrow, Brianna and Daniel will tour the Boat Works and the Cottage. We can each handle those on our own."

He nodded. Between play dates and the restoration work he'd done there, he pretty much knew the Cottage inside and out. He didn't mind skipping the tour. "Good. I could use a few hours to take care of some things."

"Me, too." Evelyn polished off the last of her soda. "Tomorrow afternoon, I'll go with Brianna to try on wedding gowns while you take Daniel to Tux or Tails. As for the rest, divide and conquer, I guess, so neither of us has too much on our plate."

He considered the schedule. It didn't surprise him one bit that Evelyn had a carefully thought-out plan of attack. But it didn't sound like they'd be spending much time together at all. Had she arranged it that way on purpose? He briefly considered asking her before he discarded the question. He nodded agreeably. "That works for me. We probably ought to touch base once in a while so nothing slips through the cracks."

"Sure. I'll call you or you can call me each evening. We'll make sure everything's covered for the next day." She grabbed the trash bags and shimmied toward the opening in the floor.

Watching her disappear down the ladder, he shook his head. He and Evelyn had been good friends once. But to protect his heart, he'd sworn to keep his distance from her. Now, she'd come up with a plan that would keep them apart throughout the Wedding-in-a-Week activities. He ought to be happy about that.

So why wasn't he?

Chapter Seven

"Hello! Anybody here?"

Ryan looked up from the ledger he'd been working on in his office at the Boat Works. He checked his fingers for telltale signs of red ink. When there weren't any, he checked the time on his cell phone. Brianna and Daniel weren't due for another half hour.

"Anybody here?" the voice called again. "Ryan?"

Evelyn? Warmth spread through his chest the moment he recognized her voice. Confusion followed on its heels. She was the last person he'd expected to see this morning. Yesterday, after the mayor had coerced them into acting as Brianna and Daniel's escorts for the week, they'd decided he'd show the young couple the Boat Works this morning while Evelyn kicked off another busy week at the Captain's Cottage. They'd agreed to trade places later, which would give him time to return the flowers he'd borrowed from Mildred and take care of a few chores. Then, this afternoon, they'd divide and conquer again—the girls would head for the bridal salon, the guys to Tux or Tails.

He shut the book containing columns that dipped

deeper into the red every day. Three days ago, those numbers had given him a headache, but not anymore. Not now that the Wedding-in-a-Week event had provided the opportunity to turn things around. Once Brianna and Daniel chose the Boat Works as their wedding venue, all his problems would be solved.

And why wouldn't they? The facility had never looked better. Throughout the building, surfaces gleamed and glistened. Ashley and Alexis had arrived before daybreak and spent hours adding festive touches to the entryway and beyond. He'd literally rolled out the red carpet in the main hall, where floral arrangements on loan from Forget Me Knot Florist lined a makeshift aisle and brightened every corner. Even the weather had cooperated by delivering a picture-perfect day. He couldn't ask for a better chance to prove to Brianna and Daniel that this was the place to hold their wedding. But first, he needed to find out why Evelyn had shown up when she wasn't supposed to be here.

Locking the door to his office, he strode quickly down the back hall to the entrance. Sure enough, Evelyn stood in the lobby, tapping one well-heeled shoe against the hardwood floor. This morning, she'd paired another of those slim-fitting skirts with a snug blouse that showed off all her curves. She looked amazing, even with her hair pinned and her pretty curls tucked into a tight knot at the back of her head.

Just looking at her spread joy like sunshine through him. He was glad they'd rekindled their friendship. One day...

He gulped and slammed the brakes on his wayward thoughts. He was not going there. He hadn't left his office to ogle Evelyn Heart. They'd agreed to work together, but things between them absolutely weren't going one step further. Not during the Wedding-in-a-Week competition, when his entire future was at stake. And not later. He'd done the math. He knew for a fact that Heart's Landing could support a dozen wedding venues. But as long as he owned the Boat Works and Evelyn was tied to the Captain's Cottage, they'd always be vying for business. Relationships faced enough obstacles without adding those kinds of problems to the mix.

Searching her face, he cleared his throat. "Hey, Evelyn. What's up? Is something wrong?"

"What? Oh, no. Everything's fine."

"What brings you here, then? I thought we were meeting at the White Dove at one." Was she hoping to undermine his efforts with Brianna and Daniel? That was something the Evelyn he remembered from high school might try.

"I had a couple of errands to run in Heart's Landing this morning. Since I was out, I ran by Parks & Rec to pick up my sapling. I got yours, too."

"Well, that was nice." And something one friend would do for another. Ashamed of himself for questioning her motives, he cast an expectant look at her feet and came up empty. "Where's the tree?"

"I left it outside, on the deck. I, um, didn't want to track any dirt in. Oh," she added like an afterthought, "I ran into Curtis and gave him a lift."

Ryan started. He'd been so entranced by Evelyn he hadn't even noticed the photographer from *Weddings Today*. Not that he was to blame. The smaller man stood quietly at the back of the room, where he hadn't attracted a bit of attention. "Hey, Curtis." He canted his head. "You didn't want to come with Brianna and Daniel?"

Curtis hefted his camera. "When I can, I get to the places on our schedule ahead of the bride and groom so I can record their first impressions. Meantime, don't mind me. It's easier for me to do my job if you ignore the fact that I'm even here."

"You got it." He left the man to his musings and turned to the redhead, who was studying the walls of the cozy entryway. A soft smile tugged at her lips.

"I love this, Ryan. You've done a terrific job with the place. I can't wait to see the rest."

The high praise sent his spirits soaring and tempted him to show her more. He gestured toward a pair of immense barn doors. He'd kept them closed in order to add an element of surprise to his tour with Brianna and Daniel, but it wouldn't do any harm to give Evelyn a sneak peek. As one friend to another. "The main ballroom and reception area are back there. Did you, um, want to see them?"

"I do, but if it's okay, I'll stay and see it with our lucky couple. You don't mind, do you?"

Evelyn's smile would melt butter, but he was on to her ploy. "Scoping out the competition, are you?" Not that he'd turn her down. Friends didn't do that to one another. And she was his friend, wasn't she? Besides, he'd been hoping to get her opinion on something else, and he couldn't think of a better time. "Curtis, if you'll excuse us for a second." When the photographer answered with a noncommittal shrug, Ryan led Evelyn to his workroom.

"What do you think?" He pointed to the sign he'd

worked on through the dead of night and held his breath.

Evelyn stared at the pair of wedding rings and horse-drawn carriage that bracketed the words *Harbor View Weddings*. Her breath caught so sharply he was almost afraid she'd choked on something. She leaned down for a closer look. "It's perfect!"

Before she could trace her hand along the letters, he cautioned, "Careful. The finish is still tacky. It'll need another twenty-four hours to dry. I'll hang it later this week."

"I love the name," she said, a heartwarming smile breaking across her lips.

Her approval meant more than he thought it should, and he coughed to cover a momentary self-consciousness. Fortunately, the sound of a car door slamming shut saved him. He angled a thumb toward the entryway. "We'd better get out there. That's Brianna and Daniel," he announced.

They made it back to the lobby just as the front door opened, admitting the young couple bathed in sunlight. In the background, Curtis's camera emitted a series of soft whirrs.

Ryan's shoulders relaxed at the sight of the couple, who looked far more at ease than they had at the train station. "Good morning." He crossed the room to greet his guests. "Welcome to the newest venue in Heart's Landing. How did you two do last night? Were you comfortable at the Union Street?"

"Oh, yes," Brianna answered, charming him instantly with her soft, Southern accent. "It's sooo nice. My room's like a picture right out a magazine. And comfortable—I can't begin to tell you. There were so many pillows on the bed, I felt like a princess."

"That's great! Everyone in Heart's Landing will do their best to make you feel like that all week." Wanting to include Daniel, he turned to the groom. "And you? Are you happy with your accommodations?" Daniel's ground-floor suite was just below his fiancée's.

"Yes, sir. Like Brianna said, the bed and breakfast is awesome." He cupped one hand at the side of his mouth. "Don't tell my mom, but Ms. Mary's a better cook than she is, and that's saying something. The blueberry pancakes she made for us this morning were out of this world." He patted his stomach.

"If she feeds us like that the whole time, I'll need to buy a whole new wardrobe." Brianna pushed her long blond hair over one shoulder.

Daniel gave his fiancée a tender look. "You probably worked off every calorie and more on our run."

"You're runners?" Ryan eyed the pair. Despite the differences in their height, they were both lean and well-toned.

"Have to be in the Marines," Daniel said solemnly.

"I ran track in high school. I've stuck with it." Brianna slipped her hand in Daniel's. "It's something we enjoy doing together."

Ryan tapped his chin. His baseball coach had insisted that running built stamina. Like Brianna, he'd kept up the habit. "If you're up for it, I'll show you one of my favorite trails. It skirts the coastline north for about five miles. There are some really pretty views along the path."

The look on Daniel's face said he was raring to go.

"Sounds good to me. Bri?" When she nodded, he suggested, "Tomorrow at oh five hundred?"

"That works." Ryan turned to Evelyn. When they were younger, basketball and soccer had been her sports. Had that changed? "Want to join us?"

"That's a bit early for me." The redhead faked a yawn. "I'll stick with my yoga class. It's better suited to my schedule. Speaking of which, ours is tight today." She tapped her watch.

Ryan clapped his hands together and gave them a brisk rub. "She's right. We need to get moving." He turned to Curtis. "Are you ready?"

The photographer checked his camera. "I have everything I need here." He looked at Briana and Daniel. "Like we did on the way down here, I'll snap some candid shots as we look around. I'll get you to pose for some more formal pictures before we move on to the next location."

When Brianna and Daniel agreed, Ryan cleared his throat. "Welcome again to the recently named Harbor View Weddings." Glad he'd taken her advice, he couldn't help tossing a smile in Evelyn's direction. "The name might be new, but this place has a long history in Heart's Landing. When the Great Depression ended in the 1930s and people had more time for leisure activities, George Farley established Farley's Boat Works. He and his sons built dinghies and daysailers up to twenty feet long. Over time, they became well-known for crafting some of the finest hand-finished wooden boats on the market." He pointed to one of the smaller vintage Farleys. He'd restored the dinghy to pristine condition and had propped it against one wall in the lobby area.

"Farleys were in high demand for a long time, but by the nineties, lighter fiberglass boats became more popular. Wooden boats that required more upkeep fell out of style. Farley Boat Works closed its doors. The building was shuttered and remained in the family until George passed year before last."

He checked the faces of his small audience. Noting that everyone listened attentively, he continued. "Heart's Landing is America's Top Wedding Destination, and it has a lot to offer practically any bride. But the one thing the town didn't have was a great waterfront location. That's where I come in. I bought this property, spent a year stripping the building down to the bare bones, and rebuilt it from the pilings up." He inhaled. His pulse thudded. The next few minutes might very well determine his future. "And here's the result. I hope you like Harbor View Weddings."

Crossing to the towering barn doors, he pushed lightly on one panel. The door soundlessly glided back to reveal the main hall. Brianna gasped in surprise and wonder. Daniel chuffed approvingly. Though Evelyn didn't utter a sound, her green eyes widened, and her mouth gaped open.

Gleaming wooden floors and sparkling chandeliers led straight to windows that overlooked the harbor. On the other side of the glass, white clouds hung in the azure-blue sky like puffy balloons. Boats bobbed at anchor. Seagulls sailed the skies. The sun sparkled off a light chop created by an easterly breeze.

"Oh! Pretty!" Brianna exclaimed.

Daniel squeezed his fiancée's hand. "I like it!" he said firmly.

Ryan launched into a well-rehearsed spiel. "The

ballroom accommodates up to two hundred guests, plus staff. For larger parties, floor-to-ceiling sliders open along the harbor side, giving access to the deck and the dock beyond." He noted the sparkle of interest in Brianna's eyes before he pointed to the ceiling. "Those chandeliers once hung in the Promontory." He'd picked them up for a song at an antique shop where they'd ended up after the Newport mansion, unlike the Captain's Cottage, had failed to stand the test of time. Answering questions and highlighting the features of the space, he showed them the side rooms, which could be used in various ways. When he sensed Brianna and Daniel had seen enough, he guided them to the spacious kitchen, which had been outfitted with top-of-the-line appliances. "Several of our best local chefs contributed to this room's design." He made sure to mention the immense Aga gas stove, the walk-in freezer, and a Subzero refrigerator that met catering specifications.

"This is all so perfect!" Brianna exclaimed when they'd moved on to the brides' dressing area, where cream-colored chairs and tables dotted the hardwood floors. A sofa at one end and several comfortable chairs provided additional seating.

Across the hall, the grooms' room featured similar seating, but there, he'd decorated the space with darker, more masculine colors that earned Daniel's approval.

"That view, man," Daniel observed when they'd returned to the main room. "It's priceless. Did you say the deck outside is yours as well?" When Ryan nodded, Daniel's head bobbed. "I'm sold." He turned to Brianna. "Did you ever, in your wildest dreams, think we'd have a chance to get married in a place like this? There's nothing like it back home, for sure."

He waited with bated breath for the bride's answer. Before she had a chance to say a word, Evelyn cleared her throat. "Don't forget," she reminded the young couple, "we're headed to the Captain's Cottage next. In the meantime, I'm supposed to remind you to keep your choices under wraps until Saturday."

He pressed his fingertips together. Brianna had been on the brink of committing to Harbor View. He was certain of it.

Evelyn handed the keys of her car to the waiting valet and hurried up the wide steps to the Captain's Cottage. Reaching the top, she concentrated on seeing the front lawn through fresh eyes. In the distance, one of the landscaping team rode back and forth across the thick, green grass. His machine created an interesting patchwork design as he mowed. Another worker trimmed the arborvitae, the precise snick-snick of his sheers maintaining a top so level she could use the hedge as a tea table. Water babbled over the rocks of a small creek that flowed under the weeping willows. She drank in a calming breath. The air carried a hint of fresh-cut grass mingled with the sweet scent of flowers. She especially loved the Cottage in the summer and made a point of stepping out onto the veranda or standing on the front steps several times a day. The sights, the sounds, the smells normally soothed her.

But not today.

Today, her shoulders were so tight, they ached. Thanks to Ryan Court and his Boat Works. Or should she call it Harbor View? As wedding venues went, the place was absolutely gorgeous. Ryan had wisely divided the floor space, providing roomy dressing areas for the bride and groom while maintaining a spacious hall that could accommodate all but the largest of weddings. Every inch of the woodwork reflected superb craftsmanship and attention to detail. He'd spared no expense when it came to furniture and appliances, either. She crossed her fingers and prayed Connie never stepped foot inside Harbor View's kitchen. If that ever happened, the Captain's Cottage might be looking for a new head chef. Throw in the spectacular views, and Ryan's building became a serious contender for first place among the Heart's Landing venues.

Which meant she'd have to redouble her efforts if she had any hope of convincing Brianna and Daniel to hold their ceremony and reception at the Cottage. She drew in another breath and flung open the front door. One look at her great-great-great grandfather's portrait strengthened her resolve. She blew him her usual kiss and marched down the hall.

Her footsteps faltered outside the dining room. She gritted her teeth. Just inside the door, crumbs and discarded napkins dotted the otherwise empty tables. On the buffet, the morning's sweet rolls had been picked over. Bits of egg and cheese clung to the sides of a nearly empty casserole dish. A lone slice of bacon sat in a tray beneath a heat lamp. She scooped up the trash and ducked into the service closet for a cleaning rag. Her feet skidded to a stop when she spotted Joelle, a new addition to the kitchen staff, at the long counter. The girl rolled silverware into cloth napkins.

With all this mess, that's what she chose to do? She fought a rising temper. Struggling to keep her voice even, she pointed out the obvious. "The dining room needs some attention."

She must've spoken more sharply than she'd intended, because silverware clattered to the countertop from the startled girl's hands.

"I'll get it, Miss Evelyn." Joelle glanced over her shoulder as she started for the door. "I was just taking advantage of the lull to—"

She held up a hand. "The egg dishes need to be replenished. Tell the kitchen to send up a fresh tray of breakfast meats," she ordered, running down her list. She studied the front room. Was it her imagination, or did the flowers on each table look a little droopy? Of all the times to skimp on details, this wasn't it. "Call the greenhouse. Have them replace the flowers."

"Yes, ma'am. I'll get right on it, but..." Her hands shaking, the young woman grabbed a bottle of cleanser from the cupboard.

"What is it?"

"Well, it's almost time for lunch. Connie and Fiona are on their way up with the sandwiches and desserts."

Evelyn felt her face heat. In her haste to make sure every detail was perfect for Daniel and Brianna's arrival, she'd forgotten the time. She checked her watch. In exactly ten minutes, housekeepers would descend on the dining room. With their usual clock-like precision, they'd sweep the floors, scour the tables and, yes, even replenish the floral arrangements while the cooks removed the breakfast items and arranged the day's lunch offerings. She took a breath. "Okay. Forget what I said about the food. But if you could tidy up out there..."

"I'm on it." Joelle grabbed a fresh cleaning rag.

Evelyn wheeled. She race-walked to the Green Room. But one look inside stopped her cold. Her mouth dropped open. When she'd left the house this morning, the ballroom had been empty. Now, rose-colored linens spilled from large tubs scattered about the room. A crew of young people moved between rows of half-dressed tables and chairs. She put a hand to her head. "No, no, no," she moaned.

She'd deliberately avoided scheduling any events in their largest hall in order to show off the wainscoting and crown molding during Brianna and Daniel's visit. The prep work ruined the effect.

"You there." She pointed at a pair of teens who were lugging an eight-top from built-in storage closets at the back of the room. "Put that back." The arm she swept through the air encompassed the entire space. "Take all this down, right away."

A young woman who'd just tied the bow on the back of a chair frowned. "Ms. Jenny told us to—"

"I'll call her right now. In the meantime, stop whatever you're doing." She tugged her cell phone from her skirt pocket.

Jenny answered on the first ring.

"We have an emergency," Evelyn said, trying not to hyperventilate. "You need to get the Green Room cleared right away. Please tell the staff to get all this stuff out of here immediately."

She disconnected. Forcing her back ramrod straight, she headed for the bridal suites. The housekeepers had worked their magic in those rooms only yesterday. They'd sailed through her white glove test this morning, but after what she'd discovered so far, she had to double-check. Her heels beat a staccato against the floor. She made it halfway down the corridor when Jenny fell in beside her.

"What's going on?" the woman murmured, her voice barely above a whisper.

"I just saw the Boat Works. Ryan renamed it Harbor View Weddings. Have you been there?"

Jenny's head bobbed as if the brief explanation answered all her questions. "Come with me."

"I can't. I have to—"

A hand grabbed her elbow in a steely grip. "Come. With. Me," the wedding planner said in a tone that made it useless to argue.

Left with no choice, she let herself be guided into a small office two doors down from Alicia's. She'd barely crossed the threshold when Jenny rounded on her, eyes blazing.

"You realize you've thrown the entire household into a tizzy, don't you?"

"I'm sorry. But the dining room was a mess. The Green Room was—"

"—lovely," Jenny cut in. "What's that you're always saying—if it ain't broke, don't fix it? There's nothing to fix here. The staff is well aware how important it is for us to win over the Wedding-in-a-Week couple. They have everything under control. Trust them."

"But they're halfway through setting up the Green Room," she objected. "I wanted Brianna and Daniel to see how spacious it is."

"They will." Jenny's exasperated sigh filled the air. "We have twenty weddings scheduled in the Cottage this week. The Harper affair is tomorrow night in the Green Room. This is the best time to set up for it. If we don't do it now, it'll set off a chain of dominoes, and we'll be playing catch-up through the weekend. You know how nervous Alicia gets when that happens. Neither of us wants that."

She shifted her weight from one foot to the other while she tried not to squirm beneath Jenny's pointed gaze. She couldn't argue. Her friend had a valid point, but the assistant planner hadn't been where she'd been. "You didn't see Harbor View," she pointed out. "It's...impressive. Soaring glass windows. Stunning views. The place is so beautiful, I wouldn't mind getting married there."

"Whooooo," Jenny breathed. "That's saying something."

"So you understand why everything here has to be picture-perfect. If it isn't, Brianna and Daniel will choose Harbor View over the Cottage."

"They're going to love it here." Despite her insistence, questions filled Jenny's eyes. "Unless there's something else I need to know?"

She inhaled. "I wish I had your confidence. Jason's counting on me to run things while he's gone, and so far, I'm afraid I'm not doing a very good job."

"Nonsense. The most important thing you can do right now is relax. Focus on the Cottage's history, its beauty, the things we offer that no other venue in

Heart's Landing can. Brianna and Daniel will love it here because you do."

Maybe Jenny was right. Maybe not. Either way, she had more riding on the Wedding-in-a-Week contest than her friend and co-worker realized. No one else had been on the phone with Jason and Tara last night. No one else knew they were nudging her aside. Or how much it hurt. True, she'd been thinking it might be time to move on, but she'd always expected to make that decision on her own. Not have it made for her. But Jenny was right about one thing—she *had* upset the entire household. Her tendency to speak first and think later had caused problems again. Her cheeks heated. She studied the floor. "I owe everyone a huge apology, don't I?"

"That'd be a good place to start. I'm just not sure it's enough."

Misery swam through her tummy. What had she been thinking? The Captain's Cottage employed only the best, people who worked hard to give each bride a perfect wedding. She snapped her fingers. "I'll stop in at I Do Cakes while I'm out and put in a special order for Nick's salted caramel cupcakes." The decadent treat was the bakery's Tuesday special. They were so popular throughout Heart's Landing, they usually sold out before lunch. "I'll leave them in the break room first thing tomorrow."

At the mention of her husband's name, stars danced in Jenny's eyes. "Nick will appreciate the extra business, and the staff will be thrilled." She nodded her approval. "You still have fifteen minutes before Brianna and Daniel get here. You could spend the time smoothing the feathers you ruffled."

She closed her eyes. Apologies weren't her strong suit, but she'd follow Jenny's advice. The staff deserved her praise, not her criticism. She set off down the hall, doling out heartfelt "I'm sorry's" to those she'd barked at moments earlier. Finishing just in time, she arrived in the foyer as a Town Car pulled under the porte cochere. Daniel took Brianna's hand as she stepped out of the car. She gestured excitedly toward the house while Curtis snapped pictures.

Evelyn wasn't close enough to make out the words, but whatever the young woman was saying, it had to be good. Brianna was practically dancing on air. The expression on Daniel's face announced to the world that he'd give his bride-to-be anything she wanted. Including a wedding at the Captain's Cottage.

A heavy weight dropped from her shoulders. Pulling herself upright, she swung the door wide to greet her home's newest guests. "Brianna, Daniel. Welcome to the Captain's Cottage."

After a brief exchange—they had, after all, only left each other a half hour earlier—she gave them a moment to absorb the impressive foyer before gesturing to her great-great-great grandfather's painting. "I'd like you to meet Captain Thaddeus Heart, the original builder of the Captain's Cottage. Thaddeus made his fortune sailing the high seas between London and New York in his ship the *Mary Shelby*, which he named after his wife. The intrepid captain battled hurricanes and pirates, raging winds and dead calm. It was a dangerous life, a hard life, and many didn't survive it. But Captain Thaddeus promised his bride he'd always make it home in time for her birthday, and his wife, Mary, never lost faith. Theirs was such an enduring love, it gave rise to the term, 'A Heart's Landing love for the ages.'" A beat later, she looked directly at Brianna when she added, "We here at the Captain's Cottage would like nothing more than to host your wedding and help you and Daniel launch your own love for the ages. If you'll let us."

The introduction was the same every prospective bride and groom heard before they agreed to hold their wedding at the Captain's Cottage. Some might call it so much patter, but the Captain's love for his wife permeated every inch of the sprawling estate. Her family had always felt it was important to provide their guests with a little bit of insight into what made the Cottage so special, why it was more than just a beautiful place to get married.

She stole a quick look at Daniel and Brianna. If the stars that twinkled in Brianna's eyes were any indication, the bride-to-be had committed every word of Thaddeus and Mary's love story to heart. Her focus shifted to Daniel. The young groom had been so enamored of Harbor View that she'd considered him the hardest to win over, but the young man stared intently at the image of Captain Thaddeus. His faraway look told her he was imagining his own life on the high seas. She crossed her fingers behind her back.

Next, she led the small entourage to one of her favorite rooms in the entire estate. "As we go through the house, you'll see we offer several options, depending on the number of your guests and the size of your wedding party. The Conservatory is perfect for smaller parties of up to twenty." She slid open the doors to a room where the sun streamed through mullioned windows to create a checkerboard pattern on the hardwood floors. Cream-colored walls and wide crown molding lent the room a spaciousness far greater than its size. A grand piano in one corner contributed to the illusion. She crossed to the instrument and plinked out the first few bars of "The Wedding March."

"Imagine a harpist and a pianist playing softly in the background when you walk down the aisle."

Daniel canted his head. "That has a nice sound for something so old."

Veering from the script, she worked hard to mask her surprise. "You know a little bit about pianos, do you?"

"My dad plays. He's always wanted a grand piano. He used to drag us to tag sales every weekend, hoping to find one he could afford. He never did, but someday—when I have a little money set aside—I'm going to buy him one."

"That's so sweet," she said, her respect for the young groom growing. She ran her fingers lightly over the Steinway's rich patina. "This particular piano has been in the Heart family since the 1800s. According to the ship's log books, the *Mary Shelby* was attacked by pirates on a return trip from London one fall. Captain Thaddeus and his crew returned fire, severely damaging their attacker. The pirates abandoned their sinking ship, which Captain Thaddeus and his men quickly boarded. They liberated several hostages the pirates had been holding for ransom. One of them turned out to be the son of a wealthy New York merchant who was so overjoyed at his son's rescue that he commissioned this piano as a gift."

"That's some story." Daniel's brow furrowed. "It's true?"

"Every word," she assured him. Tara had unearthed records of the event while she'd searched the ship's logbooks for reasons that hadn't been entirely clear at the time. Leaving Daniel to dream of adventures at sea, Evelyn turned to Brianna. Her heart ached for the young woman who'd lost so much already. Wanting to give her a perfect wedding, she said, "Personally, I love the Conservatory for intimate ceremonies. How many guests do you expect?"

Brianna's cheeks dimpled. "We're thinking somewhere around fifty or so. There's my aunt," she said, keeping count on her fingers. "She'll give me away. Her daughters, Ann and Lynn, are flying up with her on Friday. They'll both be in the wedding party. Daniel's parents will be here. His two brothers—Enoch and David—and their wives—Sissy and Melanie—are coming. A half dozen of the guys he went to boot camp with and their dates. A bunch of our friends were planning to drive up, but I'm not sure how many of them will actually make it. It's a long way from Central Florida."

"*Weddings Today* will probably send a few people. Right, Curtis?" Evelyn turned to the photographer, who'd been quietly snapping pictures from various points in the room.

Curtis lowered his camera. "Probably a staff writer. And Regina Charm, for sure. She's in charge of the Wedding-in-a-Week contest. She'll bring a date."

Evelyn nodded. Alicia and Regina had worked together on all the arrangements. "Let's say another six from the magazine, just to be on the safe side." She gave the young couple a long, appraising glance. "The shop owners and prominent citizens of Heart's

Landing would love to help you celebrate your special day, too. It's customary to invite them to attend. If you don't mind, that is. If you'd prefer a smaller gathering..." In the end, only the bride and groom could make that decision.

"The more, the merrier," Daniel said, hugging his fiancée close.

Brianna's dimples deepened. "Sounds like fun!"

"I'll let Alicia know. She'll spread the word." Evelyn tipped her head. "That means, though, you'll need a larger space than the Conservatory. Fortunately, we're just getting started. C'mon," she said, moving toward the door. "You're going to love this next spot."

A short walk down the hall took the party to the side porch, where greenery wrapped tall columns above white railings and blossoms filled the air with a heady scent. "I especially love it out here when the roses are in bloom like they are now. Many of our brides and grooms choose to marry on the Veranda. Or serve cocktails here and hold their ceremony and reception somewhere else on the property."

Or not, she thought, when someone behind her issued a series of rapid-fire sneezes. She turned to see which of the group had a problem and nearly ran into Daniel.

"Oh, gosh. Roses." A look of pure dismay crossed his face. He turned to Brianna, who'd yet to step onto the porch. "Duck back inside, honey." After his bride disappeared into the house, he explained, "She's allergic."

"That rules out the Veranda." Evelyn ushered everyone back indoors and firmly closed the door. Concern swelled in her chest. "Will she be okay?"

Daniel stared down the hall at the door that had closed quietly behind his fiancée. "As long as she doesn't touch them, she's usually fine. But direct contact"—he shook his head—"that's when things get serious."

"Good to know." Evelyn pulled out her phone. "If you'll excuse me for just a sec." She bent over the small screen, her fingers flying across the keyboard as she sent an urgent text to Alicia. Satisfied the news would get passed along to the rest of the Wedding-in-a-Week participants, she looked up just as Brianna emerged from the powder room. She scanned the girl's face for signs of distress, but Daniel's bride-to-be glowed with the same excitement she'd shown the moment she'd stepped from the Town Car. Nonetheless, Evelyn asked, "Are you sure you're all right?"

"Right as rain. See?" To prove her point, Brianna inhaled smoothly.

She eyed the young blonde. No blotches marred her clear complexion, and the girl didn't sound the slightest bit stuffy or wheezy. She certainly looked all right, but Evelyn knew her limits. She wasn't a doctor. She had to at least offer medical care. "I'd be glad to take you to the ER, if you'd like. Or the Heart's Landing Walk-In Clinic. It's just a few streets over on Boutonniere Drive."

"And miss out on all this?" Brianna whirled in a circle. "Not on your life. There's absolutely no need to fuss. I carry an antihistamine with me and an EpiPen for emergencies. I didn't have to use either. I'm fine."

Evelyn sought confirmation with Daniel, who said, "It's up to Brianna," and Curtis, who simply shrugged his approval. "Okay, then. We'll move on." Giving her self a special reminder to check on the bride frequently, she chose a roundabout path to the stairs. On the way to the bridal suites on the second floor, they lingered in the Library, poked their heads into the dining room, and forged past both ballrooms, which were hidden behind closed doors as she'd requested.

As they mounted the wide staircase, Evelyn trailed her fingers along the sturdy banister. "My cousin and I used to slide down this when we were kids. It gave my mother fits. I don't think she ever realized my dad and uncle taught us how to hold on. Just like their fathers probably taught them."

"I guess it's kind of a family tradition, then." Daniel grinned. "We had a few in ours, too. Jumping into the quarry on the first day of summer break. Floating down the Itchetucknee on inner tubes."

Brianna chimed in. "Banana splits on report card day." She turned to Daniel and they finished in unison, "Only for all A's and B's."

Evelyn laughed at their joke despite feeling a little envious. Daniel and Brianna were obviously in love, and the memories they shared made their relationship extra special. What would that be like? She'd never know. She'd known Ryan forever, of course, but they didn't have that kind of relationship.

But could they?

She shook her head. She didn't have time for a trip down Wishful Thinking Lane. Not now. Not when she was in the middle of proving the Captain's Cottage was the best place for this year's Wedding-in-a-Week couple. Squaring her shoulders as they reached the top of the staircase, she brought the little party to a halt outside the Stargazer Suite. "Each of these rooms is reserved for a bride on her wedding day." She smiled at Daniel. "We don't want our grooms to spoil the wedding by running into the bride, so we have accommodations for the men on the other side of the house."

The door opened into a sumptuously outfitted sitting area done up in pink and mauve tones. A bouquet of the suite's namesake lilies on the dresser perfumed the air.

"Goodness gracious," Brianna whispered, stepping into the space. "This is amazing!"

Evelyn gave the girl a warm smile. "But wait, there's more," she teased and led them into a second room. She gestured to the king-size bed beneath an ornate canopy. "Many of our newlyweds opt to spend their first night as a married couple at the Captain's Cottage. All our suites are fully furnished with all the comforts of a five-star hotel." She pointed out the claw-footed tub and an array of lotions and perfumes in the bath. She paused to let Brianna and Daniel marvel over the towel warmer.

"Isn't that the neatest thing? Can you imagine? No more goose bumps after a shower." Wonder filled Brianna's voice.

Evelyn cleared her throat. "Our kitchen provides room service around the clock. Someone's on duty at all times to cater to your every need."

"I thought our rooms at the bed and breakfast were spectacular, but this is...this is...I don't have the words." The bride-to-be cast a dreamy eye about the room.

Meanwhile, Daniel had propped his arm on the tall chest of drawers. He pointed to a hook suspended from the ceiling. "That seems like an odd place for a hanger," he observed.

"Oh, I know what it's for," Brianna said, as excited as if she had the winning answer on a game show. "It's for my wedding gown. It'll hang there so it won't get wrinkled."

"That's right." Sensing they'd seen enough of the bridal suite, Evelyn stepped into the hall. "The Azalea and Aster suites are on this wing." For Brianna's sake, she skipped the Tea Rose. "On the other side of the house are the Camellia, Jasmine, and Violet. Are you ready to see the ballrooms?"

"Yes, please," Brianna blurted, clapping her hands and dancing on her tiptoes beneath Daniel's indulgent smile.

A short walk took them to the grooms' dressing areas. They stopped for a moment to let Daniel view the only slightly more Spartan accommodations. Then, they were on to the Green Room. Evelyn halted her little party outside its double doors.

"Captain Thaddeus and his wife entertained frequently. As was the custom in their day, they threw lavish parties and dances. The Green Room was built specifically for that purpose. Mary insisted it be large enough to allow for the full skirts and fans that were in fashion at the time. We know from historical records that this room was used predominantly for dancing while dinner—what we'd call a buffet—was served in the smaller Blue Room."

Having delivered her final history lesson for the day, Evelyn whispered a silent prayer before she flung the doors wide. She sucked in a grateful breath at the three rows of elegantly dressed tables and chairs that had been arranged in one corner of the room. Beyond them what looked like an acre of dark hardwood gleamed softly beneath a chandelier the size of a small car. Pale green walls rose above the wainscoting. The fragrant mix of linseed oil and lemon floated in the still air.

Brianna's giddy laughter drifted over her shoulder.

"The Green Room is our largest ballroom," Evelyn said, wiping a sudden dampness from her eyes while she made a special note to thank Jenny for working absolute magic. "We can accommodate up to three hundred guests here, another two hundred in the Blue Room."

She stepped aside to let Brianna and Daniel past. Hand in hand, the couple circled the room, talking softly among themselves. When they finally returned, Brianna's eyes glistened with unshed tears above a sweet smile.

Evelyn let her gaze bounce between the bride and groom. "What do you think? Can you see yourselves getting married at the Captain's Cottage?"

Brianna pressed one hand over her heart. "I love it here. From the pictures I saw of it in *Weddings Today*, I knew I would. But being here in person, seeing everything firsthand, it's all so much better than I expected." Her cheeks reddened, and she clamped one hand over her mouth. "Sorry!" She turned to Curtis. "No offense."

The photographer peered over his lens. "None taken."

"That's not to say we're deciding on the Captain's Cottage," Daniel put in. "We both liked Harbor View, too. It had a lot to offer."

"Right." Brianna gave the ballroom a wistful glance.

"You both should take your time and mull things over." Evelyn gave herself a few extra points for sounding polished and professional while hope shimmied inside her. Brianna had clearly fallen in love with the beauty of the Cottage the moment she'd stepped out of the Town Car. The mansion's sense of history had gotten Daniel's attention. She was pretty sure that, five days from now, the couple would continue a long-standing tradition when they posed for their wedding photograph in front of the most popular venue in Heart's Landing.

Seeing them off a few minutes later, she felt guilt prickle along her spine and drew in a breath. She should be happy, ecstatic even. In all likelihood, Daniel and Brianna were going to get married at the Captain's Cottage. It was exactly what she'd wanted, what she needed to have happen. Why, then, did she feel even the tiniest bit guilty?

She pictured Ryan's smiling face. Judging from Daniel and Brianna's reaction as they'd toured Harbor View Weddings this morning, he had to be thinking they'd choose his venue. She flexed her fingers. He'd be so disappointed to learn the couple had liked the Cottage even more. She knew what that felt like from personal experience. The brides who visited the Cottage didn't often choose a different venue. When they did, the rejection stung.

Her thoughts churned. Ryan deserved a chance to prepare himself for the very real possibility that Brianna and Daniel would choose the Captain's Cottage. Should she warn him? She twisted a wayward strand of hair and tucked it behind her ear. As much as it pained her to do it, she probably ought to be the one to tell him.

Because I want to break the news to him gently? Or because I want to see him again?

To be honest, the answer was a little bit of both. Fighting a chill that ran across her shoulders, she drew her phone out of a pocket to call the man who'd shown her nothing but warmth and kindness, the one man in Heart's Landing she least wanted to hurt.

Chapter Eight

RYAN DRUMMED HIS FINGERS AGAINST the sides of two cardboard cups while he waited for Evelyn outside the White Dove Deli. The coffee from Espressly Yours was a consolation prize, his gift to her for conceding their bet. That had to be the reason she'd asked to meet, didn't it? He didn't know how things had gone during their tour of the Captain's Cottage, but Brianna and Daniel couldn't possibly have been happier there than they'd been at Harbor View this morning. Brianna had especially been impressed. Her delight with the furnishings in the bridal dressing rooms had justified every penny he'd spent on plush seating and gilded mirrors. As for Daniel, the groom hadn't been able to tear his eyes away from the scenic views. His "Wait till the guys see this" had convinced Ryan that, when the time came, the couple would choose Harbor View as their venue.

Evelyn realized that, didn't she? She had to. The fiery redhead was many things—outspoken, independent, beautiful—but she was also smart enough to know when she'd lost. In all likelihood, she'd decided to throw in the towel and admit defeat.

Doubts curled in his chest like wood shavings. After a year of pouring everything he had into the old building, was he really on the brink of success? Brianna and Daniel's wedding would be the first at Harbor View. What if something went wrong? He shook his head at the unlikelihood of that happening. *Weddings Today* had arranged for Alicia to coordinate every detail. Things always went smoothly under her careful watch.

What if he won the bet but lost Evelyn's friendship in the process? Of all the possible outcomes, that one would sting the worst. He'd missed having her in his life far more than he'd admitted, even to himself. He'd do whatever it required to keep her there. He'd even let her off the hook on their bet. Better still, he'd invite her to dinner, his treat.

Over the rim of his coffee cup, movement inside the White Dove caught his eye. Through the plate glass window, he glimpsed Brianna and Daniel sharing a quiet laugh at a table with the mayor and his wife. The love that flowed between the younger couple made his heart ache. He wanted what they had. Wanted someone to share his hopes and dreams, someone who'd sit on the front porch sipping iced tea with him while they reminisced about their day. Wanted a Heart's Landing love for the ages.

Could he have that with Evelyn?

The idea appealed; he couldn't deny it. But no. He wasn't the kind of guy who'd make a move on someone who already had a steady boyfriend. And Evelyn did. He was certain of it. She'd never actually mentioned his name, but that didn't matter. Someone as smart, witty, and fun to be around as she was could have her pick from all the guys in town. So, no. He wouldn't invite her out to dinner.

He shifted his weight from one foot to another while he resumed scanning the street for the woman who'd been so anxious to meet. And there she was, striding toward him, a warm welcome on her face and, like him, carrying coffee to share. The sight loosened something in his chest.

"Great minds," they said in unison when she neared.

Evelyn peered at the cup he held out to her. "What is it?"

"Coffee milk from Espressly Yours. With an extra shot of espresso." He grinned. Sweetened with simple syrup, the blend of coffee and milk was so popular, it'd been designated Rhode Island's official drink. When he'd worked behind the counter of the popular coffee shop one summer, Evelyn had ordered her own special version at least once a week.

"A definite upgrade from mine," she said, dropping her two cups in a nearby trash can. She reached for the one Ryan offered, removed the lid, and sniffed. "Mmm. My favorite. How'd you know?"

"It's been a while since high school, but I took a chance you still liked your coffee strong and sweet."

"You remember?" The tiniest fleck of white foam dotted her upper lip when Evelyn's mouth formed an oval.

Ryan resisted the urge to wipe away the spot and handed her a napkin. "There." He pointed to his own mouth. An uncomfortable tension eased once she'd dabbed her lip clean. "I remember a lot about those days."

"Okay, two can play at this game," she said, laughing. "No coffee milk for you. Yours is black with two sugars."

"See? You didn't forget, either."

"Actually..." The freckles across the bridge of Evelyn's nose paled as her face reddened. "Actually, I had, but that's the way you drank it in the dining room Saturday."

He tipped his cup to hers in a mock toast. The minute they sipped their coffee, though, a feeling of trepidation swept through him. Now that she actually stood looking up at him with those big green eyes of hers, he wished they hadn't been pitted against each other in the Wedding-in-a-Week contest. One of them had to lose, and he hated the idea that she might get hurt almost as much as he wanted to win. *Almost* being the operative word. He wouldn't back out. Wouldn't break his promise to stay in the contest. Not now, when he had so much at stake.

Speaking of which, why had Evelyn asked him to meet her?

"You said there was something..."

"...we should talk about."

He stopped when they finished the sentence together. They both laughed, though his sounded a little nervous. If he wasn't mistaken, hers did, too.

"You go ahead," Evelyn said, taking a long swig of her coffee.

"Ladies first," he insisted. He aimed his chin toward the interior of the restaurant, where the mayor had already handed his credit card to the waiter. "But make it fast. They'll be out in a minute."

"O-kay." Evelyn peered up at him, her brow furrowing. "I thought you should know Brianna and Daniel are getting married at the Captain's Cottage."

Ryan choked on a gulp of coffee. "They said that?" he asked when he'd caught his breath.

"Not in so many words, no." Evelyn stared into the restaurant.

"You don't know for sure," he prodded. She had to be wrong. The young couple had been over the moon with Harbor View only a few hours earlier.

"Brianna was so taken with the Captain's Cottage she was practically dancing on air. I didn't hear one negative comment from Daniel." She hesitated. Her gaze dropped. "I thought you'd want to know."

For a minute there, success had hovered so close he could've reached out and touched it. He should've known it wouldn't come that easily. He eyed his coffee. It had lost its flavor, and he tossed the cup in the trash. "A lot can happen before Brianna and Daniel announce their choices on Saturday. I'm not giving up. Are you?"

Evelyn finally met his gaze with a saucy look. "Not on your life."

He might have said more if it weren't for Curtis, who backed out of the restaurant, his camera whirring, at that very moment. The mayor and his wife came next. Brianna and Daniel joined them a moment later. At Curtis's direction, the quartet posed for pictures. Handshakes and effusive thanks followed next before Greg Thomas's focus shifted to Ryan and Evelyn.

"Well, now. Look who's here. Two of my favorite people, and your timing couldn't have been more perfect, because our beautiful bride- and groom-to-be are headed in separate directions next."

Beside Daniel, Brianna looked a little lost. The mayor's gaze tightened on her.

"Brianna, I don't have any personal experience picking out wedding gowns"—laughing, he mock-curtsied—"but I'm told it's a lot more fun when you have someone to share such a special occasion. So we've asked Evelyn to accompany you to Dress For A Day. While you're there, you'll have a chance to try on three of the most exquisite wedding gowns you've ever seen. Just remember, you must choose one—and only one—to wear in your wedding!"

"Oh, that's wonderful," Brianna breathed. Delight shimmered in her eyes. She smiled at Evelyn.

Obviously pleased with himself, the mayor continued. "Daniel, since it's bad luck for the groom to see the wedding gown before the big day, you, Ryan, and Curtis will come with me to Tux or Tails. I have the best three tuxes in the house waiting for you there."

Was he mistaken, or was Daniel less enthusiastic about the mayor's announcement? Ryan fell in beside the tight-lipped groom. Something was definitely bothering the man who, up until now, had seemed to enjoy all the wedding plans as much as his bride. Whatever it was, he'd ferret out the answer this afternoon at Tux or Tails.

"The White Dove is one of my favorite places." Evelyn linked arms with Brianna for the short walk to the car that sat, its engine idling, at the curb. Aware of the bride-to-be's nervousness, she stuck with small talk. "What'd you have for lunch?" she asked as they slipped into the back seat.

"Something called a Wedge Salad. Did you know that's just a big ol' hunk of lettuce?"

She laughed. She, too, had been surprised by how well the dish lived up to its name the first time she'd ordered one. "Did you like it, at least?"

"Oh, yes. It was absolutely scrumptious. I had a lobster roll, too. I'd never had lobster before, but I'd heard so much about it, I thought, why not?"

"How was it?" Her mouth watered. The White Dove served the best lobster salad this side of Maine.

Brianna gave a noncommittal shrug. "Like scallops? Only sweeter, maybe? We don't get food like that back home."

She nodded. Coming from a little town smack-dab in the middle of Florida, Brianna had probably grown up on Southern staples like grits and black-eyed peas and—she shuddered—okra. "Except for one trip to Daytona Beach when I was in college, I've never been south of Baltimore. Do you really fry green tomatoes down there?"

"Yum." Brianna closed her eyes. "Dip them in buttermilk and cornmeal, fry them in a little oil. That's good eating right there."

She tried to imagine the taste and failed. "People actually like them?"

"Oh, yes! We'd go through a whole bushel in a week at the diner. My mom won a blue ribbon for hers at the county fair every year. Daniel says mine are tasty, but I'll never make them as good as she did."

Evelyn watched in horror as Brianna's eyes filled with sudden tears. The girl turned to stare out the window. "What's wrong?" she whispered, worried she'd said or done something to upset the bride-to-be.

The quiet hum of the tires was the only sound for about a block. Finally, Brianna mumbled, "It wasn't supposed to be like this, you know."

"What do you mean?"

"I wasn't supposed to be picking out my wedding gown without her. Not supposed to walk down the aisle without my dad." Brianna sniffled, her face pressed against the glass. "I'm beyond grateful for what *Weddings Today* and everyone here in Heart's Landing is doing for us. But I'd be happy with a cheap off-the-rack dress if it meant..." She choked back a sob. "If it meant having my mom here to lend me her strand of pearls for my something borrowed. Or if my dad was here to give me away."

Evelyn's throat ached with unshed tears. She bit the inside of her cheek lest she, too, dissolve into a wet puddle. How would that help? When Brianna's cheeks dampened, she tugged a handful of tissues from her purse and passed them to the younger woman. Making an executive decision, she leaned forward and tapped on the glass divider. "Take us north on Boston Neck Road. We'll circle back to the dress shop in a little bit."

"You don't have to do that. I—I'll be fine." Brianna's voice thinned.

"This is your day. They can't start without us," she said while her companion blotted her cheeks. Not that it helped. When more tears turned the bride's eyes a watery blue, she reached for her phone. "I'll text Cheri and tell her we'll be along in"—she canted her head—"twenty minutes or so?"

"Ten." Brianna gave her nose a delicate swipe. "Just let me catch my breath."

"Take as long as you need," she agreed, texting that there'd been a slight delay. She paused. When Brianna continued to stare out the window, she sent another text, this time to Alicia.

911. Bring Jenny & meet at Dress For A Day. Bride needs motherly TLC.

Alicia and Jenny might have their hands full at the Captain's Cottage, but this was a real emergency. Having done all she could think of at the moment, Evelyn reached for Brianna's hand and gave it a squeeze.

"It's okay. I'm okay," the bride-to-be whispered.

Who's she trying to convince? Evelyn wondered as a fine tremble ran through the girl's fingers.

Another five minutes passed before Brianna straightened. "Geez." She sighed, mopping furiously. "It's been five years. You'd think I'd be over this by now. I am, mostly. In the beginning, I cried for days. Daniel was my rock through all of it. Holding my hand, passing me tissues. I don't know what I would've done without him. Now, I'm fine most of the time. Then, out of the blue, something will happen—like talking about Mom's blue ribbons—and it hits me all over again." She balled the tissue and stuck it in her purse with a laugh. "Fried green tomatoes. Who'd have ever thought that'd be the thing to push me over the edge, right?"

Evelyn nodded in sympathy. "It's not easy when you lose someone. Sometimes, it's the oddest things that bring back memories so sharp, they take your breath away." Like the day she'd wanted to hang a picture in her room. Rather than ask one of the staff, she'd gone to the shed. She'd found just what she'd needed there. Along with her uncle's tool belt. The worn leather strip lay on the workbench exactly the way he'd left it after he'd gotten too sick to handle even the smallest jobs around the Cottage. Sobbing, she'd run from the shed empty-handed. The next time Ryan had stopped by to visit Jason, he'd hung the picture for her.

"Thanks. I..." Brianna checked her watch. "We've been gone too long, haven't we? People are going to wonder what happened to us."

"The dress shop isn't going anywhere." The tension eased from Evelyn's shoulders. She'd been prepared to cancel the day's activities if need be, but it looked like Brianna had pulled herself together. She eyed the bride-to-be's tear-streaked face. *Uh-oh.* "We, um, might need to do some damage repair."

"Oh gosh, I must look a fright." Panic flickered in Brianna's eyes.

"Here." Reaching into her purse, she pulled out the small makeup bag she carried just for such emergencies. "You're not the first bride to ever have a meltdown. I doubt you'll be the last."

"And here I thought I was so special." Brianna paired the quip with a watery grin. "Thanks," she said, pulling open the little bag and looking inside. "You've thought of everything. You're a lifesaver."

"Nothing to it." She shrugged. With Brianna's fine complexion, the young woman needed little more than a bit of powder and a mascara touch-up.

Sure enough, when the driver braked to a smooth stop in front of Dress For A Day fifteen minutes later, no one looking at the bride-to-be would ever suspect she'd been on a crying jag.

"Whoa!" Brianna's eyes widened as she stepped from the car. She rubbed her hands together. "This is beautiful. Truly."

The brick building sat all by itself on the corner of Boston Neck and Boutonniere Drive. Tall display windows on either side of the door featured full-size mannequins in stunning dresses. Brianna wandered closer for a better look at a princess-style gown accented by a blue sash. "That's gorgeous, isn't it? I'm not sure about the belt, but I love that sweetheart neckline."

"It is pretty," Evelyn agreed. She stepped under a dark pink awning and grasped the brass door handle. "I'll bet there are even more beautiful dresses inside. Are you ready?"

"Ready!" When the bride-to-be's lip trembled, Evelyn inhaled a deep breath and prayed the girl would appreciate that she'd called for reinforcements. Holding the door, she stepped aside to let the bride pass. To her credit, Brianna walked straight into the salon.

A diminutive woman in black greeted her with a cheery, "Hello, Brianna! I'm Cheri Clarke, the owner, and this is Dress For A Day." With an expansive sweep of her hand, Cheri indicated the roomy salon. Couches and chairs clustered around separate viewing areas. Each featured its own floor-to-ceiling mirror and raised platform.

Evelyn smiled at Brianna's awed reaction to the beautiful gowns that hung in deep alcoves. Leaving her charge and the owner to get acquainted, she drank in the ambience created by cream-colored walls and burgundy accents. Not a trace of roses drifted in the air, and she nodded her approval at the honey and vanilla that scented the room.

Her attention returned to Cheri, who was saying, “It’s such an honor to have you visit my salon. In a few minutes, I’ll show you the three stunning gowns I personally selected for you to wear on your wedding day. But first, a few of Heart’s Landing’s most up-standing citizens have asked if they could join you.” At a whispered “Ladies,” more women than Evelyn had expected flocked toward the bride-to-be.

“I’m Mildred.” The florist leaned in for a quick hug. “We met yesterday at the train station, but there were so many people there, you couldn’t possibly remember all of us. This is my friend Opal Burnett,” she said as a petite woman with a towering hairdo stepped forward. “She owns The Glass Slipper.”

As soon as those two moved aside, others took their place. For the next few minutes, the women of Heart’s Landing came forward armed with their warmest wishes, broad smiles and gentle squeezes. The line moved quickly until, finally, Alicia and Jenny reached the bride.

Alicia inclined her head. “Honey, we know how much it means to be surrounded by loved ones on an important day like this. Since your family couldn’t be here, we hope you’ll let us fill in. We promise to tell you that you look divine in any one of these gowns. And if there’s anything you want—anything at all—one of us will get it for you.”

Tears once again welled in Brianna’s eyes, but this

time her mouth curved into a brilliant smile. "Thank you. Thank you all. I have to admit, I've been missing my mama a little more than I thought I would today. Having you all here, well, it's a little like having her here with me."

"All right then, ladies," Cheri said. "I have one request before we begin—let's all put away our cell phones. We don't want any pictures to ruin Daniel's surprise when he sees his beautiful bride walk down the aisle in her wedding gown."

A few good-natured grumbles followed as cameras and cell phones slid out of sight.

Next, Cheri nodded to the largest of the viewing areas. "If you'll all take your seats with Brianna on the sofas, we'll get this party started."

There was a slight juggling for position before, with Alicia on one side and Mildred on the other, Brianna sat on the center sofa. The rest arrayed themselves around her. They'd barely gotten settled when, wearing a black skirt and white blouse, a young woman emerged from the back, carrying a tray of champagne flutes. The next server carried a tray of dainty cookies and petit fours. After everyone helped themselves from the offerings, Cheri clapped her hands.

"Brianna, dear. Today, I have three gowns for you to choose from, each lovelier than the next. Thanks to the wonderful people at *Weddings Today*, who supplied us with all the pertinent information, each dress is perfectly suited for a woman of your height and build. No matter which one you choose, you have my personal guarantee, your dress will fit you perfectly on your wedding day. So, are you ready?"

The moment Brianna bobbed her head, Cheri

stepped behind a narrow podium. An approving chorus rose from the women as the first model stepped from behind a curtain onto a burgundy runner that led to the dais.

"Your first choice is a Sophie Olson original. This stunning gown features a romantic V neckline delicately trimmed in pearls and crystals." Cheri spun her finger in a circle, and the model turned. "Frosted embroidery graces the layers of tulle and organza that form a mermaid silhouette."

Evelyn gulped. The gown had to cost a king's ransom. She had to admit, though, on the right bride, it would be worth the cost.

As the first model stepped from the dais, a second emerged from the back of the building. This one wore a slightly less fitted dress with cap sleeves.

"Donna Marsha designed this fairytale-inspired gown, which hugs the upper body before flaring out at the waist," Cheri said to a chorus of happy murmurs. "Crafted from the finest of materials, the dress is adorned with delicate lace at the bodice and along the skirt."

From her seat at the end of the banquette, Evelyn studied Brianna's face. Judging from the slight tension along her jaw, the bride hadn't been thrilled by either of the first two options. She crossed her fingers and sent up a silent prayer. *Please let this final choice be the one.*

Cheri sipped water from a tumbler as the white curtain in the back of the room parted again, this time revealing a stunning ball gown. "I chose to go with a new take on a more traditional look for our final option. The square back enhances the sense of innocence and youth portrayed by this gown, while the pockets in this beautiful dress provide an unexpected functionality." The owner snapped her fingers and grinned when the model on the dais rotated slowly, her hands disappearing into the folds of fabric.

Evelyn joined in the applause that followed. She didn't know who was happier, Brianna or herself. She'd seen how the girl had straightened when the third model had walked into the room. Though she agreed with Cheri's assessment that each gown was absolutely beautiful, only one had lit a spark in the bride's eyes.

Meanwhile, Mildred Morrey tugged on one of Brianna's arms. "I simply can't wait to see you in that first gown. You'll rock the mermaid look."

"Oh, posh." Opal slipped her hand over the girl's. "The second one is my choice. You'll look like a princess in that dress."

Alicia turned to Jenny. The older woman's stage whisper sounded over the thickly carpeted floors. "Which one do you think she should choose?"

"I'm not supposed to have a favorite." Jenny folded her hands in her lap.

"But..." Alicia stared, insistent.

"But I'd have to say, I do love a dress with pockets." The event planner flashed Evelyn a bright smile while titters of laughter rippled through the room.

"Brianna, dear," Cheri said when the room quieted. "Feel like trying on a few dresses?"

Brianna went still as a statue. A statue with a deer-in-the-headlights stare that Evelyn recognized only too well. She scrambled to her feet and hustled to the bride's side. "How about if I come with you?"

Brianna tipped tear-filled eyes to hers. "Would you?"

"Of course. What fun is trying on wedding gowns by yourself?" Grabbing two flutes of champagne from a waiter, she handed one to Brianna. "Come on. This'll be fun."

Brianna rose. "Y'all don't drink all the champagne while I'm gone." She laughed.

"No promises." Mildred lifted her glass. One by one, the others followed suit in a toast to the bride-to-be.

They trailed Cheri to a dressing room painted the same soothing ecru as the walls in the viewing area. There, three gowns hung on satin-covered hangers along the wall.

"Which one do you want to try on first?" Evelyn asked when the bride-to-be hesitated.

"I guess we should take them in order," Brianna said, while her focus remained on the final gown.

"You're the bride. It's your choice."

Her voice firming, Brianna said, "In order, then." She slipped out of a simple skirt and blouse. Rapidly, she stepped into the center of the puddle of organza and tulle Evelyn helped Cheri arrange for her. Together, they pulled the strapless gown into place. As Evelyn suspected, the gown slipped over Brianna's thin frame like it'd been made for her.

Stepping back, Evelyn eyed the bride. Dampness stung her eyes. "Absolutely stunning," she declared. "Let's go show the others."

"I don't know," Brianna murmured. Staring at herself in the mirror, she raised her hands protectively across her chest. "There's way more of me outside this dress than there is in it."

"Wait a sec." Cheri bustled about. "Let me see, let me see." The shop owner tucked a piece of fabric here, pinned a bit there. In the end, the bodice rose an inch higher. "There." The shop owner's ruby-red lips widened. "That's better. Hands at your sides now," she said, demonstrating.

"If you say so." Despite Cheri's reassurances, Brianna's shoulders slumped a bit.

"It'll be fine," Evelyn encouraged. "That gown is amazing on you."

A hush fell over the room as Brianna emerged from the dressing area in front of Cheri and Evelyn. Her guests let out a collective "ohhh" when the bride-to-be stepped onto the dais.

"Oh, honey!" Mildred said, pressing a hand over her heart. "You look as pretty as, well, a bride."

"Not quite," a deeper voice responded. Stepping from behind a mannequin, the smartly dressed owner of Chantilly Veils crossed the room, his arms laden with gauzy fabric. He jogged up the stairs onto the dais. "My name's Ames. Now, this gown is absolutely stunning, and you look just as gorgeous in it. My job is to make sure your veil doesn't take away from the dress, but only complements it."

He circled around to Brianna's back. "Can you tip your head up for me, darlin'?" Doing as requested, Brianna stood stock-still while Ames fluttered and fussed. "There now. How's that?" The man stepped to one side while Brianna swung to face the mirror.

Her lips parted in a real smile. "This is real pretty,

Mr. Ames." She fingered the sheer fabric that ended at her elbow.

Evelyn dabbed at her eyes. The simple veil was so perfect, Ames must have created it just for this bride and this dress. As an added plus, it gave the illusion of being more substantial that it was, which helped put Brianna at ease. She gave a breathy sigh. Ames was a miracle worker. Seeing the transformation his veil had worked on this bride-to-be, she could hardly wait to have him work his magic for her.

Of course, there was the little problem of finding her Mr. Right. But now wasn't the time to think of that. Not when a salon full of women waited to see Brianna in the next gown.

Returning to the dressing area, she and the bride repeated the process twice more. Each time, Brianna looked more and more breathtaking in the creations Cheri had chosen. And each time, Ames added the icing to the proverbial cake with another perfect veil. There wasn't a dry eye in the salon by the time it was time to leave.

As she said goodbye to the bride, Opal leaned in to whisper in Brianna's ear.

"What'd she say to you?" Evelyn asked when she and the bride-to-be were alone and headed for the car.

"She told me to stop by her store and pick out a pair of shoes to wear in my wedding. On the house."

Evelyn felt her jaw come unhinged. She stared at the bride with open envy. "The Glass Slipper?" she screeched.

"That's a good thing, I take it?" Questions loomed in Brianna's eyes.

"I'll say. That place is amazing. They have the most gorgeous shoes. Even better, Opal recently started carrying Sophie Olsen's new line of heels." At Brianna's confused look, she clarified. "The designer of the mermaid gown. Oh. My. Goodness. If you think that dress was spectacular, wait till you see her shoes. They're to die for."

"Well, I guess I'd better schedule time for a little shopping trip." Brianna flexed her foot to show off a cute pair of flats with pink bows. "I do love new shoes."

They were back in the car again when Brianna turned to her, her mood sober. "Thanks for today," she said, her voice low. "Please tell all those ladies thank you, too. That was so sweet of them, giving up their afternoon to look at wedding gowns with me. I was touched."

Evelyn waved a hand. "I'm sure they'd thank you for the privilege. Each of them dreams of shopping for wedding gowns with their daughters or nieces one day." She leaned into the soft cushions. They'd had a few rough moments, but the day had turned out beautifully. "You and Daniel are going to make such a lovely couple. I can't wait to see his eyes when you walk down the aisle wearing one of those creations. Do you know which one you're going to pick yet?"

"I'm still thinking. I wish I could ask him about it."

Her stomach clenched when a single, fat tear rolled down Brianna's cheek. Had she said something wrong? "What is it?" she asked, tensing.

"I can't even decide which dress to wear. I—I'm not sure I can go through with this."

"The Wedding-in-a-Week festivities? They can be a

bit much, can't they?" She fanned herself, trying hard to put the bride at ease. "It was asking a lot to expect you to choose a venue and a gown on the same day. Maybe I should suggest we schedule those events differently next year. What do you think?" When the girl didn't answer, she prompted, "Brianna?"

"It's not just Wedding-In-A-Week. It's—it's the wedding, too."

The bride's thready whisper sent her stomach into freefall. Shocked, she went still as a stone. Sure, the girl had been in tears a couple of times today, but that was to be expected. Wasn't it? After all, all the brides on the reality TV shows cried. None of them called off their weddings. "Why would you even think that?"

Brianna turned a pair of watery eyes on her. "Look at me. The least little thing happens, and I fall completely apart. I'm not what Daniel needs. He's serving his country. He doesn't need a wife he has to worry about while he's away. He needs someone he can count on to keep things running smoothly at home. Somebody better, stronger than me."

"That's...that's..." She faltered as she pictured Brianna and Daniel at the Captain's Cottage that morning. "I've seen the way he looks at you, Brianna. The man is head over heels in love with you."

"Well, there is that," Brianna said with a self-deprecating laugh. "It's just sometimes I don't think it's enough."

"You said yourself he's always been your rock."

"That's the problem." Brianna's head dipped. Her blond hair fell forward to hide her face. "He's always helping *me*, lending *me* his strength. I should be able to help him, too. Shouldn't I?"

Evelyn paused for a breath. Only one question mattered. She prayed for strength and asked, "Do you love him?"

"Oh, yes," Brianna breathed. "More than anything."

"Well, there you have it, then. You're meant for each other."

"I wish I could be as sure as you are." As the car pulled to the curb in front of the Union Street Bed and Breakfast, Brianna looked up. Her eyes swam in a lake of unshed tears, but the smile she wore only wavered slightly. "You know what? I'm beat." She yawned behind one hand. "I think I'll go upstairs and take a nap before dinner."

"You do that. A little rest will do you a world of good." She crossed her fingers. Today had only been the beginning of a full week of decision-making, and Brianna had been on an emotional roller-coaster for most of it. No wonder the girl was exhausted. She rifled through the schedule. Alicia had marked tonight as a date night. A little private time with her fiancé sounded like the perfect prescription for Brianna's pre-wedding jitters. "You and Daniel have dinner plans, right?"

"Yes." Interest sparked in Brianna's blue eyes. "We're going to a steak house. It's one of our three choices for the rehearsal dinner. Daniel will like that. He loves a good steak."

"That'll be great. Get a nice rest and a good meal. You'll feel a hundred percent better. Tomorrow's another big day."

"So I'll see you tomorrow?" Brianna stepped from the car.

"I wouldn't miss it," she assured the bride through the open door. She kept her smile in place while her charge mounted the steps into the bed and breakfast. The moment Brianna slipped inside, though, she groaned. Nothing in her role as bookkeeper for the Captain's Cottage had prepared her for dealing with a bride on the verge of calling off the wedding. She needed help, needed advice. But from whom?

Not Alicia. The Event Planner had placed the bride-to-be in her hands. While she considered Jenny one of her best friends, at the first whiff of trouble, the young woman would insist on taking the problem straight to her boss. So no, asking Jenny for advice was out of the question, too.

That left only one person. At the thought, she brightened. She might not know how to handle a hesitant bride, but she did know a thing or two about weddings. And Ryan, well, he was one of the smartest people she knew. Once the two of them put their heads together, they'd come up with a plan for helping her bride-to-be remember all the reasons why she and Daniel were meant to be together.

After asking the driver to take her to the Captain's Cottage, she whipped out her phone. Leaning into the cushions, she punched Ryan's number, already looking forward to spending some extra time with him far more than she thought she should.

Chapter Nine

Snatches of conversation between busy shoppers and the sounds of traffic along Honeymoon Avenue faded as the door to Tux or Tails swished closed behind Ryan. In the well-appointed menswear shop, the soft strains of classical music broke the hushed quiet. He stepped forward, his footsteps muffled by thick carpet. At his side, Daniel whistled.

"Whoa," the groom-to-be whispered. "This sure ain't the rental shop where I got my tux for prom."

Ryan grinned. "I'm betting Tux or Tails is a little more upscale?"

"This here might be a little too rich for my blood." Daniel shifted his weight from one foot to the other.

"You're fine. Trust me."

"Easy for you to say. You ain't the one getting measured and poked and prodded."

Ryan's smile steadied. "Big, strong Marine like you? You can handle one tux fitting."

Daniel lifted a skeptical eyebrow but squared his shoulders. "I guess if I can make it through the Crucible, I can make it through this."

Before Ryan could ask for details, Greg bustled out from the back. An assistant with a tape measure followed him. Behind them, three handsomely turned-out men waited in the wings.

"Welcome. Welcome. So glad you could make it to Tux or Tails this afternoon." The owner extended his hand as if he hadn't just shared lunch with Daniel at the White Dove Deli. The groom shook hands with Greg while Curtis, who'd taken up a position beside a mannequin wearing a smart suit coat, snapped a few candid shots.

Greg rubbed his hands together. "Let me tell you a little bit about my shop. My family has owned and operated a tailoring business in Manhattan for three generations. When it came time to branch out, I chose Heart's Landing because, well, who doesn't love a good wedding?" He stopped long enough to laugh at his own joke. "I opened Tux or Tails some thirty years ago. Back then, we primarily rented and altered tuxes, but we've grown to meet the needs of Heart's Landing. While our main focus remains on providing the best in wedding apparel for the groom and his attendants, we offer a full line of men's clothing. Everything from ready-made to bespoke suits designed expressly to suit the wishes of the most discriminating customer." He paused to take a breath. "Do you have any questions?"

"Not exactly a question, sir, but…"

Ryan canted his head. Daniel stood at attention, his posture rigid as if his entire future rested on what came next.

"What is it?" Greg leaned forward. "Whatever it is, we'll do our best to take care of it for you."

"Well, sir." Daniel inhaled. "I had my heart set on wearing my uniform. Is that going to be a problem? The folks at *Weddings Today* said it was fine with them."

"Your uniform." Greg hesitated. "For the wedding." He stopped again. "Not a tux?"

"Yes, sir. I—I mean no, sir. My uniform. That's what I want to wear."

Ryan blinked as Greg's head swiveled away from the Marine to pin him with a questioning look. He answered with a blank stare. This was the first he'd heard of Daniel's request.

Greg rubbed one hand over his balding pate. He swung to face Curtis. "Did you know anything about this?"

The photographer held up a hand. "Nah, man. You'd have to ask Regina Charm. I'm just here to take pictures."

Ryan stifled a groan. He'd never met the senior editor for *Weddings Today*, but from all accounts, the woman was a piece of work. Hadn't she sent Tara to Heart's Landing with a hidden agenda? Things hadn't worked out the way the editor had hoped they would that time. Was she up to mischief again? If so, he was pretty sure she'd fail. He swiped a peek at Greg. To his credit, the shop owner hadn't flinched. His ruddy complexion hadn't gone a single shade lighter. Clearly, the mayor could handle whatever monkey wrench Regina had thrown into the works.

"You want a military wedding?" Greg asked.

"Yes, sir." Daniel snapped to attention. "My buddies from boot camp are flying in on Friday. They'll stand up front with me."

"You'll wear dress blues?" Greg peered closely at Daniel, sizing him up. "Do you have dress blues?"

"Yes, sir."

Ryan could almost picture it. A radiant Brianna in a white gown. Daniel, tall and proud. The two of them dashing hand-in-hand through the doors of Harbor View Weddings, while a line of uniformed young men and women stood at attention. It'd make for a beautiful ceremony.

"It sounds like you've thought of everything, young man. That's excellent." The mayor stroked his chin.

"You're sure it's not a problem?" A muscle in Daniel's cheek twitched.

"A problem?" The mayor's eyes rounded. "That you're honoring your country and you've answered the call to serve? How could that possibly be a problem?" At the snap of his fingers, the trio of young men disappeared into the back of the shop. "So you'll wear your uniform. And your buddies, they all have the appropriate attire as well?"

"Yes, sir. Gloves, covers, the works."

"What about swords for the arch?"

"No, sir. Not enough rank, sir. That honor is reserved for NCOs and above."

"All right, then." Greg tapped his chin. "Here's what we can do. What say we outfit you in a very nice suit? Something you can wear when you're off duty and want to take that lovely bride of yours out to dinner. Will that work?"

Daniel studied his surroundings. "I'm sorry, sir, but I don't think I can afford to shop here."

Ryan followed Daniel's gaze around the store. Two chairs flanked a hobnail leather sofa by the window.

The wood on the mahogany coffee table between them glowed. A wall of cubbies held the latest in men's shirts, while suits in rich fabrics hung from wooden hangers on recessed racks. It didn't surprise him that the young man had taken one look at the place and decided he was out of his element. But he'd change his mind once he knew Greg a little better.

"This would be a gift, son. Instead of the tux," Greg said, just as Ryan thought he might.

"I don't know." Some of the stiffness went out of Daniel's posture. "A whole suit? Isn't that too much to ask for?"

Was that a touch of wishful thinking in Daniel's voice? Pretty sure he'd heard correctly, Ryan pulled the young man aside. His voice low, he whispered, "Greg signed up to provide tuxes for you and all your attendants. In exchange, *Weddings Today* planned to mention Tux or Tails in their Wedding-in-a-Week spread. That publicity is gold for a store like this."

"Yeah, but a suit. In a place like this, that's gotta cost a pretty penny."

He held up a hand. "Let me finish. Your service is something to be proud of, something everyone in Heart's Landing is grateful for. We'll all be happy to see you in uniform on your wedding day. But if you walk out of Tux or Tails empty-handed, *Weddings Today* won't have anything about the shop to include in their article. You'd actually be doing Greg a favor by taking him up on his offer."

"You're not just saying that? You're sure?"

There was that hopeful note again. The one Daniel had tried to hide. The one that let him know the young groom recognized a chance of a lifetime when he saw it and didn't really want to turn down this one. He nodded firmly. "I'm sure."

"Okay, then." Daniel turned to Greg. "I'd be honored to accept, sir."

"Excellent." Greg clapped his hands together. "Now, I need a moment to pull together a few things. If you wouldn't mind, take a seat over there. I'll be right with you. Help yourself to a glass of wine. Cheese and crackers, too."

Leather creaked as Ryan lowered himself onto the couch. He'd shopped at Tux or Tails in the past and knew from experience that Greg didn't rush things. He settled in to wait while Daniel piled crackers on a napkin and poured himself a glass of wine.

"Have you heard from Brianna?" he asked when they were seated.

"Not since lunch." Daniel popped one of the crackers into his mouth and chewed. "I hope she's doing okay."

He smiled. He'd done some work at Dress For A Day several years ago. The place was every bit as sumptuous as Tux or Tails but decidedly feminine. He was pretty sure Evelyn and Brianna would feel right at home there. Without warning, the image of Evelyn dressed as a bride popped into his thoughts. He savored the picture for a moment before he blinked it away to focus on his young charge. "If Brianna is anything like every other woman I've ever known, dress shopping is more than just a pastime; it's a serious undertaking. From what I hear, looking for a wedding dress, well, that's like an Olympic sport. Brianna and Evelyn are in good hands with Cheri Clarke. My mother swears by her."

Daniel demolished a few more crackers. “You seem to know everyone in town. Have you always lived in Heart’s Landing?”

“Most of my life,” Ryan answered. “My family’s from around here. I was born and raised right up there.” He aimed his chin past the center of town to Cathedral Heights. His childhood home sat above the residential neighborhood overlooking Heart’s Landing. “I moved away for a few years, but I always knew I’d move back here. As soon as I had the chance, that’s exactly what I did. How about you? You plan to head back to Florida after your hitch is up?”

“Not anytime soon.” Daniel shook his head. “Lots of little kids want to wear a uniform. They dress up as firemen or police officers or astronauts for Halloween. For me, that dream never faded. It’s always been the Marines.” He took a long pull from his wineglass.

“I respect that decision.” Without thinking about what he was doing, he massaged his knee. He’d torn his ACL in a summer league football game the year he’d graduated. Surgery and months of PT had followed. He’d healed well, but the injury had virtually eliminated any chance of a military career. Not that he’d seriously considered it. He was a woodworker. Always had been. The posters in the recruitment offices didn’t exactly shout, “We’re looking for a few good carpenters!” He leaned back, his ankles crossed. “Your dad owns an orange grove, doesn’t he? You didn’t want to follow in his footsteps?”

“My dad loves what he does, but raising citrus was never in my blood.” Daniel broke the last cracker in half. “There are easier ways to make a living than in the Corps. I'm not kidding myself about that. I can handle it. It's Brianna I worry about."

He studied the dedicated young man. Daniel had clearly considered all the angles to his career choice, but from what he'd heard, the frequent moves and long separations sometimes took a toll on marriages. "You don't think she's up to it?"

"Oh no, sir. Not that. Brianna is strong. She's had to be." One by one, Daniel ate the final two pieces and emptied his glass. "It's just that, well, she's already been through so much. As soon as we get back from our honeymoon, I'll report for more training. I could be gone as long as three months. I hate to think of leaving her alone all that time. Deployments mean even more time apart. Is it fair to ask her to share that kind of life?"

Ryan leaned forward, one elbow propped on his knee. "I assume you've talked with her, voiced your concerns?"

"Sure. We've talked. She says she's on board, that whatever I choose, she's there for me. I just—I worry she doesn't really know what she's getting into. Being the wife of a Marine is a huge commitment. What if she wakes up one day and wishes she'd chosen a guy who works from nine to five, stays home on weekends, and helps coach the kids' soccer games? It keeps me up nights." Daniel brushed a few crumbs from one pants leg into his cupped hand.

"Do you love her?"

"More than anything else in the world."

"And she loves you. I can see that in her eyes every time she looks at you. They say that's all that matters." Ryan lowered his head. The young man deserved better than platitudes, but the advice was the best he could give.

"Yeah, but when I think about the things she's giving up to marry me, I, um, it's an awfully big ask. I've been on the verge of calling the whole thing off more often than I like. Sometimes I can't get past the idea that asking her to marry me was the most selfish thing I've ever done."

Every fiber of his being focused on the man sitting across from him. The one who apparently was willing to sacrifice his future happiness to give Brianna a chance at a better life. That was true love. A Heart's Landing kind of love. The kind of love he wanted for himself one day.

How could Daniel possibly walk away from that?

He wished he knew what to say to ease the young Marine's fears, but he'd drawn a blank, and his time had run out. Even as he searched for the right words, he spotted Greg emerge from the back of the shop, carrying an armload of fabric swatches.

Daniel saw their host for the afternoon, too. He leaned in. "Ah, man. Listen to me. I shouldn't have had that glass of wine. It makes me run my mouth. Forget I said anything, okay? I made a commitment, and I won't back out on Brianna. I wouldn't do that to her."

Ryan forced his back into the couch cushions. Feigning a relaxation he didn't feel, he zipped one finger across his lips. "Mum's the word if that's what you want. But, uh, you'll let me know if have any second thoughts, right?"

"Sure. But I won't. Me and Brianna, we're going to

get married on Sunday." With that, Daniel jumped to his feet, his eyes on the approaching store owner.

"I'll catch up with you in a minute," Ryan said when Greg beckoned the young Marine to a tall work table. He waited until the two had their heads together before he ran a hand behind his neck and wiped away a trickle of sweat. Heart's Landing had a lot riding on seeing the Wedding-in-a-Week couple walk down the aisle. With a photographer from *Weddings Today* on hand to snap pictures, the publicity the town stood to gain from the event was worth its weight in solid gold bullion. If that were all, it'd be reason enough for concern. But it wasn't. Not by half. Every citizen from Boutonniere Drive to Champagne Avenue was invested in giving this couple the wedding of their dreams. From Mildred Morrey at Forget Me Knot Flowers to Walter's son at the Honeymoon Cottages, every person in town would be crushed if Brianna and Daniel broke up the very week of their wedding. Not only that, but he'd personally be called on the carpet. After all, the mayor had put him in charge of shepherding the groom throughout the week. Of making sure the wedding went off without a hitch. He could just imagine the pointed questions he'd have to answer if he failed.

He suddenly wished he could talk to Evelyn. He felt certain she'd know exactly what to say to convince the young Marine he'd be making a huge mistake if he walked away from the woman he loved in the hopes of giving her the kind of life he thought she deserved. Sighing, he pulled his phone from his pocket and hit speed dial. Seconds later, he listened to a recorded message that let him know the one person he wanted to talk to, the one person he'd sworn to stay away from, was unavailable.

"Great." It was just his luck that Evelyn was nowhere to be found when he needed her the most. With no other option, he left a message asking if he could stop by her office at the Captain's Cottage later. He crossed his fingers, disconnected, and went to help Daniel and Greg design the perfect suit for a young man who teetered on the brink of leaving his bride at the altar.

Evelyn slid the first paycheck from the stack, held it up to the computer screen, and compared the numbers. They matched. She'd known they would, but it never hurt to double-check. She lowered the paper to her desk. Bending, she signed it, slipped the payment into a waiting envelope, and crossed the first name off her list. One down. Seventy-five more to go. She grabbed the next one from the pile.

Three knocks in rapid succession interrupted her routine before she got any further. She straightened, but it was no use. A two-foot-tall wall of fabric samples stacked on the edge of her desk blocked her view. Grumbling, she propped herself up on her chair's armrests to peer over the pile. Her pen clattered to the floor the instant she spied the tall figure standing in the doorway of her office. Her heart rate leaped into overdrive. *Ryan!* A welcoming smile sprang to her lips.

"Hey." She waved him in. "I didn't expect to see

you tonight." But she was certainly glad he'd stopped by. She needed to talk to him. But more than that, she'd wanted to see him, wanted to spend time with him.

"You didn't get my message?" Ryan's brow furrowed.

"Sorry. No." She lifted her cell phone from her desk. The screen, which normally sprang to life whenever she so much as breathed in its direction, stayed dark. "Battery's dead," she announced, feeling her face warm. "I've been so busy since I got back from shopping with Brianna, I didn't even notice."

"Looks like I've caught you at a bad time." Ryan lingered at the door. "Payroll?"

"Yeah. Much as everyone loves working at the Captain's Cottage, no one wants to do it for free." She grinned.

"Well." Ryan hesitated. "I'll let you get back to it."

"Don't be silly. You're here, aren't you? C'mon in." She started to motion him to a seat, but a quick glance confirmed what she'd feared. While she'd been busy with other things—like holding the hand of a weepy Wedding-in-a-Week bride—someone had stacked mail and other deliveries in the guest chair. She leaped to her feet. "Here. Let me get rid of that."

Ryan covered the distance between them in two quick strides. Her breath caught in her throat when they reached for the boxes at the same time. Their fingers touched, a move that sent tiny lightning bolts arcing up and down her arms. She told herself she should break the connection, should withdraw her hand, but she remained where she was, secrctly enjoying the steady zing of electricity that coursed through her.

"Um." Ryan's voice severed her connection to him.

She stared at her fingers. "What was that?"

"What was what?" He peered down at her, confusion tightening the skin around his eyes.

"Nothing. I must've jammed my finger." He hadn't felt the same thing she had. She pretended to examine her hand. The move bought her enough time to shake off her disappointment.

"You okay? Where would you like these?"

"What? Oh, yeah." Her hand fell to her side, and she peered up at the man who stood, his arms filled with boxes and envelopes. "Anywhere." She pointed to a bare spot on a nearby workbench. "Sorry for the mess. It's not usually like this. Well, it is, but not this bad. Things have kind of gotten out of control the last couple of weeks. But I'll get..." She trailed off when Ryan stood rooted to the spot, a silly grin stretched across his face.

"Have you forgotten we grew up together? You've always been a little on the disorganized side."

"Hey! I resent that." She propped her hands on her hips. "This may look like a mess, but I know exactly where everything is."

"Don't get your feathers in a bunch," he said over his retreating shoulder. "I've always considered it part of your charm."

At that, she straightened. "You think I'm charming?" she asked, hating the doubt that laced her tone.

"Yeah, of course. Everybody does, don't they?"

She sighed. And here she'd thought he might, just might, consider her special. *Wrong again, Heart.* So why had he shown up in her office? "Did you need something? Besides to concede you've lost our bet?"

"You wish," he said, giving her that smile that always made her stomach flutter. Unfortunately, his lips quickly straightened. When they did, concern etched its way across his brow. "Seriously, though. You got a minute? I'd like to get your advice on something."

"Funny you should say that. I was hoping to pick your brain about a couple of things that happened today." Motioning him into the chair he'd so nicely emptied, she shoved things aside on her desk until she had room to sit on the corner.

"Ladies first?" Ryan asked.

She grinned, loving the way his lips quirked as if he knew she'd argue. She wouldn't disappoint him. "I went first last time. It's your turn."

Her abdomen tightened as Ryan filled her in on his discussion with Daniel at Tux or Tails. When he finished, she felt like someone had punched her in the stomach.

"He can't be serious." Daniel's idea was so preposterous, she didn't quite know where to begin. "He loves Brianna. He wouldn't walk out on the wedding, would he?"

"I'm pretty sure he'd have the decency to call things off before the big day." Ryan held up a hand, halting her mid-protest. "I know—it doesn't make sense. But you have to admire his willingness to sacrifice his happiness for hers."

"Yeah, but..." She cupped her head in her hands and groaned out loud. "How can he possibly think she'd be better off without him? Men can be so dumb." She gave Ryan her most direct stare.

"You say that like you've never done something you regretted later."

"Okay, I'll give you that one. I've made my share of mistakes," she admitted. "To be honest, Daniel's not the only one poised on the brink of doing the wrong thing. Brianna's thinking along the same lines, but for different reasons. She thinks Daniel deserves someone stronger, someone more suited to becoming the wife of a Marine."

Ryan's lips pulled down at the corners. "She doesn't resent his commitment, does she?"

"No. Just the opposite." She rushed to clarify before he got the wrong idea. "Brianna thinks Daniel practically walks on water. She's honored he's chosen to serve his country. But she doesn't want to drag him down. Right now, the only way she can see to prevent that is by refusing to marry him."

"Hmm." Ryan cupped his chin in his hand. "It sounds like they both have the best of intentions, but they've drawn the same wrong conclusion."

"If we don't stop them, the situation is only going to get worse, not better." She didn't doubt that for a second.

"You're right. The last thing they need to do is to walk away from love."

Evelyn sighed. How had their Wedding-in-a-Week couple gotten so confused? Love meant finding your soul mate and building a life with them. Making a home. Raising a family. She wanted that. Didn't everyone?

She paused for a quick peek at Ryan. There'd been

a time when she'd thought he might be her Mr. Right. He checked all the boxes—smart, driven, independent, caring. He laughed at her lame jokes. He even thought her worst flaws were charming. It also didn't hurt that looking at him made her heart race. Like she had a dozen times over the years, she wondered why they'd drifted apart instead of growing closer. If things had been different between them, who knew—maybe they'd be planning their own Heart's Landing wedding instead of helping Brianna and Daniel with theirs.

"So how are we going to do that?"

Ryan's voice hauled her back to the problem at hand. She slouched forward. "I have no idea."

At her answer, his mouth dropped open in shocked confusion. She smiled. The man clearly had a higher opinion of her than she'd thought. But with a real love at risk, they needed to come up with a solution. And fast, before either Daniel or Brianna made a move that would lead to a lifetime of unhappiness and regret.

She tugged on her ponytail, thinking. "What's on the agenda tomorrow? Eat, Drink and Be Married?"

"In the morning, yeah. After lunch, they go to Forget Me Knot Florist." Ryan rubbed a hand over one knee. "Unless they finish up at Eat and Drink early. I mean, how long can it take to pick out a few dishes and some silverware?"

Evelyn felt her eyes go round. "You're kidding, right? You seriously did not grow up in Heart's Landing without learning the importance of a proper table setting?" At Ryan's blank look, she shook her head. For a man who was opening his own wedding venue, what he didn't know could land him in a world of hurt. "You might want to bone up. Read a few bridal magazines. Learn the ins and outs of everything that goes into a wedding."

"Why? Won't the wedding planner take care of all the details?" Ryan's eyebrows arrowed down, and he frowned.

"Have you hired one? Put one on retainer?" When Ryan shook his head, she groaned. "You're gonna need a good one, and it's not like they grow on trees." The man clearly needed a crash course in Weddings 101. Fortunately, she was more than qualified to give it to him. She plunged into the subject. "About that table setting. It's second only to the bride's gown and the groom's tux. The whole reception is built around it, so it can't be done willy-nilly. First, the couple has to choose a theme. That'll drive every other choice they make, from the centerpieces to the wine goblets."

She thought she saw a smile pass over Ryan's face, but the fleeting expression was gone in a second. Not before it raised a tiny flicker of doubt, though. Did Ryan know more than he was letting on? But no, she reassured herself, he couldn't. Not when he sat there staring with a clueless look on his face. She must've imagined that smile.

Returning to her lecture, she gave examples. "Say the couple settles on a nautical theme. Their table decor might include an elaborate display of miniature ships and oars, braided ropes and anchors. Or, for a ceremony on the Veranda, they might go with something as simple as roses." She drummed her fingers on the desktop. "Okay, where were we?"

"I have no idea." Giving off the vibe of a bored teenager, Ryan crossed one ankle over the other.

She swallowed. The man was toying with her. Why else would he flaunt those long legs of his? Well, if he thought he was going to distract her, he needed to think again. "We were talking about why tomorrow will be such a busy day," she reminded him. "Once Brianna and Daniel have their theme, everything has to support and coordinate with it. But not too close, or things will end up all matchy-matchy." She nodded, agreeing with herself. "No one wants that."

"Let me see if I've got this right. You're saying pink on pink does not make a good color scheme." Ryan threaded his fingers and stretched.

"Right." He'd caught on quick. She gave him a quick nod of approval. "Next comes china. They'll want something that looks nice when paired with the linens. But that's where it starts to get tricky because each choice limits what they can pick next."

Ryan's eyes narrowed. "I don't get it. Why is that?"

"Say the dinner plate they choose has a gold rim. They'll need to keep that in mind when they look at flatware. Silver clashes with gold unless..." She tapped her chin and waited.

"Unless they pick out silverware with a little gold trim?" Ryan asked.

"Exactly!" She let her smile widen. "Stemware—the same thing. If they chose delicate plates and cups, they'll need to look for something similar in glassware." She slid off her desk. Crossing the room, she headed straight for the spot where she kept a sample box. The cardboard flaps creaked open. Packing paper rustled as she dug for the pieces she wanted. She wrapped her hand around the stem of a chunky glass and held it aloft. "You wouldn't pair this glass with..." She pulled out a piece of bone china. The fragile plate was so fine, it was practically translucent. "With this," she finished.

"Got it." Showing far more interest than she'd expected, Ryan nodded.

"All of which explains why tomorrow will be such a long day. There's a lot to consider, a ton of decisions to make. I haven't worked with Eat, Drink and Be Married before." The Cottage had its own linens and china. For specialty items, they turned to a prescribed list of vendors, and Be Married wasn't on it. Her brow furrowed. Had Ryan even lined up his suppliers yet? She made a note to circle back and ask him. "I imagine the owners will have stacks of idea books for Brianna and Daniel to look through. It could take hours before they decide on a theme. Let alone all the stuff that comes after."

"We can skip that part," Ryan said, his expression turning as self-satisfied as a cat who'd just eaten the canary. "Daniel and Brianna want a military wedding."

"As in everything red, white, and blue?" She tried to picture the couple standing beneath an arbor draped in patriotic bunting. Her breath stalled. She couldn't breathe again until Ryan shook his head.

"That's where I went, too. But no. I asked Daniel about it. He said he was thinking more about all the gold buttons and insignia on the Marine uniform. Gold, with touches of red. He'll wear his uniform instead of a tux. The same for his groomsmen."

"That could work. It'd definitely make for a beautiful wedding." An unsettling uncertainty stirred in her chest. She tilted her head. "Does Brianna know about this?"

"From what Daniel said, it was her idea."

That decided it. If the couple had chosen their theme together, who was she to argue? She'd been right about one thing. Ryan had been keeping a secret. She slanted a look at him. Did he know how important this was? How many people needed this information? "Who else knows this will be a military wedding? Did you mention it to Alicia or Jenny?"

Ryan's sheepish grin made her heart quiver. "Never even thought of it."

"When we finish up here, we'd better make some phone calls if we want to give this couple a perfect wedding." She paused when a new thought occurred to her. Ryan had known about the theme all along, but he'd let her spend the last fifteen minutes giving him a lesson on weddings. A lesson he obviously hadn't needed. She pursed her lips. "If you knew about the theme and everything else, why'd you let me ramble on for so long?"

Ryan shrugged. "I must like listening to you talk, I guess."

She stared at him. Had his ears actually turned pink? She blinked and looked again. *Yep.* Like they had whenever he'd gotten flustered as a kid, his ears had turned so red they practically glowed. But why? They were just two friends, having a discussion. He shouldn't be embarrassed. Unless...

She picked at a loose thread at the hem of her shirt.

Unless he liked *her*.

A shiver that had nothing to do with the temperature in the room worked its way from her shoulders to her feet. Did Ryan's feelings for her go beyond friendship? The concept was so new, so foreign, she stilled. Her mind whirred with a whole world of possibilities she'd never allowed herself to consider.

"Evelyn. Earth to Evelyn. You okay over there?" Ryan began to rise from his chair.

Marshaling her thoughts, she waved him back into his seat. "What'd you say?"

"I said, I still don't understand how we're going to make sure Brianna and Daniel don't cancel their wedding."

She might not know whether Ryan liked her as, well, more than a friend, but she had a plan. A good one. "We'll double-team them," she announced, her voice firm and decisive. "Starting tomorrow, we'll go with them to every store that's participating in Wedding-In-A-Week. We'll sit beside them during the tastings at I Do Cakes and Food for A Day. We'll ooh and aah over the floral arrangements at Forget Me Knot." When Ryan rolled his eyes at the last one, she conceded the point. "Okay, you don't have to gush about the flowers. But the rest of it, definitely. While we're at it, we'll remind them why they're perfect for one another and why they'll never find another love as true as the one they've found in each other."

"She's the yin to his yang," he put in. "Where he's weak, she's his strength. Vice versa and etcetera." He waited a beat. "You think it'll work?"

"It has to. Otherwise, things like venues and who pays for dinner at Bow Tie Pasta won't matter, 'cause without our help, Daniel and Brianna will make the biggest mistake of their lives." She wagged her finger back and forth between them. "And guess who everybody's gonna blame."

"Whoa!" Ryan threw up his hands. "Neither of us wants that." For a long minute, he sat quietly. At last, a sly smile formed on his lips. "You know, there is an upside to all this."

Evelyn cocked her head. "What?"

"It'll give us"—his eyebrows rose and fell—"a chance to get to know one another better."

Her heart caught. She'd been right earlier. There was something going on between them. She swallowed. "I'm afraid we'll have to work pretty close together if we're going to save this wedding."

"Good." Ryan stood. "We were friends for a long time. Then we just..."

"Drifted apart?" she finished. Why that had happened was one of life's little mysteries.

"Yeah, that. So, friends again?"

"Sure." She let out a long, slow breath. *Friends.* He wanted to be friends. She should've known she was wasting her time hoping for something more. Despite the disappointment that pricked her chest, she squared her shoulders. Heart's Landing was counting on them. They had a job to do, a wedding to keep on track. If that meant she had to spend the next five days working with Ryan, so be it.

She'd just have to keep her guard up. She'd constantly remind herself he wanted to be friends—and nothing more. Otherwise, by the time Brianna walked down the aisle, she'd be in for a world of heartbreak.

Chapter Ten

"WOULD YOU LOOK AT THAT!" From the middle seat of the Town Car, Brianna craned her neck toward the window. "Have you ever seen anything so pretty in your entire life?"

Beside her, Evelyn felt her own face crinkle in delight. Spotting a bride all decked out in the back of a horse-drawn carriage never failed to send warmth flooding from her chest to her fingertips. But today wasn't about her. She focused on the bride-to-be. "Would you like to take a ride like that?"

"Could I?" Brianna's gaze tracked the gleaming white vehicle and its precious cargo until it turned a corner and disappeared from sight.

"We can definitely make it happen."

Giving Brianna's hand a squeeze, she smiled. Whether they deemed it necessary or not, few brides turned down the chance to take a carriage ride through Heart's Landing. She wouldn't either, when—or if—the time came. The idea of sitting on the plush bench seat while Tom Denton, regal in white tie and tails, clucked to a matched set of high-stepping horses sent a thrill of expectation racing through her. They'd circle the town before taking that final ride up Procession Avenue to the Captain's Cottage. When the driver pulled his team to a stop, her very own Mr. Right would be waiting for her. She pressed a hand to her heart. Just thinking of that day made her eyes go a little misty.

She glanced toward Ryan sitting in the passenger's seat up front. She liked that they'd renewed their friendship. Loved the way they'd slipped so easily back into a familiar relationship. More than that, working with the tall, handsome carpenter had given her a new appreciation for the man he'd become. He'd applied the same attention to detail he'd given his restoration work to providing Brianna and Daniel with the perfect wedding. His caring attitude and the kindness he'd shown the young couple stirred a desire in her for a stronger, deeper connection. Could things with Ryan go beyond friendship?

The car turned onto Bridal Carriage Drive, and she marshaled her wayward thoughts. This wasn't the time to dwell on the future. Right now, the reputation of Heart's Landing rested on Ryan's shoulders and hers. With so much depending on them, her focus had to remain on their assignment.

With that thought, she leaned forward to catch Daniel's eye. "She'll look radiant. Can't you just picture it? You in your uniform, so tall and handsome. Brianna in the perfect gown and veil. All your friends and family there to share this very special moment in your lives."

Seated by the other window, Daniel nodded. He lifted his fiancée's left hand to his lips and kissed the simple diamond that adorned her finger. "I'll do whatever it takes to make Brianna happy."

Not exactly the ringing endorsement for love and marriage she'd been hoping for, but it would have to do, she thought as the driver braked in front of a small building on a deep lot off Champagne Avenue. *Eat, Drink and Be Married,* announced a sign that swung between two posts on the wide lawn. Finer script read, "For all your wedding needs."

"You're going to really like this place," Ryan said, rounding the front bumper after they'd piled out of the car. He gave the driver a mock salute and waited until the man sped off before he spoke again. "Bev and Vi Gorman grew up spending summers with their grandmother here in Heart's Landing. When she passed three years ago, they converted her house into a rental boutique featuring linens and tableware. They've built it into a thriving business. This is their first year as Wedding-in-a-Week participants." He gave his hands a brisk rub. "I can't wait to see what they have for you."

While Brianna linked her arm through Daniel's and followed Ryan up the stone walkway, Evelyn lifted her chin. Summer was the busiest season at the Captain's Cottage. Small wonder, then, that she barely recalled the two sisters who'd spent a couple of months in town each year. But Ryan sure seemed to know a lot about the women. When had he gotten so chummy with the Gormans?

She shoved those thoughts aside for another time while they climbed the wide steps to the entrance. On a shady porch, bright pink peonies sprang from planters atop the rail. Cross-stitched pillows on white wicker chairs invited customers to linger in the shade. Nearby, a tall dispenser of frosty lemonade and a plate of cookies on a chintz-covered table added to the altogether charming effect.

"Cookie, anyone?" Ryan asked. He lifted a domed lid and helped himself.

"Thanks. Don't mind if I do." Daniel snagged a couple. He offered one to Brianna.

"I'll pass." The bride-to-be patted her tummy. "I filled up on blueberry muffins this morning. Y'all grow the biggest berries up here." She laughed. "Ours back home aren't half that size."

"There's a U-Pick place just north of town," Evelyn offered. "You and Daniel could go there Saturday." Once the couple announced their selections, they'd have the rest of the day free to sightsee, shop, or take a trip to the beach.

"Maybe," Brianna said, clearly interested.

They waited until Daniel brushed the last crumb from his hands before Ryan held the door open for the rest. Evelyn had no more than stepped foot in the store when a dynamo of a woman with short brown curls exclaimed, "You're here! You're here! Welcome!"

Smiling staffers wearing pink aprons clustered around the checkout counter. From a spot that must've given him excellent coverage of the entrance, Curtis snapped pictures. He lowered his camera to wave hello. Then, motioning Evelyn and Ryan aside, he retreated behind the lens while their hostess continued her greeting.

"Welcome to Eat, Drink and Be Married, where only the very best will do for your wedding! I'm Vi Gorman. My sister Bev had planned to be here today, but my nephew caught a cold. So you're stuck with me!" Vi spread her arms wide, exclamation points peppering her sentences. "But don't despair. Everything's ready for you." She stopped in the middle of a rushed monologue to take a breath. "You're Daniel, of course! We met at the train station." She spun to Brianna. "And this must be your lovely bride-to-be. I didn't have a chance to introduce myself when you arrived. There were so many people! Congratulations on being chosen as this year's Wedding-in-a-Week couple!"

Brianna's eyes widened in a sure sign that she hadn't expected the effusive chatter. Evelyn stepped forward to give the wary bride a chance to collect her thoughts. She stuck out her hand. "Vi, good to see you."

"So happy to have you here, Evelyn." Vi grasped her hand and gave it a firm pump. "Now I know you have everything you could ever possibly need at the Captain's Cottage, but if something in our store catches your eye, just let me know." She turned to the fourth member of their party. "Ryan! So good to see you again!"

Evelyn watched in stunned silence as the woman surged forward to embrace Ryan in a hug that, in her opinion, lasted entirely too long. Even as the tiny hairs on the back of her neck bristled and her jaw tightened, she told herself she had no right to be jealous. She and Ryan were friends. Nothing else. The more time they spent together, the more she asked herself, "What if he's *the one?*" but that was all it was—a question. She had no business poking her nose into his history with Vi.

Nevertheless, she moved to keep the visit on track.

"Ahem. I'm sure Brianna and Daniel would love to see what you've selected for their wedding."

"Right!" Vi finally relinquished her hold on Ryan. "Come right this way."

Curtis's camera whirred as they followed the owner past built-in wall units. Table linens in every imaginable color hung from velvet-covered hangers beneath the cabinets and shelves. Next came china patterns artfully arranged in individual cubbies, stacked one on top of the other from floor to ceiling. When green flames continued to flicker at the edge of her vision, Evelyn feigned a sudden interest in one of the displays and veered off from the group.

"Get a grip," she muttered under her breath. She ran one finger along the rim of a china cup. "Ryan and I are friends. Just friends." She repeated the phrase several times. At last, her heart stopped aching whenever she pictured him walking arm in arm down Bridal Carriage Way with someone else, and she hurried to catch up with the others.

"Here we are," Vi said at last. In the far corner of the shop, comfy white chairs had been arranged in front of low tables that held an assortment of bridal magazines, snacks, and beverages.

"Nice." Daniel plopped down on the first cushion. "I'm all set." Ever hungry, he reached for a plate.

Brianna slid in beside him, her eyes glued to three free-standing screens that, according to Vi, hid Eat, Drink and Be Married's suggestions for the Wedding-in-a-Week couple. "I'm so excited." She bounced up and down, clapping her hands like a schoolgirl. "I can't wait to see what you've chosen for us."

Ryan and Evelyn took the remaining chairs. She

stole a quick sidelong glance at Ryan, who watched Vi's every move as the woman crossed to the first screen. A hard knot formed in her stomach. She shook her head, but she didn't have any luck dousing the green flames this time.

"Focus," she told herself and tore her gaze from him.

Up front, Vi said, "Every item in this first table setting was chosen to honor Daniel and Brianna's commitment to his military service while celebrating this most important day in your lives. Ready?"

Vi rolled the curtain out of the way. Behind it sat a round table draped in pristine white. A satiny finish created the impression of movement in the cloth that brushed the floor in thick folds. Dark navy table runners crisscrossed at the center of the table. Light sparkled from the gold tips of silver flatware, white china, and elegant glassware. As a final touch, bright red napkins sprang from each plate.

"Oorah," Daniel chuffed.

"Nice!" Brianna pronounced.

Vi beamed.

Impressed despite herself, Evelyn had to give the woman mad props for creating a setting that was both patriotic and elegant. She listened closely while their hostess launched into a thorough description of the pieces she and her sister had chosen for the table. When it was time to move on to the next option, she looked forward to seeing what lay behind the curtain almost as much as the bride, who drummed her fingers in anticipation.

"We've designed this look to reflect Brianna and

Daniel's love for their home state of Florida," Vi announced.

Brianna's smile widened when the woman rolled the curtain aside to reveal a row of oblong tables swathed in pale yellow. Bamboo chairs matched the decor and provided seating. On the tabletop, sleek, modern flatware surrounded square china plates adorned with tropical flowers, while olive-green napkins and placemats complemented the bright colors.

Evelyn smoothed the skirt of her shirtwaist. A Florida theme wasn't exactly her style, but when the time came—*if* the time came—she wouldn't mind incorporating some of Rhode Island's best features in her wedding. A few blue violets in her bouquet. A menu built around clams and lobsters. No chickens, though. Even if they were the state bird. She smothered a laugh as Vi began to speak.

"Option Two incorporates a slightly more festive air." The owner ran a hand over the surface. As she had with the previous entry, she provided a detailed description of each item in the setting. Almost finished, Vi picked up an enlarged postcard in a gilt frame from the spot where it leaned against a candelabra. "We've chosen vintage postcards to identify each table. Miniature versions would serve as place cards."

"How fun is that!" Brianna's smile grew wider. "We want to throw a big party and meet all our neighbors once we're settled in at Daniel's next duty station. That place card idea would be a fun way to tell everyone where to sit."

"Place cards and formal dinner parties are for officers, sweetheart." Daniel reached for his fiancée's hand. “We’re more wings and beer than all this.” With a wave at the displays, he indicated the shop.

“But you like it, don’t you? I mean, it’s our wedding and…”

“Of course I do.” Daniel caught her fingers up in both his hands. “I’m just saying none of this matters as long as I get to have you as my wife.”

Evelyn swore every heart in the room went pit-a-pat when Daniel brought Brianna’s fingertips to his lips and kissed them. *That,* she said to herself. *Forget the big, fancy wedding—just give me a man who loves me like that.*

Curious, she glanced at Ryan. Was he as moved by Daniel’s display of affection as she’d been? She wrenched her gaze elsewhere when Ryan’s soft eyes touched her heart.

After a moment, Vi said, “So, to recap. The first option honors Daniel’s military career. The second is a tribute to your home state. Are you ready for your third and final option?”

“I’m already having a hard time choosing between the first two.” Brianna flounced back in her seat.

Daniel looped one hand around her shoulders. “I know which one I like.”

“Oh, you.” Brianna brushed her fingers over his upper arm. “We’re not supposed to say anything out loud.”

Her reprimand earned her a sheepish look, which Brianna followed up by bussing Daniel’s cheek.

Evelyn’s chest expanded. As they were getting into the car this morning, Brianna had whispered that she and Daniel had talked late into the night. So far, there’d been no sign of the doubts the young bride had expressed yesterday. Had the couple simply had a case of wedding jitters? She hoped so.

Up front, Vi rolled away the third curtain, and Evelyn clamped a hand over her mouth to capture a happy giggle. An olive-green runner stretched the length of a rustic wooden table. Caned-bottom chairs had been placed at regular intervals. Red dishes sat on top of gold charger plates. Silver flatware with gold handles rested on dark blue napkins. White bread plates and delicate stemware added to the effect.

This, she thought, eyeing a table that exuded charm and sophistication. This was what every wedding should be—a perfect blending of his dreams and hers. She started to comment on it, but one glance at Ryan told her something else entirely had captured his attention. Following his gaze to Vi, who invited Daniel and Brianna to give all three choices a closer look, she pressed her lips together. When he continued to stare while the couple joined hands and moved to the table settings, she leaned into her chair, her arms crossed. She sat, stewing in silence, as long minutes ticked slowly past.

Eventually, Ryan tore his gaze from Vi and leaned toward her. "Bev and Vi did a great job, didn't they?"

"Perfect. Simply perfect." She laced the words with an extra dose of sarcasm. "You two sure are awfully friendly."

"I should hope so." Confusion clouded his eyes. "When I first got back to Heart's Landing, no one would hire me except my dad. He wanted to put me to work swinging a hammer. Um, no thanks. I thought I might have to move on until Bev and Vi asked me to convert their grandmother's house into this place." His gaze wandered the walls.

"I didn't know." She studied the nearest set of closets. How had she failed to notice Ryan's handiwork? His demand for perfection was evident in the tight joints of the cubbies, the smoothly turned posts that adorned the display cases. That still left a lot of unanswered questions. Determined to learn the answers to them, she braced herself and plunged on. "Is that when you and Vi started seeing each other?"

Ryan rolled his eyes. "Is that what's got your nose out of joint?"

"Me? You're the one who's practically drooling."

Ryan shot a quick look over his shoulder at the couple, who stood at one table, their arms wrapped around a smiling Vi. Standing, he bobbed his head toward the exit. "Let's go outside."

Did she really want to end things with Ryan before they even began? She stalled by asking, "What about Brianna and Daniel?"

"Curtis will keep them busy for a few minutes." He started for the door, leaving her no choice other than to trail slowly behind him. On the front porch a few minutes later, he turned to face her. "Now what's all this about me and Vi?"

"It's no big deal," she protested. Okay, so she'd dreamed of having a deeper, more meaningful relationship with Ryan, but that was all it was. A dream. His social life was really none of her concern.

"You've been in a mood ever since we got here."

"I am not in a mood," she insisted. "I asked a simple question. How long have you and Vi been seeing each other?"

"We're not." Confusion knitted his brows. "Where'd you get that idea?"

"I thought..." Her voice trailed off. Did she really have to say it? Evidently she did, because Ryan just stood there, waiting for her to continue. Her breath shuddered. "I saw how she hugged you. How you hugged her back. Like you were more than friends. Like you were involved." She gave him her best challenging look. There, let him deny that.

"Me and Vi." A smile crept across Ryan's lips. It quickly turned into a full-fledged grin.

Whatever reaction she'd expected, laughter wasn't it. "What's so funny?" she demanded.

"You realize she's ten, maybe fifteen years older than me?"

"So what? Men date older women all the time." There'd probably been a dozen December/May weddings at the Cottage over the years.

"Sorry." Ryan sobered. His hands rose in protest despite the merriment that continued to dance in his eyes. "There's nothing going on between me and Vi. She's married. So's Bev, for that matter. But even if she was free, Vi's not my type."

"And what is your type?" The words rolled right off her tongue before she could stop them.

"Well, if you must know, I'm kind of partial to redheads."

If there'd been a wall behind her, Ryan's stare would've pinned her to it. Heat flooded her face and spread across her shoulders.

"And no." His voice dropped an octave. "Just in case you were wondering, I'm not dating anyone.

Not that it should matter to you one way or another. You're the one with a steady boyfriend."

Her head jerked up. "Wh-what gave you that idea? I don't have a boyfriend, steady or unsteady."

"You're sure about that?"

The man was so earnest, she couldn't resist teasing him a bit. "Hmm. You think I'm getting forgetful in my old age? Here, I'll check my schedule." She made a huge show of pulling her phone out of her purse and scrolling through the calendar app. "Nope. No date last Saturday. I'd better check the week before. Um, nope. Nothing then, either. Maybe last month?" She scrolled again and peered up at him. "Nothing there. You're sure I'm seeing someone?"

"Evelyn." Ryan's voice dropped to a heart-stopping growl. "Who are you taking to dinner at Bow Tie Pasta?"

"Bow Tie—oh! When I win our bet? You're worried about my dinner date?" She canted her head. Who was being jealous now?

"You're not going to win, but that's beside the point. Who?" He ground out the last word.

"Okay. Okay." No sense upsetting the man now that things were just getting interesting. "If you must know, I was planning to let Tara and Jason go in my place. I thought it'd make a nice gift for them when they get home from their honeymoon."

"So all that stuff about the lamb chops was..." He stopped to let her fill in the blanks.

"Just me having fun." She hung her head. "Sounds like we both jumped to conclusions."

"Yeah, it kind of does. I'm glad we cleared that up."

Ryan studied a spot over her left shoulder. "Maybe we should—"

Behind her, the door to Be Married sprang open. The moment it did, Ryan's mouth clamped shut. Brianna and Daniel emerged from the store. Curtis edged around them, his camera at the ready. Vi stepped into view, her staff clustered behind her.

"Of all the rotten timing," Evelyn muttered, wishing Ryan had been able to finish.

"I can't wait to find out what you've chosen for your wedding!" Vi's face beamed with pleasure. "Feel free to stop in anytime if you have questions or want to see the options again. They'll be on display all week."

"Thanks for everything." Daniel gave the shop owner's hand a final shake.

"It was all so lovely," Brianna said dreamily. "We're going to have the best wedding, thanks to you!" She sidled closer to Daniel, who slipped his arm around her. While Curtis snapped pictures, the couple headed down the steps to the car that waited at the curb.

"Evelyn, I'm so glad you visited our store today. I trust you liked what you saw." Hope tinged Vi's words.

Be Married had certainly exceeded her expectations and, after misjudging the woman so badly, Evelyn felt she owed her. "As soon as Jason gets back, I'll ask him to add your store to our suppliers' list," she promised. The offer would drive a lot of business to the shop.

"That's wonderful! I can't wait to tell Bev! She'll be thrilled!" Vi turned to Ryan. "Seeing you today was a pleasant surprise. Don't be strangers, you hear?"

"Good to see you, too, Vi." Headed for the sidewalk, Ryan added, "Give my best to Bev. Hope that little one of hers is feeling better."

"I'm on my way to check on them right now," Vi assured him.

A light beep from the Town Car reminded everyone that Alicia had planned a working lunch with Brianna and Daniel at the Captain's Cottage. Evelyn hurried down the stairs two steps ahead of Ryan. Keeping the Event Planner waiting was never a good thing.

She reached a spur-of-the-moment decision on the sidewalk. "Hey, you all go on back to the Cottage. I'll meet you at Forget Me Knot."

"You're sure?"

"Need to stretch my legs." She also needed to sort out her feelings for a certain tall, blond carpenter. Not that she was willing to share that thought with anyone just yet. "I'll grab a bite while I'm here in town."

She traded silent nods with Ryan. There'd been a moment on the porch when she would've sworn he'd been about to ask her out. Her mouth had gone dry with anticipation. Her heart had beat as fast as a hummingbird's. Then Brianna and Daniel had stepped onto the porch and...nothing. Like someone had flipped a switch, his interest had shifted. Had she read the situation wrong? Had he been about to ask her something else entirely? Something about the weather?

Ugh! Her thoughts were so all over the place, she didn't even know whether or not she'd accept. If and when he did ask her. She clenched and unclenched her fingers to release the tension. Yeah, right. Who did she think she was kidding?

Chapter Eleven

UNDER A SHADE TREE ON Bridal Carriage Way, Ryan scrolled through the messages on his phone. He scanned a text from his mom, who wanted to know if she could count on him for Sunday dinner. A muscle in his jaw twitched. He hated to disappoint her, but sharing another tense meal with his father and brothers was not the way he wanted to spend the day. Fortunately, Wedding-in-a-Week gave him just the excuse he needed. He dashed off a quick reply and scanned the phone again.

When he didn't spot a text from Evelyn, he delivered a swift kick to the mental seat of his pants. He should've asked her out while they were at Eat, Drink and Be Married. Sure, she might've turned him down—again. But wasn't it worth the risk to find out? Ever since they'd started working together, she'd surprised him with her down-to-earth approach to life. He'd been even more shocked by how much he enjoyed being around her. She made him laugh. When life threw her a curve ball, she dealt with it.

He nodded. He wouldn't hesitate again. The next time he had a minute alone with her, he'd ask Evelyn out. He smiled as a shiver of nervous energy passed through him. He could hardly wait to put this new plan into motion.

Apparently, though, his plan would have to wait because a familiar Town Car had just pulled to the curb in front of Forget Me Knot Florist. No matter how much he wanted to explore his growing attraction for a certain feisty redhead, his first obligation lay in helping to give their Wedding-in-a-Week couple a perfect wedding. He tossed the dregs of his now-cold coffee into the trash and summoned a ready smile for the couple.

But something had gone horribly wrong.

He knew it as sure as he knew his own name the instant he saw Brianna's tight expression. Emerging from the car behind his bride-to-be, Daniel didn't look one whit happier. Worry lines etched the normally cheerful groom's brow. When he reached for her hand, Brianna moved out of his reach.

Ryan tapped his foot on the sidewalk. Had they had a fight? Decided to call off the wedding? No matter what had happened, he had to intervene. He ventured a tentative, "Um, Brianna? Daniel? How was lunch?"

The question earned him a scathing look that, in retrospect, he had to admit he deserved. He jingled the loose change in his pocket. Whatever had upset the couple, he'd try to help them work it out. But standing on Bridal Carriage Way in the middle of America's Top Wedding Destination was not the place to do it. Already, the couple had drawn a few sidelong glances from passersby. If they argued, someone might whip out their cell phone and record the incident. He didn't want an awkward video to become a souvenir of Daniel and Brianna's stay in Heart's Landing. But getting the couple off the sidewalk required more than one pair of hands.

That thought had no sooner crossed his mind than he spotted Evelyn striding toward them. Relief rippled through him. He didn't think he'd ever felt happier to see the tall redhead than at that moment. He motioned for her to hurry the moment she stepped under the awning of I Do Cakes. She didn't hesitate. She simply picked up her pace. Seconds later, she skidded to a stop at his side.

Peering up at him, she asked simply, "How can I help?"

"I'll tell Mildred we'll be back. Meanwhile, you get them someplace quiet and out of sight."

"Got it." She straightened, her shoulders squaring. By the time he slipped through the door of Forget Me Knot, Evelyn had already linked arms with Brianna and Daniel and had them marching in lockstep down the street.

He shook his head. The girl had skills. Trusting that she had everything under control for the time being, he looked for Mildred among the shelves of sweet-smelling greenery. He didn't have to look far. The owner stood at the window.

"That didn't look good," the florist murmured softly when he reached her. "Did they have a spat?"

"Oh, you know. Young love. There's always drama," he joked. "We're going to give them a few minutes to calm down. Can you stall the photographer when he gets here?"

"Already done." Mildred aimed a thumb toward the

workroom in the back. "My niece has taken him on the grand tour. But the store isn't all that big. Beth won't be able to keep him entertained long. After that, we'll have to talk about flowers and hope he nods off."

"We'll be back as soon as possible," he said, offering the only reassurance he had. "You're the best, you know." He leaned down to give the plump florist a peck on the cheek.

"Oh, you!" Coloring sweetly, Mildred shook her fingers at him. "That's what they all say."

The comment brought a smile he didn't have to force to his lips and, humming a jaunty tune, he retraced his steps to the door. Outside, he lengthened his stride and quickly arrived at Bow Tie Pasta. He watched in awe as Evelyn approached the black-garbed hostess.

"We'll need a private room for a bit," she announced, her firm tone pitched too low to draw unwanted attention.

The woman behind the hostess stand swept one glance over the tight-lipped couple with Evelyn and gave a solemn nod. She grabbed an armload of menus the size of encyclopedias. Seconds later, she wove between tables toward the back of the restaurant.

Ryan let the peaceful atmosphere seep into his soul as he trailed the group past brick walls dotted with framed paintings by local artists. The good smells of olive oil, garlic, and tomato filled the air. Light filtered through narrow, curved windows and reflected softly from the glassware hanging above the bar. He passed a tuxedoed waiter, who quietly explained the day's specials to a group of businessmen at one table. The sommelier poured sips of wine for a couple at another.

He waited until they were behind the closed doors of a room reserved for private parties before he faced Brianna and Daniel. He cut to the chase. “Okay, what’s this all about?”

Brianna’s lower lip trembled. “Daniel got a phone call over lunch.”

He braced himself. “Bad news?” His head filled with images of police cars and fire trucks.

The young groom studied his toes. “Sort of. I was given an extra month of leave when we were selected for Wedding-In-A-Week. That meant I was supposed to report to Camp Geiger at the end of July. But I just got new orders. I have to report in nine days. Brianna, she’s having a hard time with that.”

“I am not!” The slim blonde tugged on her ear while she stamped her foot. Her eyes wide, she stared at Daniel. “I just asked if you told your boss you’d be in Hawaii then.”

“And I told you, I can’t argue with my CO!” Defiant, Daniel lifted his head to meet his fiancée’s gaze.

“You were going on your honeymoon,” Ryan said, fitting the peg into the hole. No wonder they were upset. No matter how committed they both were to Daniel’s military career, canceling the trip had to be a huge disappointment.

Brianna hung her head. “Daniel doesn’t think I’m cut out to be a military wife. He’s giving up on us.”

“You’re making me out to be the bad guy here.” The young man’s expression stiffened. “I’m having just as hard a time with the change as you are, Bri.” He turned away from his fiancée. “I was all set. I knew life in the Marines was going to be tough. They tell us that in boot camp—how hard it is on wives and families. But knowing what to expect is half the battle, right? That's what I thought until I got these new orders. Now, I have to report two weeks earlier than we'd planned. It's made me see how I could get sent halfway around the world at a moment's notice. It's not fair to do that to Brianna."

The kid was talking in circles. Ryan had to straighten him out. "What do you mean?"

"I think...I think we should call off the wedding," Daniel said, looking like he'd just agreed to have a root canal without Novocain.

Brianna's shoulders slumped as if she was on the verge of collapse. "If that's what you want..."

"Whoa! Wait a minute." Ryan held up his hand. He got that the news was upsetting, but how had these two people who obviously loved each other gone from disappointment to canceling their wedding in under sixty seconds? He stole a glance at Evelyn, who stood white-faced and in shock like the rest of them. As he watched, she shook herself and squared her shoulders.

"Let's all just sit down and talk about this, shall we?"

Her no-nonsense tone cut through the room like a drill sergeant's, and Daniel didn't argue. His movements stiff and unnatural, the young man headed for one of the tables. In silence, he pulled a chair out for Brianna. She slid onto it without complaint. Daniel sank onto the seat beside her. By unspoken agreement, Ryan and Evelyn sat opposite the unhappy duo.

"Okay, let's all take a breath," Evelyn began, her voice softening. Across from her, tears seeped from between Brianna's closed eyelids, while Daniel merely stared at a spot on the wall. Ryan fought the urge to drum his fingers on the table. The next time he saw Alicia, they were going to have a little talk about making Wedding Counseling 101 a prerequisite for working with Wedding-in-a-Week couples.

The silence stretched out for a bit. When he thought everyone had calmed down, Ryan cleared his throat. He directed his first question to Daniel. "Want to tell me what's going on here?"

Tight-lipped, he held up his hands, his palms empty. "She expects me to argue with my CO and get him to change my orders. Will you tell her I can't do that?"

Ryan felt his pulse thud while he studied Brianna closely. Admittedly, he didn't have a whole lot of experience with angry young women, but if he had to guess, he'd say this one wasn't demanding anything. "I don't think she's asking you to."

"Ryan's right. Isn't he, Brianna?" Evelyn interjected.

The thin blonde steadied herself with a shuddery breath. "I admit I could've reacted better when you first gave me the news, Daniel. It came out of the blue. I was so shocked, I needed a minute. That's all it was, I swear." Brianna swiped at her cheeks and straightened. "I may not know a lot about what it means to be a Marine, but I know you have to go where you're told, when you're told. And if the Marines want you in Camp Geiger, you'll be there."

"Yeah, but..." Daniel's face flushed. "I know how

much you were looking forward to Hawaii. You deserve to be with someone who can take you on a proper honeymoon."

"Daniel Johnston." Brianna tapped the table with one finger. "If you think you're getting rid of me that easy, think again. We'll take our honeymoon later. The next time you have some vacation."

"Leave. In the military, it's called leave." The harsh lines in Daniel's face softened.

"Leave, then. We'll go to Hawaii the next time you have leave."

Daniel's head swung from side to side. "That's the problem. I can't promise you we'll ever get to Hawaii. Or that I'll be home for Christmas. Or our anniversary. Or any of the other holidays or special dates. I love you. You know I'd do anything in the world for you. But you deserve a better life than the one I can give you."

"So your answer is to leave me?" Fresh tears welled in Brianna's eyes.

Ryan shook his head. He'd never taken a counseling class in his life, but he knew a thing or two about love and marriage. To begin with, if he was ever lucky enough to find his soul mate, he wouldn't walk away from her at the first sign of trouble. He might have to make some adjustments. There might be compromises. But he'd stick with it. No matter what.

The real question here wasn't whether Brianna was better off without Daniel. It was whether they cared deeply enough to make their relationship work. "I know you two love each other. But marriage takes more than that. It takes commitment. Brianna just said she's in it for richer or poorer, for sickness and in health, for the rest of her life. Can you say the same thing, Daniel?"

The young groom grasped his fiancée's hands. His voice thick with emotion, he said, "If it was up to me, I'd never leave your side."

"Well, I'm glad that's settled." Relief washed through Ryan, and he took a deep breath. A breath that froze in his chest when Daniel spoke again.

"That's why I have to break up with you. Because I'm not in charge. And I love you too much to ask you to face a lifetime of disappointment."

Ryan didn't know whether to smack his head in frustration or wring the kid's neck. Daniel clearly had the best of intentions, but he was going about it entirely the wrong way. Trouble was, Ryan didn't have the first clue about how to convince the young man he was throwing away the best thing in his life. Hoping against hope that Evelyn would, he turned to her. When she flashed him a look that said *I got this*, he turned the floor over to her.

"Around here, it's tradition to raise a toast to the bride and groom at every wedding and wish them a Heart's Landing love for the ages. Do you know why?"

"No," the young couple answered practically in unison.

"It's because of the love Captain Thaddeus and Mary shared. See, he spent his entire career ferrying merchandise and passengers between New York and London. In those days, the trip took three months each way, which meant the good captain and his wife spent more than half their married life apart from one another. Despite that, their love for one another endured."

Seeing where Evelyn was headed, Ryan added, "We're sure of it because, each fall, Captain Thaddeus presented his wife with a large stone heart he'd carved for her during that year's long voyage. A symbol of his love for her."

Across the table, Daniel and Brianna had leaned forward slightly, their interest piqued.

"Mary kept the home fires burning. Every fall, she kept watch for Thaddeus from the widow's walk," Evelyn said, her words brief and to the point. "It didn't matter if the weather was fair or foul; she scoured the horizon for the first sign of his ship."

Ryan picked up where she left off. "Meanwhile, the captain fought off pirates and endured long days when no wind filled the sails. Once, he even battled a hurricane to get home to his wife and children." Wrapping up, he got to the point of the story. "Mary could've chosen any of a dozen suitors. Thaddeus could've walked away from his career. Instead, they refused to give up on their love for one another. Their lives weren't always easy. But through the good times and the bad, whether they were apart or together, Thaddeus and Mary's love and commitment to one another remained strong."

He looked to Evelyn, who tied everything up in a neat bow. "Together, they established the town of Heart's Landing. Their legacy lives on today in the Captain's Cottage and in their great-great-great grandchildren. My cousin Jason and I are their direct descendants." She aimed a searching look straight at Daniel. "We believe you and Brianna have the same kind of love Thaddeus and Mary shared. Brianna has already endured more heartbreak and disappointment than anyone should at her age, but each hurt has made her stronger. Strong enough to be the wife you need."

Ryan's voice dropped lower. Evelyn's words had stirred an emotion deep in his chest. His eyes on her, he asked Daniel, "In what world do you think she'd be better off without you?"

"I wouldn't be," Brianna whispered. "You know how much I need you."

"Awww, man." Daniel cradled his fiancée's hand in his. His voice shook nearly as much as his fingers. "I'm sorry I ever doubted us. Can you forgive me?"

"Yes. Of course, I do." Brianna smiled through her tears. "But you have to promise me something."

"Anything. I'll do anything."

"You have to promise you won't ever do this again, you hear?"

"I won't." Daniel traced a cross over his chest. "I swear."

When the couple exchanged a tender kiss, Ryan grinned at Evelyn. He felt like someone should give them the key to the city. They'd done it, had saved Wedding-in-a-Week from complete failure. Even more important, they'd helped Daniel and Brianna forge a deeper bond.

"There's just one more thing," Evelyn said, stepping forward. "It's only a day's drive to Camp Geiger from here. That gives you two extra days before you have to report. I think I can speak for all of Heart's Landing when I say we'd love it if you spent that time as our guest at the Captain's Cottage. Consider it a mini-honeymoon."

Brianna sucked in a deep breath. "In one of the bridal suites?"

Evelyn nodded. "Yes, of course."

"Oorah!" Daniel whispered.

So much relief flooded him when Brianna and Daniel embraced that Ryan had to turn away. He didn't intend for his focus to shift to Evelyn. That happened purely by happenstance. But he was glad when it did. His gaze softened. Warmth curled in his midsection at the sight of her standing there, her hair in its familiar ponytail, the hem of her skirt barely brushing her knees. His fingers itched to take her in his arms. Resisting the urge was tougher than he'd expected.

Was he falling for her? He started and gave himself a stern reminder that such thoughts were utter foolishness. How could he fall for someone before they'd even gone on their first date?

Hoping for a distraction, he glanced toward Brianna and Daniel. No luck there. The couple continued to cling to one another. Resigned, he signaled Evelyn and counted himself lucky when he didn't have to explain. It was as if she instinctively knew what he meant. A second later, she headed out the door, and he followed close on her heels.

"You were amazing," Evelyn whispered as they headed for the exit. "For a minute, I thought they were on the verge of calling it quits."

The compliment warmed him to his core, but he hadn't acted alone. It'd taken their combined efforts to keep this Wedding-in-a-Week on track. "I couldn't have done it without you. We make a good team."

"Yeah." Light shot through him when she smiled up at him. "I guess we do."

He smiled in return, although one thing still niggled at him. Much as he hated to accuse her of having an ulterior motive, he had to know whether Evelyn's offer was an attempt to coax Brianna and Daniel into choosing her venue. The Evelyn he'd grown up with wouldn't even think of such a thing. The one he'd known in high school might. The question was, which Evelyn was she now?

"It was nice of you to offer them one of the bridal suites," he hinted.

"I couldn't very well throw them out on the street, could I?" She grinned as they emerged onto Bow Tie Pasta's covered walkway. "Besides, they'll get a one-night stay at the Captain's Cottage when they choose it for their wedding venue. It's only right to give them one or two more."

"And if they don't?"

"That won't happen." Sympathy clouded her eyes. She waited a beat. "But either way, the offer stands."

He loved that she hadn't wanted to hurt him, but she needn't worry. His shoulders were broad enough to bear it if Daniel and Brianna did choose the Captain's Cottage over Harbor View. More than that, though, her assurances helped him let go of his final doubts about her. He exhaled. "In that case..." he began.

"Yes?"

"Well, we'll both be at the wedding on Sunday—wherever it's held," he added with a smile. "What if we went together?"

Evelyn stopped dead on the sidewalk. Her feet

planted, she scoured his face with a laser-like gaze. "Are you asking me to be your plus-one at the wedding?"

"Yeah." This was it, the moment of truth. The last time he'd asked her out, she'd given him the cold shoulder. Would she do the same thing this time? He held his breath. She either would or she wouldn't. There wasn't any middle ground.

"I'd like that," she said at last.

Watching the kittenish smile play around Evelyn's lips, he groaned. Much as he'd tried to fight it, much as he'd warned himself not to let it happen, he was falling for Evelyn Heart.

Now what was he going to do about that?

Evelyn's pulse fluttered. *Finally!* A giddy rush sped through her, leaving her as excited as a girl who'd been invited to her first prom. By the quarterback, no less. She opened her mouth, prepared to throw Ryan some snark about taking so long...and her lips snapped shut. She simply didn't have the words.

Imagine that.

Lucky for her, Brianna and Daniel chose that moment to step through the door of Bow Tie Pasta. Their arrival served to remind her that this week wasn't about Ryan or her. It was about giving the Wedding-in-a-Week couple their perfect day. Which was where she needed to keep her focus unless she wanted to let down all of Heart's Landing.

"I hope you're ready for a real treat, because it's

time for floral arrangements and bridal bouquets," she announced.

"About that..." Daniel began.

"Not to worry." She waved her hand in a soothing motion. "We made sure everyone in town knows about your allergy, Brianna. I have it straight from Mildred Morrey that she's taken special steps to ensure your safety."

"I wish I had your confidence." Brianna tugged on one earlobe, a move Evelyn had seen her make a few times.

Brianna's allergy was no laughing matter, and Evelyn was fresh out of reassurances. She looked to Ryan.

"Tell you what." He rubbed his chin. "Let's see what precautions Mildred has taken. The instant you feel the least bit uncomfortable, say the word. We'll whisk you straight to the car and back to the bed and breakfast."

"Well, I love flowers, and I do want to see what they've come up with for our wedding," Brianna hedged. "As long as I can leave if—"

"You can," Ryan assured her.

"Okay, then." Despite the worry lines that crisscrossed Brianna's forehead, she slipped her hand in Daniel's and headed up Bridal Carriage Way.

Sun dappled the sidewalk between them on a walk to the floral shop that took quite a bit longer than their earlier rush down the street. Evelyn found herself growing more eager with every step. Mildred had quite the reputation for creating window displays that were sheer perfection, and knowing this one might be featured in *Weddings Today*, she'd probably pulled out all the stops. A shiver of anticipation passed through her as she imagined the possibilities. She chanced a quick glance at Ryan. Was he the kind of guy who sent flowers to a girlfriend on her birthday? Who considered them a necessary part of every wedding?

Whoa. She jammed the brakes on her runaway thoughts. Ryan had only invited her to be his plus-one. She had no business turning sappy over bridal bouquets and boutonnieres. She shrugged. It was all Heart's Landing's fault. In a town where weddings were on everyone's mind 365 days a year, who could blame her? She did her best to control her imagination as they passed beneath the chocolate-and-pink awning of I Do Cakes.

"Huh," Ryan said when Forget Me Knot came in view. "That's odd."

The comment broke her reverie. Thankful for the reprieve, she shot him a questioning look.

"Mildred never raised the curtains on her new window display," he said, discreetly aiming a finger toward the shop. "I'm surprised I didn't notice it earlier. I hope nothing's wrong. I always look forward to seeing what she comes up with, don't you?"

At his concern, a sudden wave of warm feelings rushed over her. A happy sigh escaped her lips. Not only did Ryan understand the importance of the window coverings; he was concerned about Mildred's well-being. How sweet was that? Of course, that didn't answer his question.

What was up at Forget Me Knot?

They didn't have long to wait for an answer. Mildred must've been watching for their arrival, because the moment they stepped foot on the sidewalk outside the floral shop, the door flung open. Wearing her standard dark green apron with the store's logo embroidered on the bib, the silver-haired owner rushed out. Behind her came a line of three assistant florists pushing trolleys. Small mounds draped in white sat atop each cart.

Evelyn swung a sideways glance at Brianna. A mix of relief and interest swirled across the girl's face. Holding her hand, Daniel looked completely at ease. *So far, so good.*

"Welcome! Welcome to Forget Me Knot Florist," Mildred said loud enough to make herself heard over the few cars that passed by on Bridal Carriage Way. As she spoke, two of her assistants poked long poles into the ends of the awning that provided shade for passing customers. At their touch, a banner welcoming the Wedding-in-a-Week couple to Heart's Landing unfurled. Couples who'd been browsing along the sidewalk caught wind of the excitement in the air and wandered closer. Traffic slowed to a crawl, everyone eager to see what was taking place.

"I have no idea what comes next, but I have to hand it to Mildred—she knows how to draw attention," Evelyn whispered to Ryan as people began to gather on the sidewalk. He nodded.

"Brianna and Daniel." Mildred addressed the couple directly. "I'd love to have you visit my store. But, in the interest of Brianna's health, we can't risk it. So, today, we're bringing our selections to you!"

With a flourish, the silver-haired matron pushed a button on a key fob. A second later, the thick shade covering a third of the shop's front window rolled up smoothly. On the other side of the glass, wispy vines dripped from tall pedestals that held a stunning arrangement of white, green, and peach-colored flowers. Applause from the growing crowd joined with Brianna's soft "Oh!" as Mildred sidled closer to the window.

"If Daniel and Brianna choose this option, a dozen tall pedestals exactly like the ones shown here will line the aisle at their wedding." Mildred pointed to another arrangement on a small table. "These same centerpieces will adorn every table at your reception. Your matron of honor and bridesmaids will carry bouquets of Gerbera daisies and gardenias, while this will be your bouquet." At some hidden signal, one of Mildred's young staffers stepped into the display holding a cascade of white orchids. This time, a few cheers accompanied the round of applause.

"To help you keep this option in mind while you make your decision, we've prepared this nosegay for you to keep." Mildred nodded to another of her assistants, who took a miniature bouquet from the trolley and presented it to Daniel. The florist's voice dropped. "All the blossoms you'll receive today were flown in especially for you. We've taken extra care to avoid any cross-contamination with roses by assembling the smaller bouquets offsite. We'll be just as careful with the flowers you choose for your wedding."

Evelyn read pure gratitude in the look on Brianna's face and wasn't the least bit surprised when the bride-to-be bent over the small arrangement and took a little sniff. "These smell divine," she declared.

Moving on, Mildred retracted the shade over the next choice. This one featured the most exquisite burgundy dahlias Evelyn had ever seen, surrounded by masses of purple iris and Queen Anne's lace. The last selection included a mix of blue and pink hydrangeas, carnations, and large white lilies. By the time they finished, colorful bouquets filled the arms of the happy bride-to-be, and several eager shoppers had ducked inside the store.

As they shook hands at the end of the presentation, Brianna exclaimed, "I've never seen such pretty flowers. I want all of them. I have no idea how we're supposed to make a choice." She traced the outline of one of the blossoms. "Thanks ever so much. For all of this. Thanks for that thing with the roses, too."

"My pleasure." Mildred's cheeks glowed. "Here in Heart's Landing, we do our very best to meet the needs of every bride."

Evelyn pressed one hand to her heart. She wasn't getting married anytime soon. When she did, she wanted roses. Masses of them, picked straight from the bushes surrounding the Cottage. But she didn't envy Brianna. Each of Forget Me Knot's arrangements had been better than the last. Choosing between them would be difficult. She turned to Ryan. "Which one would you choose?"

The big guy only smiled and shook his head. "I'm bright enough to know that's not really my decision."

She chuckled. "When did you get so smart?"

Their driver, who'd thoughtfully parked down the street during the presentation, pulled to the curb.

"Dinner plans?" Evelyn asked the Wedding-in-a-Week couple.

"We're meeting with the minister in an hour," Daniel answered. "Do you think anyone would mind if we skipped the restaurant tonight and ordered in a pizza? We have so much to talk about—the flowers, the table settings. We need to compare notes."

"I'm sure it's fine," Ryan assured the couple quietly. "We'll take care of notifying your hosts for the evening."

"Right. Alicia and Jenny." Evelyn whipped out her phone and texted the pair. "They won't mind making an early night of it." Between the Wedding-in-a-Week festivities and picking up the slack in Jason's absence, the event planners had been putting in a lot of overtime.

She wished the couple a happy evening, but when Brianna and Daniel had climbed into the car and sped off, she hesitated. She scanned the street, shifting uneasily from one foot to the other. The crowd had dispersed, some shoppers heading back to the inns and hotels scattered throughout Heart's Landing, others ducking into various shops before the business day came to a close. A small sign in the window of the bakery next door announced that they'd sold out for the day and invited customers to return in the morning. She waved to Nick. His cupcakes had been a huge hit with the staff at the Cottage. He returned her greeting with a jaunty wave of his own and turned out the lights. She smiled. He'd probably already heard the news that Jenny was on her way home. She probably should be, too, but she wasn't quite ready to say goodnight to Ryan. She sought his eyes while she slid one hand behind her back and crossed her fingers.

"What's next?" Hope that he wanted to spend time with her welled in her chest.

Chapter Twelve

RYAN CLEARED HIS THROAT. “WE were so rushed earlier, I didn’t have a chance to thank Mildred for all her help with Harbor View.” The owner had been busy with a customer earlier in the week when he’d returned the floral arrangements she’d lent him. “If you don’t mind waiting just a minute, I’ll walk you back to the Cottage.” He’d parked his pickup truck in the lot at the opposite end of the block, behind the White Dove Cafe, but he couldn’t pass up the chance to spend a little while longer with Evelyn.

“I’d like that.” Tiny lines around Evelyn’s eyes deepened when she smiled. “I wanted to pick up some flowers for Alicia and Jenny, anyway. It’s the least I can do to repay them. They’ve carried the load at the Cottage this week.”

“Okay, then.” Suddenly feeling as awkward as a teenager, he held the door for her.

Inside, the normally quiet shop buzzed with activity. He couldn’t be sure, but he thought more customers than usual discussed floral arrangements with Mildred’s helpers. He stopped to let the green fragrance of potted plants and cut flowers wash over him while he searched the crowded aisles for the shop's owner. In answer to his question, a passing clerk told him she'd last seen Mildred in the workroom. Promising Evelyn he wouldn't be long, he left her studying ready-made arrangements in the store's two floor-to-ceiling coolers.

Sure enough, he found Mildred sorting through stacks of new orders and scribbling names and dates on a large whiteboard mounted on the workroom's wall. He waited until she finished the one she was working on before he cleared his throat. "Mildred?"

Wrinkles wreathed the skin around the older woman's smile. "I was hoping you'd stop by. This being your first year participating in Wedding-In-A-Week, I wanted to make sure you saw what it does for my business." She fanned the stack of papers. "All these new orders? They're from today." A wave of her hand indicated the customers quietly speaking with her associates throughout the store. "They'll more than cover the Wedding-in-a-Week entry fees."

His chest seized. *There were entry fees?* The realization hit him. Of course there were. Running an event like Wedding-in-a-Week cost money. Just like renting a booth at the annual craft fair, vendors paid their share.

But who'd paid his? When Alicia had first told him they'd chosen Harbor View to participate, he'd ultimately assumed, for whatever reason, she'd filled out an application in his name and had let it go at that. But she wouldn't have covered his entrance fee. He didn't know anyone who would.

Oblivious to his turmoil, Mildred continued her

spiel. "This event is one of the most expensive ones we enter. Each year, I tell myself not to bother, but the numbers don't lie. I more than make it up in new business." Her gaze narrowed in on him. "You're lucky your dad entered Harbor View this year. It'll be good for your business, no matter which venue Brianna and Daniel choose."

My dad? He braced one arm on the worktable and thanked goodness for its sturdy support. At the moment, it was about the only thing that kept him upright. He resisted an urge to shake his head. He couldn't have heard right. His dad didn't approve of his work as a restoration specialist. He certainly hadn't liked his youngest son's efforts to turn the old boat works into a wedding venue. Every time the topic came up—and it had at every Sunday dinner for the past year—his father had insisted the project was merely a distraction, one that prevented Ryan from taking his rightful place with Court Construction. That the senior Court would part with so much as a single thin dime to support his dream was, um, preposterous.

And yet...

He aimed an appraising glance at the florist who'd been doing business in Heart's Landing since before he was born. As one of the town's movers and shakers, Mildred knew everything that happened within the city limits. Usually within minutes. If she said his dad had covered his entry fee, he had to believe her. She had no reason to lie. Still, he had to be sure.

He inhaled so deeply, his chest expanded. On the exhale, he asked, "Mildred. You're sure my dad filled out an application for me? Not Alicia?"

"Sure as I'm standing here." She stared up at him, amazement in her eyes. "You didn't know?"

"Um, no. I didn't. I guess..." He paused, unable to think of what to say next. "I guess he and I are overdue for a chat."

Mildred's face blanched, and her voice trembled. "I hope I haven't spoken out of turn."

Reassuring the older woman was easy. He ran one finger across his lips. "It's our secret. The truth was bound to come out sooner or later, but I definitely appreciate hearing it from you." He checked the clock on the back wall and patted Mildred's age-spotted hand. "I hate to cut this short, but I'm going to run. If I leave now, I should be able to catch Dad at the office before he closes up for the night." By this time of day, his brothers had probably gone home to their wives and families. His father followed a different philosophy. He believed the boss ought to be the first on the job in the morning, the last to leave at night. Which meant, if Ryan didn't dilly-dally, he could talk with his dad without anyone overhearing.

He spotted Evelyn in the checkout line, patiently waiting to purchase two bunches of flowers in elegant vases. His heart melted at the sight of her standing there. He'd been wrong to consider her a diva. People with egos the size of Texas didn't stand in line to buy thoughtful gifts for friends. Regret washed through him. He wished he could stay and walk her home, tell her how wrong he'd been, but he couldn't. He couldn't let the sun go down without clearing the air with his dad. He slipped in beside Evelyn and leaned down to whisper in her ear. "Something's come up. I need to go. Do you mind getting back to the Captain's Cottage on your own?"

Confusion flashed momentarily in Evelyn's green eyes. Her jaw tightened, but she answered with a bright, "Sure! I'll call for a car."

He knew he'd disappointed her. With anyone else he'd have taken care of business and tried to make it up to them later. But his relationship with Evelyn was so new, so fragile, he couldn't take that chance. He bent lower, aiming his voice for her ears alone, and whispered, "I just found out my dad was the one who signed me up for the Wedding-in-a-Week competition. I, um, I think I need to talk to him about it."

He'd been right to tell her the truth, he decided, when understanding turned Evelyn's eyes a shade of green he'd never seen before. "Didn't you say things were tense between you?" she asked.

"They are." He nodded. Just once. "That's why it's important that I see him. I need to know why he did it."

"You're headed there now?" She glanced toward the door. "Do you want company?"

Her support flooded him with warmth, but this was something he needed to do on his own. "Much as I appreciate the offer, no." A move like that deserved his thanks, though, so he gave her upper arm a gentle squeeze. "Thanks for understanding. See you tomorrow, okay?"

"Definitely." She nodded. "Favors Galore at ten. Then we have a tasting at Food Fit For A Day right after." A half beat passed before she added, "Call me if you want to talk or anything."

"Yeah. Sounds good." He wavered on the edge of

reconsidering her offer and asking her to come with him. He swallowed. Things were complicated enough between him and his dad without adding another person into the mix. Especially when his relationship with Evelyn was in its infancy. His dad might jump to the conclusion that things were far more serious between him and the feisty redhead. As for his mom, well, she'd made no secret of her wish to see him settled down like his brothers. She'd buy out the grocery store's entire stock of rice the next time she went shopping if he so much as mentioned he had a date.

Resisting the urge to turn back to Evelyn, Ryan forced his feet to take him to the door. He couldn't help but look over his shoulder at her before it closed. She still stood where he'd left her, her eyes locked on him. The image released a flood of warm feelings that tempted him to stay. Wishing he could, he jammed his hands in his pockets and headed for his dad's office.

Evelyn sat on the couch in her third-floor apartment in the Captain's Cottage, her legs curled up on the thick cushions. She turned the page of a romance novel that hadn't managed to capture her attention. Oh, the author had done a good job of telling a juicy story. That wasn't the problem. The problem was her mind—it kept drifting off the page to Ryan's face at Forget Me Knot earlier. From the little he'd said, she knew his father hadn't exactly supported his youngest son's ambitions. So it didn't make any sense at all for Mr. Court to enter Harbor View in the Wedding-in-a-Week festivities.

Was Ryan's father trying to heal the rift between him and his son? She hoped so. The day they'd had coffee in the Cottage's dining room, tension had gathered in Ryan's eyes at a mere reference to his family. She'd seen hurt reflected in the firm set of his jaw the few times he'd mentioned his mom and dad since then. She shook her head and thanked her lucky stars for the good relationship she had with her own parents. Even though they'd retired to Florida, she and her mom talked most every day. She spoke with her dad nearly as often. She wanted Ryan to have that same kind of relationship with his folks.

She'd no sooner had that thought than her cell phone buzzed. She hit the Accept Call button after glancing at the screen. "Hey, Ryan." She closed the book and set it aside. "What's up?"

"Can we talk?"

Her stomach plummeted at the strain in his voice. The silence that followed tugged at her heart. "Sure. Want me to meet you at Harbor View?"

"Actually, I'm right outside. I was going to come in, but it looks like there's a wedding on the Veranda. Meet me on the bike path? We'll go for a walk?"

This time of night, they'd have the trail practically to themselves. It made a good place for a quiet talk. "Sounds great. I'll meet you around back in five minutes."

In thirty seconds, she'd grabbed a sweatshirt, captured her hair in a scrunchie, and slipped her feet into comfortable walking shoes. With time to spare, she trotted down the rear stairs to the first level of the house. She spotted Ryan right away, and her heart gave the little shimmy she'd grown accustomed to feeling whenever his broad shoulders came into view. A pair of casual jeans emphasized his long, muscular legs and made her doubly glad she'd changed out of business attire and into her own comfy jeans and a T-shirt. Tying the pullover around her waist, she closed the gap between them.

A broad, winding path led from the back of the Captain's Cottage to the bike path that stretched northward along the rocky coast past Heart's Cove and beyond. They set out, her own long strides easily matching his. At first, Ryan didn't say anything, and they walked with only the roar of the ocean waves crashing on the rocks below and the first stars of the night to keep them company. A few lights twinkled from ships on the horizon, where low clouds clustered.

"Thanks for understanding about this afternoon." Ryan broke the silence as the path curved past a rugged promontory known as Peter's Lookout. "I hated to change our plans. I wanted to spend some time with you. You know, without Brianna or Daniel or Curtis looking over our shoulders."

Her heart skipped a beat. His admission raised a prickle of goose bumps along her arms. Much as she wanted to explore that feeling, she set the thought aside. "No problem, honest," she hurried to assure him. "You had to clear the air with your dad. How'd it go?" She didn't want to pry, but that was why he'd asked her out here, wasn't it?

"Not exactly like I expected." Ryan kicked a pebble and sent it skittering. "You know I've never considered myself much of a builder. A fixer, yeah. A finisher, sure. But creating something from the ground up—not so much. My dad, my brothers, they're the builders."

For a kid whose family was in the construction business, that had to sting. But Ryan was good with his hands, and she felt she had to point that out to him. "You've said that before. I didn't understand it then any more than I do now. You're really talented." He'd rebuilt their old wooden fort practically from scratch, and it had weathered several fierce Nor'easters since then. Thanks to the work he'd done at the Captain's Cottage, her family home looked better now than it ever had. To say nothing of how he'd taken the dilapidated boat works and turned it into a stunning wedding venue.

"I'm not half as good as my brothers. When we were kids, they made my efforts look sad by comparison."

"Um, they're older than you, aren't they?" She couldn't explain why she felt the need to defend him, even from himself, but she did.

"Tom was eight when Mom had me. Bruce was six." He canted his head to look down at her. "I see where you're going with this, and you're right. It does explain a lot. I don't know why I never saw it before tonight, but there you have it."

"Have what?" She squinted up at him. He hadn't explained anything.

"Yeah. I skipped a few parts, didn't I?"

"Yep." When Ryan laughed to himself, the sound triggered another round of goose bumps. "Hold up a sec," she said and stopped to untie the sweatshirt from around her waist. She tugged it over her head. "Tell me everything. This time, don't skimp on the details."

"You're sure? It might take a while."

"Take your time. We've got all night." She couldn't think of a single place she'd rather be.

Against the darkening sky, she saw him shrug. "Okay, but remember, you asked for it." He seemed to settle into himself as they resumed their walk. "It all started one Christmas when Santa brought birdhouse kits for the three of us. Dad made a big deal of our presents. He promised we'd all work on them together. I was five at the time, and I remember being so excited, 'cause I rarely got to do anything with my brothers." He hesitated. "Well, that's not right. We sat at church together on Sundays. Ate dinner as a family most nights. But Tom and Bruce hung out with their own friends. They played sports and went to school, things I was too young to do."

When she felt Ryan's eyes on her, she nodded. "I know how that feels. You and Jason went off together and left me alone a lot, too."

Sympathy shadowed Ryan's eyes. "I never thought of it that way, but yeah, I guess we did. I'm sorry."

"Water under the bridge," she quipped. Spending time on her own had encouraged her to become more independent. In the long run, that had been a good thing. "Go on."

"O...kay." Ryan's gaze flickered. "About the birdhouses. This one Saturday morning, Dad set up a work table in the basement, and we all got started. Of course, Tom and Bruce, they finished theirs by lunch and ran off to go ice skating, while I still had a long way to go. I could've given up. I wanted to. But I stuck with it." He showed her that sheepish grin she was so fond of. "My dad called me a 'stubborn little cuss.' Mom had just called us all to dinner by the time I finished." His smile faded. "My brothers' birdhouses were all sharp angles and straight sides. Mine just kind of...drooped. It had this sloped porch. The walls were crooked," he said, demonstrating with his hands. "There was a big gap along the roof seam. I was so disappointed that, if Dad hadn't been watching, I would've smashed it to smithereens."

"Awww. I wish I could've seen it. I bet it was precious." She imagined Ryan as a little tyke, his head bent over the project. She bet he'd concentrated so hard he'd bit the tip of his tongue between his front teeth. She'd caught him doing exactly that a couple of times this week when he hadn't thought anyone was watching.

"Oh, it's still around. That was the worst part. Dad took all three birdhouses to his office. He made a special shelf for them over his desk. They're still there." Hair fell onto his forehead when he shook his head. He brushed it back with a sweep of one hand. "Gosh, did Tom and Bruce tease me about that or what. They still do. 'He can't drive a straight nail to save his life.' 'What's that hole in the roof supposed to be—a skylight?'"

She'd never had a brother or a sister, but plenty of flower girls and ring bearers had trooped through the Captain's Cottage. While each and every one of them could be so sweet it made her teeth ache, she'd seen a few get into it with a younger sibling. Kids could be brutal. The lucky ones had parents who looked out for them. She sought Ryan's eyes in the fading light. "What'd your dad say?"

"Dad's always been a man of few words. He put his hand on my shoulder and said, 'Well, you tried, son. That's the important thing. You tried.' I might've only been five, but on some level, I knew I'd let him down. I've been a disappointment to him ever since." He inhaled like he wanted to suck all the oxygen out of the air. "Or I thought I was. Until tonight."

"What happened?" She kept the question simple, hoping she wouldn't disrupt his thoughts.

Ryan's footsteps stalled. She slowed, matching his stride. Up ahead, a chest-high rock wall prevented unwary cyclists from missing a sharp curve and plunging over the side and down the cliff. Ryan walked to the edge. He waited until he'd braced his elbows atop the rocks before he continued. "I told Dad I heard he'd paid for my Wedding-in-a-Week entry and asked him why he'd do such a thing, considering I'd never lived up to his expectations. He got the strangest expression on his face. Like he didn't have the faintest idea what I was talking about. I told him he couldn't deny it. I knew how he felt. I pointed to the birdhouses on the shelf behind his desk and said I knew mine was a constant reminder that I'd never be the builder he and my brothers were."

"Oh, Ryan." Her heart ached for him. She was only a little surprised by how much.

"He put his hand on my shoulder like he had all those years ago and said that wasn't why he'd kept the birdhouses. He'd kept them as a daily reminder of how proud he was of"—Ryan's voice tightened—"of all three of his sons."

Tears stung her eyes. She longed to put her arms around him. "I guess you didn't expect that," she managed.

Ryan shook his head. "Not hardly. Could've blown me away like so much sawdust when he said it."

When Ryan grew quiet, she nudged him. "And then?" She wasn't about to let him stop now. There had to be more to the story.

"Dad pulled all three birdhouses down and sat them on this huge antique desk he keeps in his office. He picked up Tom's and said it was the best of the lot, but he'd expected it to be, seeing as Tom was the oldest. Then he pointed out the deck and window boxes that none of the others had. He said Tom had always been the one to go above and beyond. Today, Dad counts on him to improve every house they build, to look for add-ons that make life better for their customers." Ryan lifted one shoulder in a half-shrug. "He's right, too. Tom's the best salesman in the family. He has a knack for giving clients more than what they asked for but always what they wanted. He and Bruce go toe to toe over that sometimes."

"Why's that?" She thought she might have some idea.

"When Bruce built his birdhouse, he followed the directions to the letter. Not one shingle out of place. The door precisely where it was supposed to be. Dad said as soon as he'd seen it, he'd known the day would come when he could hand Bruce a set of plans and six months later, he'd deliver the exact house the customer had ordered, right down to the number of shelves in the linen closet."

Her heart pounded. "And yours? What did he say about yours?"

Ryan barked a laugh. "He plunked that misshapen, lopsided thing on the table and said he'd always known I'd finish whatever I started. No matter how difficult it was." His voice grew tight again. "He told me that's how he knew I'd do whatever I set out to do. It was how he knew I'd finish the Boat Works in time for Wedding-In-A-Week. He was so sure of it, he filled out the entry form in my name and paid the fee."

"Oh, wow," she whispered. Getting into the contest involved a sizable chunk of change.

"Yeah, wow. This changes everything. It's going to take some time to overcome perceptions of the past. But I think my dad and I can finally have a real relationship. My brothers, too."

"Does this mean you'll go to work for Court Construction?" She held her breath. Ryan had put a lot of time and effort into building his own business. He wouldn't give that up, would he? She hated to think of him walking away from his dreams.

Ryan shook his head. "Dad and I both agree my place isn't in the family business. We'll find a way to work together. Refer clients to one another. That sort of thing. Enjoy Sunday dinners without feeling like we're on pins and needles the whole time."

He'd braced his palms on the rock wall. Tentatively, she placed her hand on one of his forearms. Beneath the sleeve of his sweatshirt, she felt his muscles tense. "I'm glad for you, Ryan. Truly. I know how much it bothered you that things weren't good between you and your folks."

"You did?" He swung toward her, his eyes scouring her face. "I never complained about it, did I?"

"You didn't have to. I knew anyway."

"Huh. Guess you know me better than I know myself." He turned to face her, his arm still braced on the wall. "That's one thing about you, Evelyn. We've known each other practically our entire lives. You'd think by now I'd know everything there was to know about you, but you constantly surprise me. There's still so much more about you I want to learn."

Her breath caught. She'd been thinking the same thing, but she'd never in a million years thought Ryan returned the feeling. "I was hoping you'd say that."

She welcomed his touch when Ryan put an arm around her and hugged her close. They stood for a while, their hips grazing as the twilight deepened. As they watched, a large ship steamed into view and began making its slow trip across the horizon.

Ryan aimed his chin at the big boat. "A cruise ship out of New York," he murmured. "I wonder where they're headed."

"Someplace warm and sunny," she suggested, relishing the weight of his arm across her shoulders. "The Bahamas, maybe? Or Antigua?"

"Have you ever visited the Caribbean?"

"No. I've always wanted to. It's just..." She hesitated, then shrugged. Ryan had shared his innermost thoughts and fears with her tonight. She wanted to repay his trust by opening up to him, too. "Until now, it's been hard to get away from the Captain's Cottage. When Uncle Dave died and my parents retired, Jason and I suddenly found ourselves in charge. It was a lot sooner than either of us expected and, even with a lot of help from Alicia and Connie, we struggled a bit. It took us a while to settle into a new routine. It took even longer for me to figure out this isn't what I really want to do for the rest of my life."

"It's not?" Surprise showed in Ryan's features. "I thought you liked your job."

"I love the Captain's Cottage," she corrected. "And Jason's the best. We work really well together. But I don't think the role of Maiden Aunt is a good fit for me. And you have to admit, I'm not your average bookkeeper." She touched one finger to her eyes. "No horn-rimmed glasses. No pencil stuck in my hair."

He laughed at that. "No, you're not. You're an original."

"Once Tara and Jason get back from their honeymoon, I think it might be time to move on."

Concern flashed in Ryan's eyes. "You're not...not leaving, are you? Not going back to New York?"

She gave her head a firm shake. "No. I closed that door. Like you, I've decided I want to stay in Heart's Landing. It's my home. But there has to be more to my life than numbers and inventory lists. I just don't know what it is yet."

"You'll figure it out," Ryan said. He sounded far surer of that than she felt.

"I hope so," she whispered.

"You will." His voice firmed. "You're the most capable person I know. Look how well you've done running the Cottage while Jason's been away."

"I don't know." She scuffed one foot across the cement walkway. "Alicia and Jenny have helped a lot."

"You're too modest." He eased his arm from her shoulders and stepped to the side. "Not only have you kept things going smoothly at the Cottage, you've taken on the Wedding-in-a-Week festivities. I can pretty much guarantee Brianna wouldn't be walking down the aisle on Sunday if you hadn't calmed her fears and helped her realize how much she and Daniel love each other."

"That's one thing I have enjoyed. Bookkeepers don't usually play a hands-on role in the lives of our brides. Whatever I end up doing, I'd like to do more of that."

When she stopped for a breath, Ryan's quiet, "You should. You're good at it," warmed her heart and encouraged her to go on.

"Once Jason and Tara get back, she'll take over as the official hostess of the Captain's Cottage. Which means I'm going to have plenty of time to figure out my next step."

"Is that so?" Jason leaned closer. "Maybe enough time to actually go on a real date? Like dinner and a movie?"

"Who knows? It could happen. I expect a lot will change." She paused. "Oddly enough, that thought scared me last week. Now, not so much." She had Ryan to thank for that. He'd encouraged her, prodded her, and given her the courage to start thinking of her own future. Because of him, she looked forward to this next chapter in her life more than ever.

When Ryan leaned even closer, she hoped he'd kiss her. That might be another change in a long string of them, but this was one she'd been looking forward to. She moistened her lips, her anticipation building. She sipped air. He angled his head closer to hers. But in the split second before Ryan brushed his lips against hers, his cell phone emitted an alarming chirp.

"Sorry. That's Daniel's text tone. I gave it to him for emergencies." He straightened with a grimace. In one swift move, he pulled his phone from his back pocket. His expression drooped as he glanced at the screen. "Brianna's aunt is in surgery."

"What? What happened?" When Ryan said he didn't have any more details, she pressed one hand to her forehead. A headache threatened, and her heart lurched. "We need to get to the bed and breakfast. There's no time to waste."

Chapter Thirteen

"SURGERY. THAT SOUNDS SERIOUS."

"Yeah." In the passenger seat of Ryan's pickup truck, Evelyn worried at a fingernail. "This is bound to shake Brianna's confidence. Do you think she'll call off the wedding?"

"I hope not, but you said she had a meltdown at the bridal salon." Ryan spun the wheel. The tires complained as they turned onto Officiant Way.

"Yeah, I thought she was past that, but this..." Evelyn's chest heaved. "Her aunt and cousins are her only family. They were supposed to fly in on Friday. She has to be beside herself."

"That's rough," he admitted. "I'm just as concerned about Daniel. He had cold feet before. This'll probably freeze them solid."

"He didn't say anything more? We don't know what happened?"

He jerked a thumb toward the cell phone he'd tossed onto the console. "Nothing more than that cryptic text. I pray she's all right."

"And that they don't call off the wedding."

"Yeah, that. If there ever were two people who

deserved to be together, it'd be Brianna and Daniel." Though lately, he'd been thinking he and Evelyn might have a chance at their very own Heart's Landing love for the ages.

His thoughts stuttered. *Love?* Did he love Evelyn Heart? He'd fallen for her, sure. Who wouldn't? With her masses of red curls surrounding finely chiseled features, the brilliant eyes that saw through to a man's soul, her long, lean form—what guy wouldn't trip over himself to win a second glance from her?

But love? That was something else entirely. Love went deeper than looks. Love involved the heart and soul. True love brought out the best in people. Did he and Evelyn have that special kind of bond? His fingers tightened on the steering wheel. He couldn't say for sure, but he knew one thing. She brought out the best of him. He wanted to be a better man, a more steadfast version of himself for Evelyn's sake. Whenever she was around, she made him feel stronger, smarter, more capable than he was without her. That might not be love—yet—but it was definitely a step on the right path. He couldn't wait to see where it led. But all that would have to wait. For now, he and Evelyn had a bride to console, a groom to calm, and a wedding to save.

Grateful for Heart's Landing's sparse evening traffic, he sped past Harbor View and the marina before turning west on Champagne Avenue. Less than five minutes later, he braked to a stop on the graveled parking strip behind the Union Street Bed and Breakfast.

"There's Daniel," he said, pointing. The young man paced back and forth on the back porch.

"I don't see Brianna anywhere."

"That's not a good sign." His heart sank. Whether things were going well or not, he'd expected to find the young man at his bride's side, holding her hand, calming her fears. He hurried around the truck to hold the door for Evelyn. Together, they raced up the stairs onto the roomy back porch. "What's going on?" he asked the groom, who'd stopped his pacing long enough to greet them beneath the ivy-covered awning.

"Brianna's aunt has appendicitis."

Ryan rocked from one foot to the other while he waited for the other shoe to drop. Surely that couldn't be all there was to it. An appendectomy was so straightforward, medical students often performed it as their first surgery.

"They just took her into the operating room a few minutes ago. Brianna's on the phone with her cousin. It doesn't sound like any of them will make it to the wedding."

"Oh, poor Brianna. I'm so sorry!" Evelyn choked back a sob.

Her reaction was too intense. He drew closer. He'd clearly overlooked an important detail. "What am I missing?"

"Brianna's aunt is supposed to walk her down the aisle. Her cousins are her bridesmaids."

Ah! There it was, the vital piece of information he needed but didn't want. His head throbbed as the dominos began to fall, one knocking over the next. Appendicitis, *click*. Canceled trip, *click*. No bridesmaids. No matron of honor. No one to give away the bride. *Click. Click. Click*. What was next? *No wedding*? "What can we do?" He addressed the question to Daniel but wasn't at all surprised when Evelyn answered with her usual take-charge attitude.

"Marybeth keeps beer stashed in the fridge. Why don't you grab some while I run upstairs and check on Brianna? Daniel, you'll be all right here for a minute?"

When the would-be groom nodded in the affirmative, Ryan held the screened door open for Evelyn before stepping inside himself. The hall branched ahead of them. He squeezed her hand for luck as she headed for the stairs. Seconds later, lights and a mouthwatering aroma drew him into the kitchen. After grabbing beers from the fridge and helping himself to a plate of cookies still warm from the oven, he pulled a handful of bills from his wallet and tossed them into an honesty basket on a small table. Back on the porch, he handed one of the frosty bottles to Daniel. He left two more on the coffee table with the cookies, popped the top off one, and lowered himself onto the tufted cushion of a nearby chair to wait.

Not five minutes passed before footsteps pounded down the staircase. "She's going to be okay!" Even through the screen door, he saw the joyful tears in Brianna's eyes. He heard the happiness in her voice. The bride burst onto the porch and flung herself into Daniel's arms.

Close behind, Evelyn pivoted toward Ryan. When she reached him, he slipped one arm around her waist. His heart swelled when she leaned into him. Together, they listened for details.

"She's out of surgery, and she's okay!" The words tumbled from Brianna's lips in a rush. "Ann and

Lynn have been in to see her. They should release her tomorrow. The day after at the latest."

Daniel gave his bride-to-be a tight squeeze. "Thank goodness," he said, his voice heavy with relief. "That's exactly what we were praying for, isn't it?" He led Brianna to a loveseat surrounded by climbing ivy. Together, they sank down on the cushions. "Want a beer?" When she nodded, he removed the cap with a single flick of his thumb and handed one to her.

Ryan motioned to Evelyn, who reached for the final bottle. Much as he wanted her beside him, he understood when she chose another chair. Flanking Brianna and Daniel, they sat and sipped in silence for a while. At last, he passed his half-empty bottle back and forth between his hands and offered Brianna his good wishes. "That sure was excellent news about your aunt."

"Yeah." The young woman looked at him through puffy eyes. Loose strands of hair shimmied when her head bobbed. "Ann—she's the oldest—she said Aunt Sheila woke up with a stomachache this morning, but she didn't think it was anything to worry about until late this afternoon. The pain had only gotten worse by then, so she had the girls take her to the ER. I'm so thankful she's going to be all right." Leaning forward, she grabbed a cookie from the plate and nibbled on it.

"What does that mean for the wedding?" he asked, determined not to ignore the elephant that had joined them once they knew the surgery had been successful.

"Well, I was counting on Aunt Sheila to walk me down the aisle. Now that she can't be here, I don't think we have any choice."

His breath stalled. Despite the tension in the air, he smiled when, across from him, Evelyn went on high alert, too.

"I'm going to have to find someone else to do it." The girl brushed crumbs from her hands. "Do you have any ideas?"

He wondered if the others heard the utter joy in Evelyn's voice when she asked, "So the wedding's still on?"

Brianna sought Daniel's eyes. She must've seen confirmation in their dark depths because she said, "Yes. Definitely. Daniel and I talked it over. I hate that Aunt Sheila and my cousins can't come, but we've come too far and fought too hard to back out now. Besides." She took a swallow from her bottle. "If we're going to have a Heart's Landing love for the ages, it has to start right here."

Glass clinked as the foursome raised their beers in a hearty toast.

Brianna sipped once more before she passed her nearly full bottle to Daniel. She aimed a pointed look at Evelyn. "Would you be my Maid of Honor?"

Evelyn's hand fluttered to her chest. Tears glistened in her eyes when she gave a heartfelt, "It'd be my pleasure."

"Good." Brianna leaned forward, and the girls exchanged hugs. She settled back in the crook of Daniel's arm. "I really don't want to walk down that aisle by myself. Do you think Miss Alicia would give me away? And maybe Jenny could stand up front with you?"

"Sounds like you've given the matter some thought," Evelyn mused.

"The perils of destination weddings, I guess," Brianna said, sounding far calmer than Ryan imagined possible for a bride who'd been through what she'd endured the last few hours. "All the bridal magazines advise making alternate plans in case someone gets sick at the last minute or misses their flight. So I've thought about it. Honestly, I can't think of three people who've done more for us since we've been here."

"I'm sure Alicia and Jenny would be honored to be in your wedding. We all are." Evelyn tapped her chin with one finger. "And, as my first official act as your Maid of Honor, I'll make sure JoJo and her videographer know we'll need to live-stream the ceremony for your aunt and your cousins. We don't want them to miss out."

"Oh! That'd be wonderful!" Brianna reached for Daniel's hand and gave it a squeeze.

Daniel grinned. "I bet it'll be standing-room only in Aunt Sheila's living room Sunday." He turned to Evelyn. "This is really nice of you."

Evelyn leaned forward, her expression earnest. "I'm sure you've heard that the Heart's Landing motto is 'a perfect wedding for every bride.' Everyone here works hard to make sure we live up to that promise. But I want you to know that working with you and Daniel this week has been more than a job. It's shown me what true love is all about. More than that, I'd like to think we've become friends. I know Alicia and Jenny feel the same as I do."

"Aww, careful. You're going to make me cry. I've already done enough of that today." Brianna brushed her fingertips beneath her eyes. She straightened slightly. "I know it's late notice, so don't worry about your dress or anything. I'll tell Alicia and Jenny the same thing—I don't care if you show up in shorts and a T-shirt as long as you're there."

Evelyn laughed, a sound that sent ripples of warmth through Ryan's chest. "Please," she said. "I have Cheri at Dress For a Day on speed-dial. You just tell me what color you want us to wear, and she'll take care of everything."

Brianna's eyes glittered in a way that made Ryan's mouth twitch. He braced himself. "Do you think she could whip up dresses like the green one Scarlett wore in *Gone with the Wind*?"

He had to give Evelyn credit when she barely flinched. He couldn't help it. He laughed out loud. Beside his bride-to-be, Daniel did the same. Apparently, he'd seen the same gleam in Brianna's eyes. They were in on her joke.

The puzzled look on Evelyn's face was priceless. "Wait. You're not serious?"

"No." Brianna joined in the laughter. "I think the Southern belle look is a bit passé, even for me."

"You're the bride. It's your choice..." Evelyn hesitated a second longer before her face broke into a wreath of smiles. "But I'm awfully glad you were kidding."

Ryan lifted his beer in a silent toast to the woman he was fast beginning to have deeper feelings for. Seeing Evelyn interact with Brianna and Daniel, watching her help them cope with the pitfalls of planning their wedding in a week, he'd grown to admire her kindness and caring attitude. His thoughts leaped forward, and he was powerless to stop them. Evelyn would make a great mom one day. He could almost see her kissing boo-boos to make them better and putting Band-Aids on skinned knees. She'd be the one to help their daughter get over her first heartbreak, to teach their son to take up for the underdog at school.

He pictured her walking down the aisle, not at Brianna's wedding, but at their own. He'd stand beside the minister, his palms sweating until he saw her step into view. Her curls would softly frame her face. With a rustle of lace and satin, she'd walk toward him. All their friends and family would be watching, but he'd only have eyes for her. And when she stood beside him, when she said, "I do," she'd make him the happiest man in the world.

Get a grip, Court.

He was getting way, way ahead of himself here. He and Evelyn hadn't been on their first official date yet, and he was already hearing wedding bells. Oddly enough, the thought didn't bother him in the slightest.

Not that long ago, he'd considered Evelyn nothing more than a selfish diva. Now, he knew nothing could've been further from the truth. She was everything he'd ever wanted in a woman—supportive and outspoken, compassionate and independent. Who cared if they'd reconnected less than a week ago? When it was right, it was right, and he knew in the deepest recesses of his heart that she was the one for him, the woman of his dreams. He'd always known. He just hadn't admitted it before now.

"Hey, Ryan?" Daniel peered at him from across the small coffee table.

With a start, he straightened. "Sorry," he mumbled, not sure what he'd missed but certain he wasn't going to admit where his thoughts had taken him. "I must've drifted off there for a moment."

"We were discussing the bridesmaid's gowns. Brianna asked you what you thought of pink," Evelyn coached without a hint of reprimand.

"Pink." He sought Evelyn's eyes and smiled at the amused expression he found there. Did she know what he'd been thinking? Nah. She couldn't have. He blinked away images of her in a white dress and veil. "Pink's good."

"Pink, then," Brianna agreed. "It'll blend well with any of the floral arrangements we saw at Forget Me Knot or the table settings from Be Married."

That topic behind them, the conversation drifted to other subjects. Through it all, he didn't have much to say. Whenever he thought of a few words, his mind replaced them with an image of his future with Evelyn in it. Robbed of his ability to speak, he spent the next hour pretending to listen until, finally, Brianna yawned.

"This has been fun, but it's been a long day," Daniel said less than a second later. The groom gave his arms and legs an exaggerated stretch. He hugged his bride-to-be with one arm. "Tomorrow's another busy one. What say we call it a night?"

Brianna poked him in the ribs. "You big goof. That wasn't very polite." She smothered another yawn behind her hand.

Hoping the motion would clear his head, Ryan was on his feet in an instant. "Don't give it another thought. It's time we headed back, too. Like you said, big day tomorrow."

He and Daniel traded fist bumps while the women exchanged goodbye hugs. Almost before he knew it, he was holding the door to his pickup open for Evelyn. They'd backed out of the driveway before either of them spoke.

"You were awfully quiet back there." Evelyn's voice drifted from the passenger seat. "Nickel for your thoughts?"

He harrumphed. "Isn't that supposed to be a penny?" He shifted the pickup into drive.

"Inflation. Humor me."

He cast a sidelong glance at his passenger. Confessing that he'd been picturing her in a long white dress might win her over, but it might just as easily scare her off. He needed a surer bet, a more subtle approach. *When in doubt, go with what you know,* he told himself. And what he knew was restoration. The first step in every project was to scope out the extent of the job. His heart hammering in his throat, he moved to gauge the task that faced him. "Do you ever see yourself having what Brianna and Daniel have?"

Evelyn swiveled toward him, her jeans whispering on the leather seat. "Someday, yeah. I need to figure out my next step career-wise. After that..." She shrugged one shoulder. "I want someone to love, someone who loves me. Who doesn't? I want the whole package—a home, a family."

Good. That was good. His heart rate throttled down a notch. Next, he needed to find out if that someone could be him. His mouth dry, he asked, "Any prospects?"

Evelyn crossed her legs. "There's one guy I have

my eye on. Tall. Broad shoulders. Good with his hands. He's definitely in the *Maybe* category."

Him. She was talking about him. Hope bloomed in his chest. Before he let it go too far, he stole a glance from the road to see if she was serious. The smile that played around her lips told him he'd heard right and sent a jolt of pure joy racing through him. Determination straightened his spine. For as long as it took, he'd spend every minute working to change that *Maybe* into a *Definitely.* He'd start by picking up where they'd left off on the path. He wanted a second chance at the kiss Daniel's text had interrupted.

But when he slowed to check for cross traffic at Union and Procession, Evelyn dashed cold water on his plans by asking him to drop her off at Dress For a Day instead of taking her home. "Cheri and Jenny are meeting me at the salon so we can look at gowns for Brianna's wedding."

"In pink," he added, just to prove he had been paying attention. He checked the digital readout on the dashboard, surprised to see it was well after nine. This time of night, all the stop lights in town had turned to yellow caution lights. Apparently, Evelyn had her own way of slowing things down, too. He made the final turn onto Boutonniere and stopped in front of the dress shop. "I'll wait for you," he said, letting the big engine idle.

"That's sweet, but I can't ask you to do that." She uncrossed her legs and shifted toward the door.

"I don't mind. I wouldn't want you to walk home alone this late." Even as he said the words, he knew she'd see through his excuse for staying put. Crime was practically nonexistent in the town known as

America's Top Wedding Destination. She'd be perfectly safe on the short walk to the Captain's Cottage.

Evelyn's hand on his forearm sent his pulse galloping, but her smile warmed his heart. "I have no idea how long I'll be. This could take fifteen minutes, or it could take all night. Jenny will drop me off at the Cottage when we're finished. See you tomorrow?"

Warmth flooded him at the hope he heard in her voice. He rushed to reassure her. "You can count on it. We have a Wedding-in-a-Week to plan."

And I have a heart to win.

He waited until the door of the bridal salon swung shut behind her. Then he aimed the truck for home. He had a campaign to plan, one that was sure to win the heart of the woman of his dreams.

Stop that!

Evelyn reluctantly quit doodling hearts and flowers on the paper ink blotter that covered her desk. What was she, a teenager? She had better things to do, more important things to accomplish than to sit here daydreaming about Ryan Court and being in love. She wasn't in love. Not even close.

She gave the paper sheet one last glance, sighed, and reached for her computer mouse. Maybe she was just the tiniest little bit in love, but she couldn't think of that right now. Jason was counting on her to keep things running smoothly in his absence. Heart's Landing was counting on her to deliver a perfect wedding for their Wedding-in-a-Week couple. She couldn't let them down.

She slid the cursor across the screen. Three clicks of the mouse later, she studied the schedule for the Captain's Cottage on her computer screen. While she'd been busy with Brianna and Daniel—and thinking entirely too much about a tall, handsome carpenter—Alicia and Jenny had launched four couples into wedded bliss. Additionally, Jenny had given several prospective brides tours of the mansion. Four of them had locked in their preferred dates. Housekeeping and Landscaping reported that everything was going smoothly in their departments. Even Connie had helped out. The head chef had inventoried their stock and prepared this week's supply order, relieving Evelyn of yet another task.

She tapped her pencil against the ink blotter. Much as she appreciated how much everyone had pitched in to cover for her while she focused on Wedding-In-A-Week, she had to admit their efforts only underscored the fact that the Captain's Cottage could get along perfectly well without her. She'd suspected it for some time now, but scrolling through the weekly reports without spotting a single red flag confirmed it. Once Jason returned from his honeymoon and Tara took over as hostess of the mansion that played host to hundreds of weddings each year, she'd be at loose ends.

Oh, no doubt, she'd have a job for as long as she wanted, and she'd always have a place to live. Family meant too much to Jason for her cousin to throw her out on the street. The thing was, she'd grown restless over the past year. She wanted to do more than merely manage the books and order supplies. But what? And where? Those were questions she needed to find the answers to, and the sooner, the better.

She ran a hand through her curls. She'd meant it when she'd told Ryan she was done with New York. Always hustling to make the rent, to nail even a bit part in a play...that wasn't for her anymore. The bright lights and crowded streets no longer held any appeal. As for the Captain's Cottage, she loved the history and the elegance of her family home, but helping to continue its traditions wasn't her cup of tea.

So, what did she want?

She jotted three quick notes on the blotter. She'd love to get in on the ground floor of a project here in Heart's Landing. She wanted to establish new traditions, develop her own ways of going about things. She needed to play a bigger role in providing the perfect wedding for every bride. When she finished, she studied what she'd written and nodded. Now that she knew what she wanted, she just had to figure out the how and the where of it.

She sensed the answers hovered just out of reach. But they were getting closer. Close enough that she ought to broach the subject with Jason as soon as he returned from Europe. A thrill rushed through her. Whatever happened next, it felt exciting to be on the cusp of something new.

A knock on her door interrupted her musings. She looked up to see Jenny standing in the doorway.

"You're leaving soon?" The slim brunette held a copy of today's itinerary in one hand. According to it, Evelyn had a full day of Wedding-in-a-Week activities ahead.

"Pretty quick." She glanced at her notes and smiled. *In more ways than one.*

"Cheri called. She was able to get the dresses we like from a sister shop in Providence. They'll be here in plenty of time for the wedding on Sunday."

"Great!" She and Jenny had spent hours trying on gowns before the newlywed had chosen one with a fitted waist that showed off her ample curves and was sure to put a smile on her husband's face. Evelyn had selected an off-the-shoulder model in the same mauvey-pink. The skirt of hers fell in graceful folds from an empire waist. She could hardly wait to see Ryan's reaction when he saw her in it.

"So, um, Ryan, huh?" Jenny raised an eyebrow, all the while delivering a knowing look.

Evelyn fought to keep her features neutral. "He's helping with Wedding-in-a-Week. Just like Alicia asked him to."

Her deepening feelings for Ryan were too new to share. Why, she'd barely mentioned the carpenter while she and Jenny had tried on gown after gown last night. She gave the matter a second thought. Okay, maybe she had wondered aloud whether he'd like this dress or what he'd think of that one. And she might've mentioned he was her date for the wedding, but that was all, honest. She certainly hadn't gushed about him like a high school girl with a crush.

"You're sure there's nothing more going on between the two of you?" Jenny wagged a finger back and forth.

She flattened her palm over the hearts and flowers on the ink blotter while her resistance buckled. She didn't have any idea how she'd kept the secret locked inside all through last night's fitting, but she couldn't hold it back anymore. "Well, he did nearly kiss me."

"Oh?" In three quick strides, Jenny crossed to the guest chair and plunked herself down. "Out with it. I want all the juicy details."

"I'm afraid there aren't any. The operative word here is *nearly*," she pointed out. "He had some, um, stuff to go over." Ryan trusted her to keep his secrets. She wouldn't blurt them out, not even to Jenny. "We went for a walk along the bike path, and everything was normal. Until, all of a sudden, it wasn't. There was this moment when we just connected, you know?"

"Ooh," Jenny sighed. "Tell me more."

"There's not a whole lot more to tell," she admitted, surprised by how much she wanted there to be. "He leaned in, and I had just enough time to think, *kiss!* Then his phone went off. After that, we rushed over to the bed and breakfast."

"But he has feelings for you. And you like him, too, don't you?" Jenny leaned forward, anticipation written on her face.

"I do. I always have," she admitted.

"Squeeee!"

"Hush!" Evelyn warned. "No one can know about this. It's too soon."

"Oh, but those first days of falling in love are so exciting," Jenny protested. She sucked in a breath. "Are you in love?"

She wrapped one loose curl around her finger. She found it hard to concentrate whenever she was around Ryan. When he wasn't near, she thought of him constantly. More than once, she'd caught herself daydreaming of a future with him.

Was that love? Heavy like, definitely. But something more, something deeper? How could she be sure? She shook her head. "I don't think so. Not yet, anyway."

"But there's a chance."

Jenny looked at her with such hope in her eyes that Evelyn hated to disappoint the girl, but if and when she ever did fall in love, she'd always thought her Mr. Right should be the first to know. "We'll see." That was all she could say for now. "You, you won't repeat any of this, will you?"

"I won't. I swear." Jenny crossed her heart with two fingers. "This is Heart's Landing, after all. If two of its own start making calf-eyes at each other, every shop owner will have your entire wedding planned before you go out on your second date, right down to whether you'll put mints or Jordan almonds in your favor bags."

Laughter bubbled up from deep inside her chest. Jenny might be a relative newcomer, but she knew how things worked in the town where weddings reigned supreme. She sobered quickly and worried her bottom lip. There was one other reason why she refused to get her hopes up about Ryan, and it was a doozy. "It's true that I have feelings for Ryan. I'm pretty sure he likes me more than a little, too. But once Brianna and Daniel announce their choices, everything could fall apart," she warned. Until then, she couldn't let her guard down. Not completely. She had to protect her heart.

Jenny's brows knitted for a second. They smoothed

just as quickly. "You think our Wedding-in-a-Week couple will choose the Captain's Cottage."

"If they don't, it'll be a first. I'm not sure Ryan will take the news well."

Jenny shook her head as if that made no sense at all.

"He has a lot riding on this," she explained. "He could lose everything he's worked for if they don't choose Harbor View. What if they choose the Captain's Cottage and he blames me?" She couldn't, wouldn't let herself fall in love with Ryan until then.

"You're not trying to influence Brianna and Daniel, are you?"

"No. Of course not." She swept the question aside like rice on the sidewalk after a wedding. She'd never stoop that low. Not even if it meant catching drips from the Cottage's leaky roof in pots all over the attic.

"I'm sure Ryan knows it, too. Just like you trust him not to try and sway them to his side."

She smiled. Jenny was right. She did trust Ryan. At least, as far as Brianna and Daniel were concerned. That just left her heart. She'd have to figure out whether she could trust him with that next, and she had a pretty good idea how to start. "I'll talk it over with Jason the next time he calls, but I want us to start recommending Harbor View Weddings whenever a new bride isn't completely sold on what the Captain's Cottage has to offer. Can we do that?"

"Wow! You *really* like this guy, don't you?" Jenny's mouth hung open just a bit.

True, but there was more to it than that. "Heart's Landing prides itself on providing the perfect wedding for every bride. We're either all in on that, or we're not. Now that Ryan's opening Harbor View, we can't afford to miss the 'boat'"—she enclosed the pun in air quotes—"with anyone who wants a waterfront venue."

Jenny's eyebrows dipped. "What if we start doing this and things don't work out between you and Ryan?"

She hated to think of that possibility, but Jenny was right. She had to consider it. "That won't change a thing," she said, sticking by her decision. "We have to do the right thing for our brides. It's why they come to Heart's Landing, after all." She tore the top sheet off the blotter, folded it neatly into quarters, and tucked it in her top drawer for safe keeping. "I have to run. Ryan and I are meeting Brianna and Daniel at Favors Galore. Then it's on to Janet Hubbard's place for a tasting. Tomorrow, we'll be at I Do Cakes for most of the day."

"My favorite part." Standing, Jenny smiled a dreamy smile. No surprise there, considering her husband, Nick, owned the bakery.

"We'll wrap things up on Friday with cocktails and music selections here at the Cottage. Are we all set for those?" A country-western band, a jazz combo, and a stringed quartet had offered to provide music for the wedding and reception. During the auditions, the happy couple would sip drinks specially prepared by a professional bartender.

"Yep. I can't wait to see what they choose for their signature cocktail."

"Whatever it is, that's one tasting we'll all enjoy." Evelyn licked her lips. She scooped up the day's itinerary and rose. "I hate to run, but, well, I've got to run."

She and her friend traded a few last-minute updates before they headed in different directions. Not long after, she stepped from the Cottage's car in front of Favors Galore. Ryan waited for her on the sidewalk. As she'd hoped, his eyes widened slightly the moment he spotted her auburn hair falling in thick ringlets over the pale peach blouse she'd chosen especially for its color.

Could they really have their own Heart's Landing love for the ages? Her breath quickened. Ryan was one of the kindest, most intelligent men she'd ever known. He knew what he wanted to do with his life and had set out to make his dreams a reality, even when they'd clashed with his parents' vision for their youngest son. It didn't hurt one bit that his tall, broad-shouldered frame and chiseled features made her motor hum. She liked him—a lot. She even loved him in many ways. But was she *in love* with him? She didn't know the answer to that question, but she certainly planned to enjoy spending time with him over the next few days. And who knew? Maybe she'd discover the answer to her question along the way.

Inside the gift shop, Curtis snapped pictures while Brianna and Daniel lingered over three different gift bags loaded with goodies and wine. Each contained an assortment of Ashley's hand-crafted chocolates. Evelyn tried and failed not to read too much into it when Ryan stuck close by her side as they sampled the candies and sipped the wine selections. But all too soon, it was time to head to Food Fit For A Queen.

She drank in the mouthwatering aromas of butter and spice as she stepped into Chef Janet Hubbard's domain. She'd attended enough weddings and other events in Heart's Landing to expect great food from the caterer, but in this instance, the chef had clearly gone the extra mile for their Wedding-in-a-Week couple. Evelyn's tummy rumbled, as if she needed reminding that she'd deliberately skipped breakfast this morning in anticipation of the coming feast.

After welcoming them to her establishment, Chef Janet quickly explained Brianna and Daniel's three options and then turned them loose to taste their way through the dining room, arranged to highlight their choices. In the front area, bar tables clustered around food stations that held a variety of heavy hors d'oeuvres, along with a carving station. Opposite it, a buffet offered a selection of pasta dishes before ending with a seafood bar. At a table in the center of the room, waitstaff stood ready to provide a plated dinner option. A discreet placard provided a menu that included steak, lobster, and Cornish game hens.

Evelyn grinned when Ryan headed straight for the carving station, where one of Chef Janet's assistants piled his plate high with succulent roast beef and turkey. He drizzled her signature sauces on both. While Brianna and Daniel slowly worked their way through the pasta buffet and seafood bar, she surveyed the assortment of appetizers. Evelyn couldn't resist a tasty-looking mushroom and scallop concoction and was glad when she sampled it. The combination of the earthy mushrooms with the salty sweetness of the seafood practically made her eyes roll back in her head. She loaded several of those morsels onto a dish and surrounded them with an assortment of other bite-size pieces, enough to share with the others. Gathering at the table, the foursome laughed and talked and traded bites as they worked their way through the amazing spread.

By the time everyone had declared they couldn't eat another bite and thanked Chef Janet, the sun hung low in the western sky. Brianna and Daniel opted to swing by The Glass Slipper before going back to the bed and breakfast. Other than that, their big plans for the evening included renting a movie and vegging out. Evelyn rarely turned down a chance to go shoe-shopping, but for once, she resisted joining the couple. Despite the excellent job Alicia and Jenny and the rest had done covering for her this week, she still had bookkeeping to tackle and Connie's supply order to place. When she shared that news with him, the disappointment that swam in Ryan's eyes tempted her to change her mind, but she stuck to her guns, and they headed in different directions.

Chapter Fourteen

RYAN PERCHED ON THE EDGE of a small couch in an alcove at I Do Cakes and sipped from a cup of dark espresso while Nick walked Brianna and Daniel through the process of choosing the right cake for their wedding. He rubbed his eyes. They felt gritty after a long night of tossing and turning in the bedroom of an apartment that suddenly felt too lonely, too empty.

Evelyn's decision to return to the Captain's Cottage alone had baffled him yesterday. He'd been certain she'd accept his invitation to go for another walk along the rocky coast after the tasting at Food Fit For A Queen. He'd seen her looking his way when she'd thought no one was watching and knew they shared a deepening attraction to one another. He was pretty sure she was as eager as he was to pick up where they'd left off with the kiss they'd almost shared the other night. But at the last minute, she'd chosen to return to work. The move had left him standing on the sidewalk outside Food Fit For A Queen with his head full of questions.

Was it any wonder he'd been too restless to fall

asleep? Or that when he finally had drifted off in the wee hours of the morning, he'd dreamed of her? He shook his head. The alarm had rung far too early. He gulped another swallow of the strong coffee and studied her over the rim of the cup. She'd pulled her hair off her face and had fastened it with sparkly combs this morning. The green shell she wore under a brown zippered jacket highlighted the green in her eyes.

A slight cough from the woman at the opposite end of the banquette jolted him out of his thoughts. Knowing she'd caught him staring, he gave Evelyn a sheepish smile and lifted his cup in a mock toast. No more woolgathering, he promised himself, just as Nick snapped his fingers. At the baker's signal, a tuxedoed waiter pushed a cart bearing a wedding cake through the swinging doors that separated the kitchen from the front half of the bakery.

Brianna cooed with pleasure while Daniel grunted his approval of the round tiers covered in a blush buttercream and decorated with fresh flowers. Ryan merely nodded. As they listened to Nick's description of mouthwatering flavors and fillings, he spared a single glance at Evelyn. To tell the truth, he expected to see her staring at the cake in childlike wonder. But for the second time in two days, the saucy redhead's reaction completely baffled him. Rather than sitting in rapt attention, she excused herself and hurried out of the room with her phone pressed against her ear.

A frisson of concern passed through him. He tried telling himself the call was none of his business, that she was probably fielding a mundane request from the Cottage's switchboard, but unease plagued him. Especially when her absence stretched through Nick's second option—a beautifully decorated sheet cake—and well into the gold-foiled tower that was his third. Without her there to share the tasting, Ryan pushed bites of filling that had lost its flavor around his plate.

The minutes dragged by until she finally returned to the booth. When she slipped into onto her seat, twin lines between her eyes begged him to rush to her side and do his best to fix her problem, whatever it was. Only pure strength of will kept him in his seat. Well, that and the fact that he'd have to climb over Daniel and Brianna to reach her. He forked up a final bite and mostly gave noncommittal answers to questions from the Wedding-in-a-Week couple until, finally, it was time to leave. Biding his time, he smiled and waved until the car carrying Brianna and Daniel disappeared around the corner. When he was certain they'd gone, he slipped one arm around Evelyn's waist. His concerns mounted when she didn't resist in the slightest but let him guide her to a table in the bakery's cafe.

"Okay," he said when the waitress had brought their coffees. "What's wrong?"

"Why do you think something's wrong?" Evelyn emptied half her cup in one gulp.

"You'd never skip a Wedding-in-a-Week event without a good reason. And those frown lines you're wearing? They tell me there's a problem. Is it Brianna's aunt? She's not worse, is she?"

"No," she answered, putting his biggest fear to rest. Then Evelyn reached across the table and did the last thing he expected her to do—she wrapped his fingers in hers. For a second, his world stood still while the warmth of her touch spread up his arm and through his chest. "You know me well, Ryan. I like that."

When he could breathe again, he squeezed her hand. "I like this," he admitted, aiming a look at their joined hands. When he was just a little tyke, he used to try and shake loose from his mother's firm grip whenever they crossed the street. To this day, she told anyone who asked that he'd always been independent. Now, holding Evelyn's hand, for the first time in his life, he didn't ever want to let go.

"Sheila's on the mend. She'll get out of the hospital tomorrow, but you're right. There is a problem."

"How can I help?" Keeping his arm right where it was, he straightened.

"I have to go to Newport tomorrow."

He lifted an eyebrow. "What about Wedding-In-A-Week? Aren't we supposed to stay with Brianna and Daniel while they choose a dance band?"

"And drinks." She nodded. "I spoke to Alicia. Since those activities are being held at the Cottage, she and Jenny were planning to be there anyway. They'll cover for me."

"A road trip, huh? I'm sure there's a good reason." He didn't need all the details. Those could wait until later.

"It's complicated. I'm not even sure I have all the facts straight. I do know a jeweler on Bellview is holding a strand of pearls for Brianna. I need to get them for her."

"Not quite what I expected." But a month ago, he could never have imagined he'd be sitting in I Do Cakes holding hands with Evelyn Heart. He sat back, considering. The prospect of hanging out in the Green

Room with Alicia, Jenny, Brianna, and Daniel for the better part of a day was nearly as appealing as eating wedding cake that had lost its flavor the moment Evelyn had left the table. "What time do we leave?"

"We?"

Seeing her smile sent another jolt of warmth through him. "Of course, we." He gave her fingers a light squeeze. "You weren't thinking of going alone, were you?"

"Well..." Evelyn's voice told him she had considered that exact thing.

"I'll drive. We'll take the truck and make a day of it. If you play your cards right, I might even buy you lunch while we're there." The seafood restaurants that lined Newport's wharf offered some of the best lobster and clams in the country.

"We'll need to be back in time for the rehearsal dinner," she cautioned.

"No problem." After the leaves fell in the fall, he could easily drive to Newport in an hour or so. But at the height of tourist season, they'd need to allow twice that amount of time. "If I pick you up at eight, we can be there by ten when the store opens. That'll give us plenty of time for lunch and maybe a little sightseeing." The views of the ocean and Newport mansions were spectacular along the Cliff Walk, but they'd be pressing their luck to try and take the four-hour hike. On the other hand, he could see them strolling along the shore together or exploring the cavern-like tunnels at Fort Adams.

"Can we afford to be away that long?" Though her eyes sparkled, doubt tugged at Evelyn's lips.

"We're only talking a few hours. After the week we've had, I think we both need a little break."

"It'd be a shame to drive all the way to Newport and back without at least grabbing lunch." Evelyn's lips smoothed. "Eight it is. I'll meet you out front." She thumbed through the messages on her phone with one hand. Her face softened. "I'd better go now if I'm going to be ready in the morning."

He couldn't resist giving her hand one last squeeze before he relinquished his hold. Tomorrow, he promised himself. They'd get to know each other a little better while they explored the neighboring town.

At the door, she leaned up on tiptoe and brushed her lips against his cheek. "Thanks," she whispered. And then she was off, her long strides eating up the sidewalk, her hips swaying and her head held high, while he remained rooted to the spot, rubbing a tiny spot on his cheek.

She'd kissed him. He hadn't seen that coming, but of the many curveballs she'd thrown him today, he liked that one best of all.

A shiver of anticipation passed through Evelyn the moment she spotted Ryan's pickup turn onto the long, curved driveway that led to the entrance of the Captain's Cottage. She darted through the massive double doors. The hem of her sundress swished against her knees, and her heels clicked on the stone steps as she tripped down the steps. Over one shoulder, she carried a straw bag loaded with essentials.

A thermos of coffee, a few snacks in case they got hungry, a pair of comfortable walking shoes, and a light sweater. She'd debated about the sweater. No doubt Ryan would gladly wrap his arms around her and keep her warm if the day grew cool. In the end, she decided bringing it along kept her options open, so into the bag it went.

The well-oiled door of the aging truck opened noiselessly at her touch. A rush of air-conditioned air flowed out, and she sniffed. The interior of the vehicle smelled of Ryan's spicy aftershave and his own unique scent. She drank it in, looked up at the man behind the wheel, and just like that, her mind went completely blank. She knew she was supposed to say...something. Wish him a good morning. Thank him for driving. She stared silently at curve of his chin, his freshly shaved jaw, the lips that wore an amused grin, the eyes that crinkled with good humor. The possibility of speaking actual words retreated further.

"Hey, good morning," he said, his smile widening. "How are you doing?"

"I'm good, thanks. And you? Looking forward to the trip?" Ryan's friendly greeting must've jump-started her brain, because she'd at least strung a few words together. She climbed onto the wide bench seat and rested her bag in the well at her feet.

"Ready?" Ryan asked.

She buckled her seat belt. "Ready." As Ryan followed the driveway to the main road, she pulled out the cell phone she'd already programmed. She settled it into a cup holder and hit Go. The GPS squawked out the first set of directions.

"You look nice." His hands on the wheel, Ryan aimed the truck toward Boston Neck, which would take them north along the coast. "Did you sleep well?"

The compliment warmed her, but she was pretty sure he was just being his typical sweet self. She'd had a late night. "Jason called just after I turned out the lights. He wanted me to fill him in on things here. I brought him up to speed on the Wedding-in-a-Week activities." Glad her brain and mouth had stayed in gear, she paused. "He said to tell you hi."

"He and Tara are having a good trip?"

"Sounds like it." She smoothed her skirt over her knees. "They were both going on about the churches they'd toured earlier in the day. How utterly boring." She clamped her hand over her mouth. With his interest in the history of old buildings, Ryan probably thought Jason and Tara's tour of grand cathedrals was a little slice of heaven.

But he shook his head. "You'd think I'd be itching to visit all the famous buildings throughout Europe. The truth is, I study enough architecture in my line of work. That's the last thing I'd want to do on my honeymoon."

"Whew! That's a relief." She fanned herself with exaggerated motions.

Ryan pressed his shoulders into the seat back. "Give me a sandy beach and tropical breezes, and I'm good."

Now that was interesting. That was exactly what she'd call the perfect honeymoon. But they'd gotten ahead of themselves, hadn't they? Or maybe not, she corrected when Ryan turned serious.

"You might not realize it, but I've been looking forward to spending a day like this with you for a long time. Probably ever since you started high school."

"You're kidding, right?" He was already a junior when she'd finally entered Heart's Landing High as a freshman. Back then, she'd hoped that once they were all in the same school, she and Jason and Ryan would start hanging out again. She'd quickly learned that upper classmen had little to do with the younger students.

"No, I'm serious," Ryan insisted.

"Huh." She didn't want to say anything that would dampen their time together, but she hadn't forgotten how much it had hurt when he'd ignored her. "You didn't even know I was alive in high school."

"That's not true. I've always thought you were special."

"Oh, yeah?" she challenged. "If that's so, why didn't you ever ask me out?"

"I did." Ryan tapped his fingers on the steering wheel.

"You most certainly did not, Ryan Court." Grinning, she shook one finger at him. "Most of the girls in my class had crushes on both you and Jason. They envied me because Jason was my cousin and you were his best friend. I would've remembered if you'd asked me on a date."

"But I did." Ryan turned to her, his expression sheepish. "It took a while to get up the courage. There was my friendship with Jason to think about. Plus, those other kids from the theater were always around. But I asked you once. You turned me down flat." He quickly returned his focus to the narrow, winding road.

I what? She stared at him. "Nuh-uh."

"Yessir. It was homecoming my junior year. You were standing outside Mrs. Eller's drama class, waiting for the bell to ring. I didn't want to say anything to you in front of your girlfriends, but those days, you were hardly ever alone. I knew if I didn't ask you then, I'd lose my chance and some other guy would take you."

"Really? I don't..." Something nudged the back of her mind. She shushed it in order to hear what Ryan said next.

"I had it all planned out. I'd wear my best Sunday suit, buy you a corsage. Our moms would take pictures. We'd double-date with Jason and...I think he was dating one of the cheerleaders then, wasn't he?"

"Sally Robinson. She was captain of the squad." The two of them had been an item through high school.

"Perky little blonde?" When she nodded, he said, "That sounds about right. Just a sec." Ryan focused on the road ahead until they'd passed a slower-moving car. After he pulled the pickup back into his lane, he picked up the threads of the story. "Anyway, I walked right up to you and asked if you'd go with me to the Homecoming dance, and you said..."

"What?" She held her breath. Why would she ever turn him down? She'd thought he practically walked on water ever since the day he'd taught her how to tie her shoelaces.

"You said, 'Hit the road, toad.'"

"Oh. My. Gosh." Laughter rumbled through her chest. She tried to smother it. She even held her hand over her mouth, but she was powerless against it. It bubbled out of her. She bent over, hiding her face in her hands. "That's—that's a line—a line from—from *High School Sweethearts*," she gasped.

Looking for all the world like a guy who needed to give his head a good scratch, Ryan stared straight ahead. "I don't get it," he said when her laughter died.

"It was a dreadful little script written by..." She stared past Ryan's nose to the stacked stone fences that lined this section of the road. "That doesn't matter. *Sweethearts* is about a day in the life of a couple of high school students. There's this scene where the heroine and her boyfriend have had a big fight. She's hanging out with her girlfriends when he tries to win her back. She really loves him, but she's just been telling all her girlfriends how awful he is, so she says, 'You're no frog. My kisses won't turn you into Prince Charming. Hit the road, toad.'" She shrugged. "Like I said, it was a terrible play."

"You turned me down with a line you stole from a bad play?" Ryan's voice dropped into a lower register.

Hearing his confusion, she sobered. "You're missing the point. Or I'm doing my usual bad job of explaining," she quickly corrected. "We had to perform that dreck in drama class. I played Suzie, the heroine. I must've been running my lines with a couple of the other actors—the girlfriends. It's the only thing that makes sense."

She could practically see the wheels turning in his head. She crossed her fingers, praying he'd reach the same conclusion. There really was no other explanation. Hurting Ryan was the last thing she'd ever want to do.

He lifted one hand from the wheel and plowed his

hair with his fingers. "You're saying it was all a big misunderstanding?"

"It had to be. I'd never say something like that to you on purpose."

His head tilted. A sly grin formed on his lips. "So you'd have gone to the dance with me?"

"Oh, goodness, no." Her voice softened. "I might've dreamed of us going steady, of wearing your ring or your favorite sweatshirt. But you were a junior. I was a freshman. My parents would never have let us date. Not even if we'd been friends since we were little. Maybe especially not."

He mulled that over for a few seconds before he nodded, more to himself than to her. "Yeah. I guess you're right."

"But if I'd known..." She put one hand to her chest and fluttered her fingers. "If I'd known Ryan Court, captain of the baseball team, the guy every girl in school wanted to date, if I'd known you wanted to take me to the homecoming dance?" She pressed the back of her other hand to her forehead and pretended to swoon. "I'd have climbed out my window and shimmied down the rose trellis in my party dress."

"And broken your neck in the process." His face registering shock at the mere suggestion, Ryan stared at her for a long second. "Maybe it's a good thing we had that misunderstanding, after all." His attention returned to the road. Almost as an afterthought, he added, "We can see each other now if we want."

"If you're asking me to go on a real date with you, I want you to know ahead of time, I'll say yes." Her pulse hammered in her ears. She was taking a huge leap, and she knew it. Going as his plus-one to a wedding they both had to attend anyway was a far cry from driving into the city for dinner and a movie.

Ryan gave her a grin so wide she could only call it goofy. "Well, in that case, I have a question—"

"What took you so long?" she asked before he could finish, and they both laughed.

Warm tingles rushed through her when Ryan reached for her hand. They rode in comfortable silence for another mile or so before the GPS warned of an upcoming turn. She'd made this trip often enough to know this was the first of several merges that would put them on the Jamestown and then the Newport Bridges. Reluctantly, she withdrew her fingers.

Traffic had backed up at the toll plaza before the Newport Bridge. Letting the pickup inch forward, Ryan said, "So you never told me exactly why we're making this trip. Not that I mind. I'm enjoying the company."

"Right. I promised details, didn't I? It's such a sweet story." She shifted on the leather seat, angling for a better view of Ryan's face. "Sheila Stevens—that's Brianna's aunt—she called from her hospital bed. Can you imagine? She said she was heartbroken at not being able to attend the wedding, but her doctor had given strict orders. No flying for at least ten days."

"Bad timing." Ryan tightened the gap between his vehicle and the next one in line.

"Yeah. To make matters worse, Sheila had some pearls that've been in their family for a couple of generations. Two strands. She said she and her sister Debbie—Brianna's mom—pinkie swore they'd each give one to their oldest girls on the day their daughters got married. I don't know how Sheila ended up with both sets of pearls, but she'd planned to keep the promise and give her sister's to Brianna before the wedding. Until then, she kept them in her safe deposit box. Only Sheila discovered the catch was broken when she went to the bank as soon as she found out about Wedding-in-a-Week."

"Ouch," Ryan commiserated.

"I guess Geneva's pretty small. There's just one jewelry store close by, and when Sheila took the pearls there for repair, the owner was backed up for a month. She found a jeweler here in Newport who could handle the job for her and had them sent here."

Ryan nodded. "I see where this is going." He braked to let a family in an older van cut in front of him. "She was going to stop and pick them up on her way to Heart's Landing."

"Yeah. But the surgery threw everything out of whack."

"So our job today is to get the pearls and give them to Brianna on Sunday."

"They'll be her 'something old.' Sheila got all choked up when I told her I'd take care of it for her. She said she could rest easy knowing Brianna would have a little piece of her mom at her wedding." Her eyes had grown misty. She fanned her face.

Ryan tapped his fingers on the steering wheel. "Do you know what time the jewelry store in Newport closes?"

"Five o'clock. I checked the website." She noted the concern in his tone and frowned. "What are you thinking?"

"I think it's time for a change of plans."

She held her breath, afraid he might want to cut their trip short. "Do you want to head straight back to Heart's Landing?" she whispered.

His eyes tender, Ryan studied her for a long moment. "No. Not that. But I'd feel awful if anything happened to that necklace while we had it. It's a family heirloom. For all we know, it might be the only thing Brianna has left of her mom."

Tears pricked the corners of her eyes. Ryan was being incredibly understanding.

"I think we should do our sightseeing first, eat a late lunch, and pick up Brianna's pearls on our way out of town. What do you think?"

Words failed her for the second time that day. Ryan's kindness and concern went far beyond what she'd expected of the man. At this rate, she'd be permanently mute by the time their second date rolled around.

Oh, boy. She was in big trouble. No matter how much she'd told herself she wouldn't risk her heart on the tall, handsome carpenter, she'd already fallen more than a little in love with Ryan Court.

Chapter Fifteen

RYAN STOOD, HIS ARMS CROSSED, toes sinking into the cool wet sand while Evelyn searched the waterline for shells. Not that she'd find any. The tiny beach at Fort Adams was far too popular with tourists for anything to wash ashore other than thick, red seaweed and the occasional broken bits of sand dollars. That didn't mean he wasn't enjoying himself. Watching Evelyn prowl the shoreline, strands of her hair catching the cool breeze, the wind ruffling her skirt, her long legs in constant motion, it loosed a torrent of unfamiliar emotions in his chest. Much like Evelyn did herself whenever she was near.

He'd meant it when he said she was special. From the time he'd grown old enough to realize girls were cut out of a different, finer cloth than men, he'd known she possessed attributes that set her apart from all the other girls. That they were spending the day on an errand for someone she'd never met, for a bride she'd known less than a week, spoke volumes about her compassion. Her willingness to put in long hours and do hard work showed in her dedication to maintaining the Captain's Cottage as the area's number one wedding venue. Her outgoing nature and downright friendliness brightened the lives of everyone around her.

"I found one!" Evelyn's shout rose above the sound of the waves that lapped the sand in the protected cove.

"What do you have there?"

She raced toward him, her fingers curled around her find. When she reached him, joy suffused her face as she opened her palm to reveal a shiny orange toenail shell in near-perfect condition.

"That's a nice one," he agreed. *Sometimes, it's good to be wrong.*

"I'll save it," she said, tucking it deep into the pocket of her sundress. "A reminder of the day we spent here." She peered up at him. "I've had a great time."

"Same here." From the moment he'd pulled to a stop in front of the Captain's Cottage and she'd climbed into his truck, bringing sunshine and the faint blend of vanilla and citrus with her, the day had been nothing less than perfect. Conversation flowed naturally between them during the two-hour ride and later while they browsed Newport's crowded shops and streets. They feasted like royalty on fried clams and scallops at an outdoor café and laughed aloud at the seagulls and pelicans who vied for their scraps. When they made one last stop at the little beach, they both kicked off their shoes and danced along the wet sand, laughing when a rogue wave soaked his jeans and drenched the hem of her dress.

"It doesn't have to end with today," he said, finally speaking the words he'd never thought he'd hear himself say. “I was serious about what we were talking about in the truck. I want to see you again. A lot.”

Happiness bloomed within him at her whispered, “I’d like that.”

Her hair felt like silk as he threaded a strand between his fingers. “There’s just one thing.” He searched her face. “I need you to make me a promise.”

Her gaze never wavered. “Sure. What is it?”

Her trust turned his insides to jelly. More than ever, he wanted her in his life. However, the very circumstances that’d drawn them together might very well drive them apart. He needed to do whatever he could to prevent that from happening. He let Evelyn’s sleek curl slip through his fingers. “I want you to promise that, no matter which venue Brianna and Daniel choose, it won’t affect our relationship.”

“Ooh!” Mirth danced in her eyes. “Are we in a relationship now?”

He tilted her chin up until she had no choice but to face him squarely. “I’m serious. If Brianna and Daniel choose Harbor View, we can’t let it tear us apart.” Given proper nurturing, one day their love would be as strong and sturdy as The Ash in its glory. They’d serve as an example to others who were starting out on their own love journey. Right now, though, their bond was only a sapling. A strong wind, a flood, could damage it. They needed to do whatever they could to protect it.

“Not a problem. Because they won’t.” She shrugged. The motion sent one of the thin straps on her dress sliding off her slim shoulder. “I’m more concerned about how you’ll react when they pick the

Captain's Cottage." She stared up at him, her certainty showing in the firm set of her jaw.

He nudged the fabric back in place. Just for a moment, he let his hand linger on her shoulder. "I won't lie to you. If they don't pick Harbor View, it's going to hurt. It might take me a minute or two. I just have to keep reminding myself that whichever venue they pick, it's their wedding. First and foremost, their happiness is what matters."

Concern stitched tiny lines across Evelyn's forehead. "Do you really mean that? Or are you saying it for my benefit?"

"I mean it. You've helped me see I have options." Things might not go the way he wanted them to. That didn't mean he had to fail. He could approach the bank. They might be willing to renegotiate his mortgage. Or, now that they'd resolved their differences, his dad might cosign a loan to keep him afloat until Harbor View turned a profit. Neither of which would be necessary if Brianna and Daniel opted for a waterfront wedding.

A shift in the wind blew a strand of Evelyn's hair across her face. She pushed it aside. "I know you're counting on the publicity from the *Weddings Today* article to drum up new business. But what if there was another way?"

"Are you talking about advertising?" He'd looked into placing ads in magazines like *Weddings Today*. He'd thought the cost of a backup generator was high. He'd been wrong about that. The expense of running a national campaign would leave him up to his eyeballs in debt. And it came with no guarantees. At least with a generator, he'd get one of those.

"The Captain's Cottage could send you some referrals."

The suggestion stunned him to his core. "That'd be..."

Evelyn grinned up at him. "I think *awesome* is the word you're looking for."

"Why would you do that?"

She waved a hand, dismissive. "You've taken a derelict structure and turned it into a gorgeous building. I have faith you'll succeed with it as a wedding venue. Maybe with a little help from your friends."

"One particular friend." There'd been a time when he'd been convinced she didn't care about anyone but herself. He'd been so wrong about that. He pulled her to him for a quick embrace. Or he'd planned to make it quick. But once he had her in his arms, letting go was harder than he'd ever thought possible. Standing there with his arms wrapped around her, her head on his shoulder, he wanted the moment to go on forever. His heart thrilled when she seemed as reluctant to let go as he did.

"Wow!" Evelyn smiled. "If I'd known my little announcement would get that reaction, I'd have said something sooner."

His fingers itched to draw him to her again, but he resisted. There was one more matter he needed to clear up. "I thought you were worried about the competition."

Evelyn turned serious. "I've been thinking about that a lot lately. You know how everyone in Heart's Landing works together to give each bride their perfect wedding?"

Not sure where she was headed, he nodded.

"That's one of the things I love most about our town. To tell you the truth, it's the main reason I left New York."

"I'm not sure I follow." What did the Big Apple have to do with Heart's Landing?

"When I first got to New York, I was totally focused on my career." A chagrined smile played across Evelyn's lips. "I don't know if you realize it or not, but actors can be pretty self-centered."

"So I've heard." He'd caught a few glimpses of that when Jenny had been planning her movie star cousin's wedding.

"They have to be." Evelyn shrugged. "Competition for roles is fierce, and if you don't put yourself first, you're never going to make it. Maybe once you've made a name for yourself, maybe then you can afford to give another actor a leg up. But it's pretty dog-eat-dog down in the trenches. When Uncle Dave got sick, I think it was easy for me to come home because, deep inside, I'd already decided I didn't like how the constant struggle was changing me. Didn't like the person I was becoming. I'm not proud of it, but finding out about Harbor View stirred some of those old, cutthroat feelings. I had to remind myself people aren't like that in Heart's Landing."

He whistled. "You've changed."

"I didn't have a choice." Her face crinkled. "Someone pointed out that we hadn't fulfilled our promise to deliver a perfect wedding to every bride who wanted a waterfront wedding. From now on, we will…by recommending Harbor View Weddings."

There was one more thing he had to know. "You're certain Jason will be onboard with this?"

"I've already talked it over with him. We both want every bride to have the wedding of her dreams. Most want to walk down the aisle at the Cottage. For those who have something different in mind, Jason agreed it was a great idea to refer them to you."

The news was so astounding and so unexpected, it deserved a celebration. Unfortunately, he didn't have a bottle of champagne handy. Instead, he lifted Evelyn up and swung her around in a circle while she laughed out loud. Once he'd set her down, he rocked back on his heels, stunned.

Minutes passed while they discussed the difference this new opportunity could make. It'd only take a handful of referrals to get the ball rolling. Once Harbor View had hosted two or three successful weddings, he had no doubt that word of the newest venue in Heart's Landing would spread.

The breeze shifted while they talked. The beach narrowed on an incoming tide. The first gentle waves lapping at their feet told him it was time to go. As much as he wanted to stay right where he was, he and Evelyn needed to head for the jewelry store to pick up Brianna's pearls and hightail it back to Heart's Landing in time for the rehearsal dinner.

They held hands on the walk back to his truck. Halfway there, he realized they'd never finished talking about how Brianna and Daniel's decision might affect them. Hating to put a damper on things, he brought the conversation back to where they'd started. "I know you're positive they'll choose the Captain's Cottage. But let's say, for the sake of argument, they don't. If they choose Harbor View, what then?"

"Then we'll go on with our lives." Evelyn leaned

against him, her warmth filling his soul. "The sun will still come up the next day. The stars will come out at night. Heart's Landing will continue to be America's Top Wedding Destination. Life will go on."

"And us? Will we be okay?"

"You and me, we're like this." She wrapped her middle and index fingers around each other. "Nothing can break us apart."

He liked the sound of that and pulled her close for another one of those delicious embraces. He'd been wrong to doubt he'd recognize love when he found it. He knew what it was now. Love was staring into Evelyn's face and seeing his own feelings for her reflected back at him. He'd fallen head over heels for the saucy redhead. He loved her, plain and simple. Without doubt. Without reservation.

He wanted, needed to tell her. And he would. Soon. Soon, but not today. Confessing his love for the woman of his dreams was a momentous occasion. One that called for candlelight and soft music. He wanted to hold her in his arms when he said those three little words that would change everything. He glanced at Evelyn and knew he had to wait.

Evelyn smiled brightly while Curtis snapped off several pictures of her with Jenny and Brianna. When he finished, the three of them sat together on the podium that'd been erected in the shady park across from the Union Street Bed and Breakfast. Hoping to find Ryan, she scanned the crowd that had gathered for the unveiling of Brianna and Daniel's Wedding-in-a-Week choices. She spotted the man of her dreams guiding Daniel's frail grandmother to one of the folding chairs on the front row, and her insides went all soft and gooey. They positively melted when he kneeled in front of the aged matriarch and laughed softly at something the woman said.

Yep. She was in love—definitely, hopelessly in love. Just thinking about Ryan sent ripples of delight through her. The mere mention of his name could stop her in her tracks and steal her focus. How had that happened? If someone had told her two weeks ago that by today she'd be so in love with Ryan Court, her heart would squeeze every time she thought of him, she'd have told them they needed to have their head examined. But here she was, crushing on him so hard she didn't want to be apart from him for a single moment.

With a final word to the older woman, Ryan stepped into the aisle between the rows of folding chairs. He glanced in her direction, and their eyes locked. The look only lasted an instant, but she felt the connection between them deepen. She crossed her fingers, hoping and praying he wouldn't be too disappointed today. She'd wanted to stand beside him, to lend him her support when Brianna and Daniel announced their Wedding-in-a-Week selections. Only things hadn't gone quite the way she'd planned. The arrival yesterday of Daniel's large, happy family, plus all his groomsmen and their dates, underscored the absence of Brianna's aunt and cousins. The bride smiled bravely through all the hugs and greetings. Still, Evelyn and Jenny promised each other they'd stick close to Brianna's side until she walked down the aisle. Which was why she and her friend stood in front of a very large crowd, flanking the girl who wore a wedding tiara and an I'm-the-bride T-shirt, instead of standing next to the men they loved.

She hummed a few bars of the music from last night's rehearsal dinner. She'd been positively giddy when Ryan had taken her into his arms at the beach yesterday. But that feeling—as good as it had been—didn't begin to compare with how she'd felt as he led her out onto the dance floor last night. She'd never forget the solid feel of his hand at her waist or the steady beat of his heart when she laid her head on his shoulder during the slow waltz. It had been...magical.

Reluctant to let go of the memory, she forced herself to focus as Mayor Thomas stepped to the podium. A few last-minute arrivals hurried to find seats. The mayor tapped the mic, and the crowd quieted.

"Welcome to Decision Day for our lovely Wedding-in-a-Week couple." Greg's voice boomed out across a sea of eager faces. In the front row, Daniel's family sat in rapt attention. Behind them, his attendants—six young, uniformed Marines—straightened, pulling their usual erect posture even tighter. The townsfolk of Hearts Landing loved nothing more than a good wedding. They, along with shop owners from miles around, had crowded the park. Here and there, families with young children had opted to spread blankets on the grass for the event.

"Let's start by thanking everyone who contributed to this year's Wedding-in-a-Week festivities, beginning with a special round of applause for our sponsors, the good folks at *Weddings Today*."

Regina Charm and an associate rose from their chairs on the podium and bowed while hearty applause thundered from the crowd.

When things quieted, the mayor moved to the next item on his list. "How about the shop owners who contributed to the success of this year's event? Let's show them some love."

Greg didn't have to ask twice. Throughout the crowd, people expressed their appreciation with hearty applause.

For the next several minutes, applause came in waves as the mayor thanked everyone for their contributions. Finally, he reached the end of his list and the honored guests. "Last, but not least, let's give a big hand to Brianna and Daniel, who we've all come to love and adore this week."

Chairs creaked and fabric rustled as the crowd surged to their feet to deliver a standing ovation. Brianna, who'd nearly fled at a much more subdued greeting at the train station, beamed. On the other side of the podium, Daniel nodded his thanks.

When everyone had taken their seats again, the mayor pointed to the immense board behind the podium. Images of each vendor's three options lay on a nearby table, he explained. As Brianna or Daniel announced each choice, they'd pick up the corresponding placard and hang it from a hook beneath the store's logo. Eventually, they'd fill the entire board with their choices.

He clapped his hands. "Ready to get started?"

Brianna approached the table. After selecting a placard, she held it up for everyone to see before she carried it to the board and hung it on the hook beneath Eat, Drink and Be Married's logo. The crowd erupted in applause while Vi and Bev jogged up the steps and onto the stage to congratulate the young couple. Meanwhile, the mayor announced, "For their first choice, Brianna and Daniel have chosen to drape their tables in floor-length white tablecloths. Navy table runners, silver flatware tipped with gold fleur-de-lis and gold-rimmed crystal adorn the table. Red napkins complete a look that's sure to make their wedding spectacular."

Concentrating on keeping her smile firmly in place, Evelyn buried clenched fists in the folds of her dress. She'd have sworn Brianna and Daniel would choose the tropical color theme. They'd barely glanced at the red, white and blue option at Be Married. What had changed? And, more important, what other surprises lay ahead? She stopped herself before she went too far down that rabbit hole. As long as they were happy with their selections, it didn't matter what choices Brianna and Daniel made. All of them would look perfectly lovely in the Green Room of the Captain's Cottage.

Next, Daniel approached the table. Tucking a placard under his arm, he approached the podium and stepped to the mic. "I want to give a special Marine thanks to Greg Thomas for going above and beyond this week. See, I surprised the mayor a little when I announced my intention to wear my uniform, rather than a tux, for the wedding. He could've said 'fine and dandy' and let it go at that. Instead, he insisted on tailoring a suit for me as his gift from Tux or Tails. And here it is." The instant Daniel held up the poster, his six attendants issued a crisp “Oorah!” which was quickly followed by yet another round of applause.

And so it went, with Brianna and Daniel slowly building their wedding from the ground up while those watching noted their approval with round after round of applause. Evelyn joined in the fun with each choice. As they neared the end, she eyed the board. The couple had tossed a few surprises into the mix, sure enough, but every option they’d chosen would look stunning in the Cottage.

Finally, only one empty peg remained. Brianna and Daniel joined hands at the table, and Evelyn knew the moment she’d been waiting for had arrived. She found Ryan in the crowd. The man she loved wore a confident smile, but she knew his insides were shaking, his palms damp. To be honest, so were hers. Mustering a wide smile, she blew him a kiss for good luck, caught the one he sent her in return, and pressed it to her heart. More than anything, she hoped and prayed he’d been honest when he’d said whichever location Brianna and Daniel chose, he wouldn’t let it drive a wedge between them. She clung to that thought when the young couple approached the mic.

“Before we announce the venue for our wedding, Daniel and I just want to say how much we appreciate what y’all have done for us this week.” Brianna brushed a few wisps of her straight blond hair over her shoulder. “Evelyn and Ryan have been godsends. I seriously don’t think I’d have made it through the week without Evelyn’s help, especially. She held my hand, lent me her shoulder, and wiped away my tears on more than one occasion this week.”

My pleasure, Evelyn mouthed. She pressed one hand to her heart and swallowed past the lump that had formed in her throat. She and Brianna had grown so close, she was going to hate to say goodbye when the time came.

"Ryan lent me his support and offered advice," Daniel said, taking over the mic. "They've become more than mentors to us. They've become good friends. Which makes having to choose between them doubly hard."

Brianna stepped forward again. "We'd be blessed to hold our wedding at either of their gorgeous facilities. Everyone here already knows about the Captain's Cottage—it's a Heart's Landing institution, and rightfully so. You may not know Harbor View Weddings as well yet, but you will. I encourage you to visit there soon. It's a beautiful place to get married."

The lump in Evelyn's throat melted. It was just like Brianna and Daniel to soften the blow for Ryan. She, for one, would forever be grateful to them for singing the praises of Harbor View, something they wouldn't do if they'd chosen it as their venue. She flexed her fingers and straightened, preparing to step forward and deliver hearty handshakes and hugs the moment the couple hung the placard featuring the Captain's Cottage on the board.

His arm around Brianna, Daniel leaned into the mic. "In fact, it's so beautiful, we've chosen to hold our wedding"—he paused—"at Harbor View Weddings. We hope you all will join us this Sunday for the first-ever wedding at Heart's Landing's very own waterfront wedding venue."

Wait. What? She couldn't have heard right, could

she? She scoured the crowd for Ryan, finally spotting him moving toward the podium, a beaming smile on his face.

Evidently, she'd heard correctly, after all. She slumped against her chair while Daniel crossed to the board. When he hung a picture of Harbor View from the final hook, all the air escaped from her lungs. Almost before she knew it, Ryan had mounted the few steps onto the stage. Brianna enveloped him in a hug. A few seconds later, he shook hands with Regina Charm while the mayor grinned and patted him on the back.

He was standing in *her* spot. Accepting the congratulations that should've been *hers*. Ryan had sworn Harbor View would never take the Cottage's place. And yet that was exactly what had happened.

Someone stepped in front of her. She tried to look around them, but they blocked her view.

"You're dangerously close to looking like a sore loser," Jenny whispered. "Stand up right now. Go over there and tell Brianna and Daniel you're happy for them. Give Ryan your best wishes. We'll commiserate over pizza tonight."

It took a good friend to step in at a time like this. Thankfully, Jenny was one of the best. The newlywed was also right—she could do this. She had to. She stood, glad when her legs didn't buckle beneath her. Plastering a smile on her face, she headed first for Brianna and Daniel, who stood chatting with the mayor. Her arms might've felt like lead weights, her mouth stiff and unnatural, but she hugged Brianna and offered her congratulations to Daniel.

That done, she looked around for Ryan. She found

him quickly enough. Wearing an all-too-pleased-with-himself grin, he stood between Regina Charm and her assistant while Curtis shot pictures that would no doubt be included in the *Weddings Today* article.

She told herself she couldn't intrude on his moment in the spotlight. In truth, she needed time. A moment. Maybe a week. He glanced toward her, but she turned aside. She couldn't look into his eyes. Her cousin had left the Captain's Cottage in her hands while he was gone. He'd trusted her to preserve its reputation as the top wedding venue in Heart's Landing. But she'd gotten so distracted by Ryan that she'd let Jason down. And not just him. From the Cottage's newest hire to Connie, who'd been there the longest, she'd let them all down.

How had she been so foolish?

Chapter Sixteen

RYAN'S HEART THUMPED. BRIANNA AND Daniel had done it; they'd had chosen Harbor View Weddings for their venue. As a result, here he was, shooting the breeze with Regina Charm and her cohorts as if it was the most natural thing in the world for him to do when, two weeks ago, he'd worried whether he could even hold on to the building he'd painstakingly restored. Money wouldn't be an issue anymore. Not with an article in *Weddings Today* proclaiming Harbor View as the...how had Curtis put it? *The fabulous new venue in America's Top Wedding Destination.* His phone would be ringing off the hook.

But Evelyn hadn't stopped by to congratulate him yet. He hoped she would. He wanted her beside him when he asked Ms. Charm to mention the Captain's Cottage in the article. His building might be the newest, and with its beautiful views of the harbor, it was certainly one of the prettiest places to get married, but the Captain's Cottage would always be an iconic venue in Heart's Landing.

Turning, he was just in time to catch a glimpse of Evelyn as she left the podium. In the split second before she disappeared into the crowd, he registered the bright spots of color on her cheeks, the tears in her eyes. His heart sank. He'd tried to warn her, had tried to get her to at least consider the possibility that Brianna and Daniel might opt to hold their wedding at Harbor View. He'd tried, but he'd failed. Now she was hurt, and instead of turning to him, she was running away. He had to stop her.

"Ms. Charm, I'm sorry but, uh, something's come up that I need to take care of."

The senior editor for *Weddings Today* frowned. The straight black hair she wore in a precision cut rippled. She swung away from Curtis's camera to face Ryan, her lips pursed. "I'd like to get a few more pictures for the magazine."

He shifted uneasily. Regina Charm had a legendary temper. No one needed to tell him how important it was to maintain good relations with her. But Evelyn had a knack for acting and speaking first, thinking later. And while he loved her spontaneity and wouldn't change that about her for all the world, he couldn't let her leave without making sure everything was all right between them. He swung a look to Curtis. Did the photographer know more than he let on? He took a chance. "Hey man, you got what you need there?"

Curtis lowered his camera. His gaze swung from Ryan to the woman rapidly making her way through the crowd. "More than enough. I'm good."

Ryan didn't wait. He reached for the editor's hand and gave it a firm pump. "It's been a pleasure, Ms. Charm. I'll see you at the wedding, if not before." With that, he bounded down the steps, leaving one of the most powerful women in the industry with her mouth agape.

Over his shoulder, he heard her mutter, “Why, I—”

“Don’t mind him. Love makes you do crazy things,” Curtis cut in. “You know, I don’t think I like this image of you and Brianna…”

By then, Ryan was too far away to hear the rest. Not that he cared. Only one woman mattered right now, and she was making a beeline out of the park. Deep in his heart, he knew if she reached the Captain’s Cottage before him, if she climbed the steps to her apartment on the third floor, if she closed the door behind her, she’d close the door on their love as well. He had to catch up with her before that happened.

He scanned the park. Most of the attendees had dispersed as soon as Mayor Thomas delivered his closing remarks. Now, loud snaps echoed beneath the trees. A crew from Public Works had already begun folding chairs and loading them onto carts. He caught sight of Evelyn near the last row. He was in luck—Mildred Morrey had pulled her aside. The delay gave him just the chance he needed. He jogged toward the women, reaching them just as Mildred said her goodbyes.

“Evelyn,” he said, closing the gap between them in two final strides. “Where are you off to? I wanted to introduce you to Regina Charm.”

Evelyn swung toward him. “No need. We’ve met.”

Like the hearts that hung from buildings throughout the town, her expression could very well have been chiseled from stone. Instinctively, he held his hands up in a gesture of surrender. “Hey, don’t shoot the messenger. I was going to ask her to mention the Captain's Cottage in the article, but if you don't want me to..."

With visible effort, she straightened. Her expression softened. "Sorry. I did it again, didn't I? I don't want to ruin your moment. You must be thrilled with Brianna and Daniel's decision. Congratulations. You won."

Ryan gulped. Evelyn's voice sounded as stiff and unnatural as the text-to-speech function on his phone. As he watched, her face crumpled. Tears dampened her cheeks. Wanting, needing to fix things for her, he stepped forward. His footsteps halted when an unfamiliar gleam flickered in her green eyes.

Was she playing him?

He shook his head. Once upon a time he'd believed she was capable of manipulating a situation to get what she wanted. But that was before. Before he'd gotten to know the real Evelyn. The one who went out of her way to buy flowers for her friends. Or plan a daylong trip so a bride-to-be could have her perfect day. "You want to tell me what's really bothering you?"

She pressed a hand to her throat. "Jason trusted me to take care of the Captain's Cottage in his absence. He counted on me to convince Brianna and Daniel that the Cottage was the best place in Heart's Landing to get married." Her shoulders slumped. "But I didn't do my job, did I? I lost." She inhaled. "I lost, and it's all my fault. I should never have let myself get distracted. By you. By us."

"Whoa! Wait a minute." Talk like that moved her dangerously close to a line that, once crossed, would mean the end of them. His heart ached. He had to stop her before she said something she'd regret. He held up a hand. "You don't think you're taking too much responsibility for something that was never under your control?"

Looking miserable, Evelyn shrugged. "This is the first time *ever* that another venue will be featured in the *Weddings Today* article. What else am I supposed to think?"

"Oh, I don't know. How about trying this on for size—Brianna and Daniel wanted a waterfront wedding. No matter what you said or did, the Captain's Cottage couldn't give them the wedding of their dreams." Pulling himself to his full height, he towered over her. "A certain redhead told me that's what we do here in Heart's Landing. We create the perfect wedding for every bride...and groom."

She stared at him, her green eyes wide. The ghost of a smile played across her lips. "Well, there is that, I guess."

Relief, pure and cleansing, washed through him. He got that she was upset. He'd figured she needed a moment to calm down, just like he'd known he would if the shoe were on the other foot. Now that she had, he held out his arms. In an instant, she sagged against his chest. "It'll be all right. Everything will work out. You'll see," he murmured into her hair. Evelyn was the most capable person he knew. She might not have figured out all the answers for her future, but she'd accomplish whatever she put her mind to when the time came.

"Are we still friends?" she asked, tipping tear-stained cheeks to him a few moments later.

He needed every ounce of his will and then some not to kiss away her tears. But workers were dismantling the stage. The sound of drills and hammers filled the air. Standing in the middle of all that wasn't exactly where he wanted them to share their first real kiss. A first kiss deserved moonlight and violins. He settled for brushing his lips against her forehead. "I'd like to think we're more than friends. I want us to have a future together."

"Even now that you know how much trouble my big mouth can get us in?"

He shook his head. "I've known that since the day I met you. Besides..." He slung one arm around her shoulders and steered her in the direction of the Captain's Cottage. "You owe me a dinner at Bow Tie Pasta. You haven't paid up yet. I won't give up on you until you do."

They laughed then and cut through the park, arm in arm. The soft grass whispered beneath their feet. Birds chirped in the trees. From the street came the steady clop-clop-clop of horses' hooves as another bride rode past in the back of a carriage. With Evelyn at his side and a recommendation from *Weddings Today* in his pocket, everything was right in his world.

Well, not quite. There was one debt he needed to repay. Unless he was sadly mistaken, Curtis had covered for him with Regina Charm. The photographer might prefer to blend into the background, but he'd watched the man work. Ryan doubted very little escaped his notice. He stuck his hand in his pocket and whistled. He owed Curtis a drink. It was a debt he'd gladly pay tomorrow, after Brianna and Daniel said their "I do's" at Harbor View Weddings.

Chapter Seventeen

ACTIVITY HUMMED IN THE BRIDE'S dressing room of Harbor View Weddings. A makeup artist from Perfectly Flawless Day Spa brushed a final dusting of powder across Brianna's nose. Seated in a plush white styling chair, the bride practically glowed in a puffy white robe. Her hair in large rollers, she waited for the stylist to work a miracle by turning her straight locks into masses of ringlets around an elegant updo.

Thunder rumbled, the noise more ominous than it'd been a short time earlier. A distant flash of lightning caught Brianna's attention, and she stirred nervously. "Do you think the storm will hold off until after the wedding?"

Not likely. Evelyn, who'd been checking the weather reports on her phone every five minutes, tucked the device in her pocket. An isolated thunderstorm was predicted to hit their area within the next half hour. With any luck, they'd have clear skies again in time for the reception. Not that it mattered. The building was sturdy—Ryan had made sure of that. The cake, the flowers, the gift bags had already been delivered.

He'd even drafted Daniel's groomspeople to form an umbrella brigade, if necessary.

"You never told me if you and Daniel enjoyed the day yesterday," she said, trying to distract the bride from the darkening skies. "What did you end up doing?"

"First, we went for a long run along that path Ryan showed us. We'd skipped our usual run the last couple of days, so it felt good to get out and stretch our legs. Then we had a couple's massage at the spa, and I got a mani/pedi." She splayed her fingers for Evelyn to see. "My first ever!" She laughed. "After that, we took a carriage ride to the rehearsal and back. Then, on to dinner."

"Aww! That sounds wonderful! I'm glad you had time to enjoy yourselves after all the stress of the past week."

"We did. I..." Brianna cast a worried look out the window as another peal of thunder sounded. "Um, how does everything look out there?" She indicated the area beyond the door.

"Beautiful," Evelyn offered, her conviction strong. "The colors you picked, the floral arrangements, the gift bags, they look stunning together. Mildred Morrey and her crew are nearly done with the bower. I have to admit, I've never seen burgundy dahlias used in a wedding before. These are absolutely gorgeous. They go perfectly with the rest of the color scheme."

Brianna nodded. "I can't wait to see it!" She glanced at the confection of appliquéd lace over matted white silk hanging from a hook in the ceiling. "Is it almost time to put on my dress?"

Evelyn gave her an indulgent smile. The ball gown

would stay right where it was for a while longer. "Relax. Enjoy your day. It's still hours before the ceremony. We'll get you into your gown an hour or so before. Curtis will want to take photos of before you walk down the aisle." At Brianna's disappointed face, she suggested, "You should probably eat something. Can I make you a plate?" A small table draped in Brianna's colors held a sampling of Chef Hubbard's favorite dishes.

"I'm not sure I could eat a bite. I'm so nervous." Outside, thunder rolled across the sky. Brianna stared out the window. On the other side of the glass, rain pelted down at a good clip. "Daniel's already here, isn't he? And his friends? Have you seen him?"

"Yes, he's here, and I've seen him. He looks, oh—" She pressed one hand to her chest. "So handsome in his dress uniform. His attendants are all in the groom's dressing room with him. They're a good-looking bunch." She fingered the thin box in her pocket. "If you're ready, I have a special something for you."

Brianna bit her lower lip. "You've already done so much. You didn't have to get me anything."

"Oh, this isn't from me," she corrected. "I guess I could've phrased that better. It's a gift from your aunt."

"Aunt Sheila?"

Nodding, she slipped the slim box from her pocket. She closed the short distance between them and placed it in Brianna's hands.

"What is it?" The woman gave the box a tiny shake.

"You'll have to open it."

Careful not to ruin her manicure, the young bride

removed the lid. She sucked in sharp breath and stared down at the pearls nestled in soft cotton.

"They were—"

"My mother's," Brianna finished. She looked up through tear-filled eyes. "But how? Where?"

"Your Aunt Sheila planned to give them to you today. When she found out she couldn't make it, she asked me to act in her stead."

"I thought they were lost," Brianna whispered in an awestruck tone. She held up the strand. The pearls glowed in the light. "After Mama and Daddy..." She swallowed.

"Your aunt has been keeping them for you. I'm sure she can fill you in on all the details. She said your mom dreamed of seeing you walk down the aisle wearing these pearls."

One fat tear rolled down Brianna's cheek. Evelyn handed the girl a tissue.

"Can you help me with them?" The young woman held out the strand.

"Of course." She moved swiftly to the bride's side. In seconds, she'd fitted the metal V into the clasp and *snicked* it shut. She tugged it gently to make sure it held. When it did, she stepped away.

Brianna stared into the mirror, her fingers tracing the lustrous pearls around her neck. "If y'all will excuse me for a minute, I need to call Aunt Sheila." She turned to the makeup artist, her smile tremulous. "Don't wander off. I think I might need a touchup by the time we're through."

The other women blotted their own eyes as they filed out of the room. Evelyn gave Brianna's hand another squeeze and pressed the girl's cell phone into her hand. She'd taken two steps toward the door when a particularly loud roll of thunder crashed overhead. Immediately on its heels, lightning flashed outside the window. In the ensuing silence, a loud boom shook the windows. Evelyn flinched. Brianna squealed. The lights flickered once and went out.

"It's all right," Evelyn called into the darkness. Rather than rushing to Brianna's side, she headed in the other direction. While she and Ryan had been setting up yesterday, she'd tucked a box of battery-powered candles into one of the cabinets. Now, she felt her way along the wall to the bank of storage closets. Sure enough, the box was right where she'd left it. In minutes, a soft glow filled the room. She carried a candle to Brianna.

"We lost power," the girl said in case no one else had noticcd.

"We did."

"How can we have a wedding with no electricity?"

"Well, that could be a problem," she conceded. Quickly, she added, "But I'm sure Ryan has everything under control. Go ahead and call your aunt," she said, giving the girl's hand a reassuring squeeze. "In the meantime, I'll see what's going on."

Ryan took advantage of the momentary break in the chaos to lean against one of the cedar support beams in Harbor View's ballroom. He and Evelyn had been hard at work getting the hall ready for the wedding since shortly after Brianna and Daniel's big announcement yesterday. He didn't think he could've made it without her help. She seemed to do things by instinct, but he knew hers was an instinct honed by a lifetime spent at the Captain's Cottage. She was the one who'd insisted they sort through every cabinet and closet, every dish cupboard and the pantry, checking and double-checking the supplies for the Harbor View's first wedding. It'd required more than one run to the store to stock up, but she'd made sure they had every single thing they needed. She'd even insisted on purchasing a supply of foul weather gear, which she'd hung on hooks in his office. At the time, he'd thought she was overthinking just a bit. Now, looking at the threatening sky, he had to admit having the rain gear handy didn't hurt.

As for the rest, he breathed easily. Bev and Vi had arrived at eight sharp and had immediately begun arranging tablecloths, runners, and sparkling china on three dozen tables. After lunch, they'd set to work covering two hundred chairs in navy spandex, which Evelyn had declared the best possible use for the stretchy material. Mildred Morrey and her crew had shown up at ten with two vans filled with flowers and arrangements. Ashley and a young teen had pulled into the parking lot next. In short order, they'd piled hundreds of gift bags into the old Farley boat on display in the front lobby. Soon after, Janet Hubbard and her crew had taken over the kitchen. Since the chef had helped design the layout of Harbor View's counters and appliances, she'd set to work with few questions. From then on, the front door had opened and closed at least a thousand times as stylists and musicians and deliveries had arrived. Nick Bell had rolled in with a wedding cake so tempting it'd been all Ryan could do not to swipe a bit of icing. JoJo Moss and her videographer roamed back and forth, taking preliminary shots of everything.

In well-timed movements, the shop owners and their helpers had transformed the empty hall into space truly fit for a Wedding-in-a-Week couple. Dark purple flowers clustered around the bower where Brianna and Daniel would stand to recite their vows. The same floral design echoed down the rows of tall pedestals lining a carpeted aisle. It was repeated in the centerpieces on each of the tables set with gold-rimmed glasses and gleaming gold-tipped flatware.

In a matter of hours, guests would begin to trickle in. His parents, his brothers, and their families would be among them. He'd called his dad on the way home from dropping Evelyn off at the Captain's Cottage yesterday. The old man had rallied the entire family to attend the wedding tonight and celebrate Ryan's success. Even if they all got soaked in the process.

He eyed the dark clouds overhead. Distant lightning flashed. In the short time he'd been standing next to the window, a light drizzle had given way to a downpour. According to the weather reports, they were in for a blow.

The building didn't worry him. It was sound. The people, though—they might need reassurance. He'd barely turned away from the window when a tremendous crack of thunder roared overhead. On its heels, lightning arced down from the clouds. A loud boom rattled the windowpanes. He had a split second to wonder if they'd been struck when the lights flickered. Then, the room went dark.

"Gosh! That sounded close." JoJo scampered down from the stepstool she'd been standing on. She clutched accessories for the photo booth in both hands.

"I think it might've hit nearby." Ryan raised his voice to be heard over the rain that sluiced down by the bucketful, turning the world outside into gray soup. "Is everyone okay?"

A smattering of "Yeah's" and "Fine here's" answered.

Curtis appeared at his elbow out of the gloom. "We lost power," the photographer announced, as if Ryan had failed to notice the sudden lack of light.

"I see that. Hang on while I call the power company." He was already scrolling down the contacts list on his phone. "Hopefully, it's something they'll fix in a jiff." He punched a few numbers and was immediately put on hold.

"Is your backup generator on manual? It hasn't kicked on yet."

"There's a reason for that," Ryan said, trying to remain upbeat. "We don't have one."

"Uh-oh." Curtis pulled out his own phone. "I, um, I need to check in with Regina. Let her know what's happened."

"Can't you just wait until..." A voice sounded in his ear. He paused to listen. By the time he realized it was just a recording telling him that call volume was heavy at the moment and asking for his patience, Curtis was already talking with his boss in low tones.

People streamed toward him from wherever they'd been when the lights had gone out. A door opened and closed somewhere at the front of the building. Six sturdy Marines in dress blues joined the small crowd. Speculation buzzed.

"Hold on." Ryan raised his voice to be heard above the hubbub. "I'm on the line with the power company. Let's see where things stand before we start jumping to conclusions." He turned away from the group when another voice, a real one this time, asked him for the address. In response, a few beeps sounded through the earpiece. A recording followed.

"A power outage has occurred in your area."

"Tell me something I don't already know," he muttered.

"The problem appears to be with a transformer. One hundred customers have been affected. Time to repair is estimated at..." A bead of sweat trickled down his neck. "Six hours."

Six hours! *Oh, crap!* The words struck a harsh blow to his gut. His thoughts swam.

"We appreciate your—"

He didn't bother listening to the rest. Panic gnawed at his center. He searched for answers in the faces of those around him and found only more questions.

Outside the bridal suite, Evelyn rested her back against the door. She'd done her best to put Brianna's fears to rest, but she couldn't ignore the uneasy feeling in the pit of her stomach. Surely by now the backup generator should've kicked on. Why hadn't it? Determined to learn the answer, she headed through the barn doors to the reception hall, where gray skies and pouring rain cast the large room in semidarkness despite the floor-to-ceiling windows.

A small group had gathered in one corner. She spotted Ryan standing off to one side, his phone pressed to his ear. Across from him, Curtis likewise had his cell phone out. The tiny screens bathed their faces in a greenish glow. Jenny and Alicia stood apart from the group, whispering, their heads close. In between, Daniel and his groomspeople, Mildred Morrey and her assistants, and Janet Hubbard all spoke at once.

"When's the power coming back on?"

"What about meal prep?"

"Will the wedding go on as scheduled?"

"What do you mean, there's no backup generator?"

That last ominous question sent Evelyn's stomach into freefall. She shuddered, crossed her fingers, and prayed the electric company would be Johnny-on-the-spot with their repairs.

She'd no sooner finished than Ryan lowered his phone. His face pale, he announced, "A transformer blew. The earliest estimate for repairs is late tonight. It could take longer."

Shock echoed through the room. The electricity couldn't possibly be restored in time for a wedding that was only hours away.

"Quiet, everyone," barked the least expected voice in the crowd. At Curtis's firm command, silence rained down like the deluge on the other side of the windows. "I have Ms. Charm on the line." He rocked his phone away from his ear and back again. "She wants me to remind you that, due to deadlines beyond our control, there can be no delay in tonight's festivities." He scanned the faces crowded around him. "Does anyone have a weather report?"

One of Daniel's groomsmen spoke up. "I do. The storm should move offshore within the next thirty minutes."

"Good. That's good news." Curtis relayed the information to his boss. After a brief pause, his chest heaved. Sliding the phone into his pocket, he took in his surroundings. "The bad news is, we can't have a wedding here without power. We'll have to move to a different location."

"Now, wait a minute," Ryan began.

Curtis shushed him with a chopping motion. Holding up his fingers, he counted off problems one by one. "There's no electricity. The sun's going down. By seven, this room will be in total darkness. No light means no photographs. No photographs means no special wedding edition."

Before anyone could count to ten, the significance of Curtis's reasoning sank in. Everyone began to talk at once. Evelyn held her breath. Many of the vendors counted on the article in *Weddings Today* to drum up new business that'd help them recoup substantial investments in Wedding-in-A-Week. They had every right to complain.

Though Ryan fumed, his shoulders slumped. Evelyn shot him a sympathetic glance. But she wasn't ready to throw in the towel quite so easily. There had to be a way to save the wedding for him.

Curtis aimed a pointed look in her direction. "Evelyn, you reserved one of your ballrooms for tonight's festivities in case Brianna and Daniel chose the Captain's Cottage, didn't you? I trust you haven't rented it out on such short notice."

Is he serious?

The heavy weight of failure melted from her shoulders. Relief shivered through her midsection. For an instant, she imagined Jason's face when she told him they'd won a coveted spot in the *Weddings Today* article after all. She pictured herself standing in the background holding Ryan's hand while Curtis snapped pictures of Brianna and Daniel.

Ryan.

She couldn't snatch success from his hands. She wouldn't. But according to Curtis, things were headed in a direction that left a sour taste in her mouth.

When she failed to respond immediately, the photographer phrased his question more sharply. "Is the room available or not?"

"It is," she answered, wishing the floor would open up and swallow her.

"Good." Curtis's head bobbed as if he'd been expecting her answer. "We'll move everything there."

"No!" Ryan shouted. His voice dropped to a growl. "You can't do that. Daniel and Brianna chose to get married here. Everything is nearly ready." A few last-minute details were all that remained.

"No!" She added her own protest. Curtis expected them to pick up and move an entire wedding to a different location and still have everything go off without a hitch? The idea was ludicrous. She eyed JoJo Moss. Her photo booth alone required at least ninety minutes to erect. Then there were the floral arrangements to transport, the wedding arch, the bride. She stopped, her thoughts in a jumble. How were they supposed to get Brianna and her dress clear across town in the pouring rain? It couldn't be done.

"You have no electricity." The man who'd insisted on staying in the background all week now overruled every objection in a flat, matter-of-fact tone. "There are only two choices: move to the Captain's Cottage, or cancel the ceremony." He singled out Daniel. "It's your choice."

The groom's features twisted into a stricken expression. His gaze darted to Ryan and then to her. The starch went out of his posture. "If those are my only two choices..."

She held her breath while Curtis nodded.

"Then I choose the Captain's Cottage."

"You heard the man, people." Curtis clapped his hands together. "Let's get moving. We're on the clock here."

As if he'd fired a starting pistol in a race, the group dispersed, each person heading in a different direction.

Ryan's voice rose above the sounds of the rain and the sudden clatter of feet. "Wait. Let's talk about this."

"There's nothing to talk about," came Curtis's curt response. "The decision's been made."

She watched Ryan's mouth work wordlessly. Pain lanced her chest. Her eyes welled. She wanted to go to him, sling her arms around him, comfort him. But she couldn't. They'd agreed to keep their relationship under wraps until after Brianna and Daniel's wedding. *I'm sorry,* she mouthed.

Ryan either didn't hear her or he chose to reject her sympathy. A muscle in his jaw twitched. His expression collapsed. "You know I'll lose everything unless the wedding takes place here. And it'll all be your fault." His shoulders rounded as if they carried the weight of the world. "Congratulations. I guess you won our bet after all."

With that, he spun on one heel, shouldered his way past Curtis, and marched to the vestibule. He didn't stop when he hit the door but stalked out into the pouring rain. Moments later, his truck tore out of the parking lot.

She stared after him. She'd been in Ryan's shoes. She knew exactly how he felt. In New York, every time another actress had landed a part she'd auditioned for, she'd been crushed. When Brianna and Daniel had announced their decision to wed at Harbor View, for a moment she'd thought her whole world had collapsed. Ryan needed time to come to grips with what'd just happened. She'd give it to him. Her heart broke for him, but there was nothing she could do or say at this point to help. He'd have to deal with this disappointment on his own. For now, she had a wedding to save and not a minute to spare. She wrenched her gaze from the main entrance.

"Stop," she called. "Everybody, just stop!"

Curtis growled a warning. "Evelyn, we don't have time for this."

"We don't have time to move this wedding to the Captain's Cottage, either," she replied in her best, all-business tone. Mentally crossing her fingers, she focused on Daniel. "Curtis overlooked one option. We can still give you and Brianna the wedding of your dreams here tonight. What do you say?"

"Harbor View has always been our first choice."

The groom snapped to attention. "If you say you can do it, I'd say, 'ma'am, yes, ma'am.'"

With the groom's support in her pocket, she scanned the room. Halfway to the kitchen, Janet Hubbard had halted. Evelyn singled her out. "Chef, that gas stove, does it still work?"

"Yes." Understanding glinted in the chef's intelligent eyes. "We can cook on it whether we have power or not."

Her heart in her throat, she pressed. "How much time will you lose transporting everything you need to the Cottage?"

"Honestly?" The chef swept her toque from her head. "It'll take an hour, maybe more, to load everything back into the van. Unloading on the other end will eat up another hour." The tall, angular woman followed Evelyn's lead. "I'd say we'd be running about three hours behind by the time we plated the meal."

"Thank you, Chef." Relieved, she breathed deeply.

Her relief short-circuited when Curtis intervened. "What if you serve everything buffet-style? Eliminate some of the dishes?"

The chef shrugged. "That would save some time. We might be able to make it."

She blinked. Okay, a buffet wasn't ideal. Nor was it Daniel and Briana's first choice. But she'd let that one slide for now. She carried on, determined to show Curtis why his plan wouldn't work. Moving on to the next item on her list, she turned to Mildred Morrey. "Will you be able to transport the floral arrangements to the Cottage and recreate all this?" She waved a hand toward the room that looked exactly like Brianna and Daniel wanted.

One of the centerpieces in her hands, Mildred let a rare irritation creep into her voice. "We've been working on this room since ten this morning. We'll never get everything to the Cottage and set up in time. Some pieces, like the bower, were assembled on-site and can't be moved at all."

"They'll make do without the arch," Curtis said as if the hours Mildred's staff had spent on it were of no consequence. "I'm sure there are flowers left over from another wedding or two there at the Cottage."

"Why don't we just fill the room with roses while we're at it?" Mildred shot back. Grumbling to herself, the florist shook her head.

Bev from Eat, Drink and Be Married caught wind of what was going on and chimed in. She gestured toward the tables and chairs. "It'll take all night to break down these place settings and move them to the Cottage. If we had another day, maybe..."

Jenny added, "The Green Room isn't set up for a wedding. At least, not this wedding."

"Look, it won't be perfect," Curtis admitted, "but you'll make do."

That was the last straw. Evelyn put her foot down. "No," she said through gritted teeth. "That's not how we do things in Heart's Landing. We deliver a *perfect* wedding for *every* bride. With a little bit of creativity and some help from our friends, we can give Brianna and Daniel the wedding of their dreams on time and right here." She gulped air. She was putting everything on the line, but this was for all of them—for Brianna and Daniel, for Heart's Landing, and for the man she loved. "Tell Regina the wedding will go forward as scheduled at Harbor View."

She didn't see the person who started clapping first, but she wanted to hug them. As one by one the others joined in, she thanked her lucky stars for letting her live in a place where people truly believed in creating a perfect wedding for every bride.

Curtis glowered and threw out one last warning. "I hope you know what you're doing. If you mess this up..."

Tears stinging her eyes, she added her own reassurances to those of the shop owners and workers who chorused, "We won't!"

The photographer was smart enough to know when he'd been defeated. "All right, then." He waved a hand for silence and got it. "I'll let Regina know."

The minute Curtis stepped to the opposite end of the hall to call his boss, Evelyn wiped her cheeks and signaled to Chef Hubbard. "Carry on, Chef. I know you have a lot to do in a short amount of time."

Janet crammed her chef's hat on her head. Without stopping to ask questions, she strode toward the kitchen. In seconds, she began issuing orders in a calm, detached voice.

Evelyn moved to the middle of the room. Ignoring the way her knees trembled, she called out over the rattle of pots and pans. "If you're still working on something that needs to be done for the wedding, continue with whatever you were doing. When you finish, come see me." She turned to Jenny. "Take my place with Brianna. Reassure her that we have everything under control out here."

Daniel and his groomspeople stepped forward. "We're here to help, ma'am. Tell us what to do."

"There are umbrellas and a rack of foul weather

gear in Ryan's office. Get whatever you need and gather at the front door. In about"—she glanced at her watch—"fifteen minutes, people are going to start dropping off items we'll need for tonight. If you and your squad could meet them and bring everything inside, it'll save us a lot of time."

"Yes, ma'am." Daniel turned smartly to his friends. "You heard the lady."

The group double-timed it across the hall and out of sight.

"The rest of you," she said, eyeing about a half-dozen volunteers, "break out your cell phones and start calling every person you know in Heart's Landing. This is what you're going to tell them to do..."

Chapter Eighteen

RYAN DROVE THROUGH THE POURING rain, his wipers swishing back and forth across the windshield faster than a jigsaw blade. Not a single street lamp illuminated the sidewalks around the marina. Nary a traffic light blinked along Officiant Way. With only his headlights to guide him, he crept along, despite a nearly overwhelming need to put as much distance as possible between himself and the woman who'd betrayed him.

How could she? More than anyone, Evelyn knew how much holding Brianna and Daniel's ceremony at Harbor View meant to him. How much it meant to his future. Yet she hadn't even hesitated when Curtis suggested they move the wedding.

As he drove past the Captain's Cottage, lights glowed from all the windows. Powered, no doubt, by the mansion's very own backup generator. His grip on the steering wheel tightened. When he got right down to it, this was all his fault. He should've taken Norman's advice, should've had the electrician install a generator even if he'd had to max out his credit card. Doing so would've saved him a world of hurt.

Because hurt was all he felt right now. His stomach twisted into knots every time he thought of Evelyn's betrayal. Ice ran through his veins when he considered what it might mean to him financially. Worst of all, his heart had splintered into a million pieces when he'd realized she didn't love him like he loved her. Because she couldn't, not and stab him in the back like she'd done.

The rain slowed by the time he reached a parking area above Heart's Landing. Pulling into the empty lot, he shut the wipers off and peered through the windshield. The fast-moving storm had moved well offshore. Lightning arced on the distant horizon, so far away, the rumble of thunder had faded completely. He exited into a light drizzle, pulled his collar higher on his neck, and climbed onto the bike path.

A five-minute walk took him to the rock wall overlooking the cove. Propping his arms on the wet rocks, he stared down at the rough sea. The tide was in. Water surged against the cliffs that sheltered the spot where Captain Thaddeus had once anchored the *S.S. Mary Shelby*. His thoughts churned along with the waves.

He had no choice. He had to accept that Evelyn had never changed. By turning her back on him when he'd needed her support the most, she'd proven she was still the self-centered, demanding diva he'd known in high school. Going along with Curtis's idea to move the wedding to the Captain's Cottage made it abundantly clear she'd go to any lengths to come out on top.

No, wait. That wasn't right.

A particularly rough wave struck the rocks below

with enough force to send up a spray that doused him in salt water.

Evelyn cared for those around her. Rumor had it she'd bought I Do Cakes' entire stock of salted caramel cupcakes earlier this week as a surprise gift for her staff, her way of thanking them for all they'd done. And that wasn't all. She cared for the people around her. She'd come home from New York without a moment's hesitation after her uncle had taken sick. More recently, she'd called in the cavalry when Brianna had melted down the day she'd chosen her wedding dress. He and Evelyn had both heard the news about the bride's aunt, but Evelyn had been the one who'd insisted they rush to the young woman's side. When he doubted himself, she encouraged him. He might never have healed the breach with his parents without her support.

Those weren't the actions of a selfish, egotistical diva. They were the actions of someone who put others first. Someone who sacrificed her own hopes and dreams for the good of Heart's Landing.

His shoulders slumped. He blinked salt spray out of his eyes and forced himself to start over, take a fresh look at things.

When Brianna and Daniel had chosen Harbor View over the Captain's Cottage, Evelyn had been hurt and surprised. Who wouldn't be? But she'd been quick to do what was best for Heart's Landing. As a result, she'd worked side by side with him into the wee hours yesterday and all day today in order to get Harbor View in tip-top shape for its first-ever wedding.

Going along with Curtis's plan to move the ceremony to the Captain's Cottage was more of the same. All of Heart's Landing would've suffered if they'd canceled or postponed Brianna and Daniel's wedding. Evelyn must have seen the move as the best option for Mildred Morrey, for Bev and Vi Gorman, for Greg Thomas and a hundred more who'd invested so much in Wedding-In-A-Week. She had to have known the change of venues might destroy any chance they had of happiness together. But she'd agreed to do it...for the good of Heart's Landing.

Only a strong, savvy, completely unselfish person could see all that was at stake and make the decision she'd made. And how had he responded? He'd blamed her. Had accused her of using the circumstances to her own benefit. His stomach twisted.

He'd been such a fool.

Earlier this week, he'd told Evelyn his shoulders were broad enough to carry the load if Brianna and Daniel chose the Captain's Cottage. He'd meant it at the time. But when push came to shove, he'd failed. Now, he needed to prove there was more to him than the petty side he'd shown at Harbor View.

But he wouldn't lie to himself. He'd ruined things between him and Evelyn. He'd seen her tears. He knew he'd hurt her. He'd thrown away the one thing that mattered most—her love.

Could he win her back?

He shook his head. He might be the best restoration specialist in the state, but he couldn't undo this damage. The words he'd spoken in the heat of the moment had burned like acid. He might never earn or deserve Evelyn's forgiveness. That wouldn't stop him from spending the rest of his life trying to atone. He'd start right now. For the sake of Heart's Landing, he'd help salvage Brianna and Daniel's wedding…wherever it took place. His hurried to his pickup.

Minutes later, he turned off one darkened street onto the equally dark side street that led to the marina. He hit the brakes. The truck rolled to a stop. His hands on the steering wheel, he stared at the spot where he'd expected to see the dim outline of the old manufacturing plant. Instead, light glowed from the windows of Harbor View. Unable to believe his eyes, he rubbed them and stared again. The one bright spot in the darkened night shone like a beacon. How was that possible? He put the engine in gear and rolled forward. His heart, which he'd been sure was broken beyond repair, beat slowly.

Only a few vehicles sat in Harbor View's parking lot. Flickering lights from a dozen lanterns illuminated a path that led straight to the main door. He pulled into an empty spot and headed for the entrance. His rain-soaked jeans made swishing noises with every step. He drew a ragged breath, grabbed the doorknob, and stepped inside.

In the lobby, a cluster of lanterns surrounded the Farley skiff, which overflowed with wedding favors. Flameless candles shed light on the guest book that stood open on a small podium outside the barn doors. From there, his gaze followed a white carpet lined with floral arrangements and lanterns. The runner led to the wedding arch. There, flickering tapers stood in tall candelabra. With the soft glow of lantern and candlelight reflecting off the tall glass windows, the effect was stunning and far more romantic than he'd ever dreamed possible.

He gulped. *What? Who?*

In an instant, he knew. Evelyn. It had to be. She was the only person who'd dare stand up to Curtis or Regina. The only one who could've saved Brianna and Daniel's wedding. Apparently, she'd done exactly that while he'd been off throwing a pity party for one.

Noise in the lobby wrenched his gaze from the scene. Muted laughter and masculine voices drifted from the groom's dressing area. A soft cough came from somewhere close. Movement drew his eyes to a table where postcards had been arranged like a seating chart. Wearing a purplish dress, Alicia sat at the table. Otherwise, there was no one in sight.

Water dripping from his clothes onto the welcome mat, he eyed Alicia. "Evelyn did all this?" he asked simply.

"Sure did. She put out a call for lanterns and electric candles. Dozens of people responded. It was like a fire brigade there for a while—Daniel's young friends meeting the cars and bringing the items inside, everyone else placing them all over the building. You should've been here."

That last bit punched him in the gut. "You're right. I should've been."

Accusation filled the wedding planner's dark eyes. "You hurt her." The harsh whisper echoed through the nearly empty lobby. "You need to fix things."

Ryan gulped. If Alicia only knew how much he wanted to do exactly that. He gave his head a mournful shake. He had to face facts. He didn't deserve a second chance. "She'll never forgive me."

"You won't know until you try."

"Right again." He glanced toward the bride's dressing area. "Is she in there?"

Alicia's head tilted in the opposite direction. "Last I saw, she was headed for the kitchen." When he moved toward the barn doors, the older woman's voice softened. "Um, Ryan, you might want to clean yourself up a bit first."

"You're batting a thousand tonight, aren't you?" He ran a hand over the T-shirt that rain had plastered to his chest. His shoes squished soggily on the carpet. "If you see her before I do, tell her I'm looking for her, okay?"

"I will. But you don't have a lot of time. Guests will start to arrive any minute."

He nodded, reversed direction, and hurried down the back hall to his office. Earlier, he'd hung his wedding attire on a hook behind the door. In his private bath, he traded soggy clothes for a navy suit and a crisp white shirt. Ryan glanced in the mirror and quirked one eye at his reflection. Satisfied that he looked as presentable as possible for a man who had broken the heart of the woman he loved, he went to search for her.

He had a lot of explaining to do.

And after that? After that, he'd dedicate the rest of his life to redeeming himself in the eyes of the woman he'd loved and lost.

Evelyn slipped into the kitchen. She'd been hoping to find a quiet space where she could regroup, but the kitchen was not it. The final prep for the meal service was underway, and the crew operated at full tilt. Pots rattled. Knives flashed. Cooks and assistants talked constantly. Requests for more carrots, added salt, directions to stir this or taste that created a low buzz liberally peppered with, “Yes, Chef.” Janet must’ve spotted her, for the busy chef appeared at her elbow.

“You look like you’re at the end of your rope.”

She managed a tremulous smile. Thanks to the generosity and quick response of the citizens of Heart’s Landing, preparations in the ballroom were complete. Daniel and his groomspeople were tidying themselves up after dashing into the pouring rain to meet what had to have been a hundred vehicles bearing the finest of Heart’s Landing, who’d loaded every lantern and electric candle they could find into cars and trucks and had delivered them to Harbor View. Alicia had stationed herself in the lobby. She’d direct arriving guests and family—friends of the bride to the left, of the groom to the right. Jenny was helping Brianna while Curtis shot photos of the bride in her gown.

Which had finally given her a moment all to herself. But the second she’d let her guard down, tears had threatened.

“Come with me.” The whispered order carried no farther than her ears.

A hand at her elbow propelled her through the kitchen and out the back door. Here, the roofline had been extended to protect a small porch from the elements. She sucked in a breath of air that smelled of freshly washed earth, salt spray, and the crisp smell that lingered after a lightning strike.

"Stay here as long as you need. I'll fend off any wolves who come looking for you."

Evelyn gave the chef a grateful smile. "Not wolves so much as eager puppies. So many questions." She'd answered more of them in the past hour than she had in the last year.

"Where do you want this lantern? Do you want candles on every table? Where are the extra batteries? Where do you keep the mops? The umbrellas?"

"Thanks, I—"

"Been there. Done that. Take a breath. Recharge."

If only it were that simple. Tonight, she'd saved a wedding. In the process, she'd lost the only man she'd ever loved.

The first had opened a world of new possibilities. All week, the sense that change was on the horizon had built within her. With Ryan's help and encouragement, she'd discovered she had a bigger purpose than keeping the books and tracking the supplies at the Captain's Cottage. Thanks to him, she'd learned how it felt to be actively involved in giving brides their perfect day. She wanted more of that.

She'd hoped that, somehow, she and Ryan would be partners in that effort. But after seeing the disappointment and pain in his eyes when he'd looked at her earlier, she knew that would never happen.

Which hurt more than she'd ever thought possible, because she'd fallen in love with the tall, blond carpenter. He made her heart sing in a way no starring role in any play ever had. He filled her with hope and dreams of a better day, a future filled with happiness and love. Only she'd destroyed any hope of that ever happening when she'd chosen to put the Captain's

Cottage first. She pressed one hand over the missing pieces of her heart.

For one long moment, while Curtis had ranted about moving the wedding to the Captain's Cottage, she'd wavered. She'd only agreed with the man for a second. It'd been long enough to ruin everything. She'd broken Ryan's trust by once again letting her mouth get ahead of her head. She'd come to her senses mere seconds later, but by then it was too late. Ryan was already gone. For the past two hours, she'd done her best to rectify her mistake. Not that it mattered. He'd never look at her the same again. The words she'd spoken in haste had seen to that.

How was she going to live without him?

She couldn't, not in Heart's Landing. Not where they'd constantly see each other on the streets, or attend the same weddings, or sit next to one another at town hall meetings. Losing Ryan left her with no choice. She'd have to leave. She'd have to move to a different city, a different town, where she'd never see him again. Where she wouldn't have to watch him meet someone new or fall in love with a woman who wasn't her. And she'd need to do it soon, while her heart was still so broken over losing the one man she ever loved that she'd hardly notice she'd left behind her home, her town, her friends, and family.

The door leading to the kitchen creaked open. Chef Hubbard stuck her head out. "There's someone here to see you."

"I—I'm not ready to see anyone just yet." She blotted her eyes.

"I tried to explain that, but he's quite insistent. I can't hold him off any longer."

"Evelyn, we need to talk." Ryan's head appeared over Janet's shoulder.

At the words known for introducing the big breakup scene in every romance novel she'd ever read, she took a ragged breath. He was right. They probably should talk and get it over with. Once they got everything out in the open, they could move on with their lives, start to heal. *As if.* She stifled a laugh. Recovering from this breakup was never going to happen. "It's okay, Janet. Let him by." She braced herself.

Ryan barely waited for the chef to step aside before he shouldered his way through the door. She swallowed hard. She'd always thought he looked good in jeans and a T-shirt. Dressed in a suit with his hair slicked back, he was practically irresistible. But resist she must. Though every fiber of her being fought against it, she motioned him to keep his distance. Much to her sorrow, he did as she asked.

"I thought you'd moved Brianna and Daniel's wedding to the Captain's Cottage." He spoke in clipped tones, his voice strained. "Didn't Curtis insist on it? Or did I hear wrong?"

"I..." Afraid anything she said would only make things worse—if that was even possible—she simply nodded. "That was the plan."

"What happened? When I left, you were all set to follow Curtis's lead."

There it was, the hard part. Yes, she rallied the town to come to Ryan's aid, but that hadn't been her first thought. Her temples throbbed while she searched for the words that would end things between them. "I'm not proud of that," she said at last. "For a minute there, I was only thinking of myself. Of what it'd mean for me if we held the wedding at the Captain's Cottage. But then I realized it wasn't what Brianna and Daniel wanted. They've had their hearts set on a waterfront wedding from the moment they stepped foot in Harbor View." She stopped. "By the time my brain caught up with my mouth, I'd already said I'd go along with Curtis's plan. I know that hurt you. I know you can never forgive me, but I want you to know I didn't mean it. I'm sorry." A tear rolled down her cheek. She brushed it away.

In the shadows, she saw Ryan shrug. His voice softened. "I won't lie to you. That did hurt, but you weren't the only one who made mistakes tonight. We both did. I should never have left the way I did. I rushed back to help, to beg you to forgive me—"

She stared at him, her eyes widening. "You were going to help move the wedding to the Captain's Cottage?" She wished she'd known.

He nodded. "Curtis was right. With no power, no electricity, moving was the only option. But then you did all this." He gestured toward the kitchen and the ballroom beyond.

She twisted her fingers together. "I had a lot of help. I could never have done it all on my own. Practically everyone in Heart's Landing pitched in."

"It takes a village."

"Yeah, a village."

"There's one more thing." Ryan stepped closer. "I said some things I didn't mean. Words I'll regret to my dying day. I want you to know how sorry I am. I know I don't deserve it, but I'm asking you to forgive me."

She batted the air with one hand. "You don't owe me an apology. More than practically anyone, I know what it feels like to say something and a minute later wish you hadn't."

"Hear me out, okay?" He closed the gap between them. "It's just that, well, when you went along with Curtis's plan, I was so concerned about losing Harbor View that I didn't see I was losing the one thing that meant the most. The one thing I couldn't afford to lose."

Her breath stuttered. Was he about to say what she thought he might? She crossed her fingers and slipped her hand behind her back. Tilting her face up to his, she whispered, "What was that?"

"You."

This was sounding less and less like the breakup and more like the beginning of something she hardly dared to believe. She threw caution to the wind. "I don't want to lose you, either."

He reached for her free hand. "I love you, Evelyn. You've always had a special place all your own in my heart."

Air slipped slowly over her lips. She managed to draw in enough to repeat his declaration back to him. "I love you, Ryan. It's always been you. From the time we raced through the halls of the Captain's Cottage and slid down the banister, there's only been you."

His eyes met hers then, and she gazed into their deep blue pools. In them, she saw the depth of his love and knew he loved her as much as she loved him. They closed the short distance between them. Ryan's hands around her waist felt like coming home. His lips on hers tasted sweeter than the richest chocolate, spicier than the hottest peppers. She drank in the scent that was his alone and knew she'd never tire of it.

Moments later, they sprang apart when the back door to the kitchen opened. Chef Hubbard stuck her head out. "Oh!" she exclaimed, her eyes darting between them. "You two?"

"Yes, but hush. We're not telling anyone until after Brianna and Daniel's wedding." Evelyn grinned while Ryan slipped one hand around her waist.

Janet studied first Ryan and then her. "Good luck with that. The way you're both glowing, everyone in town will figure it out before the bride walks down the aisle."

"You're probably right about that." Evelyn laughed through happy tears.

"Speaking of which, it's about that time." Janet pointed to her watch.

"We'll be right there, Chef," Ryan assured her. He waited until the door shut before he turned to her. "I don't want this moment to end. I wish we could stay here forever."

"Me, too." She glanced at the water. Light from the windows danced on the ripples. Harbor View had never looked so lovely. "This really is the perfect place for a wedding." She sighed, content at last.

The string quartet played Handel's "Air" while Evelyn started down the carpeted aisle to take her place beside the floral arch. She scanned the rows of chairs on either side. Friends and neighbors in their Sunday best filled every seat. She'd heard their murmurs of approval, had watched doubtful expressions change to delight as the first guests arrived. She'd known then that all of Ryan's hard work, all his efforts, had been worthwhile. Harbor View was a hit. She'd be surprised if he didn't find a dozen messages from prospective brides on his answering machine Monday morning.

There'd been a time, not so long ago, when that thought had filled her with trepidation, but no longer. Heart's Landing staked its reputation on providing the perfect wedding for every bride. Not every one of them dreamed of getting married at the Captain's Cottage. Some wanted a waterfront wedding. Ryan had been right about that. As he'd been right about so many things. Their love for one another among them.

Up front, Jenny smiled out at the crowd. Opposite her, gold buttons gleaming against the blues of their dress uniforms, Daniel and his attendants stood at attention. The groom stared over Evelyn's shoulder, waiting for his first glimpse of his bride. As Evelyn hit her mark and turned, the musicians reached the end of their piece. An expectant hush fell over the crowd. The bass player struck a note, and the violinists played the opening bars of "The Wedding March." Chairs creaked and clothing swished as two hundred guests surged to their feet, their eyes focused on the back of the room.

Ryan slid the barn doors wide, and there she stood. Radiant in a white gown made of matted Makoto silk, her hair a mass of ringlets anchored by a wispy veil, her mother's pearls around her neck, Brianna beamed. One hand rested lightly on Alicia's arm. The other held a cascade of burgundy dahlias and purple irises. White bows on the shoes she'd chosen at A Glass Slipper peeked out from beneath her hem.

Evelyn wiped a sudden dampness from her eyes. Who would've thought she and Ryan would fall in love while they'd helped create a perfect wedding for this Wedding-in-a-Week couple? Would they have a perfect wedding of their own one day? Watching Brianna walk down the aisle, she could hardly wait to see what the future held in store.

Epilogue

EVELYN LINGERED AT THE DOOR of Harbor View Weddings while Josh Anderson and Lacy Martinez practically floated down the sidewalk to their car. As Evelyn knew she would, the bride-to-be stole a final peek at the converted Boat Works where, next June, her friends and family would watch her walk down the aisle and into the arms of the man she loved. The dreamy smile that played across the bride's lips sent a contented sigh sifting through Evelyn's chest. She waved goodbye to the couple, satisfied that in several months' time, she'd help them have the waterfront wedding of their dreams.

"Are you finished for the day?" Dressed in jeans and a flannel shirt, his tool belt hanging low across his hips, Ryan stepped into the lobby from the back hallway.

"Yes." She closed the heavy double door and locked it. Butterflies took flight in her midsection at the sight of Ryan's tall figure striding toward her across the polished wood floor. "I had appointments with six couples today. Four of them reserved their dates."

Ryan whistled softly. "That's pretty amazing."

Ever since the *Weddings Today* article ran—well, before that, to be perfectly honest—brides and grooms had flocked to the newest venue in Heart's Landing. Their names and wedding dates crowded the once-barren whiteboard in the office.

She nodded while she tugged a few pins from her hair. Loving the way Ryan's eyes lit up when the thick curls fell around her shoulders, she grinned. "How'd your day go?"

"Awesome," he said, his features softening. "I should finish with the vestibule at the church before the weekend." He'd been restoring the entryway after the rector discovered termite damage in the century-old building overlooking Heart's Landing. "That'll free me up to help you with the Morgan/Simpson wedding on Saturday."

"Great!" At first, she'd questioned whether working side by side with the man she loved was the wisest move. But in the six months since she'd stepped into her new role as the event coordinator at Harbor View, she'd never been happier. She and Ryan quickly developed a routine that freed each of them to pursue their dreams. Throughout the week, while he spent most days working on various restoration projects throughout Heart's Landing and nearby towns, she found a greater satisfaction than she'd ever expected in managing the venue. Weekends, they worked together to fulfill the Heart's Landing promise of providing the perfect wedding to every couple who'd chosen to exchange their vows on the waterfront.

"Are you still up for going out tonight?" Ryan shot her a look filled with concern.

"Absolutely. I can't wait to find out what your big secret is." Ryan had planned a special evening, but despite her teasing, he'd refused to divulge a single detail. She gave his hand a playful tug and gave him her best pleading look. "Where did you say we were going?"

Ryan's eyebrows rose. A lazy grin spread across his face. "I'm wise to your ways. I'm not going to spill the beans. It's a surprise."

She faked a pout. "How am I supposed to know what to wear if you won't give me a hint."

"Okay, okay." His gaze met hers, and her knees went weak. "Someplace nice, but that's all I'm telling you." He zipped his lips. "I'll pick you up at seven."

She glanced at the time on her phone. Five o'clock. "I'd better get moving." She wanted to look her best for their date. Not that she cared where they went. A walk on the beach or the fanciest restaurant—either was fine as long as they were together. Intending to gather her things and head home to the Cottage, she stepped toward the office. "I guess I'll see you then."

"Hold on a minute." Ryan slipped his arms around her waist and pulled her toward him. "We have time for one kiss, don't we?"

"Mmm." She tipped her head to his. "I thought you'd forgotten."

"Never."

After a kiss that left her yearning to spend more time in Ryan's arms, she grabbed her purse from the office and headed across town. With the holidays right around the corner, things were quiet at the Cottage. She stopped by Jason's office to say hello, but her cousin had already left for the day. Over breakfast this morning, he'd mentioned he and Tara would be performing as the Captain and his wife at an event that evening. Alicia and Jenny's offices were dark, as well. Evelyn smiled, glad that Alicia's transition into retirement was going well. She didn't expect any problems once Jenny took the reins in the New Year. Evelyn stopped in her office next. She still spent one day a week at the Cottage, tending to the books and accounts, and wanted to check her inbox. It was empty, other than a few receipts that could wait until next week. Satisfied, she dashed up the stairs to her suite.

A shiver passed through her. Between getting Harbor View off the ground and his booming restoration business, she and Ryan stayed busy. So busy that it'd been a while since they'd gone on a real date. She couldn't wait to have him all to herself for an entire evening.

In her room a half hour later, she slipped into the new red dress she'd been saving for a special occasion and stepped into the tall boots she hadn't been able to resist during her last visit to the Glass Slipper. She didn't need much makeup—just a little powder and some lipstick—but she took extra care applying it. As a final touch, she retrieved the dangly dragonfly earrings from her jewelry box and slipped them on. The gossamer wings made her feel feminine and girly and, looking forward to seeing Ryan, she hummed a few bars of a love song.

She trailed her fingers along the banister on her way down the stairs. At the stroke of seven, she stepped into the entryway just in time to see Tom

Denton pull a horse-drawn carriage to a stop under the porte cochere.

She pressed one hand to her heart. “Oh, I didn’t expect this!” she said when Ryan, so handsome in a suit coat and tie, stepped lightly from the carriage steps.

His cheeks reddened slightly. “I overheard you recommending Your Ride Awaits to the Peterson bride. It sounded like the perfect way to celebrate our six-month anniversary.”

She sighed. He’d remembered their special day. That was something else she loved about him—Ryan was the most romantic man she’d ever met. She leaned forward and pressed her lips to his cheek. “I’ve wanted to do this forever.”

His hand at her side felt warm and secure as he helped her up the single step and onto the plush cushions. Joining her, he tucked a warm blanket over their knees in deference to the crisp November air. Once they were settled, Tom clucked to the horses, and they headed down the long, curving driveway.

With Ryan’s arm around her shoulders, she leaned into him. “This is a wonderful surprise,” she murmured. “Thank you.”

Ryan stole a quick glance at the gleaming carriage. “I can’t believe we’ve waited so long to do this.”

They rode in silence, listening to the steady clop-clop of the horses’ shoes against the pavement while metal jangled. The carriage swayed. Overhead, stars twinkled in the clear sky.

Tom led the team onto Bridal Carriage Way. As they passed Forget Me Knot, Ryan pointed out the colorful red poinsettias surrounding a mannequin dressed in white. The darkened windows of I Do Cakes came next, and they both laughed when their tummies rumbled. A tiny spotlight shone down on a display of heirloom jewelry in the window of Something Old, Something New, but Evelyn focused on the carved stone heart that hung over the door. She blew a kiss to the symbol of her great-great grandfather's love for his wife and squeezed Ryan's hand. Her love for him grew deeper every day, and she hoped one day they'd build a future together. The mouthwatering smells of basil and garlic permeated the night air around Bow Tie Pasta. She half expected their ride to end there. But they continued on past Statue Park, which still looked oddly vacant without The Ash.

Her brow furrowed when Tom steered them onto Champagne Avenue. In the distance, lights gleamed. She canted her head. "Is something going on at Harbor View tonight?" He hadn't scheduled an event at the venue without telling her, had he?

Ryan snugged her closer. "I must've forgotten to turn out the lights when I closed up. Let's swing by. It'll only take a minute." Moments later, Tom reined the team of high-stepping horses to a halt in front of the building. "Come with me," Ryan said, extending a hand to help her down from the carriage.

Unwilling to spend even a little bit of their date apart, she gladly complied. But instead of heading directly for the front door, Ryan detoured to a spot not far from the entrance. There, protected by stacked stone fencing, a small tree stood in the center of a circle. Ryan squeezed her hand. "The baby Ash is doing well."

She nodded. More than a dozen saplings had been

planted throughout Heart's Landing. One day, the tall trees would tower over the town.

Ryan cleared his throat. "You know, lately I've been thinking a lot about The Ash...and us. That tree was around forever. Kind of like we were always fixtures in each other's lives. For a while there, we drifted apart, and I thought our friendship had died like The Ash did earlier this year. I'm so glad helping Brianna and Daniel brought us back together again."

"Me, too," she whispered. Her heart fluttered. "I can't imagine my life without you in it."

"Same here." Ryan brushed a kiss through her hair. "You make me want to be a better man, a better person. I love you more than I ever thought possible."

"I feel the same way," she assured him.

His eyes met hers then, and she gazed into their deep blue pools. In them, she saw the depth of his love. She kept her eyes locked on his as he went down on one knee. "Evelyn Heart," he said. "My love for you is as strong and steady as The Ash in its glory. I want to spend every waking minute looking into your eyes, hearing your voice, standing beside you. If you'll have me. Will you marry me?"

Words failed her. But then, Ryan often had that effect on her. She answered him the only way she could, with a kiss. Pulling him to his feet, she moved into his arms.

At last, both breathless, they pulled apart. Her heart thudded again when Ryan tugged a small black box from his coat pocket. He opened it to reveal a diamond solitaire that sparkled brighter than the prettiest star in the sky. His hands trembling slightly, Ryan plucked the ring from the box and slipped it on her finger. "So is that a yes?"

"Yes." Laughter spilled from her lips. "A thousand times yes." She leaned in for another of Ryan's amazing kisses.

They stood, cradled in each other's arms until, finally, one of Tom Denton's horses stomped his feet. Ryan slipped his hand around her waist. He smiled down at her with a smile she knew she'd never grow tired of. "I guess we'd better shut off those lights. We can't expect poor Tom or his horses to stay out here all night."

"You're right," she agreed. She glanced toward the carriage. As she did, she noticed the cars that filled all the parking spaces in front of Harbor View. "Ryan?"

"C'mon. Let's go inside for a minute."

She shrugged aside her concerns when he slipped one arm about her waist. Together they covered the short distance to the main entrance. The instant Ryan opened the doors to the lobby, shouts rang out.

"Congratulations! We're so happy for you!"

Jason and Tara, dressed in period garb, surged forward, offering congratulations and well wishes. What looked like half the population of Heart's Landing trailed in their wake. In seconds, Evelyn was enveloped in hugs and promises that hers would be the best wedding Heart's Landing had ever seen. At her side, other people shook Ryan's hand and patted his back. She glimpsed the absolute happiness that danced in his blue eyes, and her heart melted.

"This," she whispered. This was what she'd always wanted. To stand beside the man of her dreams, surrounded by the people she loved. One day, in the not-so-distant future, she'd look out over the sea of these faces—friends, family and relatives—people who'd gathered to celebrate the beginning of a new journey. When that day arrived, she'd only have eyes for one person. Ryan, her very own Heart's Landing love for the ages. On that day, she'd say "I do" in a waterfront wedding of her very own.

Champagne bottles popped. Someone pressed a glass into her hand. She and Ryan clinked their glasses together while all around them, friends and neighbors raised their voices, offering up the words that had echoed through the ages in Heart's Landing.

"The best is yet to be."

Truer words had never been spoken. Her heart overflowed with love as she gazed at Ryan and dreamed of their future in the town devoted to delivering the perfect wedding for every bride.

The End

Slow-Braised Lamb with Apricot Madeira Sauce

A Hallmark Original Recipe

In *A Waterfront Wedding*, Evelyn and Ryan fall in love while competing against each other for the chance to host the Wedding-in-a-Week contest. They've even placed bets on it—loser pays for a romantic dinner at Bow Tie Pasta. Both of them have their sights on the most expensive item on the menu—the slow-braised lamb. You can make it at home for your own romantic dinners, or for no occasion at all: the apricot Madeira sauce makes it truly special.

Prep Time: 15 mins.
Cook Time: 210 mins.
Serves: 6

Ingredients

- 2 tablespoons olive oil
- 1 (3½ to 4 lb.) lamb shoulder, boned, rolled and tied
- 1 teaspoon kosher salt
- 1 teaspoon coarse black pepper
- 1/4 lb. bacon, cut into 1/4-inch strips
- 1/2 yellow onion, chopped
- 1 carrot, peeled, fine chopped
- 1 celery stalk, fine chopped
- 1 tablespoon garlic, chopped
- 1 tablespoon tomato paste
- 1 cup Madeira (can substitute Marsala wine)
- 3 cups chicken stock
- 3 tablespoons apricot jam
- 2 sprigs fresh thyme
- 4 tablespoons cold butter, cut into pieces

Preparation

1. Preheat oven to 350°F.
2. Heat olive oil in a heavy bottom roasting pan over medium high heat; season lamb with salt and black pepper and brown on all sides. Remove from pan and set aside.
3. To same pan, add bacon and cook over medium-low heat until cooked. Add onion, carrot and celery; sauté until tender, stirring frequently. Add garlic and sauté 1 minute.

4. Add tomato paste, Madeira, chicken stock, apricot jam and fresh thyme and stir to blend.
5. Return browned lamb to pan, cover and braise in oven for 3 hours.
6. Transfer lamb to platter and cover with foil.
7. Carefully strain braising liquid through a sieve into a bowl, using the back of a spoon to press out any remaining liquid. Transfer liquid back into roasting pan. Simmer liquid on stove top over medium-low heat until liquid has reduced by 50 percent.
8. Reduce heat to low. Slowly add cold butter pieces to braising liquid, whisking constantly, until all butter has melted and sauce is thick and glossy. Return braised lamb; keep warm.
9. To serve, remove strings from roast, transfer to platter and spoon sauce over the top.

Thanks so much for reading
A Waterfront Wedding. We hope you enjoyed it!

You might like these other books
from Hallmark Publishing:

A Simple Wedding
A Cottage Wedding
A Country Wedding
Beach Wedding Weekend
Love on Location

For information about our new releases and exclusive offers, sign up for our free newsletter at hallmarkchannel.com/hallmark-publishing-newsletter

You can also connect with us here:

Facebook.com/HallmarkPublishing

Twitter.com/HallmarkPublish

About the Author

Leigh Duncan, an Amazon bestselling author and a National Readers' Choice Award winner, has written over two dozen novels, novellas and short stories, including *A Simple Wedding, A Cottage Wedding, Journey Back to Christmas, A Country Wedding*, and her own Orange Blossom series. Leigh lives on Central Florida's East Coast where she writes complex, heartwarming, and emotional stories with a dash of Southern sass.

Leigh loves to stay in touch with readers through social media. Find her at www.facebook.com/LeighDuncanBooks, or visit her website at www.leighduncan.com.